MAN DOWN

Other Titles by Irma Venter

Hard Rain

MAN DOWN

IRMA VENTER

TRANSLATED BY KARIN SCHIMKE

AMAZON CROSSING

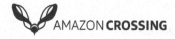

Previously published as *Skrapnel* by NB Publishers in South Africa in 2013. Translated from Afrikaans by Karin Schimke. First published in English by Amazon Crossing in 2021.

Published by Amazon Crossing, Seattle

www.apub.com

ISBN-13: 9781542018173
ISBN-10: 154201817X

Cover design by Shasti O'Leary Soudant

Printed in the United States of America

For Jacci
And for Esta and Sca

ALEX

1

The first shot kicks up dust ten, twelve yards to my left, too far away to convince me to take cover. The second one makes me drop to my haunches on the hard, dusty ground. Somewhere, above my head, it explodes through the galvanized steel of the squatter shack and travels all the way into the hut next to it, hitting something solid with a dull thud.

A child screams, but from a few shacks farther down the winding, rubbish-strewn dirt road.

Movies lie. Nine-millimeter bullets rip through everything.

"Move!" the policeman shouts.

Constable Ndebele, if I remember correctly. First name Dumisani. Or "just Dumi" he told me this morning when Captain Burger introduced us.

From the shack next to the one where I'm hiding, the policeman urges me with two fingers to move on to the next row of houses, away from the firefight.

I do as he says.

Earlier, over rusks and a flask of coffee in the back seat of the freezing police car, he told me he came from a small place near Ulundi, in the province of KwaZulu-Natal. His uncle is a traditional healer. A *sangoma*. He could have stayed in the village if he'd wanted to, he joked, but the boredom would probably have killed him.

I wonder whether some part of him doesn't wish he were back there today.

"Come on," he calls, indicating that we need to move even deeper into the sprawling shantytown.

Fine dust eddies up around his black boots as his feet dig into the soft sand. The bulky front-row rugby legs in the blue uniform betray the hours he must spend in the gym.

I focus on his black helmet. The barrel of the R5 automatic weapon swings behind his back as he runs.

We sprint to the next shack.

The next one.

Another.

The gunfire has stopped. There's a sudden, eerie silence.

Then the shots ring out again, fired in rapid succession from somewhere behind us.

The bastard had been reloading. Or is there more than one, running with us from house to house?

I dive for the cover of the next hut, roll, and sit up on my knees. Look up at the sky. It's an almost unnatural deep blue. Why is the sky always so much more beautiful in the Free State than anywhere else in South Africa?

I force my breath to slow down. I don't want to draw the gunman's attention with my panting. I glance through the window of the shack.

The wallpaper is made from sheets of labels that were once destined for Lucky Star sardine cans. The sagging double bed is neatly made. A baby in a red T-shirt is sitting on the orange duvet cover spread over it. The golden earrings in her earlobes are sparkling in the morning sun falling through the small rectangular window.

Where's the girl's mother? She must be less than a year old.

I squat down again. Dumi is young and fit, but he's breathing heavily beside me. He's twenty-two, he told me. Considerably younger than my almost forty. Must be all the equipment he's carrying that's making his lungs work so hard. All I have on me is a notebook in the back pocket of my jeans, a pen hooked in the front pocket of my shirt, and an uncomfortable bulletproof vest announcing in big white letters that I'm from the *PRESS*.

Not that it's of any help today.

The next bullet hits the kettle in the corner of the hut.

Water streams down the makeshift table and onto the floor. Steam rises up slowly through the dusty yellow light inside, disappearing on its way to the low roof.

The baby starts to cry, her arms reaching out for someone to pick her up.

No way. If something happens to this kid, it would be our fault.

"Come on." I tug at the policeman's shirt and point to the next hut. "That way."

Dumi shakes his head. Silently juts his chin in the direction I want to run.

He's right. Just after the next few ramshackle huts, about fifty yards down, the row of houses ends abruptly. On the other side of that is a fire-blackened, rubbish-strewn veld that signals the edge of Chris Hani Park.

"What now?" I say in a low voice. "We can't stay here."

I shift uncomfortably in the vest. I didn't want to wear the damn thing this morning, because it chafes my shoulders, but now I'm grateful for the heavy Kevlar.

"I've radioed the others," Dumi whispers. He peers around the corner of the shack. "They're two minutes away. They say we need to sit tight. There's big shit going down. AK-47-size shit. Bigger than we anticipated."

I wish my isiZulu were as good as his Afrikaans is.

An automatic weapon stutters nearby, as though to emphasize his statement. The shots are coming from the left somewhere, near where we've just been.

I look at Dumi and see he's thinking what I'm thinking: there's at least one man with a big gun between us and his colleagues. Illegal gold miners are syndicate men. They often carry bigger-caliber weapons than the police do.

I push my notebook deeper into my back pocket. A camera would have been more useful in a situation like this. A lens makes people think twice. Makes them more willing to state their case, to negotiate before they pull the trigger.

The thought sneaks to the surface, too quick to stop: Photos. Ranna Abramson.

Fuck. She's the last person I want to think about right now.

"We have to do something," I urge Dumi, nodding toward the house beside us. "There's a kid in there. We're drawing the gunfire toward her. We have to move."

Dumi stands up, looks through the window. Swears like he did earlier, when he realized we'd strayed from his colleagues. He and I had been yakking away all morning, not paying attention, which is why we're stuck here now.

He looks down at me, then back at the baby inside. "That's all we need." He turns his head toward the veld, as though measuring the distance mentally. "How long ago was the last shot?"

"I'm guessing ten seconds."

"Not more?"

"Maybe," I say, standing up. Nothing makes time more relative than the threat of a bullet to the brain.

We glance at the child again, her little hands urgently opening and closing, her mouth wide, pleading for someone to pick her up, to take her away from here.

"It doesn't help that she's screaming like that," mutters Dumi. "Fuck it. Let's hope our shooter's attention is on Captain Burger and the others. They should be close by now."

He points at the burned grass at the end of the line of shacks. "We'll run that way, around the squatter camp, and see if we can get back to the rest of the group."

"Okay." I nod and check that my notebook is firmly stowed in my back pocket. I can't afford to lose my notes.

"Go!" Dumi urges me. "I'll cover you."

I drop my head between my shoulders and run toward the field, Dumi's size twelves stomping the ground behind me.

Fifty yards.

Forty.

No shots.

Twenty.

Ten.

My breathing accelerates, adrenaline fueling my legs. We hit the veld, turn right, and race on, the houses flipping past us. An emaciated dog, chained to a fence, barks nervously as we speed by.

Three shots ring out. They are more measured than the staccato sounds from before.

Nine mil?

Someone screams. It's not the child, thank heavens. It's a shout of surprise at an abrupt death, the umbilical cord cut without warning.

Whoever it was, was right in front of us.

"Go right," Dumi calls. "Right!"

We turn back toward the shacks again, running for the cover of a narrow dirt lane sandwiched between two rows of houses.

More shots, closer this time. Morse code. R5?

Ahead of me the lane splits in two. I swerve right and run down an even narrower passage. Jump over a wobbly fence separating two houses. Storm through damp laundry hanging in a neatly swept yard.

The shots are getting closer. I hear someone shouting over Dumi's radio: "I see him. Yellow shirt, yellow shirt. Go, go, go!"

Dumi stumbles, calls out: "Stop, Alex!"

I do as he says. Lean with my hands on my thighs, trying to catch my breath. Pat my back pocket. Notebook's still there. Pen's still where I put it too. I look up. We're standing next to a house that looks out over a dusty, deserted soccer field. Thousands of people living in Hani Park, and suddenly there's no one to be seen.

Dumi taps my shoulder for me to turn around. His finger's resting on the trigger of his R5.

"Stay put," he warns. "It's not safe. I'm going to see if there's a way out of here."

I shake my head. "*Aikona.* I can't do the story if I'm not there."

He pushes two fingers into my chest. "It's not safe, Alex. Stay here, out of sight."

He heads off before I can argue. I watch him running and ducking all along the row of shacks.

I drop my hands onto my knees again. He is probably right, but I'm still going to follow him as soon as he's out of sight. There's definitely a story here. There are hundreds of ways a police operation can go wrong, and this one feels as though someone knew we were coming. Someone warned the bad guys. Someone in the police?

I take another deep breath and stand up straight again.

The sudden silence is overwhelming.

It rings in my ears in a high-pitched whine. I sweep the claustrophobic lanes and alleys for any sign of life. Search the shack windows.

This is not an it's-all-over silence. This is an oh-fuck silence.

Something's wrong. Something big. Something . . .

I turn around.

A man in a yellow T-shirt is pointing what looks like an Astra pistol at me.

"Move and you're dead."

No need to say it. The pistol has my attention. There's blood on the metal. And on the yellow cotton of his Superdry T-shirt—a fine spray, like when you shoot someone at close range.

I watch as he shuffles restlessly in his pointy black shoes. I notice the gold chain around his neck, the sweat on his forehead. Somehow I don't think he'd mind shooting more people today.

I put my hands up slowly.

"Don't," I say softly in English. "Just take it easy." I point at the letters on my chest. "I'm not from the police."

"What the fuck are you doing here, then?" The pistol accentuates every syllable of the heavy, out-of-breath English. His accent sounds French. West African French.

"A story. I'm a journalist. I'm just doing my job. That's all."

His eyes jump around, scouring the alley behind me. He looks like a trapped animal, his breath rattling nervously through his body. He glances over his shoulder, but there's no one behind him.

The silence remains. All the running, shooting, and shouting has stopped. Are the cops closing in on us?

The man in the yellow shirt takes a step toward me.

I step back.

Again.

We do the absurd dance one more time, my hands still in the air. There is no way I'm going to be taken hostage, and I definitely don't want to end up in the sights of a police sniper. They're good, but we all have our off days.

"Stop it! Come here." The barrel of the Astra is calling me closer. "Here!" He glances over his shoulder again.

I shake my head. "You don't want me. The police will shoot right through me. I'm not one of them."

"Keep quiet."

He looks around when we both hear footsteps. Careful, measured steps closing in from our right and left.

"Let me go." My voice is surprisingly calm.

"Keep quiet!" he shouts. "And get your fucking ass over here."

I shake my head again. Slowly, resolutely.

"Va au diable!" he swears. *"Merde!"*

I see it before it happens. The finger on the trigger pales.

I jump to the right, to the safety of the nearest squatter shack.

The sharp crack of two, three shots follows, then a blow to my back that knocks me down, face-first, into the Free State dust.

2

"Ouch."

"Don't be such a wuss." Dumi moves toward me as though to examine the bruise on my back again.

I turn away from him and the cop car and step over my bulletproof vest lying on the ground. Slip back into my shirt. The wintry air, like the adrenaline, is cooling quickly.

"Wuss, my ass," I say. "Be careful, man. It was a gunshot, not a goodnight kiss from your grandmother."

He laughs, lifting his hands in surrender. "Okay, okay. Let's get you to a hospital, then."

"I didn't ask to go to the hospital. It's only a bruise. All I'm asking is that you not break-dance on it."

Dumi shakes his head. "Nope. I think we have to go, to make sure there's no internal bleeding. It happens more often than you'd think. And we can't trust you media types. Before we know it, you'll be writing a front-page story on how we dropped you off at your bed-and-breakfast and left you to cough up blood all night."

"Of course. You know how it is: everything's a front-page story." I want to laugh to show I'm joking, but it hurts too much. Maybe the bullet cracked a rib or two.

Dumi must have noticed. He comes closer and gently squeezes my shoulder, careful not to touch my back. "You sure, Alex?"

"Yes."

"You were lucky."

"I know." I look at the body lying in the distance under a silver space blanket, a uniform respectfully standing guard beside it. Probably waiting for the coroner.

"Did you know him?"

"His name was Jerry Ndaba." Dumi looks down at his shoes, frowning. "We finished our training on the same day in Pretoria."

"I'm sorry." Seems like the constable got caught in the crossfire.

Dumi shrugs as though it means nothing, but his hands betray him. They become white-knuckled fists doing a quick rap against his thighs. Then he relaxes again, drops his shoulders. Hooks his thumbs into his blue belt.

"You did all right today," he says. "You've done this before?"

"Yes. Few times. And not always with the same result. I'm just glad you guys got him." Farther back, behind us, is another silver blanket. Yellow shirt.

"*Ja,* me too," says Dumi. "But you know what? Tomorrow there'll be someone to take his place. Someone else desperate enough to dig down in the old mine shafts for leftover gold. To join the gangs who have no issue gunning down anyone who gets in their way. And all of it so that someone in their Sandton or Cape Town penthouse can buy their second Ferrari."

"I'll write the story."

"Won't make a difference."

"We can't just all lose faith."

"The pen-mightier-than-the-sword thing? Who are you trying to convince?" Dumi leans forward and takes something out of my shirt pocket. He's holding up my pen. Or rather, one part of the silver-and-blue pen.

I look down at the ink staining my left pocket. The Parker must have shattered when I dived to the ground.

Dumi raises his eyebrows. "And with that lovely theory now completely fucked, you're going to have to think carefully about what you're going to sell me next." He offers me the piece of pen he's holding.

I take it and give a sour little laugh. "Yes. All right."

He motions for me to follow him. "Come on, I'm taking you to the hospital. I'm not going to let you drop dead on my watch."

I pick my bulletproof vest up off the ground and open the police car's passenger door. "You're a good shot. They tell me you got the guy in the yellow shirt with your first bullet. Between the eyes. With a fifteen-year-old service pistol."

"It's nothing. It's why we get paid the big bucks."

"Is this the first time you've killed someone?"

"Is that for your story?" His hand hesitates on the driver's side door, his body halfway in the car already.

"No."

"I believe you."

"It's not for the news sites or the paper. I promise." I get in.

He slides into the driver's seat. Turns the key and adjusts the rearview mirror. "Third time."

I try not to show any emotion. Reach for the seat belt. "How does it feel? How do you feel?"

"Too much. Too little."

"Makes no sense."

"Precisely."

3

The guesthouse I'm staying at is just outside Welkom's somewhat weathered heart. The town started emptying out some years ago as the gold grew scarcer and mines were forced to shut down. Many of the residents moved to Limpopo and North West, in search of work in the platinum mines.

The Zama-Zamas—illegal miners—remained, as well as one or two of the mining companies that believed there was still enough gold under their feet to keep going, albeit at slimmer margins.

At least the horizon is still open here, and the air fresher than it is in Johannesburg. And you can see the stars. That's always a good thing about sparsely populated places.

A sudden gust of cold wind blows a handful of dry leaves through the open window. I get up and close it. Check the date on my watch. July 16th. Wasn't it April just yesterday?

I fiddle with the pieces of the broken Parker pen. Puzzle them together. Take them apart again. I can't sleep. I've written my first in-depth feature about illegal gold-mining in the Free State and sent it to the paper's news editor, and now my head is full of unwanted memories.

Is Ranna also lying awake somewhere? In whose bed?

How do I feel about the photographer who disappeared from my life last year? Angry? Or do I still miss her?

Pissed off, I decide. You don't just disappear like that, no matter how many times you declare it to be in the other person's best interest. That's the kind of thing you say to make yourself feel better, to silence the guilt about running away. Again.

We could have worked through the police investigation into Tom Masterson's death. Stuck it out together. At the very least, Ranna could have stayed in contact until the worst had blown over.

The room phone rings, arresting the familiar rage that's building up again.

"Derksen."

"I have something for you, Mr. Derksen. Something important."

"Okay," I say slowly, tentatively.

The unfamiliar voice, with a distinct nasal quality, belongs to an older man.

It's late. Half past eleven. Which means just one thing: someone may have information to share.

"I'm listening," I say when there's no response.

"Today's raid? Radio says it was a fuckup. Two people dead. I knew it was going to happen. Someone tipped off the syndicate."

"And you are . . ."

He laughs and then pauses, as if to think. "Call me Gaddafi."

"Fine. Gaddafi. Why aren't you going to the police with your information?"

"I can't. There's too much at stake. Too many people being paid to look the other way."

I'm trying to place his accent. It sounds a touch Eastern European, with a tendency to broaden the *s* to a *z*. Unusual. Illegal gold-mining in this country is normally the domain of undocumented immigrants from the rest of Africa and a number of entrepreneurial South Africans. But things are always changing.

"What do you want me for? And remember, my newspaper doesn't pay for stories."

"I'm not looking for money. I'm just a concerned citizen. That's all."

"Okay, then. I'm willing to listen."

"Good. Go to Long Street. There's a pub on one of the side streets. Shafts, it's called. Everyone knows it. I'll meet you there in fifteen minutes."

He ends the call as I open my mouth to respond.

I use the Google Maps app to locate the bar. It's a five-minute drive to Shafts. Does that mean Gaddafi knows where I'm staying? Or is everything five minutes away from everything else in Welkom? Probably. This is not exactly Paris or London. Just a small mining town in the center of South Africa.

The decision is easy. I pull on a jacket and ram my laptop into my backpack. It'll be safer on me than here in the room, in case Gaddafi—or whatever his real name is—is actually just getting me out of here so that he can break in.

I hesitate for a moment when I pick up my cell phone. Should I stick to Sarah's rules? Rules the redheaded hacker invented because she says I've been reckless of late. Should I let her know where I'm going?

It's probably best. She'll be awake anyway.

I throw the phone into the backpack and zip it shut.

Nah. You don't walk away from one woman simply to fall under the control of another. Too many women. Too much trouble.

It's twenty-five to twelve. I'm wasting time.

A small group of people is milling about outside Shafts's blackened windows, most of them drunk and seemingly immune to the cold. I stand across the road, in front of a closed-down furniture store, surveying the run-down bar.

Sturdy security gate at the door. Purple neon lighting spelling the name over the bright yellow outline of a miner's helmet. White shoe polish writing on the window advertising a Monday special: two Black Label beers for the price of one.

Today is Tuesday.

I drop my head when two men rush by. My pickup is parked in an almost empty parking lot to my left. The security guard let me drive in without asking any questions. Seems most people who drink here walk to the bar.

Three young men wearing cheap, shiny shirts rush into Shafts. A striking woman with waist-length braids, wearing an impossibly short silver dress and carrying a purse as small as her fist, walks out. Her experienced eyes notice me immediately. She smiles, as though she's assessing my bank balance and my interest in one go. The smile dims as she seems to decide that my bush jacket, dusty brown boots, and Levi's wouldn't be able to afford her.

A few seconds later, she gets into a gray BMW that has stopped in the middle of the road. As she opens the door, the sound of Sho Madjozi rapping something about John Cena spills into the street, and then disappears again when she closes the door behind her. The driver, a round man with dark glasses, kisses her. Drives off as if he's in a rush.

Everything looks okay so far. Time to go in. It's getting damn cold out here anyway. My breath's turning white in the cool night air.

I didn't ask Gaddafi how I would recognize him, but it shouldn't be a problem. If he knows where I'm staying, he'll know what I look like. He may even be a policeman. Maybe I got the accent wrong.

The door hinges squeal as I walk in. The man behind the counter, drying a row of beer glasses, looks up, but it's too dark to read his eyes. There are far more people outside the bar than inside it. Only one table still has drinkers around it—the shiny shirts who walked in earlier.

Shaggy is pulsing a steady, scratchy beat through the loudspeakers attached to the ceiling. A gas heater in the corner is stripping the night of the worst of its chill.

"You still open?" I ask.

The man behind the counter motions with his shaved head past my shoulder. "Door's closed."

"It's not midnight yet. And I'm thirsty."

"Then you better be a quick drinker." He looks at his watch to make sure I know he's in a hurry.

I sit down at the end of the bar, in the corner, so that I can keep an eye on the door. The wooden countertop is full of carved graffiti. *Casper Digs Cindy*. A newer one says *Thabo loves Lungile*, with Lungile's name scratched over with something sharp.

"Castle, please."

A few seconds later I have my beer. The barman takes my money without saying thank you or offering me change.

"Ten minutes," he declares.

I nod. It solves my problem. If Gaddafi arrives on time, that's good. If not, I go back to the bed-and-breakfast. I have to be at the police station early tomorrow morning for a one-on-one with Dumi's commander, then on to an interview with a shift boss at a nearby mine.

My phone rings, but I ignore it. It's the news editor, Jasmine. I'm not in the mood for her right now. Especially not for a lecture about having gotten myself shot.

The shiny shirts pay their bill and leave.

The barman looks at his watch and juts his chin at me. "Waiting for someone?"

I look around me. The room is empty. If the barman was Gaddafi, he would have said so by now.

I shrug. "Not sure." The last of the beer slides down my throat. I get up. "Guess not. Goodnight."

"Night."

The door slams behind me. Seconds later, the lights inside go off, leaving the flashing neon of the bar's name to illuminate the darkness.

I walk to the pickup, hands in my pockets. Inhale the cold air and wonder what happened—or rather, what didn't happen. Why did

Gaddafi bring me here? Maybe he did just want me out of my room. But why? It's not like I have cash stashed under the mattress. And I have the most important things with me: Mac, cell phone, wallet, notebook, recorder. All he'd find in the room would be dirty clothes and a toothbrush.

I've been living like Ranna for months now, rootless, no ties.

Ranna.

Fuck.

I step onto the sidewalk across the road and nod at the security guard standing by the gate. He gives me a half-hearted salute from his six-by-six wooden hut. At the pickup, I dig for my keys, only to freeze when I feel something hard digging into my back.

"Don't move."

It sounds like the voice from the phone—older, and high, as though it's being forced through his nose. Whoever it is, he moves silently.

Where's the security guard? Or is he the one standing behind me now? Shafts is closed, and I'm alone in the parking lot. Not a bad trap. Quiet, efficient, out of the way.

I turn slightly to try and see the man behind me. "What do you want?"

The pistol's grip strikes me on the back, close to where I was shot this morning. Pain snakes down my spine. The doctor said nothing was broken, but now I'm not so sure.

"Shut up!"

"Okay, okay," I say, gritting my teeth against the knot of pain in my kidneys. I put my hands on the pickup's door. "Are you Gaddafi?"

"If that's what you want to call me, yes."

"Why didn't you come and talk to me at the bar? What's this crap?"

The man's laugh is brittle, dry. "Talk is not really my thing." The barrel pushes into my back again. "Get in. We're going for a drive."

"What do you want?"

"Everything."

Surely he knows that journalists earn little more than pocket money. And I'm worth zero as a hostage.

"There's money in my wallet. A few hundred bucks. I can take out more if you want. There's an ATM nearby." I don't want to get into the pickup with this man. Anything could happen.

"I don't want money, Alex. I am after something far more valuable."

What is he on about? Why would the syndicate be interested in me?

"You've got the wrong end of the stick, buddy," I say.

He nudges me with the gun. "That's what you think. Move. Get in the car. Now!"

Sarah

1

Mumbai feels like more of the same: just as chaotic, noisy, dirty, and steaming hot as Nigeria was. And I could see the litter on the roads as the plane descended. Not a little—tons of it.

But the people look different, and the man stamping my new, almost empty passport is a little friendlier than the burly official in Nigeria.

I'd been in Lagos nine hours when I discovered that she'd been gone for weeks. *Weeks*. Thank the freaking stars for the sudden, unexpected notice that she'd used her credit card in Mumbai. I rushed my guide back to the airport before I'd even checked in to the hotel.

How she got to India, I have no idea. She must have used cash. Caught buses. Hitchhiked, swum, snuck across borders. Maybe she even got herself a new passport. You have to give her credit: she knows how to disappear.

I'm lucky she swiped her credit card at all. She'd bought nothing on it for months. She's smarter than that. But something must have happened. A crisis. A fuckup of major proportions. Or maybe she'd used up her cash. The few thousand dollars she had couldn't have lasted forever.

"Miss?"

The voice pulls me back into the stuffy airport, the air heavy with heat and humidity.

"Yes?"

"Why have you come to India?" asks the middle-aged man behind the passport counter, possibly for the second time. He blinks at me through his glasses and chews at his bushy mustache with his bottom teeth.

I can feel the sweat trickling down my neck, forming a rivulet between my breasts. Behind me, a throng of hot, irritable tourists is lined up, eager to exit the building. It's almost five in the morning, and a suffocating mugginess hangs over everything like a wet blanket, slowing every movement to half speed. It's probably ten times worse outside.

I pull the clingy green T-shirt away from my body in an attempt to cool my skin. Wipe my palms on my jeans. My feet, in thick-soled military boots, feel like they're on fire. This is the price you pay for the vanity of wanting to appear a little taller.

First Lagos, now here. And Lagos was difficult enough.

No. Lagos was hell. Plain old hell for every one of the nine hours I spent there. It feels like half of everything happens under the table in that city, and I don't have the people skills to deal with it.

"I'm coming for a visit. To see a friend," I tell the patient official, remembering to smile.

"Sounds nice. And how long will you be here, Miss De Freitas?" He pages through my passport to find my visa and then peers at it.

I hold my breath. The false travel document is a good one, but you never know. "About a week. I'm just here to see the sights. Have a bit of a holiday."

He lifts the green book higher to study the photo, looks at me, then peers at the photo again.

I comb through my messy, short red hair. It was a little longer in the photo. Hopefully it's not going to be a problem.

He closes the passport.

I swallow. My throat is dry. I need a Coke. And a cigarette. The sooner, the better.

The man pushes the passport over the stained counter toward me. I want to take it, but his hand remains on the document.

"It's going to be the festival of the Lord Ganesh soon. If you stay long enough, you can enjoy it. It's very colorful. People all over the streets." He smiles so widely his mustache bounces up.

I want to ask who Lord Ganesh is, but I vaguely remember something about a Hindu elephant god. I smile again. Wonder how people do this all the time.

"Who knows. Maybe I'll be lucky. Thanks. Goodbye."

He nods, apparently satisfied, and waves the next passenger closer, blissfully unaware of the $30,000 in cash and the two false passports in my baggage.

Getting a cab outside the airport is easy. A black-and-yellow car brakes sharply when the driver spots me smoking outside the building. A stout older man jumps out and trots over.

"Taxi?" he asks.

I consider whether his little cab is big enough for me, my computer backpack, and my suitcase.

"Okay." I nod.

He smiles widely and tips toward me in a little bow. "You are welcome."

A similar cab stops behind us as he's loading my suitcase into the trunk. A much younger man comes rushing toward me.

"Taxi for you, madam?"

I shake my head and gesture at the older driver, who looks like he's steeling himself for a brawl. "I already have one, thanks," I say, grinding my Marlboro under my sole.

He continues looking at me.

"No," I say more loudly. "No. Really. I'm fine."

He retreats reluctantly.

Lagos taught me a thing or two. Never sound uncertain in a foreign country, especially not if you're a woman. Say yes and no with conviction. And don't wear white if you're planning to travel thousands of miles.

And now I've learned another lesson: don't try to look taller by wearing boots. When you're in a country where the temperature averages in the high eighties, accept that you're only five foot two and wear flip-flops like everyone else.

The driver wants to take my backpack, but I shake my head. It stays with me. He shrugs and opens the door for me. I get in, grateful for the air-conditioning. He settles himself in the driver's seat and turns to me with his wide grin.

"Where to? Anywhere. Your wish is my command."

I want to give him the name of my hotel, but I reconsider. Maybe he can help with the thing I most desire right now.

"I need a Coke. An ice-cold Coke."

The last liquid I consumed was just before we landed. A testy flight attendant finally brought me a lukewarm can after the third time I asked. She looked as though she would have preferred to pour it over my head instead of into a cup.

I give the driver a roll of rupee notes as an incentive to hurry up.

He nods vigorously. "Of course. The heat is bad when you're not used to it. I'll be right back."

He hops out of the cab, leaving the A/C on.

I've been worried about my equipment since we landed. Computers don't like heat. I need to get my business here wrapped up as quickly as possible.

The driver returns ten minutes later. He opens the trunk and closes it again. He gets in and holds out a Coke to me.

"This what you wanted?"

I take the drink, open it, and swallow. It's cold enough. "Perfect. Thanks." I don't care that it's just the one can. He probably helped himself to a tip.

"And now . . . where to?"

"The Taj Mahal Palace Hotel. Colaba."

Traffic is heavy despite the early morning hour. At the hotel, I pay him and get out. He indicates he'll bring my luggage in for me. I take my backpack, leave him at the vehicle, and walk to reception. Check in.

The concierge hurries over to me. "May I take your luggage for you, ma'am?"

"It's miss. And I'm fine. It's just a suitcase and a backpack."

He frowns and adjusts his gray tie uncomfortably. "And the other stuff?"

"What other stuff?"

He points past me. "Is that not yours, ma'am? Miss?"

I look around. It's a crate of Coke.

How much soda did the driver buy? How much is a rupee worth? I never checked. Just hopped on the first flight out of Lagos.

I hitch the computer backpack's strap over my shoulder and act nonchalant. "Yes. Of course. Yes, please bring it up."

2

The shop where Ranna Abramson used her credit card is long and narrow, and is packed from floor to ceiling. Pradeep & Sons, near the Colaba Causeway Market, seems to sell just about everything. It isn't far from my hotel, but it took the cab fifteen minutes to get here. Traffic laws mean zip here. Whatever is biggest gets right of way. Or whoever leans on their horn the longest.

The street smells as though someone left cooked cauliflower or fish out in the sun.

I hope the shop is air-conditioned.

From the outside, it looks like all the other shops on the street, except there are no people inside. Which probably means it's a good time to go and do what I must do. But I'm hesitant. Maybe I should just back off and let whatever happens happen.

Nope. Can't do that. There's too much at stake. Too many promises and too much guilt. Too much of this thing in my chest that keeps interfering with what should have been a much simpler life.

I wish I could reboot it. Upgrade it. Even give it away.

A bell at the front door of Pradeep & Sons announces my arrival. A tall man sticks his head through a curtain at the back of the shop and waves me in. His face, set in a scowl, slips into an easy, practiced smile, one I suspect he reserves for tourists. His shoulders are disproportionately muscled compared with his legs. He looks oddly familiar, as though I might have seen him in a movie.

"How may I be of assistance?" he asks. "We have beautiful saris, made right here in Mumbai. Handwoven pashminas, all the way from Nepal." He sounds perfectly British.

He glances down at my torn jeans and my boots, then his eyes linger for a moment on the six silver rings in my right ear, one for each member of my family.

"Or some silver jewelry perhaps? I don't have anything in platinum."

"Perhaps another day." I pull the black-and-white print I pulled off CCTV footage months ago from my back pocket. It's not a perfect likeness, but it will have to do. I move the backpack to my other shoulder. Hand him the photo. "I'm looking for this woman."

He takes the image from me.

"She's an old friend of mine," I explain. "Her mother is seriously ill. I know she was here, in your shop, because she used her credit card here."

He shakes his head, but not before the corners of his mouth twitch briefly, nervously. His gaze flickers away, to the door behind me, then back.

Jackpot. That's one thing eighteen months in prison have taught me: I'm not great with people, but I know when they're lying. Or counting exits.

The man shrugs, but it's a slow, stiff gesture. "I don't know who she is."

"It's really important that I find her. Her mother is very sick."

He shakes his head again, quickly.

Too quickly.

"As I say, I don't know her. Sorry."

He turns around and takes a green shawl off a shelf. "This one, perhaps? For your eyes. You have beautiful eyes. I'll give you a good price."

"Maybe later."

I take a business card off the pile lying on the counter and leave the cool air of the shop for the hot morning sun.

Colaba's stores are busy. Three tourist buses are off-loading their passengers on my right. Most of them are wearing big brown hats, shorts, and white sneakers. They sound American.

Beggars with dull eyes and banyan trees with roots as thick as telephone poles clog the street.

The cab driver said earlier that it might rain later today. Anything would be better than this heat. I prefer the cold. Snow, even.

I light a cigarette and wave down a cab. It's eleven o'clock. Time to go to bed. I came directly to Pradeep & Sons after checking into the hotel, and I can no longer keep my eyes open. I didn't get any sleep on the flight.

Once I've had some shut-eye, I'll take a look at where the first domino fell.

I wake a few hours later in the middle of a hotel bed I could comfortably share with four other people. I drink a Coke, take a shower, and make a few phone calls.

My parents are okay. Everything is fine at my home. The third call is short and sweet.

"Everything all right?" I ask.

My skin contracts under the cool breath of the A/C. I'm sitting naked on top of the starched bed linen, toweling my hair while I listen.

"No change."

"You're being careful, right?" I ask.

"Always." The old man coughs. "They don't know a thing. Promise."

I swallow, and my shoulders relax. "Thanks for doing this, Uncle Tiny," I say.

"Anytime."

I get my laptop out. It's quick and easy to snoop around on the Indian telephone system. Within half an hour, I have what I need. The Sylvester Stallone clone from Pradeep & Sons made a call seconds after I left. Looks like he was phoning someone in an apartment block near his store.

I fetch another Coke from the minibar and light a cigarette. When would be the best time to go and knock on that apartment's door? I wonder.

It's half past four. Why not right now?

It takes five minutes to get dressed. I'm instantly hot. I've only been in Mumbai a few hours, and I already know that I'm going to be drenched in sweat as soon as I walk out of the hotel.

I peer through the window at the sky. No sign of that rain the cab driver was hoping for. Just a few light clouds moving aimlessly over the city.

I take the stairs down to reception two at a time. Cabs stand lined up outside the building. The hotel's doorman calls the one in front of the queue and explains to the driver where I want to go.

This time the drive takes more than half an hour.

I sit back in the car and close my eyes, to signal that I don't want to make small talk. There are just too many people and vehicles in this place. I suddenly have a pang of homesickness for Pretoria. Its thunderstorms and its wide, open roads. I miss my home and my dogs and my computers and my very expensive A/C—and the relative peace and quiet that came before this mess knocked on my door. Most of all, I miss the feeling of having a modicum of control over my life.

The cab drops me in front of a tea shop. The driver, with a beard as long as my arm, jerks his head for me to get out.

It doesn't look like it could be the right place.

"Here?"

He nods vigorously.

I peel a few rupee notes from the roll in my hand, about the same as I paid for the previous cab, and mumble a thank-you.

The tea shop is tiny and busy. I take a deep breath and walk inside. I hate small spaces. Hate crowds. Hate people I don't know. The way they smell, the way their bodies take up all the space around me.

Inside, a handful of local clients moves patiently around a group of Chinese tourists all carrying yellow umbrellas. There are also three shop assistants. The place is jammed. The droning of the voices around me seems to get louder and louder.

No. No way.

I rush out, onto the sidewalk. Stand there, my back against the store window, breathing deeply. I look up at the sky, which is suddenly, half-heartedly releasing a few drops of rain. Surely this can't be the famous monsoon rain? Not the way I understand things.

Five minutes later, I'm still standing there wondering what to do. I was right about the rain. It's already disappeared. I step toward the edge of the sidewalk, turn, and look up at the building in front of me. The trees. The people walking by.

Next to the tea shop is an electronics store, and next to that one is an exact duplicate, except for the name and a front door of a different color. Just below the tea shop's name, a hand-painted sign assures me that I am indeed on Lamington Road.

It's the right address, but there are no homes here. Just a long row of shops. I take another step back, onto the road. Errant raindrops falling from the trees along the sidewalk leave big, round spots on my T-shirt. An impatient horn blares at me to get out of the way.

I jump to the right. A man on a motorbike loaded with baskets shakes his head at me and then smiles unexpectedly.

I look up again. Above the shops, beyond the thick foliage of the trees, are three floors of apartments. Mold and pollution have patterned the walls in green and black.

That must be the place, but how do I get up there?

A little ways down the sidewalk I find what I'm looking for: a narrow lane hidden behind a rusted gate, which has been left ajar. It looks as though there are stairs at the end of the dark passage. I stand near the entryway, waiting for someone to notice me, but nobody does. Seems I'm just another tourist moving in and out of the row of shops.

I slip through the gate, walk down the alley, and jog up the stairs. The ripe, rotten smell of a tropical city and its garbage is worse here than on the street.

On the first floor, I start the search from left to right. It takes me three minutes to realize I'm never going to find the apartment the Stallone clone in Pradeep & Sons called. There are no numbers on any of the doors. What now? Will I really have to ask someone for help? I think I'd rather go back to Lagos.

The apartment door nearest me is slightly open. I knock softly, then a little louder.

Nobody stirs inside.

Next one.

Another one.

The same silence greets me at every apartment until, at the fifth door, a woman in a green sari opens at the second knock and eyes me suspiciously. I push the photograph through the gap before she can close it.

"I'm looking for this woman." I point at the picture. "Please. It's urgent. Her mother is very sick."

The old woman has a thick gray braid hanging over her shoulder. She's as short as I am. Deep laugh lines fan out around her eyes as though they have been there forever. A red bindi adorns her forehead.

"You look just like my granddaughter."

She's pointing, with a finger buckled by arthritis, at my red hair and combat boots. At the faded, torn jeans.

"I wish she would dress decently." Her eyes are twinkling.

I clear my throat, a little uncomfortable.

"I'm sorry?" I offer. "It's urgent," I say, trying to get the focus back to the picture in my hand. "This woman . . . her mother is really sick."

The old woman stares at me as though assessing my true intentions. Eventually she points to the door of the apartment on her left. "That one is hers. But she's not here now."

Finally. Got her. Thank goodness.

I look at the apartment in the corner, then return my gaze to the woman. This might be the best chance I'll have to get in there. "Are you sure she's not home?"

The old woman rolls her eyes at me. "She's hard to miss. It hurts my neck to look at her. And my granddaughter's crazy about her. She's there more than she's here. I would have known if she was home."

I nod. That's good news. Very good news.

"Thank you," I say. "I appreciate your help."

The woman nods and retreats into the apartment, closing the door. But something tells me she's going to keep an eye out for any funny business. I don't think she trusts my story about Ranna's mother.

Okay. What are my options?

I can come back later, when Ranna is home, or I can wait at the apartment—inside the apartment—until she gets back.

I walk to the corner apartment's front door, looking over my shoulder. No movement from the old woman's place. I rest my hand on the polished copper doorknob. It turns easily, quietly.

The door isn't locked. Why not? Is Ranna home? Was the old woman lying?

I push the door open and walk in slowly. My boots squeak faintly on the white tiles.

"Ranna?"

No answer.

I walk to the middle of the small lounge, stop, and look around. Alex told me Ranna wasn't domestically inclined, but this is just plain weird. It makes sense that the door wasn't locked. The apartment is empty. Well, almost empty.

There's a double bed in the corner, by the window. The white bedding is old but pristine, just like the floor. The freshly painted walls are bare. No sign of the books Ranna's supposed to always be reading.

A T-shirt hangs from a length of wire strung across the window. A microwave oven rests on top of a mini fridge near the bathroom, which itself is no more than a cramped box. The blue shower and the toilet are both scrubbed clean. A tube of toothpaste rests on the basin.

Not a purse, backpack, passport, or camera in sight.

I groan with frustration. Perhaps this is another Lagos. Maybe Ranna's moved on to her next hiding place. Could be the cops know about the credit card with the new name I gave her last year—and have realized too that she's used it.

Or does she know somehow that I'm looking for her?

I inspect the tube of toothpaste. I would also have left it behind. It's almost empty. The medicine cabinet reveals a few more items. An unopened bottle of sleeping pills on the top shelf and what looks like a container of pain pills on the one below it. A yellow toothbrush behind a pack of tampons.

I put the toothpaste on the shelf next to the toothbrush and close the door.

Open it.

Check: the toothbrush is wet.

Another realization dawns on me. The room is still cool, as though someone has only recently switched off the air-conditioning.

Shit.

As I start to turn a voice stops me: "Don't move."

The steel is cold on my neck. A quick warning, then it moves away. I can sense it's still there, not touching me, but too far to reach should I want to turn around and knock it out of her hand.

I once got a knife in my back. In jail. It was the closest I ever came to dying. And it was strange: the blade was cold when it pierced my skin, just like this weapon, but burning hot as it hit muscle. People underestimate how violent women can be.

I clear my throat in search of my voice. Lift my hands slowly. I'm aware of Ranna's itchy trigger finger. "I'm not here to cause trouble."

"Then what are you doing here, Sarah? Need something for a headache?"

"I'm here to see you."

"Why?"

"I need your help."

The steel touches my neck again, as though she wants me to put up a fight, but this time it stays there. Cold. Still. Like her voice.

The last—and only—time the two of us met was in Pretoria West, and I wasn't particularly nice to her. I happily supplied her with a new passport, glad she was leaving Alex to get on with his life. She was desperate to get away. To keep Alex safe. To make sure everyone knew that she was the one who had killed her stalker, Tom Masterson, and that Alex had had nothing to do with it.

I never imagined I'd be forced to come looking for her.

"You must be in some really deep shit to come all the way to India," says Ranna. "You with your control issues."

I shake my head. "I'm not in trouble. It's Alex. He's disappeared."

She withdraws the pistol.

I turn around slowly, my hands still in the air. I study the woman in front of me. She's changed. Become harder, the lines of her body more strongly defined. All the muscles you would use to move—to run—are finely carved out on her arms and under her tight jeans. It's like she's spent a lot of time making sure she would be ready for a day like today, when the past would come knocking on the door.

There's something new in her eyes too. The blue is cold and distant. And her shoulders are tense and stiff, as though she's been treading water forever. As though she's been holding on to something with great difficulty, something that's threatening to consume her.

Must be hard to live with the stress of being wanted for murder. Of being suspected of multiple murders.

No. No, that's not it.

Ranna Abramson is angry. The casual, almost irresistible sensuality I was so envious of has been replaced with a white-hot rage.

Maybe coming here was pointless. Maybe there's nothing left of the person Alex loved so much.

Loves.

Let's be honest.

Ranna's right hand urges me to start talking, the gun in her left hand still pointed at me. Her long black hair is shorter, and it's tied back. The silver bracelets on her right arm and the military watch on her left are still the same.

"Well? Are you just going to stand there, or are you going to tell me what's going on with Alex?"

I drop my hands slowly. "How did you know I was here?"

The Glock doesn't move. "In my apartment? Amita."

"Amita? Is he the man in the shop?"

"No. Amita is a woman. My neighbor. What man are you talking about?"

"Pradeep & Sons."

"Who the hell are—"

"Wait, just hang on a bit," I say, scrambling to keep up. "The old woman—Amita—said you weren't here."

"That's what I told her to say if anyone came looking for me. And to then call me immediately."

"Nice of her."

"I'm teaching her granddaughter photography."

That is the first bit of good news I've had since walking through Ranna's front door. It means there may still be something human behind those icy eyes.

"Put that thing away," I say. "It's hard to think with a gun in my face."

She hesitates but then drops the weapon, her finger still on the trigger.

"I came alone. I promise."

She barks a short, loud laugh. "Why should I trust you? You've never liked me. Not since Alex and I started dating. Who says you didn't bring the police with you? With me out of the picture, you can get Alex right where you've always wanted him. Where he probably was before I arrived on the scene."

"It's been a year since you disappeared. Don't you think he would have moved on by now in any case?"

I regret the words the minute they're out. This is no way to convince Ranna to come back to South Africa. "I mean . . ."

"Don't . . ." She shrugs half-heartedly, but a bitter curl of her lips betrays her.

I remember this about the old Ranna, that Morse code of emotion that gives her away no matter how hard she tries to hide her feelings.

"But you're right," I admit. "I'm not crazy about you."

She lifts the Glock and flips the safety on. Slips it into the back of her jeans. Pulls her blue linen shirt over the weapon.

"What do you want, Sarah? And don't bullshit me. You told Amita my mother was sick, but now you're telling me Alex is in trouble. What's going on?"

"I lied about your mother. I thought people would be more willing to help if it was your mom. Alex is in trouble, and he needs your help. Our help. And that's the truth."

Her frown tells me she's not convinced. "How did you know to come to Mumbai?"

"Your credit card. You used it at a shop nearby. Pradeep & Sons."

"I'm not stupid. I did no such thing."

"Well, someone did."

She turns around and walks to the fridge, opens the door, shifts things around, and lifts out a brown leather wallet. She rifles through its contents.

"Damn. It's gone."

She closes the wallet and throws it back into the fridge. Slams the door and wipes away the thin veil of sweat on her forehead with the back of her hand.

"Must have been Nikhil," she says. "Some of his friends are the 'Sons' in Pradeep & Sons."

"Who's Nikhil?"

"Amita's grandson. He and his sister, Karishma, live with her. Nikhil is a problem. He doesn't like me. Says I put funny ideas in his sister's head." Ranna stomps a sneakered foot in anger. "I live like a hermit so no one can find me, and then he goes and steals my fucking credit card. I can't believe it."

"Hey, I'm sorry. But I'm also glad, otherwise I would never have found you. You've been extremely careful. No cell phone calls, no accounts in your name. Never on anyone's official payroll."

I pause for a moment. "How do you actually survive?" I wave my arm at the sparsely furnished flat. "It's not the Hilton, but it's a fairly decent roof over your head."

Her jaw tightens as she squares her shoulders again. She doesn't want to talk about it.

"Okay. Fine. Leave it."

If she doesn't want to say, I probably don't want to know. In any case, that's not why I'm here. Who she's sleeping with and what she's selling to put food on the table is none of my business.

She unties her curly black hair, then fastens it again, tighter this time. She walks to the bed and lifts the mattress. Sticks her hand into a hollow cut into the foam, takes out a red backpack, and starts throwing things into it from a closet next to the bathroom.

She zips the bag shut. Looks around the room as if she's going to miss the place, and then jerks her thumb at the front door. "Let's go."

"Where to?"

"I'm going to get my credit card back, and then I want to know about Alex."

"Why can't we talk here?" There's air-conditioning in here. And I saw a Coke in the fridge.

Ranna lifts an eyebrow. "I can't come back here. You found me. And if you were smart enough to do that, someone else might have also figured it out. And that would be very, very bad news."

"You don't trust me," I say as I scramble to keep up with Ranna's long-legged stride.

"Not for a second." She walks down the corridor to Amita's door.

I stand next to her as she knocks, trying to look as though I belong there, as though we're old friends. Then I step back a little. My father loves Laurel and Hardy, the mismatched comedians of the 1930s. I can't help thinking that we look a bit like them. Ranna is more than six feet tall, and I don't even reach her shoulders in my boots.

Pity I never mastered the art of walking around in high heels. My life would have been so different if I'd practiced that, instead of sitting in poorly lit rooms staring at computer screens all the time.

Ranna knocks again. Amita opens the door. Her face confirms what I've just been thinking: Ha-ha. Very funny.

Ranna doesn't seem to notice. "Hello, Amita. How are you?"

"Fine." She nods at me. "So, she found you. No trouble, I hope?"

"Not too much, no. Thanks for the warning. It was very helpful."

"It's nothing." She folds her hands over her green sari, a question mark in her eyes.

"Amita, do you know where Nikhil is?" Ranna flashes her a thin, forced smile.

"He was just here. What do you want with him?" Her curiosity turns into vague suspicion.

"I want to ask him a favor. I don't mind paying."

"Oh, okay. He's probably at Jagan's store." Amita sighs. "Doesn't matter how often I talk to him about it, he always ends up there. I wish he would go to college. Or find a job. Do something with his life. He is so different from Karishma." She pulls her shoulders up to her ears in an exaggerated show of exasperation. "What do you want him to do for you?"

Ranna smiles again, managing a little bit of warmth this time. "I'm going away for a while. To my mother's place. In Paris," she lies. "With Petra. She's an old friend." She points a thumb at me. "I want him to look after my place. I know Karishma is away right now."

Amita shakes her head. "It's going to cost you a lot of money. You know him."

"It's okay. I'll sort him out." Ranna's eyes are hard, though her mouth clings to the smile.

I'm almost tempted to warn the old woman.

If Amita has an inkling that Ranna's intentions aren't honorable, she's not letting on.

The old woman nods. "I wish you would. When you find him, tell him to come home. Jagan is bad news."

"I will."

Ranna leans forward and embraces Amita. Unlike the verbal exchange between the two women, the hug is real.

Just before we take the stairs down to the street, Ranna turns back to her neighbor, who is still standing at her front door, watching us.

"Tell Karishma not to give up photography. She's really good." She hesitates a moment. "Tell her I'm sorry I have to leave without saying goodbye."

3

On the sidewalk, people scatter left and right as Ranna charges ahead. She turns to me impatiently, indicating that I must step it up.

"Jagan's cell phone shop is that way. Five hundred yards." She points up the street.

Men in flowing white clothes shove past me. I try to keep myself as small as possible.

When you're tall, people keep their distance. Ranna moves in her own vacuum. Quiet. Brooding. Irresistible to watch, like weather building.

Which makes me think.

I look up at the sky. The wispy clouds are still there, but no sign of rain.

Sweat streams down my back. I am beyond irritated. "Let's get a cab."

Ranna pinches her blue linen shirt, fanning herself so that air can move between the fabric and her skin. I spot her stomach. Nut brown. She's caught some sun somewhere along the way. She rakes a hand through her hair, untying it. Unhooks the Ray-Bans from the front of her shirt and puts them on.

A tourist walking by, Asian, stops and takes a photograph of her. Then he looks at me and starts talking to the woman next to him, indicating with his hand high above his head. Then to somewhere at his knees. Laughs uproariously.

His companion is unimpressed.

"We're walking," Ranna says when the man lifts his camera again. "It's quicker."

"And hotter."

"You'll survive." She waves a warning finger at the tourist and strides away.

"I can cancel your credit card," I offer to her retreating back.

Did she even hear what I said about Alex, that he's gone missing? Was I wrong about her? About her relationship with Alex? The way the two of them acted last year, you'd swear they were the first people on earth to fall in love.

"I want my card back," she says without looking at me.

"Why? What's so special about that card?" I'm jogging to keep up. I swing my backpack onto the other shoulder.

Fifty yards down the street I realize she's not going to answer me.

"What happens when we have the credit card?" She is seriously starting to piss me off.

"Then we can talk about Alex."

Okay. That sounds better.

She slows down a little, and we walk the rest of the way in silence. We push through crowds of people and knots of cabs and ancient trucks going nowhere. There are fewer tourists now, and eventually they trickle out altogether. I hold my breath every time a pile of garbage comes into sight. There's definitely more than just paper and plastic in those heaps. It smells like there might . . . I swallow against the bile rising in my throat. It feels as though the smell is invading my lungs, seeping into my skin.

We turn left. Right. Walk past a boy without arms. A girl with a baby on her hip starts to approach Ranna, but the tall woman shakes her head almost imperceptibly, and the girl turns away to beg from someone else.

I walk past her quickly and follow Ranna around a corner. Wish I could also look like I belong here. Anywhere, really. I've always been the perpetual outsider. Never had sleepovers or sweet-sixteen parties or late-night victory parties for a hockey team. Lots of men paying attention, though, even when I shaved my head at sixteen. Not that my current short hair is much better, according to my mother.

Ranna makes a sudden right turn. I want to follow, but stop dead when the black pebble eyes of an ox with long gray horns loom before me.

"Shit."

Ranna stops and turns around. "It's fine. Just walk around it."

"There's a bull in my way. In the middle of the sidewalk in the middle of a fucking city."

Suddenly I am enraged. Unreasonably angry. I crave the order of 0s and 1s. Codes and programs that do your bidding.

"Actually, it's a cow," says Ranna.

"I really don't care."

"It belongs to her." Ranna points at a thin woman in a faded blue sari squatting down next to the animal. Her long hair hangs all the way down her back.

"It's okay," says Ranna. "Certain animals have a special status here." She waves a hand around the cow. "You're going to have to go around it. It's not going to make way for you."

Enough. I wipe the sweat off my forehead and swing the backpack down to rest on the toes of my boots. Take out my Marlboros.

Ranna pushes her sunglasses onto her head. "What are you doing? Just walk around. There's a café on the other side of Jagan's shop. You can smoke there."

I light up a cigarette and draw the smoke slowly and deeply into my lungs. Thank the bloody stars for nicotine.

The cow takes a curious step closer.

"Stop right there if you don't want to end up a medium-rare steak." I wave the smoke in the animal's direction. The old woman, who has been watching us, starts to laugh.

Ranna throws her hands in the air. "Sarah. Really . . ."

"I'm smoking." The anger and frustration of the past weeks boil over. "I am tired. This city smells like shit. I've just had a pistol poked in my neck, and Alex is gone and you don't care. And now there's this animal in the middle of Mumbai on a sidewalk with more people than I can bear, and it's 104 in the shade. I'm smoking. Deal with it."

I crunch the empty Marlboro pack in my left hand. "This is just about the only thing that still makes sense right now. Look." I jam the cigarette between my lips again. "Breathe in. Breathe out. In. Out."

People are stopping around us, staring from me to Ranna and back again. I feel like Hardy. Or was Laurel the short one?

"You really don't get out much, do you?" Ranna asks.

It's not an actual question, so I don't answer her.

Ranna folds her arms, immune to the attention we're getting. Not that it would make any difference, since we're speaking Afrikaans.

"You really need to learn to chill. Stop and smell the roses. You can't have everything your way all the time. And watch what you say about Mumbai. These are some of the nicest people you will ever meet." Ranna puts her hands on her hips. There's a softening around her mouth that looks almost friendly.

"If I don't get out much, it's because I don't want to. Besides, it's pretty hard for people in prison to travel."

"You've been out for what, three, four years now?"

"Yeah, but I've never traveled much."

"Never?" Now she's smiling openly. "How many times have you been outside South Africa?"

"Does Lesotho count?"

"That little landlocked country in South Africa? No."

"Okay, then. Twice. This is the second time."

"What was the first time?"

"Lagos. Looking for you."

She raises her eyebrows. "Lagos? Right. Then I get it. It isn't exactly the best advertisement for travel. Abuja is better." She looks me up and down. "Come to think of it, you don't look like the type to get amped about flying in little airplanes and staying in tiny hotel rooms."

"There are very few places you can't go with a computer." I don't want to concede that she's right. The Taj and all its Saracen revival-style glory is costing me a small fortune. I took the biggest room the hotel had available.

She stops nagging me and points at a store behind her. "Finish that cigarette. I'm going to get water, before we both dehydrate."

4

Ranna decides that we need to wait and see if we can spot Amita's grandson, Nikhil, at Jagan's cell phone store before we barge in there. I still have no idea why we're chasing this credit card. Can't we just get on a plane and leave? I can cancel the frigging card remotely.

The café across from Jagan's is a small relief. Two fans are whirring noisily from left to right to keep the few square yards at a reasonable temperature. The linoleum floor and the counter clearly used to be white but haven't been for a long time. I don't mind. All that matters right now is that it is a few degrees cooler inside than out there. Plus, I'm allowed to smoke in here.

We both drink Cokes while I finish a cigarette from a fresh pack of Marlboros. Then Ranna sends me to the cell phone shop to see whether Nikhil is there, but I don't see anyone matching his description: shortish, carrying a few extra pounds around his waist, bangs that hang over his eyebrows, and low-slung jeans with Calvin Klein underwear peering out. The only person there is a friendly older man with a beard. He asks whether I'm looking to buy a cell phone so that I can call my mother.

I'm seriously starting to consider buying a pair of stilettos.

I walk back to where Ranna is sitting, drinking sweet, milky tea from a small glass, despite the heat.

"Nikhil's not there," I say.

"Then we wait."

I don't argue, though the fear and impatience about Alex gnaws away at me.

Ranna finishes the tea, asks for another. "Tell me about Alex. What's going on?"

She leans back in the red plastic chair. We're at a table that allows her to keep an eye on the cell phone store across the road.

Her expression is a mixture of curiosity and distrust. I was hoping for concern, but I'll take what I can get.

"Alex did a series of stories in Welkom," I say. "Illegal mining. The Zama-Zamas. Syndicates that mine the old shafts for leftover gold. Something like that."

"Sounds like a story he'd be interested in."

The café owner brings over our drinks. Ranna takes her tea, pushes another Coke toward me.

"Probably, yes." I pop open the cool drink and insert a straw into the can. "The way I understand it, he met a contact at Shafts—a bar with a bad reputation. Someone called him late one night and asked him to meet there. The barman says it looked as though Alex was waiting for someone, but nobody turned up. He drank a beer and left. No one has seen him since then."

"How do you know all this? Did you go to Welkom?"

"No. I went over the phone records. Police reports. Newspapers. It was a big story for a while. Especially because of his relationsh—his connection with you. You were all over the news last year, you know."

Ranna looks perplexed. "I don't get it. Why are you here? The police are already involved, and they're better at that sort of thing than I am. What do you want me to do?"

Irritation is bubbling up in me again. "A lot. You love him, Ranna."

"Loved."

"What?"

"I loved him. But in the end, he was just another man who cost me everything."

"I don't believe you."

"Believe whatever you want."

I want to shake the nonchalance out of her.

"Ranna." I take a deep breath. "Remember what you did for him last year? You gave up everything so that he could carry on with his life. So that no one would know he was with you when Tom attacked you and you killed him. Or that he helped you get rid of Tom's body."

I slam the Coke down on the table and stub out my cigarette. Grit my teeth before I venture, more calmly, "To the cops, Alex is just another person who disappeared. To me and you, it's something different. Something more. And I've never met anyone as stubborn as you. You don't give up. Ever. I mean, look at your history. All those years running from Tom. Other people would have checked out a long time ago."

I take a sip of Coke and light another cigarette, unsure if she's interested enough to answer me.

Ranna crosses her legs slowly, pointedly, and then studies me as though I'm something she's observing through her camera lens. With objective interest. As though wondering what light to cast me in for the best shot. Or whether to abandon the project altogether.

"His newspaper must have made a fuss. They always look after their people," she says eventually.

"They did. But it's been seven weeks, and there's still no news. He's become a weekly footnote on page eighteen. The last story on the website. His poor parents. His wonderful career. His bed gymnastics with you. Blah blah blah."

Finally. A response other than disinterest.

Ranna sits up straight. Her eyes soften with an emotion I can't quite name. Long fingers grip the glass of tea.

"Seven weeks is a long time. You never said it's been that long."

"I've been looking for you for more than a month." I blow out a furious stream of smoke. "And don't you follow South African news anymore? I kept hoping you'd contact me to find out what was going on."

"Why bother reading about a place I'm never going back to?" She shakes her head slowly. "I still don't get why you came here. Why can't you find Alex? Find other people who can help you? Surely you still have contacts from your time in prison. From the work you're still doing?"

This is the one question I was expecting. I hope I can lie convincingly. "I don't know people who can kick open doors, just a bunch of garden-variety white-collar criminals with computers. You care about Alex. And you make things happen. Face it. And in any case, you're already . . ." I run out of words.

Ranna smiles wanly. "And I'm already a criminal. I killed Tom Masterson, so I probably won't have any problem when it comes to doing whatever is necessary?"

It sounded better in my head somehow.

"Yes. Something like that."

"Don't worry. I know. I've learned. I learn fast. That's the only way you survive."

"What do you mean?" What has this woman been doing in Mumbai?

Ranna shakes her head briefly. "Never mind." She sips from her glass of tea. "So, in this grand scheme of yours, what was I supposed to do?"

I don't like her use of the past tense. Push on anyway. "The police have pretty much moved on. They're already overworked. But I have a lead. Perhaps if we work together, we can find Alex."

"So, you're the brain and I'm the brawn?" She raises her eyebrows sarcastically. "I'm not sure I'm flattered."

"Whatever. Sheesh."

She finishes her tea and looks over toward Jagan's again. A couple walks in, their arms around each other.

"Why didn't you give your lead to the police?" she asks.

"I did. They went to the address I gave them, but there was nothing. Just an abandoned building in Welkom, near one of the old gold mines."

"How did you get the address?"

"I tracked Alex's laptop. I had him download an app so I could trace his machine in case it was ever stolen."

"And?" Ranna looks irritable. "I don't get it. The police went there; there was nothing. What's the lead?"

I grit my teeth. "I traced the laptop again. Someone really likes that thing. I think it's the same people. This time it looks like it's at an old steel factory in Sasolburg. It's been sitting there for a day now. I don't want to tell the cops again, because I have a feeling that one of the policemen on the team looking for Alex is part of the syndicate that kidnapped him. It's the only explanation I have for what happened in Welkom."

"A laptop signal? It's a pretty thin lead. These syndicate men might have kept the laptop, or sold it off, and gotten rid of Alex ages ago."

"Maybe. Or the laptop might take us somewhere. Give us a fresh lead. And for that I need help. Someone I can trust to have Alex's best interests at heart."

"And you have nothing else? No other leads? No fingerprints or DNA or anything?"

"No."

Ranna chews her bottom lip. "Okay. Next question. How do I get back into South Africa? As you say, I'm front-page fodder."

"I've organized a new identity for you. Everything. Bank account, passport, ID. I've even set up a business for you. And the money that's in your account is yours to keep. All you need to do is say yes."

"I don't need money," she says, somewhat defensively.

"You do. Just take it."

She runs a contemplative hand through her hair. Fiddles with the sunglasses hooked into the front of her shirt. "Sarah . . ." Her voice wavers. "Don't you . . . I was actually serious before. Who's to say Alex is still alive?" There's something bright in her eyes, melting the icy blue. "Someone has his laptop, but how do we know they didn't get rid of him a long time ago? Throw him down a mine shaft? Syndicates like those don't kidnap people. They kill them."

"Maybe they're keeping him alive as a bargaining chip. Who knows?"

"Has there been any ransom demand?"

"No."

"Then maybe . . . maybe you need to start considering that that's not the case."

"It's not . . ." There's a lump in my throat I try to swallow. I look down at my feet. I don't want Ranna to see me like this.

"Then I want to see his body," I say. "I want to give him a proper burial. A place for his mother to go and grieve."

I look past her at the restaurant owner reading his newspaper. The fan at his feet, turning left. Right. Left.

"Okay," she says, nodding. "Let me think about it."

"That's not good enough. Yes or no."

She sighs. "Okay. Fine. I'll help you look for Alex. I don't have anything better to do anyway. And I can't stay here. Not now that you found me." She wipes a hand over each eye. "You want another Coke?"

I nod. She gets up and orders two Cokes from the man behind the counter.

I open my laptop while we're drinking and start looking for the next flight back to South Africa.

5

Ten minutes later, a chubby man in jeans, a red cap, and a Yankees T-shirt walks into Jagan's shop.

Ranna gets up, her eyes on fire.

I close my laptop. Must be Nikhil. "What's the plan?"

She looks at me in mock surprise. "We need a plan?"

"Are you just going to walk in there and ask him for your credit card?"

Ranna puts her sunglasses on. "Why not?"

"That's not a plan."

She smiles and picks up her backpack. "Stay here if you like."

I get to my feet. I'm not letting her out of my sight until we have Alex.

We jog across the road, dodging bicycles, motorbikes, and cabs.

The two men sitting behind the counter freeze when Ranna pushes open the glass door of the shop. It's the friendly bearded man from earlier with the man in the Yankees shirt next to him.

So this is Nikhil. Up close, he looks like a pimp in a B movie.

"Quinne," he calls when he spots Ranna.

He's doing his best to sound friendly, but his voice is thin and wary. His right hand, a gold ring on each finger, quickly sweeps a pile of SIM cards off the counter onto the floor.

It takes me a second to remember that Ranna's name changed to Quinne after Tom died. I was the one who changed it.

Ranna closes the door behind us. Pushes a box full of cell phone chargers in front of it. And then another.

She turns back to the men. "Nikhil."

I move to the right. I get the feeling Ranna has a plan after all.

Nikhil gets up from the stool. Then sits down again. His eyes dart from me to Ranna to his colleague and then quickly glance down at a spot below the counter.

Bad news. All of it. Bad, bad news.

Sweat starts trickling down my temples, my back.

Nikhil gives a weak little laugh. "What can I do for you? Everything okay with Karishma?"

Beside him, the older man—Jagan?—shifts uncomfortably in his seat. One hand strokes his beard nervously, the other one is out of sight.

"Everyone's fine," Ranna says in a soothing voice. "I just want to have a quick word."

"With me?" asks Nikhil, faking surprise.

The old man is shaking his head. "I don't want any trouble."

"Then I'm going to have to assume those SIM cards aren't stolen."

Jagan's face freezes. His hands slide under the counter, right where Nikhil had glanced just a minute before.

"Stop right there."

When I look at Ranna, she's got the Glock in her left hand.

I glance at the door to make sure it's closed, though I have a strong inclination to open it and run away. Ranna seems to have learned a few new tricks since I last saw her. Her hands are dead steady, and her face is calm, as if aiming a gun at a person isn't at all hard to do. It looks like she wouldn't hesitate to pull the trigger.

She signals for Jagan to put his hands in the air. "Up. Come on. Quickly."

He doesn't move.

Four long strides and she's up against the counter. "Come on now, Jagan. Don't be difficult." She sounds like she's ordering tea. She looks at Nikhil. "And you can put your hands where I can see them too, thank you."

Nikhil's face contorts with anger. "You won't get away with this. Everybody's going to know you were here. How many people in Mumbai look like you—tall, white, and pissed off?" His eyes slide down her body as though he's putting a price on her. "If I owned you, we would make movies. Get rich." He looks past her at me. "And your little friend isn't too bad either. In fact . . ."

Ranna slams the butt of the gun into his face before he can get the rest out. His head whips to the side.

To her left, Jagan is suddenly on his feet, a revolver in his hand.

"Ranna!" I yell.

She swings the Glock until the barrel is resting calmly against Jagan's forehead, her right hand gripping Nikhil by the throat.

"My credit card. That's all I want," she tells Nikhil calmly.

Nikhil wheezes. Jagan shakes his head, side to side, up and down. The gun in his hand drops to the floor.

"What credit card?" Jagan squeaks.

"Your friend here stole my credit card." She tightens her grip on Nikhil's throat, and the wheezing increases. "Where is it, Nikhil?"

"Ranna . . . ," I say.

Her fingers become a white claw around Nikhil's neck. His hands are fighting them for release, for balance, as she pulls him over the counter, rage etched on her face.

"Ranna," I try again. I'm not going back to jail. And definitely not for murder. "He can't answer you if he's dead."

She opens her hand as if she's touched something disgusting.

Nikhil collapses onto the stool and then falls forward, his head banging against the counter. He is gasping. He wipes the blood off his face.

Looks like Ranna crushed his nose with the blow to his face.

"You bitch," he puffs.

The pistol is still aimed at Jagan. "Look at you. Your grandmother went to so much trouble to teach you manners." She smacks the side of his head. "My credit card. Now."

"It's in the back," Nikhil grumbles, motioning toward whatever is behind a curtain of blue and white beads. "I'll go and get it."

"You're staying right here," Ranna says. She calls to me over her shoulder in Afrikaans. "Can you go and see if you can find it?" She turns back to Nikhil. "Where is it?"

He sniffs, wipes more blood from his nose and mouth with the back of his hand.

"Nikhil," Jagan pleads, the Glock still aimed at his head.

"In a box." He spits out the words. "Behind the cigarettes."

I hop onto the counter, swing my legs over, and jump off. The quicker we get out of here, the better.

It's chaos in the cramped storeroom. Piles of cigarette cartons and cell phones are stacked as high as the ceiling. *Behind the cigarettes.* Very funny, Nikhil. Ha ha ha.

I've also had it with his miserable ass. I stick my head through the curtain.

"Strangle him again. It's just phones and cigarettes in here. Where am I supposed to look?"

Ranna grabs his shoulder.

"Wait, wait, wait! The Dunhills. The Dunhills!"

I turn back. Dunhills. Oh, good. On my left. I put a hand behind the pile of cigarette cartons and push them to the ground. Spot a green metal box in the corner. Locked.

I throw it down and stomp on it with my boots. Again and again. Eventually the lock pops open. Inside are two bundles held together by elastic bands. One credit cards, the other passports.

I squat down and shuffle through them to find the silver card I gave Ranna so many months ago. *QS Daniels.*

I walk back through the curtain. "Got it."

Ranna nods.

I jump over the counter and catch Jagan glaring at Nikhil.

"We don't do credit cards," he hisses at him.

Nikhil snorts. "*You* don't do credit cards."

Ranna smacks his head again. "Have some respect for your elders."

He stares at her angrily.

She takes the credit card from me and slips it into the back pocket of her jeans without taking her eyes off the men. Moves back a slow, careful step.

"You've got your card so you can fuck off now," Nikhil snarls. "And take your Chihuahua with you."

"Watch it, you pile of shit," I hiss. "I'll . . ."

"Wait. Wait now," says Ranna. She puts her hand on my shoulder and pushes me toward the door. "You just go and make sure no one bothers us." She shifts the pistol to her right hand and rummages blindly in the side pocket of her backpack. She takes out another credit card, a gold one, her eyes never leaving the two men. "We're not done here."

"What do you mean?" Nikhil looks from her face to the Glock, worry seeping into his eyes. "Don't do anything stupid now."

"Shut up," snaps Ranna. She puts the gold credit card on the counter and shifts the gun back to her left hand.

She asks me, in Afrikaans again, "How long till we can get away from here?"

"Day after tomorrow."

"Vietnam?"

Vietnam? What the hell? Then I notice Nikhil's paying close attention. Vietnam sounds the same in English and Afrikaans. Ranna's making sure he understands and remembers.

So, this was her plan. Finally, I know what's going on.

"Yes." I play along. "Halong Bay."

She looks back at Nikhil. "In three days you're going to buy something big with this credit card." She pushes the card toward him.

Nikhil takes it and turns it over. "Why? Whose is this? Who is *R. Abramson*?"

Not bad, I have to admit. Nikhil has no idea what this means. If the South African police and Interpol are on the ball, they're going to track him down as soon as he uses it. Ranna's laying a false trail, so we can slip back into South Africa.

"Doesn't matter," says Ranna. "I want you to buy Karishma a camera, and Amita a new living room suite. And if there's anything left, buy yourself whatever your heart desires."

"Why?"

"Because I want to thank them. You know how often I had dinner at your grandmother's."

I look at my watch. We're pushing our luck hanging around here. "We need to get going."

Ranna nods and starts walking backward slowly.

I push the crates away from the door.

Ranna still has the pistol trained on Nikhil. "In three days, you hear? And if you don't, I'll inform your grandmother and the police about what you and your friend over here are up to. Three days."

I open the door, slip out. Watch as Ranna reverses out of Jagan's store.

The glass door slams behind us. We walk quickly, crossing the road diagonally. Two blocks down the road Ranna stops and hails a cab.

Thank goodness. I was starting to think we were going to have to walk everywhere.

"Do you think he's going to listen to you? On the three-day thing?" I ask.

"No. We probably have two days, maybe less. Luckily, Amita is a formidable woman. He's wary of her."

A cab stops next to us, tires screeching. It's a three-wheeled motorbike with a black bench behind the driver and a black awning over the seat.

Ranna climbs in and makes space for me as best she can, her long legs at an awkward angle. Couple of million in investments, and I can't ride in a cab with air-conditioning and wider seats.

"I hope Nikhil gives us two days, at least," I venture. "I checked while we were in the restaurant. The flights are all full."

"Are you trying to book direct flights? We could go via Dubai or Istanbul."

"I got you a new passport, just in case. The woman who did it is good, and you've been careful about showing your face, but I don't know if I want you moving through airport security more than once."

"I thought you did all the passports," says Ranna, sounding surprised.

"No. Someone helps me. There's lots I can do with them, like open a bank account, but I don't actually make them myself. Passports, identity documents, driver's licenses—they're a skill set all on their own. The best is if you get blanks from Home Affairs or from the government printers, and for that, you need contacts. It works even better when you can apply for those types of documents using falsified papers. Then they are one hundred percent legit."

I rummage in my backpack for a bottle of water. Take a few thirsty sips. "I definitely prefer two direct flights," I say. "But if we have to take a connecting flight, I want to go through someplace we don't need visas."

Ranna frowns. "Do you really think anyone is still going to bother about me that much?"

"Oh yes."

She opens the backpack at her feet and takes out her own water, swallowing down half of it before she says, "Why? It's been a year since Tom's death."

"Your disappearance was big news. More than I think you realize. South Africa hasn't had a female serial killer for quite a while."

She freezes, the water bottle halfway to her mouth. "Serial killer?"

"That's what Interpol calls you. Even though they only have proof of Tom's death." I wonder if I should tell her everything. It might scare her out of flying back with me. I push on anyway. "The media calls you the Black Widow."

Her eyebrows shoot up.

"*You* magazine," I explain. "*Sunday Times. The Daily Sun.*"

"That's not terribly original."

"They really ran with the story. Peter, Gerard, Tom, Billy—all your dead boyfriends. Men I'm sure you don't even know were quoted on their opinions about you. Sergeant Boel de Jonghe became the cop who almost caught you."

Ranna exhales sharply. Takes another swig of water from her bottle. "And you want me to go back?"

Guilt rises in my throat, making it hard to swallow. It's an unexpected emotion. It's not as though Ranna and I are best friends or anything. All she's managed to do is ruin Alex's life.

"I already told you: I don't know who else to ask," I say, looking at the heavily laden bicycles squeezing past the cab on the left. "No one else cares about Alex enough to help. And we're talking syndicates here, not one guy acting on his own. The odds aren't exactly in our favor. In any case, Alex's mother . . . she's convinced that you're the only one who can help. Maybe I wouldn't even be here if she hadn't asked."

That's the truth, and a card I didn't really want to play.

"Sophia? This is the first time you've mentioned that to me."

"Yes, well, I didn't imagine it would be necessary to blackmail you."

She barks out a little laugh.

I sigh. "Aunt Sophia likes you. She says that if you were able to sort out Alex's dad, you can do anything. She still talks about the day you decked Francois Derksen."

"How is she?"

"Fine. Apart from this mess, of course. Alex is all she has. You get that. You and your mom only had each other after your father died."

Ranna opens her backpack and puts the water bottle away. Looks at her feet for a second or two. "You're right. You don't need Sophia as a trump card. Hearing you ask for help is almost enough." She gives a vague smile, wipes her forehead, and takes a deep breath. "I hope this woman's passports are good. In fact, they better be perfect."

"She's the best there is."

"Good, because I'll need another set of documents as soon as I get to South Africa. Before we do anything else."

"Why?"

"In case I need to get away quickly. I can't use the same passport you're going to give me to get away. Too easy to trace. And you have to filter the money from my existing account to a new one."

I shouldn't have told her about the Black Widow thing. "That's going to waste time."

"It's seven weeks later, Sarah. Seven fucking weeks in the hands of a gold syndicate. An hour or two isn't going to make much difference. And when we land in Johannesburg, we'll be close to your contact. I'm pretty sure you use someone close to home. It'll be quick."

"Can we decide when we get there?"

"No. Alex might be in trouble, but that doesn't mean he's forgiven me for leaving him last year. Helping him doesn't mean that he and I will just pick up where we left off. He is pissed off at me, and you know it. He tackles problems. Me? I run away. And I need new documents to do that. As soon as we have him—if we get him—I have to disappear again."

I swear inwardly. How can I agree to this?

"You know I'm right," she insists. "It's not . . . Alex is still . . ." She turns her head away from me, up at the sky, where the clouds suddenly hold a definite promise of rain. "I would do anything to help him, but I have to help myself too. Otherwise I'm just going to be that woman hiding in Dar es Salaam again. The little girl in my father's study."

"I understand, believe me, but time is really not on our side," I plead.

"I don't want to be difficult, Sarah, but I'm not going to allow myself to be locked up for the rest of my life. You do this, or I'm staying put."

"All right," I agree reluctantly. "We'll do it your way, then. But we're going to track Alex immediately after that. And you better not have any excuses then."

Ranna

1

My father's calling me.

"Isabel?"

He's using my first name, the one I hate. The name he insisted on: his mother's name.

"Isabel?"

He's in the living room, as he always is this time of the evening, but something's not right. He's afraid. I could see that when we were eating dinner earlier. He got up twice to check whether the back door was locked. And he closed the curtains before it even got dark. His suitcase is at the door, ready for when he leaves later this evening on one of his business trips.

I don't know what he's afraid of. Usually, it is my mom and me who are petrified. Of him.

Maybe he's sick. He was rubbing his chest while we were having supper. A heart attack, maybe? A stroke? That's what happens when you eat too much salt. And he's always after more salt.

If he's sick, it's not having any effect on how much he's drinking. My mom usually counts the number of glasses of brandy he's had. That's how she knows when to tell me to go to bed, no matter how early it is in the evening. The glass in his hand now is number five, one before I usually get sent to my room.

At this time of the evening, he's usually only on number three. The TV news hasn't even come on yet.

"Isabel, for goodness' sake, I'm talking to you!"

He's shouting now.

I walk to the living room. He's in his armchair, his legs stretched out in front of him. When he sees me, he puts the glass down on the coffee table. Summons me closer.

My mother's on the sofa. "Say goodnight to your father." She looks at me, her eyes warning me to do as she says, and then nods in the direction of my room.

"Goodnight." I turn around to leave.

His voice stops me. "Where are you going? Did I say you could go?"

I always loved his voice when he used to read me stories, but that doesn't happen anymore, not since I was five. I'm eleven now. I still love stories, though now I read them to myself. And not fairy tales anymore.

I stand in the doorway. Look at my mom. She silently urges me to answer him.

"I'm going to bed," I say. "Goodnight."

My father gets up. "Come here a minute first. I want to show you something."

I stand stock-still.

"Come on." He walks toward me and takes my hand.

I look at my mother again. She's frozen on the sofa, her eyes resting on my father's unfinished glass of brandy on the coffee table.

I know that look. She's no help to me now. I will just have to go with him and hope he gets bored soon.

I follow his unsteady footsteps across the thin carpet in the corridor.

People who have children shouldn't drink. Ever.

In his study, he tells me to sit down on the leather chair at the desk. There's a copper plate on the desk with his name engraved on it: Hendrik Kroon.

He goes to the shelf and takes down a few books to reveal the dull steel of the safe. He turns and gestures for me to look away. I already know the code, but I play along. People often use their birthdays, I've read. Especially men. But I did see him put it in once, and I seldom forget a number.

I sometimes wish I could forget. Two weeks ago, he hit my mother when they both thought I was asleep. When it was done, she came into my room and sat there crying. I carried on faking sleep, too afraid to open my eyes and have another image I can never erase.

It's been like this forever, it seems. I was going to have a baby brother, but my father took him away from us, from me. With three angry kicks to my mother's stomach.

Lucky him, I suppose. Who wants to grow up in this house anyway?

What I don't understand is why my mother hasn't taken us away from here.

You'd think losing a baby would be enough to get her to go, but even that didn't make her leave.

He hurts her, then gives her lots of flowers, a new dress, some perfume, and just like that we're back where we started.

"Here," says my father, putting something down in front of me.

It's a slim, flat red box, longer than my hand. I don't move. Sometimes it's hard to know what the right thing to do is.

He points impatiently at the box. "Open it."

He turns to the bar cabinet in the corner and pours brandy into a new glass.

I don't want to open it. Ever. I wish he would stop drinking. I'd rather have that than this box. Stop drinking. Stop being angry.

And why am I getting a gift? My mother usually gets the presents, when he's been away or when he's hit her. Not me.

He bends down toward me. "Come on now." His breath is sour. "Say thank you."

I stare at the box. I don't want anything from him.

"Do you have to be as difficult as your fucking mother?" He slams his empty hand on the desk. Some of the brandy sloshes onto my pajama top. "Open it!"

Instead, I slip off the chair.

"Isabel, what are you . . ."

I run toward the door, but he's quicker. Slams it shut so hard the house seems to shake.

I hear hurried footsteps in the house. Is my mother trying to escape?

He yanks me by the arm. "What the fuck is your problem, you ungrateful little bitch?"

He drags me toward the desk.

"Stop it," I say, trying to twist out of his grasp. "You're hurting me!"

His face contorts. He shakes my arm. "How dare you speak to me like that!"

I duck, but not fast enough. His fist explodes against my shoulder. He always hits my mother like this, where the bruises can't be seen.

This is the first time he's hit me.

I refuse to cry, even though the tears are right there.

He shouts at me. His nose is red. His eyes are red. The loose skin around his neck trembles with every word he spits at me.

I focus on the side of his head. On his temple.

The door opens slowly.

My father turns around. "What? What do you want? Must you always interfere?"

"I made us some coffee," says my mother.

My father snorts. "Coffee? Go and drink your coffee. Isabel and I are busy."

My mother touches her hair, then the earrings he gave her earlier this evening. She seems out of breath. Nervous.

"No."

She says the word so quietly, I'm almost sure I misheard.

My father drops my arm and turns to her with his hands on his hips.

"What did you say?"

"No. Leave Isabel alone. I'm a grown woman. I can take it. But you're not touching my daughter."

"Your daughter?"

I stop listening to them. I slip away, deeper into the shadows. Where can I hide? Behind the chair. Under the desk. Maybe this will all stop. If I keep quiet and close my eyes, maybe they'll forget that I'm here.

As I move toward the desk, I notice that the safe is still open.

It's never open because, my father always says, it has dangerous things in it. Like his revolver.

I look from the safe to my parents. They're in the middle of the room, on the green rug my mother loves so much.

It's always strange to see them close together. She's so much taller than he is. I take after her and my grandmother. I'm as tall as my father now. My mother says he always liked that she was so tall, but then, one day after they got married, he stopped liking it.

They've forgotten about me. I pull my arm into my sleeve. I finished reading a book yesterday about all the mistakes this woman made when she murdered her husband. She wasn't close enough. If you're not close enough, the angle looks all wrong.

I walk to the shelf. Stand on my tiptoes and take the revolver out of the safe. All I need to do is cock the gun. That's what I read. The click is soft and metallic, and my mom and dad don't hear it, because they're so busy shouting.

I walk closer. The gun is heavier than I thought.

My father's hand is around my mother's throat. His left fist is pulled back. She sinks to her knees, crying. I move toward his other side. He is left-handed, like me. They don't see me.

I take long strides. The rug feels like wool beneath my bare feet. I lift the revolver and put it right up against his temple and pull the trigger.

2

I wake up. The room is bathed in the moody light of a single lamp burning in the corner. I try to steady my breathing. Blink my eyes until the outline of the TV becomes clear. The curtain. I wait for the soft drone of the A/C to register; the white sheets rustle as I move my feet.

The dream was so clear, it feels like it happened yesterday.

When will I ever forget? Is it possible to erase the fact that you shot your father?

I look from the bed toward the circle of light in which Sarah is still working at her laptop, cigarette in hand. The room reeks of smoke. Judging by the pile of cigarette butts in the ashtray next to her, she hasn't stopped working since we ordered room service for dinner—curry, hot enough to burn the skin off a goat.

Girl can certainly hold her hot stuff. I felt like my head was on fire after the third bite.

I yawn, turn around, and pull the duvet up to my shoulders. Shiver. The air is chilly. Sarah has set the A/C at 62. It's ridiculous to feel this cold in Mumbai.

I've learned a few things about Sarah. She doesn't like heat or crowds. Actually, she dislikes people in general. And I was right about small spaces. She climbed the stairs to her hotel room instead of taking the elevator.

Perhaps her issue with confined spaces is related to her time in prison. I'm not sure why she dislikes people. I suspect it's just a personality thing.

Apart from these observations, I don't know much about her. I am aware of her history with Alex, and that she served time for theft and fraud, but that's about it. She is surly and uncommunicative. And it's not that she's shy. Most shy people would have lost some of their reticence amid the shouting and upheaval in Jagan's shop, but not her. She just got angry. And anger is not an emotion. I would know. It's like sand: You use it to bury other—truer—things. Hate. Jealousy. Love.

Love.

I look back at the desk. Sarah's fingers are flying over the keyboard. The tapping is nonstop, almost rhythmic. She's still wearing torn jeans, but with a fresh T-shirt. Her red hair is a little longer than I remember. It's curling around her ears. Elfin ears. Elfin hands. She's the type of woman almost all men like. The type of woman men take to bed.

I wonder whether anything happened between her and Alex while I was gone. She's gorgeous. Rich. Tough as nails, but she has a soft heart for Alex. She walks like a woman who knows how to make men stop and look, but she's not aware of it. Doesn't know she's beautiful. Or doesn't give a shit.

And me? What's left of me after so many years of running? I'm interesting, at most. I've traveled. Covered a war or two. Taken some interesting photos. And I've read just about every book I've ever come across. But I am tired. And old.

Older.

Would Alex have been able to resist Sarah? And why would he have had to? I'm the one who left.

I turn away from Sarah. No use thinking about these things. Sarah and I have to find Alex—if he's still alive—and then I have to hit the road again. That's my immediate future, and it's pointless torturing myself with speculation. Or comparison. Focus on the syndicate. On how to get Alex out if we find he's still alive.

I can't believe he got himself mixed up in such a mess. What was he doing getting involved with people like that? Did he just go to cover a story, or did he become reckless after what happened? After us?

Stop it. Stop thinking.

I suppress a yawn and look at my watch. Half past one. It's the second of September. The earlier stirring of memories morphs into an unpleasant jolt. It's my mother's birthday today. And the anniversary of the day I shot him—Hendrik Kroon.

Explains the dream.

I turn to lie on my back. Stare at the ceiling and consider my options. Can I get away with "forgetting" my mother's birthday?

A voice in my head reminds me that this is the only day of the year I ever call her. I've long stopped calling at Hanukkah and New Year's and on every other day that means something to her.

I do the math in my head. It's three o'clock in New York now.

I get up, take my phone, and walk to the bathroom. I don't want Sarah to be privy to this conversation.

"I have to call someone," I say as I walk past her.

"Is the phone on the other side safe?"

"Think so."

"How sure are you?"

"I've done it before, so yes."

She shakes her head. The cigarette she was about to draw on hovers near her lips. "You know they track your mother's phone calls, right?"

"How do you . . ." Of course. Sarah deals in information. That's how she makes her money.

"Relax. I know what I'm doing."

I close the bathroom door behind me. This annual phone call is hard enough without first having to negotiate with someone else about making it.

I call the number. The phone rings and rings.

I look at my watch. Fay Frost, the woman who lives in the apartment above my mother's, should be home. I dial her number again. Her phone rings. She's over eighty now, and her knees aren't what they used to be. I know I have to wait patiently for her to get to the phone.

She answers. Same nasally Brooklyn accent I remember, like something from the movies. Fay married up six decades ago—into the Upper East Side—and not for the money, she always says. Never for the money.

"Mrs. Frost?"

"Yes?"

"This is Isabel. Karla Abramson's Isabel."

"I've been wondering when I'd hear from you again."

This is probably the seventh or eighth time I've called my mother via Fay. The first few times was so that Tom wouldn't find me. Now it's to sidestep the police. I have no idea how my mother explained the situation to Fay, and I'm not sure I want to know. The only thing that matters is that I can trust her. Time has taught us that.

"How are you, Mrs. Frost? Is the rheumatism still bad?"

"How would it not be? I'm getting older, not younger."

"I'm sorry to hear that."

"Such is life." She coughs wheezily and takes a deep breath. "But enough of these morbid things. Tell me, where do you find yourself this year?"

It's become a game between us. She's always wanted to travel, but never really made time for it.

"Bangkok," I say, lying as I do every year.

"Is the sun shining?"

I look out of the bathroom window, which can't open, at the darkness outside. "Yes. And it's wonderfully warm."

"Ah." She sighs. "At least one of us is getting to see the world." She coughs again, longer this time. "Let me get your mother," she says.

I listen to her put the phone down and shuffle off.

Ten minutes later she comes back on the line. “Here she is, then. Look after yourself, dear. And come and visit us. Your mother misses you.”

“I will.”

“You say that every year.”

I don’t know how to answer her. She’s right. But even if I did want to visit, if I forgave my mother for making us stay in that house long after we should have left, I wouldn’t be able to do so. Not now, after everything that has happened. Not with the police in tow.

I wonder whether my mother knows what’s going on. Would the cops have contacted her? Gone to look for me at her and Moshe’s posh apartment?

“Are you still there, Isabel?”

“I really do want to visit, Mrs. Frost. I’ll try and make a plan.”

The old woman laughs as though she knows I’m lying. “Well, then. I hope to see you one day. Your mother shows me pictures of you, but they’re all from when you were little. Look after yourself.”

Photos? I thought she went to New York with hardly anything from her old life.

Then it’s her voice on the line. “Isa.”

It takes me by surprise. She sounds so fragile and old. I do the math in my head. She’s sixty-four. It’s not that old. Is she ill?

“Are you having a nice birthday, Ma? Everything okay?”

She laughs. It’s reassuring.

“My birthday is tomorrow, Isa.”

“Yes, but you’re already having a birthday here,” I say, looking at my watch. “And you’re almost having your birthday in South Africa.”

“Where are you?” She sounds worried, her breath up in her throat like it always is when she’s nervous.

“Bangkok.”

“Fancy that.”

I smile. That's what she used to say to me when I was little and she knew I was lying.

"How old are you this year, Ma?"

"Twenty-nine. Same as every year."

"I remember twenty-nine. It was a good year. I was very happy." I'm teasing her, but she doesn't laugh.

"And are you happy?" she asks. "Wherever you are."

"As happy as can be expected."

"That's not an answer."

"No. It probably isn't."

She clears her throat. Swallows audibly.

"I had two detectives visit me a few months ago. They were looking for you."

"Did they say why?"

"Not really." She sniffs lightly. Is she crying? "They wanted to know where you were. When I'd last spoken to you. Moshe was most upset."

"What did you say?"

"That I didn't know. That I hadn't heard from you in a long time. Which was not a lie."

An uncomfortable silence. Then she speaks again. "Are you sure you're all right? Is there anything I—we—can do to help you? Moshe will. You know he will. Do you need anything?"

"I'm fine, Ma. It's just a misunderstanding I need to sort out."

"Murder is not a misunderstanding."

The police clearly did more than just ask where I was.

"Whether you believe me or not, it really is just a misunderstanding, Ma."

"I've often wondered what your life would have been like if I'd been a stronger woman. If you hadn't pulled the trigger." The words tumble out, though her voice is quiet.

This is the first time she's spoken to me about my father's death since the night it happened, when she'd warned me to keep quiet. That she would do the talking.

The police asked surprisingly few questions when they arrived. They treated us for shock and whispered to one another that it looked like a suicide after Hendrik Kroon had taken a wild shot at my mother. It almost felt like there was relief in the room. As though they knew what a bad man he'd been. Perhaps they gleaned that from the strangle marks around my mother's neck, and the other, older injuries.

"Wondering how things might have been is an exercise in futility," I say.

"Yes, but . . ."

"Sleeping dogs, Ma. Let them lie."

She stays quiet. Then, so quietly I can hardly make out her words, "I miss you, Isa. I would love for you to come and visit us. We can go see *Hamilton* on Broadway. And there's this fabulous deli I know you'd like that opened just around the corner."

This is the first time in the fourteen years I've been away from home that she's asked me to return. I think we both understood that I needed to get away from her in order to forgive her. That I needed distance to bring her back into focus again.

But when did that turn into an excuse to keep running away from her?

Is something the matter? Is she sick? Moshe had a cancer scare three years ago, but other than that they've both been healthy. As far as I know.

"Ma, how are you really? Mrs. Frost also put pressure on me because I haven't been back for so long."

"I'm getting old. Moshe's getting old. We want to see you before we die."

"You're not that old."

"I'm turning sixty-four, Isa. Your grandmother died when she was sixty."

I say nothing. When she speaks again, there is a pleading tone in her voice. "Can't we please just put this thing behind us? Move on?"

Maybe she's right. Maybe it's time to put away all that has happened between us. But forgiveness and going to visit her are two very different things. It would be impossible to get to New York right now. I'd be locked up the minute I set foot on US soil.

Unless . . .

"How about we meet in South Africa?" I hear myself saying. "I can't come to the States right now," I try to explain. "The police there . . . the airports . . ."

"Isa, what's going on? I know about what happened before, in Paris and San Francisco, and that the police were looking for you. But this is new. Something happened. Something else. Something really bad."

I swallow the lump in my throat. My eyes are burning. "Nothing. Really. It's a misunderstanding. That's all it is. Why don't we meet in Cape Town in a few days' time?"

I stare at the date on my watch. How long will it take to find Alex? If we ever find him.

"How about next weekend?" I offer. "Next Sunday? Not this coming one. The next one."

"Next weekend?"

"Is that too soon? It's easy enough for you to get there, isn't it?"

"Yes, it's just . . . Are you serious?"

"About Cape Town?"

"I mean about us meeting."

"Yes. Aunt Lena lives in Paternoster. Maybe you can go and visit her too."

She starts crying. The sound is jarring, familiar.

"Seeing you would be a wonderful birthday present," she says quietly. "And I haven't seen my sister for a very long time."

"Hey." I try to lighten the moment. "We have to do something special. It's not every day you turn twenty-nine."

3

"Maybe you should cut it. And you're going to have to color it. I manipulated your passport photo and made you blonde."

I look at Sarah in the bathroom mirror. The bright morning light melts softly through the windows, promising another scorcher of a day. "Women often dye their hair. I'll get away with black hair."

"Your photograph was everywhere after you left—newspapers, websites, TV. Did you not follow the story at all?"

"No. It never made the news in Lagos."

"Well, you're going to have to go blonde before you get to South Africa."

Sarah drinks the last of the Coke in her can. She slept for three hours after she finished working this morning and was bouncing around like a rubber ball again before I'd even finished showering.

"Cut it." She squints at me in the mirror, a thing she does, I've realized, when she's thinking. "Then dye it and blow-dry it straight."

"Straight?"

"Yep."

"Do you have any idea how long it will take to do that? Can't I just get a wig? Mumbai has excellent wig makers."

She shrugs. "If you want. But get a good one."

"I will. I know where to go. What else?"

"A dress and some heels."

"You might as well ask me to wear neon yellow."

"You won't stand out. Trust me. We're flying business class." She wrinkles her nose as though she's smelling something bad. "And even though lots of business class people wear jeans these days, I don't want you to look the way you usually do."

I can't help laughing. "How would you know what business class people wear these days? You, who have never really been out of South Africa?"

"I have eyes," she grumbles. "And common sense. Buy a dress, shoes, and a simple wedding band. Take on a different look. Smile. Get rid of the backpack." She pushes out her chin as though to challenge me.

I'm not in the mood for arguments.

I turn away from the mirror and rest my backside on the sink. Take in the picture before me. "And you? Sticking to black-is-the-new-black, I see."

She's wearing black skinny jeans, black boots, and a loose, low-cut T-shirt as green as her eyes. No jewelry, except for a silver watch on her wrist and a row of earrings in one ear. To be honest, she doesn't need much more. At twenty-three she's got youth—and everything it has to offer—on her side. Agility, suppleness, and smooth, unlined skin. Gravity hasn't won the battle yet. And then she has those unexpected genetic gifts no one has control over. A face that could grace the cover of *Cosmopolitan*. A deep, husky voice. A body with everything in perfect proportion.

I'm thirty-six, and I am tired of my empty bed and living out of a backpack. And I'm angry. About my backpack and my empty bed. And then there's the nagging suspicion that my face is doing nothing to hide the anger. Or my age.

Fuck it. I stand up straight.

Sarah tugs at her T-shirt, shakes her head. "Don't worry about me. Focus on yourself. We won't be sitting next to each other on the plane.

And I'm not the one trying to evade the cops. You are." She adds an ironic grumble. "In any case, everyone will probably think Mommy and Daddy bought me my business class ticket."

I cross my arms and look down at my bare feet. "Do you remember how it felt? The police. The stress. The fear of being caught."

I don't know why I ask the question. Am I looking for a flaw in Sarah's armor? In her impenetrable perfection?

I turn back toward the mirror, but my eyes stay on her. I still find it hard to read her. As soon as I think I understand a little about what drives her, she withdraws into her surly, untouchable self. She seems to work hard at remaining a ghost. A rumor no one would believe.

She jams her hands into the pockets of her tight jeans. "All I remember is that I promised myself no one would ever catch me again."

"Then you're doing well so far. Here we are, in an executive suite in a five-star hotel in Mumbai."

She gives a sour little laugh. "Prisons come in many shapes and forms. Trust me."

"What do you mean?" I turn around. Finally. Something that feels like it might be the undiluted truth.

But she turns away, her face inscrutable.

"Nothing." She taps her watch. "You need to go shopping. Time's running out."

Three hours later, when I push open the hotel room door with my hip, arms laden with shopping bags, Sarah is almost done packing.

"What time is our flight?" I dump the bags on the bed. Roll the new black suitcase to the three-seater couch. Enjoy, for a moment, the cool air spilling over my body.

Shopping in Mumbai is a nightmare. No matter how long I've been here, I still hate the constant bargaining.

"In five hours, but we can leave as soon as you're done. I don't trust the traffic. We were lucky to get flights out of here. I don't want to lose them by being late." She looks unhappy for a second. "I had to get us flights via Hong Kong. The direct flights are full. I don't want to hang around here any longer, not with Nikhil and your credit card."

"I'll be ready. And don't worry. We'll be okay," I say testily. I'm exhausted from the shopping throngs. I need a break. A drink. Silence.

"We better be," snaps Sarah. "We have a shitload of stuff to do at home. We have to get your documents, like you asked, and then we have to go to Sasolburg, as soon as we can. I keep worrying that Alex's computer signal will disappear again. It died for two hours and then came back online again. Luckily still in the same place."

She packs a pile of T-shirts into the suitcase lying open on the bed, followed by jeans and socks.

"There's something else we need to think about."

"What?" she asks irritably.

"I'm not going to go chase down Alex empty-handed. Those Zama-Zamas know how to shoot. And didn't you say a cop was also involved? Our lives mean nothing to them."

"What do you . . . oh." She throws a tube of hair gel into the suitcase. "You should have said something sooner."

"And you could have planned better. Thought harder. What did you imagine we were going to do? Walk in there and ask the syndicate to please let Alex go? I've just been to the business center downstairs. I read the reports about his disappearance. These aren't small-time criminals."

Sarah rests her hands on her hips. "Did you think I was lying to you?"

"No. But I want to make sure I understand what we are getting ourselves into. And it's certainly worse than I thought. If we don't plan this properly, we don't have a hope in hell."

"You keep coming up with new ways to waste time." She's angry. "Passports. Weapons. What the hell next?"

"We can't help Alex if we're dead."

"Do you even care about him anymore? And be honest."

I sit down on the bed beside Sarah's suitcase, suddenly exhausted to the bone. "When Alex met me in Dar es Salaam, I was still on the run. Do you remember? Tom hunted me like a shadow from country to country. Alex saved my life. Gave me a few moments of normalcy. Happiness. Balance. I owe him more than you can imagine. If it weren't for him, I would be dead. Or—maybe worse—crazy. Literally."

"Then help him."

"That's what we're doing. But you need to get your head straight and start thinking. Planning. That's what this past year has taught me. What Alex and Tom taught me."

Sarah's shoulders seem to tighten with every word I speak.

"I can't believe you won't get off your ass," she explodes.

I don't want to hear one more assumption from this woman's lips. "Sarah, you and Alex are friends. He helped you when you were in prison. Wrote all those nice stories about you. But don't for a minute assume you know what happened between me and him. What happened in our bed and at our table. What he means to me."

She doesn't like this. I knew she wouldn't. She doesn't want to know. Not about any bed or table Alex and I shared.

She turns away, moves the clothes around in the suitcase. Takes a deep breath before she speaks again. "Why do you still want to get another passport, then?" she asks tersely. "Why not just stay in South Africa if Alex means that much to you?"

"I've told you. Finding Alex isn't going to be like waving a magic wand. It won't buy his forgiveness, and it certainly doesn't put food on my table. I can't just start handing out my résumé looking for a new position as a photographer. I'm still wanted for murder. Would you want to go back to prison?"

"No."

"Well, I don't want to go to prison either."

"Getting a new passport will take time."

"Then stop whining and make sure it happens quickly. Ditto with the gun."

She slams the suitcase shut and walks to the desk. She opens her laptop and sits down.

"What type of weapon do you want?"

"Glock 33 Pocket Rocket. It's small and easy to carry, but reliable. I'm going to have to leave mine here."

"Okay."

"Two extra magazines."

"Fine."

"Six mercenaries."

Her hands pause over the keyboard. "Very funny. It's not like the entire syndicate is guarding him. They have day jobs too, you know."

"You don't have a day job."

She ignores me and carries on typing.

I empty one of the shopping bags on the couch. "While you're at it, what's the name of the woman doing my passport? The new one I want when we're in South Africa."

"It's the same woman who did the passport for this trip. And the one you left South Africa with last year. Adriana."

"Adriana? You thought that up quickly."

She doesn't say anything.

"How long have you known her?" I walk to the fridge, take out a Coke, and go to stand behind her. When she doesn't answer, I move a little closer, crowding her personal space.

She moves her chair to the right, away from me.

"Long," she says.

"Do you trust her?"

"With my life."

"I bet you don't say that often."

"More often than you do."

That hurts.

I walk to the bed and put my new suitcase down next to hers. "Remind me again why you didn't ask your prison friends to find Alex."

I start opening all the bags. I didn't hold back on the spending. It was muggy and crowded in the shops, but it was nice to pay with someone else's money.

Sarah shakes her head, closes the laptop, and starts undoing the laces on her boots.

"We've been through this. They don't care. They might do it for the money, but how much would be enough? Ten thousand? More? And what if they tried to get a better deal from the Zama-Zamas? There's a huge difference between how far you'll go for money and how far you'll go for love."

"Like you. All the way to Lagos and then to Mumbai."

She says nothing, but her neck turns pink. She gets up from the desk, now barefoot and tiny. Takes something out of her laptop backpack.

"Here." She tosses a passport onto the bed. "It might be a good idea for you to page through it. Make it look a bit more used."

I open the green book, half full of visas, and read the name on the last page: *Elizabeth Gouws*. Another new name. How many have I had now? Seven?

I thumb through the pages. Stop. "What was I doing in Hong Kong?"

"You own a travel company. You organize exclusive tours for rich people." She points at the passport. "That's why you travel so much."

I try out the name. "Elizabeth," I say.

"Is it okay?"

"Elizabeth was my grandmother's name. My mother's mother."

"Is that a good thing or a bad thing?"

She doesn't wait for an answer. Walks to the bathroom, turns on the shower, and closes the door.

I stare at the blonde woman in the picture.

"It's a good name," I whisper.

My grandmother told me she knew Hendrik Kroon was bad news the day she laid eyes on him.

4

The plane parks about half a mile from passport control at OR Tambo International Airport in Johannesburg. The flight was delayed by two hours, and most of the passengers—including Sarah—are irritable.

We weave briskly through the throngs of businesspeople and tourists, cabin-friendly suitcases rolling behind us.

I run my hand over the soft material of the flowing blue dress. I've avoided dresses in the last year or so. It suddenly seemed like they are all designed to make a woman feel more vulnerable. More careful—more aware—of how she moves. And it's hard to run in a dress. Damn impossible in heels.

But there's something else too, I have to admit. A sense of self-satisfaction, of control. Like how I felt when I weighed my cabin luggage at Chhatrapati Shivaji International Airport in Mumbai and the middle-aged man behind the counter told me he'd booked the best seat in business class for me. I could feel his eyes on me as I walked away. I admit I enjoyed it.

Behind me, I hear footsteps approaching.

"Elizabeth!"

It's Sarah. It's the same test as in Hong Kong, just before our connecting flight. Again, I remember to respond to the name.

Sarah gives me a satisfied nod. "Good. You're still on the ball."

"I take it you still go by Sarah."

"Yes. But my surname is different."

We turn right, go down a set of escalators, and enter the passport queue.

This is the part of flying that makes me break out in a sweat these days. It's usually the little things that give you away. Being too friendly. Too eager. An official who is bored and just a little too inquisitive. Too alert.

I know, at least, that Sarah's papers are good. Or this Adriana woman's, rather. I've been through quite a few immigration checkpoints with the passport she sourced for me last year.

I turn toward Sarah. "What do you do, officially, for a living? You know, on paper?"

"Shares. Buy and sell."

We move forward five yards. Sarah uses her boot to push her suitcase across the tiles. The computer backpack never leaves her shoulder, a thumb protectively hooked into the strap. She travels surprisingly lightly for someone who doesn't do it often.

Another three yards. Behind us, a woman laughs loudly, the sound echoing through the arrivals hall.

"Have you heard from Adriana?" I ask.

"Do you always talk this much?"

"What else are we supposed to do?"

She mumbles something unintelligible. Then: "I don't know how you can be this calm." She waves her hand around her, whispers, "You're an international fugitive."

Is that why she's been so tense all day?

"I suppose you get used to it," I offer.

"Or addicted to it."

We shuffle forward. Almost there. It helps that we disembarked ahead of economy class.

"What do you mean?" I ask.

"I watched you in Jagan's shop, with Nikhil. And now. You're on edge, but you're also enjoying it a little. As though it makes you a little high."

The queue moves and we're at the front. No need for me to reply.

I move past a well-dressed European woman who doesn't know which counter to choose and put my passport down in front of a bored-looking man with a shaved head.

He takes my passport and gives a half smile.

"Welcome."

"Thank you. It's nice to be back."

"Where did you fly in from?"

"Hong Kong."

"Ah. Messy there at the moment."

"You're telling me. I'm glad to get out of there."

He stamps my passport and closes it. I want to take it, but his hand stays on the document, his smile suddenly faltering.

He cocks his head at me, his eyes searching. "Your hair looks different."

The damn wig. I couldn't find a single one in the style Sarah gave me, so my hair is shorter than in the passport photo.

I look at his wedding band. "What can I say? My husband was a bit cross when I cut it short. I'm trying my best to grow it back."

He smiles slowly and pushes the passport toward me. Waves the next passenger closer.

We wait for the Gautrain to Pretoria. I make sure to stand in the middle of a group of people milling around on the platform. I turn my face away from the security cameras, pretending to look for something in my handbag while I talk to Sarah.

"Where to when we get there?" I ask.

"My car's parked at Hatfield Station."

She's still irritable after the two flights.

"And then?"

"I've spoken to Adriana. We'll see her late tonight, after work. That's the soonest she's available. And it seems like the gun might be a problem."

She looks at me as though expecting me to tell her not to bother with it, then.

I say nothing.

The train arrives and we get in. We stand near the doors as the rest of the passengers filter through to the seats, eager to get off their feet.

"We can drop the gun and leave for Sasolburg immediately," she whispers once the train pulls away.

I shake my head. "No way. We're not going after Alex empty-handed."

That is not the answer Sarah wants. She's quiet for the rest of the journey, moodily staring out the window at the spring day outside.

As we pull into Hatfield Station, she storms off the train. I grab my suitcase and follow her.

"Why do we have to wait until tonight to see Adriana?" I ask. "Where does she work?"

Sarah ignores me.

"And what are we going to do until then?"

Still no answer.

I take three long strides to overtake her and then stop in front of her. Impatient commuters are forced to veer around us.

Enough now, for goodness' sake.

Her eyes bore into mine.

"I'm sorry everything is not going as smoothly as you had hoped."

"No. You're not."

"I am." I sigh tiredly. Then give up apologizing. It's been a long thirty-six hours, and I don't have the energy to make nice. "I'm hungry."

"There's a Steers on the way to my flat."

"I don't want a burger. I want proper food. Green beans. Karoo lamb." My mouth starts to water. "Things like that."

"I don't cook."

"I didn't think you did. I can barbeque some meat and make a salad."

She shakes her head vigorously, as though I'm being ridiculous. "We have more important things to think about. What . . ."

"Relax," I say in a measured voice. "It's just food. We need to eat. We don't all live on Coke and cigarettes. In any case, how were you planning on killing time? Comparing shoe sizes?"

She steps around me and walks off. We take the escalator up and step into the bright sunlight.

"We ate on the plane," she says as we walk toward the parking lot.

"That's not food. I could have knocked someone out with that omelet."

"I wish I had."

"I know. Everyone knows."

The Gucci-clad kid in the seat in front of her on the plane kept wanting to see what Sarah was doing on her laptop.

"I'm really not interested in food right now. Not in the least," she insists.

I take a few long strides to stand in front of her again. Raise my eyebrows to show her that I'm serious about this one. She throws her hands in the air and rolls her eyes.

"Fine, then. I'll call my mother. Maybe she can make us lunch."

5

The black Mini Cooper with the red racing stripes comes to life with a growl, snarling throatily when Sarah puts it into first gear. In the confines of the third floor of the Hatfield Station parking garage, it sounds like an angry, caged animal.

I buckle up and push my feet into the car's footwell as Sarah hurtles toward the exit and around the corner, quickly leaving the station behind as she races west.

"Not afraid of traffic cops, I gather."

"There's no law against how quickly you get to twenty-five miles per hour."

She rams the Mini into fourth gear, then brakes sharply to squeeze into a nonexistent gap between a Toyota and a BMW.

I clear my throat uncomfortably.

"Tell me about the car."

"It's a 2008 John Cooper Works, 250 Nm. Top speed of 150 mph. Zero to a hundred in six seconds. She's not supposed to be quite that fast, but my dad and I souped her up a little."

There is obvious pride in her voice as she takes a sharp left onto Soutpansberg Road, speeding past three trucks and cutting in front of a fourth one.

I exhale sharply.

She glances at me, her green eyes shiny with adrenaline. "What?"

"Nothing. Pollen. Spring. Must be hay fever."

I do what I do on airplanes: switch off. I close my eyes. I might as well try and sleep.

When the car slows down, I open my eyes again. The familiarity of Pretoria—the avenues of jacaranda trees that will soon explode into purple bloom, the lazy pace of the pedestrians chatting as they cross the roads—stirs a strange emotion. Something like longing.

Why can't I rid my body of this place? It's the same every time I return. Ten emotions before you've even left the airport—yours and other people's. Not the cool, polite vacuum you encounter in so many other countries.

Sarah turns right onto what used to be Church Street. Seems it has been renamed WF Nkomo Street. Nkomo was an apartheid struggle hero, if I remember correctly. We drive past the Tshwane Events Center and turn right, and stop in front of an apartment block.

White letters set against the face brick announce the name of the three-story building that looks like it's in desperate need of a coat of paint: *Acacia*. A six-foot wall hugs the perimeter. Lush bougainvilleas in full bloom grow at the base of the electric fencing.

Sarah opens her car window and waves a gray plastic disk at an electronic eye on a stand on the sidewalk. A little door next to the eye pops open, and she presses her thumb to the glass inside it.

The heavy black gate slides open to the left. The speed with which it moves, the quiet, efficient whisper, belies the building's somewhat ramshackle look.

Inside, Acacia looks completely different from the outside. The lawn is neatly, expertly trimmed. A row of rosebushes—red, hip-height—runs along the front wall of the building. A sprinkler sifts back and forth over the flower beds carrying the first blooms of spring.

I look at Sarah. The relief on her face seems to wash all the way down to her hands. She releases her tight grip on the wheel and steers the car lightly toward a second gate, leading to a parking garage under the building.

"Lots of security," I say. "Bad neighborhood?"

"Not really. We have the occasional murder, like any other suburb."

I search her face in the half-light of the garage to see whether she's joking, but it's difficult to see past her happiness. Sarah is home, and nothing else seems to matter right now.

We park beside the elevator. Other than a powerful silver Audi sedan and a bright yellow Suzuki motorbike, the place is bare.

This is all hers, it dawns on me. The entire three-story apartment building and everything in it belongs to Sarah. Does she stay here on her own, or does her family also live here?

"Nice collection," I say, pointing to the vehicles.

She doesn't answer, just jerks her thumb at the Mini's trunk. "Let's hustle. I'm dying for a shower."

With her backpack on her shoulder and her suitcase in hand, she summons the elevator using another fingerprint reader. When the doors open, she hesitates a moment, taking a deep breath before stepping into the small metal box.

I remember the Taj Mahal—how she watched me get into the hotel's mirrored elevator, and then turned around and took the stairs.

"Why do you even have an elevator?" I say, as I follow her in.

"It's safer. Never know who's waiting for you on the stairs."

"What happens if you're in it on your own and it gets stuck?"

She glares at me. "There's a backup generator. And I make sure it gets serviced regularly. You never know about other elevators. Anyway, there is a hidden staircase if I want to use it."

She places her thumb on yet another scanner and then presses the button for the third floor.

Wonder what's on the first and second floor. No point asking, though.

She fiddles with her backpack's zipper.

"There's something I have to ask you. Before we go in," she says.

What now?

"Yes?" I say warily.

She smiles almost shyly. "Do you like dogs?"

I'm on a three-seater sofa, too afraid to move. When Sarah said "dogs," I imagined something small, an ankle biter that yapped and slept on the bed and ate expensive dog food from an expensive little bowl. A dog fit for an apartment. Not these two monsters.

The two Dobermans lying at my feet in the "stay" position Sarah ordered them into are gazing at me with what looks like gastronomic interest.

"Sarah!" I call gingerly.

She doesn't answer. She disappeared into the bathroom and left me here with these enormous, silky black beasts that almost bowled her over when they saw her.

They were less than happy to see me—one of them growled and the other barked.

Sarah said they would quickly get used to me. I'm not so sure. I didn't grow up with dogs. Strangely, though, other animals don't make me as uncomfortable as dogs do. I think it has something to do with their dependence on humans. And maybe all those teeth.

I angle my wrist so I can read my watch. It's later than I thought, earlier than I hoped. It feels like a lifetime before we'll get to see this Adriana woman.

I try to push my impatience aside. Put it next to the terror that's simmering just below the surface, threatening to overwhelm me.

I take a quick, deep breath. Exhale slowly. I really, really hope Alex is still alive.

Then I shush the little voice that keeps reminding me how unlikely that would be.

No. I need to focus on something else.

The dogs. I lean forward slowly so as not to alarm them. Try to read the name tag around the neck of the one closest to me. Something with a *B* and a *T*.

"Hello, Bit," I say.

"Byte." Sarah appears behind me in jeans and a clean T-shirt, toweling her hair.

I turn toward the other, smaller dog to try and determine her name. She starts growling. I sit back with my hands up.

"No, Megs. Stay," says Sarah firmly.

The dog backs down.

"Megs? Megan?"

"Megs."

Ah. I get it. "Cute. Megabyte."

Sarah pats her thigh, and the dogs trot over to her. She rubs their heads, then disappears into her room again.

I use the opportunity to try and get up without being noticed. I can't get over the fact that this is where Sarah lives. It might as well be a state institution of some kind, with the main decor various shades of black and white. One wall is just windows. Interior walls are nonexistent, except for the bedroom and bathroom walls. I think there are two bedrooms, judging by the number of visible doors.

The open-plan kitchen is white, as are the fridge, microwave oven, dishwasher, and washing machine. No TV anywhere. The two sofas are worn black leather. Comfortable, though. A gallery of photographs hanging over a workbench with three computers on it provides the only splash of color in the enormous space.

The most striking of the photos is a grainy shot of a bald white man. A silver tag on the frame says it is *Gordon Moore*. All the other pictures look like family photographs. One immediately draws me nearer. It is a photo of Sarah and a slim man, both of them in dirty blue overalls, standing next to the black-and-red Mini Cooper. They look pleased with themselves. A tiny woman holding two mugs is standing off to one side, wearing a beige apron and a big smile.

Must be Sarah's parents. The resemblance is clear, especially the prominent cheekbones. Also, the strong bond between them seems to shine from the photos.

I'm almost jealous. I wonder how it feels to grow up in such a happy home. Why throw it all away by becoming a hacker? Is it because her family was struggling financially? Isn't that what Alex intimated in the articles he wrote about her?

The doorbell rings. It's an old-fashioned sound, shrill and loud.

The dogs don't bark. They move toward the elevator, the front door next to it.

"It's me, Sarah!" The voice of a boy sounds over the intercom.

I walk toward the elevator. The intercom has a small screen. It shows a young black boy with glasses far too big for his face standing on the sidewalk. He is peering up at a camera I failed to notice at the first entrance gate.

Sarah walks out of her room. I stand aside as she types in a code to open the gate, a smile on her face.

Who the hell is our mystery guest that he can wring such joy from Hacker Girl?

Minutes later, the boy gets out of the elevator. He looks ten, maybe eleven. I'm not good with kids' ages. He's wearing the gray shorts and collared white shirt of a typical South African public school uniform.

He waves at Sarah across the room. "Hello. How was your business trip?"

"Hi," she says. "I'm glad you managed to slip away. Just give me a sec, will you?"

"No probs."

Sarah disappears into her bedroom. The boy walks over to the sofa, the dogs milling around his legs.

“I’m Daniel,” he says earnestly as he offers me his hand. “Are you a friend of Sarah’s?” The glasses keep sliding down his nose, and he seems to sigh every time he pushes them back up.

I have no idea what to say. Where is Sarah when you need her?

“I work with her,” I say. At least that’s not a complete lie.

“Oh.” Daniel rubs Byte’s head. The dog’s eyes close in pleasure.

“And you? How do you know Sarah?” I ask.

Sarah’s head pops around the bedroom door. She looks worried, as though she suddenly realized that Daniel may just be tempted to spill some juicy tidbits about her private life.

I wave her off.

Daniel adjusts his shirt, pushes his glasses up again. He sits down on the sofa next to me. Rubs his left hand over his slightly round stomach.

“I live in the apartment block next door,” he says. “I mow the lawn and make sure everything is okay when Sarah’s not here.” His eyes sparkle behind the black-rimmed lenses. “Sarah’s teaching me about computers. And she lets me do all my school projects here while my mom’s at work.”

“That’s nice of Sarah. What is she teaching you exactly?”

Sarah clears her throat. Daniel glances in her direction, pursing his lips before answering. “Google. Coding. Firewalls and so on,” he says. “Nothing serious.”

“Ranna, I’m not teaching him . . .” She stops, mumbles something, shakes her head, and walks toward us. She holds out a roll of blue notes to Daniel.

“Six days’ worth, Dan. Did you manage to sort out the problem with the irrigation system?”

“Yes. There was a power surge, so the timer was fried, but I fixed it.”

He takes the money and pushes it deep down into his long gray sock. He pulls both socks up to his knees.

“You don’t want me to save it for you? A few more hundred and you’ll have enough for that laptop you saw the other day.”

He shakes his head. "My mom's tips haven't been great this month. This will help." He pushes the glasses up and sighs again.

Sarah gives him a look. "You can eat here whenever you want. You know that, right?"

"She doesn't like it when I come here to visit." He rolls his eyes toward the apartment block next door.

"She doesn't like me, does she?"

He laughs until his chubby stomach shakes. "She doesn't like anyone who sleeps until twelve every day."

6

I feel like a new person when I get out of the shower. I used everything on offer in the guest room: shampoo, razor, soap. All of it expensive stuff, brands I could never afford myself. That's what happens when you live out of a backpack for years on end. The only decent thing I've spent money on in the last few months is perfume. Juliette Has a Gun. And underwear. The two things that drove Alex crazy when we were in Dar es Salaam.

I have no idea what prompts me to wear black lace every now and then. Maybe it reminds me that I'm still alive. That I'm still a decent-looking woman with some prospects.

Ha. Liar.

Somewhere between drying off and getting dressed—jeans and a black T-shirt—I stop pitying myself. I need to speak to Sarah, and there's no doubt it's going to be another difficult conversation. It's as though the two of us simply cannot get on the same wavelength.

I wander out of the guest room. She closes her laptop when she sees me.

"What are you up to?" I ask.

"Best you didn't know." She sits back and folds her arms, raising her eyebrows questioningly. "And that?"

I look around me. "What?"

She points at my T-shirt. "*ISIS can kiss my ass*. Poetic."

I look down, dusting off the cotton that is looking somewhat worse for wear after six years of being packed in and out of bags.

"It was a gift from a Canadian photographer in Afghanistan. He had them made for all the female journalists. Not that anyone was crazy enough to wear them over there."

"And you do know there are Muslims in South Africa, right?"

"This is a reference to ISIS only. Not to all Muslims. Not by a long shot. In any case, I'll change before we go and see this Adriana woman." I dig my hands into my pockets. "When are we leaving, by the way?"

"Later."

I suppress the urge to say something sarcastic. There's only so much conflict one can deal with in a single day. I walk to the kitchen and switch on the kettle, leaning against the counter while it comes to a boil. I stare at my bare feet. I could do with a pedicure. Paint my toenails red, maybe. Something bright.

As I start the search for coffee cups, I say over my shoulder, "There are a few more things we need before we go to Sasolburg."

Sarah groans. "What now? We've already been through this. You need a gun and a passport. What more could you possibly want?"

I open a cupboard on my left. Rows and rows of cans of salt-and-vinegar Pringles. Instant soup. The next cupboard is filled with cans of Coke. Where might the cups be? And the coffee? Anything to eat that's not marinated in preservatives?

Sarah must have picked up on my thought. "I don't drink coffee," she says. "There's tea. Rooibos. Top drawer."

I switch off the kettle. I don't like rooibos tea. It's too healthy, even for my liking. How on earth did it end up here, in Sarah's heat-and-eat kitchen?

"We need a car," I say. "A white pickup, preferably. A Toyota? Something that's not going to draw attention in the Free State. And it needs to be clean—no outstanding fines."

"I have wheels."

"The ones parked downstairs?"

She nods.

"Forget about it. Turn the ignition and every man and his dog will know you're on your way."

She nods again, more stiffly this time. Her mouth is a thin line. "Fine. As you wish."

She starts typing. She's obviously opened a new document to make a list.

"A pickup," she says. "What else do you desire, Your Majesty?"

I ignore her sarcasm. "Printed Google maps of the area where Alex's laptop is. Front, back, aerial, the works. Binoculars. First-aid kit. Just in case. Water. If we find him, he might be dehydrated, or we might need to stay put for a long time. And don't forget extra magazines for the Glock. And something for you. A revolver, maybe? It's easy to shoot."

The typing pauses. "For me? No way. Guns are for stupid people. And they're unnecessary. Like gyms and spending hours cooking. If nobody had guns, nobody would get shot."

I laugh, though I suspect she's right. But I can't resist asking: "You don't exercise? What about all that Coke you mainline?" I point to a trash can filled to the brim with empty soda cans.

"I run with the dogs," she says. "And only because the shrink my mother insisted I see when I got out of prison told me to. And Megabyte likes it."

"Well, think of the revolver as another thing you have to do."

"I don't want a weapon. In any case, adding a second gun to the list is going to take time we don't have."

"What do you want us to do? Walk in there and ask nicely if Alex can come home with us?" I sit down at one of the barstools at the kitchen counter, craving coffee. Something stronger.

"That's not what I meant. You're being ridiculous."

"Can you even shoot?"

"I can probably hit an elephant at fifty feet, like everybody else."

"That's good to know. Get a gun you can handle. A .38 revolver."

"We won't need it."

"How do you know?"

"Shit, Ranna."

"You can say what you like, but we have no idea what the situation is like in Sasolburg. Or is there something you're not telling me?"

She looks at me for a long time before speaking again. "Alex never mentioned that you were this big on guns. What exactly did you do in India?"

"Nothing. I survived."

She stares at me without saying a word.

I give in. "I did exactly what you told my new identity to do. Elizabeth? I led tour groups. I helped businesspeople. I wandered around with CEOs and their bored spouses. I showed them wild India. Exotic Mumbai."

"That's it?"

"That's it."

She starts typing again. "Adriana has a pickup. I'll make sure we get a Glock and a revolver. And everything else you need." She points an angry finger at me. "And your list better be done now."

"Since we're doing a bit of straight talking, remember . . ."

She doesn't look at me.

I rap my knuckles on the kitchen counter to draw her attention. I don't think she's getting what I've been trying to tell her all this time. It's time for me to say it again. To say it loudly.

"Alex could be . . . It's been more than seven weeks. He could already be . . . We could be in danger. We're not playing cops and robbers here. You could get seriously hurt, you know. Or worse. It's important for you to know that. To plan accordingly."

Like I do. I carry a letter for my mother in my backpack in case of my sudden demise.

Sarah stares at me, her eyes unreadable. Then she starts typing again, something like guilt flashing across her face.

Tired of fighting, I turn around and put the kettle back on. Pilot a new search for cups, which I find in a cupboard near the fridge. Open the fridge in the vague hope for milk. Maybe I can stomach rooibos tea if I can sufficiently dilute it with something fresh.

7

We drive east, toward Sarah's parents' house. It's a lazy Sunday afternoon in Pretoria. The streets are quiet, the sun warm. The heat here, in the north of the country, is dry, not like the wet blanket Mumbai sweats under.

I watch the inner city zipping past. Shopwindows, gas stations, hopeful minibus cabs waiting for passengers on street corners. It feels like I've never left. As though I've never breathed any other air.

I absentmindedly rub my thigh where the poet N. P. van Wyk Louw's words are inked onto my skin, snaking all the way up to my heart. Words about change. Loss. Rebirth.

You can love a place too much. Love a person too much. Sometimes you can measure that "too much" by the number of times you run away from them.

This thing about Alex keeps wanting to break free from my head and make its way to my heart. Is he okay? Is there any chance he might still be alive?

I must have made a noise because Sarah turns her head toward me, her eyes hidden behind aviator sunglasses. She flicks the cigarette butt in her right hand out of the window.

"You okay?"

I nod.

She gears down and rounds a corner. We drive past the National Zoo. *Capital Park,* a board on my left announces.

"Alex never let you go, you know," she says.

"I struggle to believe that."

She laughs, sounding a bit surprised. She rakes a hand through her hair. Opens the window wider. The air rushing in smells like new leaves. Like grass starting to grow again. Jacarandas waiting to burst into bloom.

"He was like a junkie. He couldn't stop talking about you. Then he went quiet one day. Not a word. But he never dated again. And now he's gone."

Worry strains her voice on the last sentence. Without thinking, I put my hand on her forearm. She pushes the Mini's rev counter into the red, pulling away from my touch.

"We'll find him," I try to reassure her, although I know it's a pointless exercise. "He'll be fine. He's a tough bastard."

She looks at me, and I see my tired face reflected in her lenses.

"You'd better be right," she says.

"Oh, you know me. I'm always right."

We stop in front of a square, cream-colored house perched close to the street in a large yard. It has a red zinc roof and a wide porch. In size and simplicity, it is a typical sixties South African house. A tall white stinkwood tree stands guard near the front door, young leaves on its branches. A yellow ribbon flutters among the green, perhaps a remainder from a recent neighborhood children's party.

Sarah leaves the Mini to idle in front of the gate and gets out of the car.

"Stay here," she says, before closing the door.

Instead of opening the gate, she jogs away toward an old Toyota Corolla parked on the street, two houses away. The driver rolls his window down as she approaches. I recognize his leathery face immediately. It's the same man I saw last year at the Palace Hotel when I got my new passport from Sarah.

He and Sarah chat briefly, animatedly, and then she turns around and comes back to the Mini.

"What's he doing here?"

"You remember him?"

"Of course. Tommy . . . no . . . Tiny. *Uncle* Tiny."

Sarah is surprised. "You have a good memory."

"You're not answering my question."

"He stays down the road. I just went to say hi."

"And he always sits in his parked car like that because . . ."

"A private project," she warns. "And certainly none of your business."

She fiddles with a remote control on her car keys, and the black gate slides open. Three woolly white dogs stampede toward the Mini as we drive in, and Sarah parks under a carport, behind a Fiat 500.

We get out with the dogs yapping and tumbling around our feet—more her feet than mine—until a roundish woman wearing a demure blue dress and a pair of black lace-up Green Cross shoes rushes toward us, shushing them. She kisses Sarah and then looks at me expectantly.

Sarah stiffly waves her hand in my direction. "This is Quinne. Thanks for letting us come by on such short notice."

Wasn't it supposed to be Elizabeth?

"Hello, ma'am. I'm sorry . . ."

She shakes my hand and then rubs my forearm as though she's restraining herself from hugging me. "Oh, please, just call me Aunt Nellie."

Her voice is lighter than Sarah's. And much friendlier.

She runs a hand over her dark hair, which is heavily streaked with gray, and waves us toward the front door. "Come in. You're the first to arrive. Sarah's brothers are on their way."

Sarah looks upset. "You shouldn't have, Ma. Why invite everyone? I said we were just going to pop in for a quick snack."

It's clear that Sarah was hoping we'd be in and out of here as quickly as possible.

Nellie, as short as her daughter, steers us onto the porch. "It's still Sunday lunch, even if it's a little bit later than usual. And I'm used to cooking for seven people. Eight makes no difference."

She shoos the dogs, still milling about our feet. "Come in, Quinne. I want to know all about you. Sarah never brings friends home. Not even when she was at school."

The house is cool and spacious. A polished wood floor leads us from an enormous lounge down a short hallway and into a yellow-and-white kitchen that could probably host a dinner party for twenty people.

One of the kitchen walls is filled with family pictures. A little girl, who looks like she might be Sarah—wearing a shy, gap-toothed smile and a blue uniform—is standing in a garden with a brown school suitcase at her feet. The next photo is of the same little girl in running gear. There are boys playing rugby and cricket. A black-and-white wedding photo—Sarah's parents, most likely. A young gymnast, hands in the air, right foot forward, in the flourish of a completed routine. She looks like Sarah, but her face seems softer, her eyes happier, more carefree.

"Your brothers will be here soon," Nellie says over her shoulder as she puts on the kettle. She takes cups out of a cupboard above the counter. "They're driving together from college. Hannes sent a text. And Miekie is in Germany. She called last night."

"Is she okay? Is everyone okay?" Sarah is standing at the round table in the middle of the kitchen, car keys clenched in her fist.

Nellie looks at her, a little surprised. "Yes. Why wouldn't they be?"

"Just asking." Sarah shrugs, turning to hang her car keys on a hook on the wall. I count at least three sets of car keys, excluding the Mini's. She gestures for me to sit down at the table.

"Miekie sent me an email yesterday," she says, walking over to stand with her back against the counter, where her mother is making coffee and tea. "She says it's freezing in Berlin. She also said she's nailed her floor routine. But you know how she lies to me sometimes. Like about that boyfriend of hers last year."

Nellie smiles, wrinkles around her mouth and her brown eyes deepening. "You worry too much. Everything's fine. I have a feeling she's going to get at least silver this time. That Hungarian isn't there. Apparently sick of gymnastics."

She lifts the lid on a pot on the stove and starts stirring the contents. The wonderful smell of meat and vegetables fills the kitchen.

"I think I must be missing her, because I made oxtail stew." She looks over at me a little anxiously. "I hope you eat oxtail. Sarah said you like traditional food?"

The smell from the heavy-bottomed pot reminds me just how hungry I am.

"Most definitely," I say. "I love oxtail." I point toward the table. "Would you like me to start setting the table?"

Sarah frowns. "Shit, you don't have to suck up to my—"

"Sarah!" Nellie signals a warning with the spoon. "Not under my roof."

"Sorry, Ma."

The older woman, still cross, waves her eldest toward the passage. "Go and say hello to your father. The emphysema . . . I don't know. He's not great today. And make sure he doesn't try and sneak a cigarette. You two and your bad habits. That's why we are where we are now."

Sarah mumbles something and shoots me a warning look.

I raise my hands, giving her a small nod. I get the message: Behave; say as little as possible; don't be nosy.

Nellie urges Sarah toward the passage. "Go on, then. You don't like helping in the kitchen anyway. Quinne and I will call you when we're ready."

She puts the spoon down and shakes her head. Looks at me. "I hope you don't mind helping me?"

"Not at all."

She points toward the open back door and a wooden table under a big oak tree in the backyard. "We're going to eat outside. Come, let me show you where everything is."

I take my shoes off and stretch out, pulling a brown blanket hanging on the back of the sofa over my legs. I sigh contentedly. Sarah's mom is a wonderful cook.

The Fourie house is quiet. Only the zinc roof creaks now and again as the cool night settles in. Sarah's parents have gone to bed, and her three brothers are back wherever it was they came from. Sarah has plunked herself down in the living room, put on her headphones, and started wiping out heavily armed muscle men on her laptop screen.

For someone who thinks weapons are for stupid people, she certainly likes shooting people online.

Nellie invited me to enjoy a bath, but Sarah intervened. She said we only had an hour or so before we had to leave again to go to some club whose name she produced slickly, apparently unwilling to let on that we were on our way to see this Adriana woman.

Considering how Adriana makes her money, I would probably have done the same.

I turn on my side. Then onto my back again. I want to sleep. I need to sleep. I need to rest before we saddle up this wild horse Sarah and I are about to ride.

I didn't sleep too badly in Mumbai. Probably managed two to three uninterrupted hours a night. Something about the constant traffic soothed me. The voices of Amita and her family—all the families around me.

I count the pressed ceiling panels above me. Seven. Eight. Start again, on the left. Eleven. Back.

Again. Again. Again.

Sigh. I lean down and take a bottle of Temazepam out of my backpack. Weigh it in my hands. A doctor in Lagos gave these to me a few months back when I thought I was going stir-crazy. But I've never unscrewed the lid. I put it down next to my bed every night as a warning to myself that if I don't sleep, I'm going to have to take one.

It usually worked. The thought of having to swallow one—of losing control, of being unable to wake up if I needed to—scares me so much that I usually managed to doze off without any help.

I put the tablets next to my head and stare at the small gray plastic bottle until sleep arrives.

Just before eleven, Sarah wakes me so we can leave. She waits impatiently while I put on my shoes and pack my bag. She has exchanged her combat boots for red sneakers. The jeans and the black T-shirt are also fresh.

"Where does this Adriana woman live?" I ask as I tighten the laces on my sneakers.

"Where are you two going?"

I turn sharply at the unexpected voice.

"It's very late to be driving somewhere now. And don't tell me again that you're going to a club, Sarah. None of my children have ever liked going to clubs."

Nellie is standing in the archway leading to the bedrooms. Her arms are crossed over the front of a yellow terry-cloth bathrobe. Her eyes are red, her hair undisturbed by sleep.

"We're going out." Sarah looks down at her shoes, then at her mother.

"At this hour?"

"Yes?"

"Where to?"

Sarah shrugs sheepishly. "We're going to see Aunt Adriana."

Aunt Adriana?

Sarah glances at me with a look that urges me to play along. "She asked us to come by and say hi. She hasn't seen Quinne in more than a year. And she couldn't get away earlier because of the restaurant. It was fully booked tonight."

"I see."

Nellie releases the two words slowly. They hang meaningfully in the air between us. The silence thickens, becomes a white noise that hums in my ears.

Sarah holds out her hand to take my backpack. "I'm going to put this in the car while you say goodbye."

She walks over to her mother, kisses her quickly on the cheek, and gives her an awkward hug.

Nellie grabs her and forces her back into a proper embrace.

"Well, then, you two, be safe. It's late."

"We will be, Ma."

"I love you."

Sarah stops halfway to the front door and smiles. "I know."

Nellie and I watch her unlock the door and disappear, heading toward where the Mini is parked. When I turn toward Sarah's mother, she holds a fist out toward me. At first, I have no idea what she's doing, but then I see the paper clenched between her fingers. I want to take the printouts from her, but she doesn't let go. She puts her other hand over mine.

"Sarah is my favorite child, but no one must ever know that." She swallows, as though suppressing an emotion that is threatening to overwhelm her. "She doesn't always know the difference between right and wrong. She makes up her own rules as she goes along. And she either loves with her whole being or feels nothing at all. The problem is that she'll do anything for the people she loves. Which is why she took that money when she was seventeen. She wanted her brothers to go to college. For Miekie to do all the things she couldn't do. For her dad and me to not struggle so much to make ends meet."

The hand on mine shakes ever so slightly. "If you're here for Alex, you have to be careful, Ranna. Please don't let Sarah get hurt."

The white noise becomes a roar, a living, breathing fire.

Nellie lets go of my hand and gives me the article. No. Two articles. The first is about me: "Suspected Serial Murderer May Be Back in SA." The other says, "Well-Known Journalist Disappears in the Free State."

Both are about seven weeks old, from before the confrontation with Nikhil in Jagan's shop. The first article speculates that I might have come back in order to murder Alex after he escaped me last year. The photo is grainy and old, but it's still very clearly me: tall with long black hair and a tired face.

The second article is pretty much what I've seen online. Alex's abduction. His link to me.

"I trust Sarah to look after herself, and I know enough . . ." Nellie inhales sharply. "I know enough to know that things are not always as they seem. I know Sarah is not nearly as bad as she was made out to be, so I can only hope that you are not the woman the newspapers have made you out to be. I saw you with my children. I don't think this person in the papers is you."

How do I answer her? What can I possibly say to put her at ease?

"It isn't," I finally manage.

She bites her bottom lip. The gesture reminds me so much of her daughter.

"I can't imagine that Sarah would have anything to do with you if your intention was to hurt Alex," Nellie says, her hands closing the bathrobe over her chest. "I was at Sarah's court appearances. I read the reports, and I met Alex. I saw what happened after Sarah got to know him. What he broke down in her, and what he built up."

Her hands search for mine again. They are cool, calloused from a lifetime of hard work. "My sister . . . if that's who you're going to see now . . . Something's about to happen. I know that. Everyone thinks I'm a stupid old woman, but I'm not blind. I know enough to know that something's about to happen."

Her hands clamp around mine forcefully. "Please look after Sarah. Even when she's being stubborn. I can see that you know how to look after people. That you know about . . . about loss. The way you looked at all of us around the lunch table? It's as though a small part of you envied us."

"I'm sorry. Sorry for being here. I didn't mean to . . ."

She shakes her head. "Don't. Just look after Sarah. That's all I ask. I can't make her stop whatever she is planning. I know that much."

"What did my mother want?" Sarah flicks the cigarette out of the window and lights another one. We're driving toward the city center.

"Nothing much." I fold the newspaper clippings and stuff them into my jeans' pocket. "Chitchat. I thanked her for lunch. Her hospitality."

"My mother doesn't do chitchat."

"How well do you know her?"

"My mother? We don't always know what to do with each other, but we get along."

She shifts to second for a sharp left turn, then takes a right onto the next street to head for the N1 freeway south.

Get along?

"She loves you," I say, "and she's more observant than I think you give her credit for."

"Why do you say that?"

I shake my head. I'm not going to get caught up in this family's business. "Why don't you tell me about *Aunt* Adriana," I say, emphasizing the honorific. "That was a bit of a surprise."

Sarah runs a yellow light. And another.

"Adriana is my mother's youngest sister. Half sister. There are four of them. Same mother, two different fathers. Adriana is the black sheep. My mother says every family has one."

"Why is she the black sheep?"

"She ran away from home when she was eighteen and came back much later. With lots of money. She said she'd been a member of a circus troupe—Bulgarian or Russian or something. She was a knife thrower. My mother never believed her." Sarah hits the highway. She selects top gear, pushes the Mini well over the speed limit. "When I was in jail, Adriana visited me often. She offered to help me when I got out. Said she knew what it was like."

"What does that mean?"

Sarah smiles. "Don't know. That's all she said. When I had to go to Lesotho for business two years ago, she helped me get a passport. Not that I actually ever used it. We've worked together now and again ever since then."

"Is that what she does? Passports?"

"And a few other things."

Sarah shoots past a black BMW and a white Mercedes, then slows down as though remembering we're not supposed to draw any attention to ourselves. She leans back in the driver's seat, staring at me with concern.

"And that look?"

"Be careful tonight," she says. "Keep your distance."

"Why?"

"Because you're the type of person Adriana finds interesting. In fact, she's been interested in you since the first time she had to do your passport. Don't ask me why. She may not let go until she knows what makes you tick."

8

We take the Grayston off-ramp and turn right over the bridge, then left, toward the bright lights and tall buildings up on the ridge, many more than I remember. When did Sandton start looking like a bright-eyed young Manhattan?

It's almost midnight, but there are still a few cars on the road. Sarah has to brake sharply for a stumbling pedestrian, an inebriated young man wearing a tight black suit. He scrambles to get himself back onto the sidewalk.

Finally, Sarah turns the Mini down a ramp, disappearing under one of the high-rises. She waves an access card at an electronic eye and drives down three levels to park in a spot marked *A De Klerk*.

We walk to a glass-and-chrome elevator. Again, the access card. Inside, Sarah pushes the button for the seventeenth floor. She is visibly anxious. Her eyes remain closed all the way to the top.

When the doors slide open, the word *Penthouse* is engraved on a pewter plate on a wall painted a gentle slate color.

"This aunt of yours definitely does more than just passports," I remark.

"You'll have to ask her yourself."

Sarah stops me before we knock on Adriana's front door. "I'm in a hurry, Ranna. I want to get everything we need and leave immediately.

The laptop is still in the same place. I checked just before we left my parents'."

"About that. Sounds a bit like someone who's not very computer literate. Doesn't that worry you? Like it may be a trap?"

"There are lots of greedy idiots around," she says, despite the worry in her eyes. "Just about everyone, actually. And why still be careful after seven weeks?"

"Pity you can't see how many people there are in the computer's vicinity. Now, that would be helpful."

My sarcasm is lost on her. "I don't think there'd be many. Probably just one or two Zama-Zamas keeping guard."

"If we're lucky. And again, who's to say Alex's laptop's not with some Sasolburg kid who bought it without realizing it had been stolen?" I ask.

"Because I've been tracking the cops investigating the case as well," Sarah says. "I don't trust them, like I told you. One guy, a constable, has been spending a lot of time in the vicinity of that laptop, which tells me it's not just some dumb kid watching porn."

"So, the cops are involved, like you suspected?"

"Seems like it, yes."

Sarah knocks, pauses, then knocks again.

The dark wooden door swings open. In the doorway stands a barefoot woman, only slightly taller than Sarah, probably in her forties. A black silk evening dress drapes down her body from spaghetti straps over her tanned shoulders. A long slit up the side reveals perfectly formed calves.

She looks fit in a way that two Pilates classes a week couldn't possibly produce.

Straight dark-brown hair frames a face with a strong jawline. Her eyes are a flinty brown with sparks of yellow in them. But it's the scar that runs from her right eye toward her ear that makes the biggest impression. A sharp, clean cut, though it's clear it was seen to by an expert plastic surgeon a long time ago.

The total effect is stunning.

No. *Intriguing* is a better word.

"Well, well, well. Your photos do you a disservice."

Adriana de Klerk's voice has the same smoky, husky tone as Sarah's, but she wields it in a way that makes it clear she knows how potent it is when used correctly.

It's disarming. I put my hands in my pockets and smile. "I wish I could say the same, but Sarah's kept you a secret until tonight."

Sarah sighs, rolls her eyes, and pushes past us into the apartment.

"She also doesn't greet people properly," says Adriana dryly. "Ever."

I wait for her to turn so that I can follow her in. If her face is not her strongest asset, her confident body more than compensates. She moves like someone walking on a high wire strung three feet above the ground. She turns around and smiles again. Wide mouth. Good teeth. Teeth that have had work. Too white, too perfect.

"Can I offer you something to drink?" A perfectly manicured hand gestures toward the kitchen counter, where her own glass is waiting. It looks like a cognac glass. Next to it are two knives and a bunch of carrots and leeks. Steam rises from a cast-iron pot on the stove.

Strange hour to be making stew. Or soup.

"Do you have beer?" I ask.

"Heineken?"

"Perfect."

Adriana opens the fridge door and looks at Sarah. "And you?"

"Nothing."

"Not even tea?"

"A Coke, maybe?" Sarah asks.

It's Adriana's turn to roll her eyes. "One day your insides are going to dissolve from all the soda. And your metabolism is only going to save that figure of yours until you're thirty. If you're lucky."

"Whatever."

Sarah sinks down into a deep purple sofa. A silvery cat jumps on her lap. She strokes it until it starts purring. I turn around, away from the shelves full of vinyl records, to admire the view.

Johannesburg is on my right, a second-class skyline next to Sandton, which looks like a lit stage. Pretoria—or is that Midrand?—slumbers farther away, to the north.

I imagine there are new lights every few months as Sandton expands. One billboard we passed on the way here said Sandton was Africa's richest square mile.

Looking at the extravagant architecture of the tall buildings around us, I believe the marketing.

"This is beautiful. How long have you lived here?" I ask.

Adriana appears next to me with a beer in a tall, cold glass. "Long enough. Come. Let's sit down."

I take the glass from her and walk toward the two plum-colored sofas that dominate the living area. Some people's photographs—the photos in my head, the things I notice—take a long time to develop, but others are instant Polaroids: immediately available, the colors bright and overwhelming.

Adriana is a full-color photo. Her apartment is decorated in shades of dark purple, brown, and white. The paintings are oils, large and abstract. Fearless strokes in yellow and orange impasto. She loves texture. The paintings, the expensive cross-grained fabric of the sofas, the afghan carpet with its thousands upon thousands of delicate knots. Nothing is smooth and sterile. And even though I've only known her a few minutes, I've noticed two things. First, she never has both hands full at the same time. She left her drink on the counter to bring me my drink, then she fetched Sarah's Coke, then she went back to fetch her cognac.

The second thing is perhaps more interesting. Something in me instantly recognizes Adriana. She is used to being unattached. Alone. She has that same something that is always alert to trouble. That has seen trouble and can spot its silent approach a mile away. That is slightly addicted to the rush it brings.

Sarah said she owns a restaurant. I find that hard to believe.

"Here are your papers," she says, putting a black folder down on the mahogany coffee table.

Sarah opens it and pages through the contents. "This is more than I expected. There's even a birth certificate." She closes it. "I only gave you money for a passport."

Adriana warms the cognac in the palm of her hand, takes a sip, and puts the glass down. Crosses her legs. She leans back on the plum couch. The cat makes itself comfortable in her lap.

"I didn't even want your money," she says, shaking her head. "When I saw who I had to do this for—do this for *again*—I knew it was going to have to be outstanding work." She points at the folder, looks at me. "These are the best documents available. I used someone from inside Home Affairs. And you're just in time. The new ID smartcards we're all supposed to get are much harder to copy, so take the green ID book in there and apply for your ID card as soon as possible."

Sarah pushes the documents across the table toward me. "I'll pay extra."

I pick them up. Everything looks completely legit. "Thanks."

"No need to thank me." Adriana smiles at me. "One day I might need your help. You never know." She gently coaxes the cat off her lap when he starts pawing at her hands. "I knew your father, by the way."

"You did?"

"Perhaps *knew* is the wrong word. Our paths crossed briefly. Once, a long time ago. He spoke to me. Flirted, actually. Told me to stop my nonsense. Eventually, he even dropped the charges against me. I didn't know he was your father, not until the newspapers started pulling your life apart at the seams."

I wonder why she would have had a run-in with a state prosecutor but decide not to ask. It wouldn't change a thing, especially not the fact that I am now effectively on her books. Even if Sarah doubles the price she's paid for these documents, Adriana de Klerk will call me sometime in the future to collect on this debt, and I will have to oblige.

I pick up the passport and look at my new name. "Francis Beekman." How many names do I have now? How am I going to remember this one? I put it away and tuck the folder into my backpack. "Thank you. I mean it. Both of you."

Ice clinks against the glass as Sarah sips her Coke. She fishes for her cigarettes in her backpack. Adriana raises her eyebrows and points her eyes toward the balcony. Sarah grumbles and tosses the pack onto the coffee table, deciding against the nicotine hit.

You'd think she didn't trust us alone together.

"There's something else," she says, looking peeved. "We need a pickup. Can I leave the Mini for you and use the Hilux?"

Adriana's hand stalls as she brushes the cat hair from her dress. "I hate that car of yours. You can hear it coming for miles. And how am I supposed to do stock runs for the restaurant in that little matchbox?"

"What restaurant?" I ask, no longer able to contain my curiosity about this woman.

"Crow's Feet. It's not far from here. You should come and visit. The food is excellent." She holds her hands out toward me, palms up. "I'm the chef. Good with my hands. Always have been."

"Adriana," Sarah says, sighing dramatically, "we don't have time."

"You're just like your mother." Adriana leans back and picks up her drink. When she speaks again, she is looking past us, at the city lights. "I assume she didn't send anything for me. Her regards? Her oxtail recipe?"

Sarah says nothing.

Adriana gets up and walks toward what I assume is the bedroom. When she comes back, she's carrying a set of keys and a black canvas bag.

"Please bring the Hilux back safely and without any traffic fines. Don't drive like you always do. And look after the USB stick that's in there. It's Nina Simone, *Precious and Rare*. The early recording from the 1950s."

"Is that the album you told me about last week?"

"Yes. Another one of my pointless attempts to get you to appreciate real music."

"You're not doing too badly. There are a few people I've really started to like. Especially that Hooker guy."

"Yet nothing warms your heart as much as the ping of a computer," Adriana says wryly.

Sarah holds out her hand for the keys, but Adriana doesn't pass them over. "Please be careful. I don't know what the two of you are up to, but don't get hurt. Your mother . . . Oh. You know."

"I know," says Sarah.

"She'll never forgive me."

"Yeah, I know."

Adriana runs one long red fingernail over her bottom lip. "I will be sure to say at your funeral that it was all your fault. That you blackmailed me into giving you the Hilux and that I had no idea what you were planning to do with it."

"But you don't know anything in any case."

"And is it better this way? Is it really better this way?"

Sarah looks at her red Converse sneakers. "I think so."

"Okay, then." Adriana hands over the keys, then the canvas bag. "This is the revolver. It's a Taurus. And the Glock you asked for." She looks at me. "Perhaps you should take this," she says, referring to the bag.

I take it from her.

"Aren't you going to open it and make sure it's all in order?" Adriana asks.

I give a half shrug. "No need. I trust you."

I may even mean that.

Sarah opens the double-cab pickup and gets in, adjusting the seat. Forward. Then up a little. Up some more.

I look away, taking in the cold concrete of the garage, the pillars painted orange to mark parking level 3B. I look anywhere but at Sarah, because I want to smile. She can hardly see over the dashboard.

"Fuck it," she says, getting out again, slamming the door so hard, the sound echoes through the cavernous space.

I unbuckle my seat belt, get out of the 4x4, and walk around, my hand held open for the keys.

"Do you even know how to drive?" Sarah asks.

"No. I walk everywhere." Her bruised ego is amusing. "Come on," I say. "It's not that bad. Sasolburg's not too far."

She hands over the keys and walks toward the passenger door with short, angry strides. "I should have asked for the Merc."

Alex

1

"Get up."

The sudden bright light is too much for my eyes. I blink against the early morning sun streaming through the broken windows on the other side of the room. The old man has always had newspapers covering the windows. Why take them down now? Why expose himself? Are we going somewhere? Again?

Or is this the end? Finally. I look at the markings on the wall counting the days that I've been held captive. Almost eight weeks? Has it really been that long?

I swing my legs over the side of the bed. No point asking. Gaddafi's not going to say anything. I still have no idea why he abducted me that night in Welkom. Perhaps the syndicate is keeping me alive for some unknown reason. Or maybe someone is negotiating my release. Maybe those perennial good guys, Gift of the Givers? Who the hell knows?

I could have saved them the trouble. My family is dirt-poor, the farm on its last legs. The newspaper I work for is equally broke. It would be more lucrative to write up my death, sell a few more newspapers, and get a hundred more hits online than break the bank trying to buy my freedom.

"Journalist Dead after Eight Weeks." Nope. The news editor would do something more juicy. "Derksen's Body Found in Old Mine Shaft."

I grimace. Touch the raw skin on my wrist gingerly. The handcuffs are eating into my flesh. The old man cleans the wounds every night, even alternates the arm tied to the steel bed frame, but my wrists remain sore.

It's clear he's been to prison. He understands the power that belongs to those who hold the keys. The power they have over time. He gets to say when I eat, when I rest, when I shit. And he watches me all the time, as though he knows he needs eyes in the back of his head.

I need to get to the bathroom. "Gaddafi!"

The old man with the bald patch and the pigeon-feather hair comes sauntering around the zinc wall. He's carrying an enamel mug with tea in it. He puts it down on the table by the door, bows deeply. "What is it, Your Highness?" he asks in his nasal voice.

"Toilet. A bath. Food. Fucking hell."

He comes over and pulls an enamel bucket out from under the bed using his foot, then walks out cackling.

I pull the bucket closer and unbutton my Levi's. I wish I could kick Gaddafi and that infernal cup of fucking tea, but it's the only liquid I get till lunchtime.

There's no bathroom here. We're in a derelict factory. The empty steel shell has one cold-water tap. I doubt the facilities are better at any of the other factories in this abandoned industrial area.

There are no cars or people around. Or rather, no nine-to-five people. The old man keeps vagrants at bay with a shotgun. I get to go out once a day for fresh air. Fifteen minutes before bedtime. Not a minute more.

The old man has disappeared four times—that I know of. The only way I figured it out was because I slept like the dead for ten hours each time. He must have put sleeping pills in my tea or in my food.

I don't know much about Gaddafi. He's the only one who guards me. Probably has to do the syndicate's boring work. Too old for anything else. There was someone else here once, long ago, but they didn't come in and I couldn't hear what they were discussing with the old man. Might even have been my imagination.

Gaddafi seems to communicate with his bosses via email. As far as I can see, he has no cell phone.

He struggles with the laptop. It's an old Dell. He took my Mac apart, almost like a child who wanted to see how it was put together.

He types using his two index fingers. And he only understands the most basic actions: switch on, connect to the Internet using a dongle, open email, read messages, switch off. That's it. No browsing the news sites. No Facebook and no porn. That's all he does. Every evening since he brought me here.

His laptop habits are like everything he does. Regular as clockwork. Supper happens in the late afternoon. Breakfast as soon as the sun is up.

His hands are covered in tattoos. Crude, homemade drawings creep up his arm and disappear under his sleeves, only to reappear on his neck.

The one of the spider's web, spread over his Adam's apple, was made a few years before he was released, he told me one night when he was unusually talkative. It was after the prison system had transformed in '94, along with everything else after apartheid, and he'd joined a gang, the 28s, to survive.

He has patience to wait for his prey, he said. Like a spider. Prison made him patient, and he could wait as long as he needed to wait for whatever it was he wanted.

I wish I knew what it was that he was after. I also wish I'd let Sarah know where I was going that night in Welkom.

I button up my jeans and push the bucket, which I will have to empty myself this evening, under the bed again. Judging from the color and smell of my urine, I'm dehydrated. That and the headache that makes me dread any sudden movement.

Gaddafi has no idea about water. He drinks gallons of cheap beer and sweet tea, so sweet you have to wonder whether he was deprived of sugar in prison.

Speak of the devil. He peeps around the zinc wall again. "Game of chess?" The Eastern European accent nudges through his prison Afrikaans, making him sound strangely exotic.

I incline my head toward the windows and the light shining through them. Regret it immediately as the pounding inside my skull becomes a brisk tap dance.

"Now? What's going on?"

His fingers fiddle with the zip on the cheap black tracksuit jacket he's got on this morning. Must be cool outside.

I notice that the black T-shirt has been replaced with a clean red one. And he's shaved. The beard of the last few weeks is gone. The hair is still standing up at all angles, though.

"Are we expecting guests?" I try to laugh—anything to glean something from him—but laughing hurts.

I hold my side with the hand that isn't cuffed this morning, the left one.

On the second night here, I managed to wrestle Gaddafi and knock him out, but he didn't have the handcuff keys on him. And the hospital bed I'm tied to is anchored to the floor. I had to sit around waiting for him to wake up. He was livid when he did. He spat out two teeth and kicked me in the back, near where the bullet hit me in Welkom. His clothes may be cheap, but his boots aren't. Steel tips. Big fucking worker's shoes. I think some of my ribs are fractured.

Gaddafi doesn't answer me. He just walks out and comes back with a small table, the chess set balanced on top. He puts it down next to the bed. Then he brings a wooden chair that looks like it was stolen from a school. All the while he whistles a tune I don't recognize.

He walks out again and comes back five minutes later, carrying a mug of tea and a saucer with rusks.

"Well, something's definitely different today. Chess in the morning. Rusks." I sit down on the thin mattress and the cheap dog blanket. Take the tea he passes to me.

"You talk too much. Play."

"I'm not in the mood."

"And I'm not in the mood to hold a gun against your head all the time."

"Then don't. Don't you have a home to go to? Someone who misses you?"

He leans back in the chair. Drinks his tea slowly while he stares at me. His Adam's apple moves up and down as he swallows, bobbing inside the spider's web like a trapped insect.

"Fifteen," he says finally.

"Fifteen what?"

"I was fifteen when I last had a place I called home."

"Why fifteen? What happened?"

"Play."

"Gaddafi. What—"

"I answered you. Now play."

He puts his mug down on the ground and makes the first move. I balance my mug between my thighs and clumsily dip a rusk. I'd kill for bacon and eggs. And proper coffee.

Eight weeks. Eight fucking weeks.

Gaddafi takes my pawn. I can't believe I'm playing chess. I truly hate chess.

He looks up and smiles. What the hell is going on? There's a sparkle in his watery blue eyes. He puts his hands, racked by age and arthritis, on the knees of his worn-out jeans.

"Your move, Alex. We don't have all day."

2

I can hear the old man snoring from all the way over here, his breathing rhythmic, like someone in a deep sleep. This is how he always snores. Living in close quarters for weeks on end gives you these banal insights into someone else's habits.

Gaddafi's bed is about thirty feet from mine, next to the wooden school chair and a crate he uses as a makeshift desk for the laptop. I'm inside what probably used to be the office part of the factory.

I turn on my side, careful not to let the cuffs rattle against the steel. I feel around for the broken piece of a saw hidden inside a small slit in the mattress. I found it in the sand outside one night, and I've hidden it in here ever since.

Every night I saw at the rusted weld that fixes the headrail to the bed. If I succeed in cutting through it, I'll be able to slip the cuff free.

I've always only worked at night, but something's up today. After breakfast and chess, Gaddafi announced that we had to rest to prepare for later, but gave no details about what was going to be happening.

Well, he can sleep if he wants to. My time is running out. Quickly. Something is about to happen. That's clear as daylight.

I pull my T-shirt over my head and feed it down to my hand, muffling the sound of the blade. I try to keep the sawing as rhythmic as Gaddafi's snoring. The pain in my left hand, which I've been vaguely aware of for a while, is rapidly getting sharper.

My fingertips are covered with blisters I have to try and hide from Gaddafi by dirtying my hands in the dust.

It's a narrow piece of blade so there's not much room to hold it securely. But I saw and saw until I feel blood between my fingers, thick and sticky. Not long after, there's a soft give, a gentle breaking sound.

Was it the blade?

I lift the T-shirt.

It's the bed frame. I did it.

I move the handcuffs down the metal bend with my right hand as slowly as I can, careful not to make a noise.

Immediately there's a problem. The gap I've made is substantially smaller than the cuffs. I'm going to have to get up and pull the headrail away from the bed so I can push them through.

I swing my legs over the side of the bed, trying to keep my breathing even. I can't start getting excited now. I'm not out of the door yet.

Free myself. Get Gaddafi's Beretta, get the car keys, and get myself out of here. That's the plan.

I plant my feet on the ground, ignoring the pain in my ribs, and pull at the headrail with my right hand while feeling my way down with my left hand.

Fuck. There just isn't enough room.

Stay calm. I need to stay calm, though what I really want to do is upend the bed and yank at the steel until the cuffs slip through.

Try again.

I put my right foot under the mattress, against the frame, pull the headrail with my right hand, and try to feel my way through the gap with my left hand. I pull harder, a sharp pain bulleting through my chest.

Frustration burns in my throat.

The handcuffs suddenly swing free.

Got it!

My breathing is rapid and shallow. I concentrate hard to slow it down, listening to the sounds of the morning around us. Same as usual, except for Gaddafi's snoring.

I walk to the doorway that separates my part of the factory from his. I peek around the corner toward the bed where he's sleeping. I need to get the keys for the factory and the keys for the car, and I need the Beretta. Where would they be?

I can't spot anything on the crate next to his bed. Nothing in his hands.

I gauge my chances of escaping quietly. Can I get through one of the windows? No. Nothing has changed since I first assessed them. They all have burglar bars in front of them. And the large sliding door is still padlocked.

Finding the Beretta is my best option. With that, I may be able to get the keys for the padlock and the car from Gaddafi.

Can't see those either. Probably under his pillow.

I exhale my frustration. I'm going to need to find something to hit him over the head with. The chair will do.

I'm going to have to take my chances. I approach the makeshift desk carefully.

A few yards from the chair, a voice stops me in my tracks.

"When I was in prison, I would fake sleep every night. Didn't help much, but I still tried. Every night. It's not that I wasn't good at it, it's just that no one cared."

Gaddafi hoists himself up on his elbow. I lurch forward. There's something in his hand. Not the Beretta.

Then everything goes black.

SARAH

1

We drive in darkness until the first light starts to seep over the horizon at around six. The early morning traffic slows as we approach Sasolburg, but there aren't many cops on the road. Thank goodness for that. The last thing we need right now is someone to pull us over.

Say what you like about the South African police, but most of them are good people who know what they're doing. People who think. People who might wonder what two women are doing on the road early in the morning carrying liters of bottled water, binoculars, a revolver, a pistol, and a few too many passports with the same face on them. Clearly we are not suburban moms lugging around kids with their book bags and sports gear.

Ranna's impatient in the peak-hour traffic. Probably better that she's driving anyway, because there are way more cars than I'm used to sharing the road with. I'm usually still asleep at this time of the day. If I were sitting in this, I'd get frustrated and do something stupid.

Story of my life.

I focus on the person in the white overalls with the pointy ears in the Camry next to us. There's a flask on the passenger seat beside him. A boilermaker, perhaps, on his way to the bright lights of Sasol's industrial complex. Or maybe on his way home after the night shift. To his family. Sleepy voices. Weet-Bix with warm milk around the kitchen table.

I believe in family. There's not much else I believe in.

No. There is one other thing.

Gordon Moore, one of the founders of Intel, once famously said that processor power in computers would double every two years.

Every two years. Faster. Better.

Never the fastest. Never the best.

And that's how it is with everything. You never get ahead of things. All the crap you have to deal with doubles every year. Suddenly you have a property to look after. Dogs. Your father has emphysema. And you've found love. Or something resembling it. Something that feels different from the clumsy wrestling in the back seat of an old Alfa when you were sixteen years old.

We pull away at the same time as the Camry. I look from pointy ears to Ranna.

Does she know? Does she know what's going to happen? Can she sense it coming? Is that why she keeps hammering on about the syndicate? About tracing the laptop? Why she wants a gun?

Alex says Ranna sees things other people aren't even aware of. Says she sees through their bullshit. And she remembers. She remembers to never forget.

Does Alex—her thing with Alex—make her blind this time? Have I concealed enough of what's really going on?

We pull even with the Camry again at the next traffic light. The middle-aged man behind the wheel looks toward me and smiles half-heartedly.

We stop at a gas station to get something to eat. The morning light reflects off the shop's glass doors as they glide open with a whisper to swallow us.

The air inside is cool. Sterile. Wonderful.

I walk to the coffee machine while Ranna heads for the bakery. I want tea, and she's asked for a double espresso. I really can't work out why people like coffee. It tastes like poison.

As I'm putting sugar in my tea, she comes and stands next to me.

"Look," she hisses in my ear, holding a newspaper so I can see.

"'Bloodbath as Seven Rhinos Poached in Kruger.'"

"No," she says impatiently, tapping her thumb below the fold.

Her head seems to sink into her shoulders, her hand over her mouth and nose as though she is doing her best to hide. "Nikhil used the credit card."

I look again. "Isabel Kroon in India" reads the headline on an article on the lower-right side of the front page.

I scan it quickly. It says Isabel Kroon used her credit card to buy a motorbike in India. It is suspected that she's on her way to Vietnam.

"I thought he was supposed to buy a camera."

"We'll have to go back and shoot him."

I look at her. There's a faint smile on her lips. "You're on your own," I say.

"Come now. Be a sport."

I turn to page two. Nothing more on the Black Widow serial killer. "There's no photo of you. That's good news."

"I know. I've made sure never to have one taken, and you wiped whatever you could find. We make a good team."

Another joke. Ha-ha.

I put milk and sugar in the tea and clamp a plastic lid on the paper cup.

She mumbles something and folds up the newspaper. Holds up two ham-and-cheese sandwiches for me to see.

"I've already paid for this. I'll wait in the car."

I finish my tea while I smoke a cigarette in an attempt to calm my nerves. So close and yet so far. So much that could go wrong. I lean against the passenger door, blowing smoke into the air in a thin, steady stream, watching as it disappears into the cool morning air.

The driver's side door opens. Ranna walks around the vehicle, looking at me quizzically.

"You okay?" she asks. She aims, throws her empty cup into a trash can a few yards from us. Lands the shot.

"Yeah. Just nervous."

She parks her body next to mine, crossing her arms. "I'm also worried. What if your rogue cops are out there with Alex? They'll probably be armed to the teeth."

I pull at the cigarette, before I say something irrational and stupid.

Ranna turns to face me. "I want to double-check Alex's laptop trace. Show me exactly where it is and if it's still active. And it wouldn't hurt to see where all those cops hunting for Alex are either."

"Now?"

"Yes. Now."

2

The tar road disappears. Becomes a white gravel stretch that peters out into nothingness ahead of us. It's as if the developers of this particular industrial precinct on the outskirts of Sasolburg ran out of money long before they could complete most of the infrastructure.

It couldn't have helped that the complex was built on a road the municipality never connected to anywhere else.

The Hilux travels at twenty miles an hour, then slows to ten. Comes to a complete halt as Ranna hits the brakes and parks underneath the shade of an acacia tree.

I point at the set of three buildings about two hundred yards away, then back at my computer screen. "Alex is in the middle one, over there."

In the field, the other two half-finished buildings look like carcasses chewed on by wind and weather. The recent recession was insatiable.

Ranna looks at the screen, nods. "That's what your machine says, yes, but we're still not just going to storm in there blindly."

Fuck it. More time being wasted.

Ranna opens the car door and surveys the landscape. She points to a rocky hill next to the buildings. "We can scout the building from there. See if we can spot Alex or if the laptop signal is just some kid playing *Fortnite* on a computer he bought off the back of a truck."

"Can't we just go? We've checked the signal and tracked the phones of the cops looking for him. The laptop is here, the cops are not. What more do you want? Everything is fine."

Ranna shakes her head, the corner of her mouth twisting bitterly. "First we take a look around, and then we go in—*if* Alex is in there. I'm not going to jail, and I'm sure you don't want to go back either. We've waited this long. It's no use rushing now."

We collect the two backpacks and jog to the hill. I'm forced to lengthen my stride as Ranna keeps a steady pace.

She stays as close to the tree line as possible, never giving anyone a clear shot at us.

I play along, if only for the sake of getting this over and done with as soon as possible.

Just short of the top of the ridge, she stops and kneels down. Unrolls a cheap sleeping bag and takes out a set of binoculars. She lies down slowly, careful not to disturb any rocks so they won't cascade downhill and alert our prey.

I squat down at her feet, drinking water from a bottle in my own backpack. I watch as a handful of flies swarms around a dead bird a few feet away. The wind shifts, and the stench from the rotting animal invades my nose and mouth.

I look left when Ranna makes a noise in the back of her throat.

It's the sound I imagine this bird made as it died. Shocked and primal and hurt.

I have no doubt what she's discovered.

I step closer to where she is lying on the shoulder of a ridge in the shade of a Port Jackson tree. The ground under the tree is still damp from the cool night, even though the sun is halfway up the cloudless sky.

I lie down next to her, roll to one side to move a stone under my hip, and then settle down. "Here you go." I offer her my water bottle, but she ignores it. I push it into the sandy ground next to her.

She hands me the binoculars, and I do a quick sweep of the buildings.

Alex is in the abandoned factory in the middle, just as the laptop signal said. He is lying on a steel-frame bed in the building's office. I watch anxiously until I see his right hand move, the one cuffed to the bed. He is thinner, and barefoot, and his jeans are dirty. There's a smear of something on his face that looks like it could be blood.

The relief is almost overwhelming. I turn my head, just in time to see a single drop work its way down Ranna's nose, her chin.

She scrambles up and walks away. When she comes back a while later, her eyes are on fire. She looks pissed off.

"I'm sorry. You were right," she says, "I should have left the damn passport for later."

She lies down beside me again and picks up the binoculars, but this time the Glock is out, lying on top of her backpack as though she is expecting to use it soon.

"I only see one man," she says. "The others must be out. I can't imagine there would be only one guy here. And such an old man."

"Maybe the others went back to Welkom? Alex is cuffed. I don't suppose you need more than one person to keep an eye on him."

Who am I trying to convince?

"It's possible. I just don't get why they've kept him alive. What do they want?" Ranna murmurs, half to herself.

"Can we speculate about that later? And can you please stop wishing him dead?"

She ignores me. Her attention seems nailed to the factory with the two men inside.

"I think the old man's been in prison," she says.

How would she know that?

I take the binoculars from her. "Why do you say that?"

I focus on the man, who is fiddling with a laptop. He's sitting hunched over a crate. It looks like he's about thirty feet away from Alex, on the other side of a second bed that stands in the main hall. Next to the factory, near an open sliding door, a green Nissan Sani sport utility vehicle is parked under a rickety lean-to. Two bags lie on the ground beside it.

"The ink," says Ranna. "Look at his neck. And his forearms. They're gang tattoos—28s, I'd say. The really bad boys. Looking at the number of them, I'd say he was behind bars for a long time. And he's still alive, which means he's a loyal soldier. Must have been in for murder."

I peer through the binoculars. She does seem to see everything, just as Alex said. I nod as I spot the crude ink. "Okay. I see them."

Beep. My cell phone.

Ranna looks at me. She'd said we should put our phones on silent. I drop the binoculars, make a sorry face, and pull it out of my pocket.

All good, says the message.

I look back down the ridge. "I don't see anyone else. Just the old man. We should move, before his friends show up."

Ranna looks at the factory, pushing her curls out of her eyes.

"We can't afford to waste time," I prod again.

She looks at me, her blue eyes almost purple. Intense. Careful. They've been like this since Mumbai. As though she knows.

"We can do it, Ranna. One old man. That's it."

"Why don't we call the police?"

"And what about Alex?" I say. "It means you won't get to see him. And you're here now. All the way from India."

"The police's flying squad will get here quickly. And then he'll be safe. That's all that matters."

But she doesn't sound all that certain. Is she afraid to see Alex again? Worried that he's still mad at her?

I point at the old Sani. "The car looks like it's loaded and ready to go. We can't . . . I don't want to wait . . ."

Suddenly there's a tremor of rage in my voice. I bite my lower lip so hard I taste blood. She can't start this crap now. What she doesn't know is that I'm as glad as she is that Alex is still alive. All I had was a promise. A useless, shitty promise.

I shake my head. I want this thing over. "If you want to stay, fine, but I'm not sitting around here any longer."

I jump up. She lifts the binoculars I left on the ground to her eyes and stares at the building below us. Calls to me quietly.

"Okay. We go in. But you do as I say. Or someone's going to get hurt."

She waves me down the ridge on the left. Indicates she'll walk around the right to the sliding door.

I do as she says. The revolver is heavy in my hand. "Guns are for stupid people," I'd told Ranna. And now I'm one of them.

This entire mess is ridiculous. I know that. But I don't have any choices. I'm the puppet dancing on strings someone else is pulling.

How did I end up here? I promised myself after prison that no one would ever do this to me again. That no one would ever again tell me what to do, when to do it.

I'm at the bottom of the ridge. Sweat trickles down my spine, and it's not only because of the sun. Fifty yards to the right I spot Ranna taking three long strides to stand with her back against the factory's corrugated steel walls. Her tread is light, her hands sure around the Glock's grip. She waves me over. I walk quietly and quickly toward her, my breath shallow. Ranna looks up at the window above us and then at me as though she's weighing me.

I wave at the sliding door. Whisper, "It's open."

"Too obvious."

I walk past her toward the door.

"Sarah," she hisses.

I go on walking. This stupid game has gone on way too long.

The footsteps behind me approach quickly. I start jogging. Slip through the door.

It's time to get Alex back.

Just inside the door she catches up to me. Yanks me brutally by the back of my T-shirt, then quickly grabs my upper arm with the same hand.

"What the fuck do you think . . ."

She stops when she feels the barrel pushing into her back.

I saw him coming. How he knew we'd use the door, I don't know. Maybe it was obvious. As Ranna said.

"Drop it. Now."

Ranna hesitates.

"Do it."

She complies.

"Kick it away from you."

Again she does as he says.

The old man shifts back a step, the gun still pointed at Ranna. He moves like she does. Softly, carefully, as if to make sure no one senses his approach.

She waits, breathing heavily with pent-up emotion, then frowns.

I watch as the realization dawns on her face. The disappointment. The impotent, white-hot anger edged by a hint of fear.

He didn't tell me to drop the revolver.

Her hand digs into my arm. "Why?" She shakes her head slowly.

I try to twist out of her grip, but her fingers dig into my flesh.

"Why, Sarah? For fuck's sake!"

I look down at my sneakers.

She lets go of my arm, as if in disgust.

I take a step away from her, away from him.

"Had to," I whisper. I don't know where to look. "It was you or Alex. And if Alex had never met you, he wouldn't be here now. Neither would I. And in any case . . ." I shake my head, annoyed to be explaining. It doesn't matter anyway.

I look at the man behind her and nod. Take two more steps away and to the side. Ranna is standing between us now. I wonder whether I could shoot him. But the truth is, I don't shoot well enough.

He clears his throat and speaks in the nasal, singsong voice I've become familiar with.

"Hello, Isabel. I've waited such a long time to see you again."

Ranna

1

If I had to take a photo of Sarah, it would be ice. Black ice. Hard to spot. Camouflaged, hidden. Something that would take you down before you even knew it was there.

Betrayal has a color: it's a chilly, dirty black.

I should have shot Sarah that day in my apartment in Mumbai. Was Alex even kidnapped? Is there a syndicate? Is he in on this? What *is* this?

And how the hell does this old man know me? I'm one hundred percent sure I've never seen him before.

Sarah walks around me warily, out of reach. I follow her with my eyes. Wish I could get my hands around her neck and strangle her.

She's on my left now—me between the two of them—mute, the revolver unwieldly in her hands, as though she doesn't know whether to aim it at us or drop it.

"Okay. You have her now. Where is Alex? Next door?" Sarah nods toward the office in the corner of the building.

The bastard nods and smiles.

No. He's grinning. One of his front teeth is chipped, another is missing. His eyebrows are thick and woven together across the top of his nose. He takes one, two steps back.

"Alex is here. Don't you worry."

He speaks Afrikaans, but his accent is unusual, his tongue dragging through the *s*'s. It sounds like he was forced to learn Afrikaans late in life. Probably in prison.

Sarah waves the gun in his direction. "Where is he? In there? We saw him there. If you've done anything to him . . ." Her voice is hard and impatient.

The old man ignores her. Instead, his sunken eyes burn into me.

I watch him with equal intensity, calibrating what I'm up against. Stringy arms. Yellowish skin. Years of malnourishment have carved out his shoulders and hollowed out his cheeks. His skin is tired, sagging off his face, leaving his mouth looking wholly disappointed. Up close, it's clear that one of the tattoos running up his neck is of a naked woman with long hair. There's a 28 on his one hand. Looks like someone recently tried to cross it out with a cut.

The fingers around the Beretta say he is familiar with the shape and heft of his weapon. And there's a wariness in his eyes, like someone who is used to the fact that anything can happen, even when it seems like everything is under control.

He's still grinning. "Done looking, Isabel?"

I don't react.

Again the gap-toothed smirk.

"I don't have time to wait." Sarah speaks up again, her voice fraying at the edges. "Where is Alex?"

"We can all go see him once you drop the gun."

"No way. Not until I've seen Alex."

"I'm not negotiating with you. Drop it."

"Alex first."

He considers her words and then gives in. "Fine. But if you do anything funny, I'll kill you, her, and Alex."

He indicates that I have to turn around and walk toward the office. "Keep your hands where I can see them. Up." He jerks his chin at Sarah: "Walk next to her."

She hesitates, then obliges, gun still in hand.

We walk through an open doorway, into what was once the factory office. Alex is lying on the bed we saw earlier. Asleep?

Alive?

I look over my shoulder. The old man is two steps behind me, his pistol trained on my back. Sarah is to the left of him, her jaw clenched tight.

If Alex is sleeping, perhaps I could wake him and he'd be able to help me. Louder than necessary, I say, "Why, Sarah? What the fuck is this?"

The old man steps forward, punches me in the kidneys with the gun, and steps back again. "Shut it!"

Pain shoots through my body, a thousand pins pricking my palms. I am hugging myself to try and make it stop. I have the sudden urge to laugh. I've been so stupid. Not just now—I've been naïve from the minute I found Sarah in my bathroom in Mumbai. I should have known she was up to something.

"If I ever get out of this, Sarah Fourie," I say through clenched teeth, "I swear I will—"

"Sarah? Ranna? Is that you? What the . . ."

The raspy voice from the bed pulls me up straight. It's the voice I've been waiting for, but also not. It's tired, short, angry. Much like the last time we spoke.

I stare into eyes that look confused, dazed. Probably drugged.

Alex is handcuffed to the bed. He looks terrible. Much thinner than the last time I saw him. His lips are chapped, and his beard and brown hair are long and wild. His right eye is swollen shut, and there's a smear of dry blood at the corner of his mouth. But he's alive.

He sits up slowly, swings his legs over the edge of the bed as if unsure about its dimensions.

I forget about the old man and the gun and rush over to Alex, kneeling down in front of him, my hands on his legs. I search his face, feeling clumsy and afraid. Not of the old man, but of Alex. He has every reason to hate me.

"Ranna?"

"Yes."

He frowns in disbelief. "No way. Can't be."

"It's me. It's really me."

He reaches out with an unsteady hand. Stops, as if afraid to find out that I may simply be a product of his dazed mind. "What are you doing here?" he asks, a slur in his voice. "Are you crazy?"

"A little. Still."

He works hard to produce a crooked smile, then leans his head forward until his forehead rests against mine. I breathe him in deeply. He smells of sweat. The whole place smells of something I don't want to name, but it doesn't matter. He's here. Still. Obstinate as ever. Stronger than anyone else I know.

"You're alive," I whisper.

He shakes his head slowly, the spark of life in his dark eyes dulled. "You shouldn't have. Not here. No."

I kiss his mouth. Taste him, under everything, the way he was in Dar es Salaam when we first met.

He groans as he tries to move forward. He's in pain, something more than the bruising on his face. My hands search his neck, his body, to find the source of whatever is making him wince. Halfway down his back, I find it and press softly. He sucks in his breath noisily.

"Your ribs. Your face," I try to joke. "I rather like this cowboy look on you."

"Comes for free." He nods toward his prison guard and the Beretta. "He knows how to use that thing."

He touches my hair, my arms, finally resting a hand on my neck, as though he is checking for a heartbeat.

The old man steps closer, snuffing out the emotion. "He wouldn't have looked this bad if he didn't keep trying to escape. But he's stubborn.

And stupid as fuck." He taps an index finger against his temple to make his point. "Each time I have to show him why he shouldn't try again. And each time I have to make myself a little clearer."

"Not going to stop," Alex says, giving that crooked smile again. He leans over my shoulder and gives the man the middle finger.

I sit down on the bed next to Alex, trying to wipe away some of the blood around his mouth. I refuse to look at the Beretta. I refuse to be afraid.

"I'm going to kill you," I tell the old man.

"How touching," he says dryly.

He waves his pistol to show me to move over on the bed, away from Alex. There's another set of handcuffs hanging off the steel frame at the foot of the bed. "Go on, chain yourself to the bed."

Alex scrubs a hand over his head as if he's trying to shake the cobwebs from his mind. "Let them go. Tell me what you want, but let them go."

He hasn't figured out yet that it was Sarah who brought us here.

"Cuff yourself," the old man says to me, his voice deceptively soft, but the pistol talking loud and clear. "Now."

I do as he says, but don't close them too tightly. He's no idiot, though. Without taking his eyes off me, he tells Sarah, "Make sure she's done a decent job."

Sarah doesn't hesitate. She steps toward me and jams the cuffs tight around my wrist.

He nods approvingly and then points to the Taurus in her hand. "And now it's time to hand that over."

Sarah holds the weapon up uncertainly. "I'm here for Alex. That was the deal. I bring you Isabel, you give me Alex."

"The deal hasn't changed, but how am I supposed to trust you with that thing while we talk?" He beckons her to put the revolver in his hand. "Come on. Hand it over."

"And my family?"

"I'll call. Soon as we're done here. Nothing will happen to them."

"Is there even anyone to call?" Sarah sounds bitter.

He laughs.

The realization of what is happening finally dawns on Alex. He gets up slowly, a frown between his eyebrows.

"Sarah? What's this? Gaddafi?"

"Will everyone just shut the fuck up!"

Looks like Granddaddy's patience is all used up. He rushes forward, pushes Alex down onto the bed, and grabs him by the hair. He pushes the pistol into his temple and looks at Sarah. "I'll say it again: give me the revolver."

"That was not the deal!" she explodes.

"Boo-fucking-hoo. The revolver. Now!"

"If something happens to my family, if you do anything to Alex . . . I'll . . . ," Sarah hisses.

I feel tempted to laugh. Her face is pathetic. "What deal, Sarah?" I ask. "Why don't you tell us? Tell everyone here how you screwed me over for your own selfish interests."

"Shut up," she spits at me, her voice tight with panic. Things are clearly not playing out as she envisaged.

I wish she or the old bastard would get a little closer.

"What did you think was going to happen, Sarah?" I say mockingly. "Did you really think he was going to keep his promises? How stupid are you, exactly?"

Alex tugs at his handcuffs, looks at us in confusion. "I don't . . . What have you done, Sarah?"

"It was my family or her. You or her. And you wouldn't have been in this mess in the first place if it wasn't for her . . ."

"Quiet." The old man's voice snaps like a whip. His blue eyes are ice cold. Then he says evenly, "Revolver."

"Go, Sarah," says Alex, his voice raw. "Go and see if your people are okay. Run and don't come back."

It doesn't sound like freedom he's offering her. His voice is too disappointed for that. It's more like he's chasing her away.

Sarah shakes her head and straightens her shoulders. She walks toward the bed and places the revolver in the old man's palm.

2

Alex and I sit perched on the bed, like birds on a wire, waiting for whatever will happen next. Alex is cuffed to the one side, me to the other. The old man has given Alex some sweet black coffee, as if he wanted to wake him from his lingering confusion. He looks slightly better than when we first walked in. More alert, and increasingly worried as he realizes Sarah and I have walked into a trap.

Sarah sits handcuffed to a heavy, rusted steel chair, upholstered in blue nylon, placed between us in front of the bed.

I would strangle her if I could. There were at least ten different ways we could have gotten Alex back. Adriana looks like someone with friends. Even I might have been able to improvise something given more time and if I'd known, from the outset, what was really going on. But no. This was the quickest, easiest route open to Sarah. Screw me over and perhaps have Alex all to herself. She never liked me. Never wanted me near Alex.

What I still don't grasp is why I was lured here. What could the old man possibly want from me?

He's sitting before us on a fragile-looking wooden chair, sipping tea from a yellow enamel mug. Behind him, on the floor, are Sarah's revolver and my Glock.

His own Beretta rests on his lap.

"Let's start at the beginning," he says. "My name is Adorjan Borsos."

I laugh at the absurdity of the introduction. "I'm sorry I can't get up and shake your hand."

"Ranna," says Alex, reaching out his left hand to plait his fingers through mine behind Sarah's back. "He's the one with the gun, remember?"

"So, we just have to—"

"Wait. Wait," says Borsos. He seems amused. "You've always been so impatient. Even as a little girl you were never able to wait for anything. Christmas. Birthdays."

Little girl?

"Who are you?"

"You don't remember me at all?"

I search the watery blue eyes. He must be over seventy. No. If he was in jail for a while, he would look older. Maybe he is in his sixties. He doesn't look like anyone I know. But then again, he must have looked very different when he was younger.

In any case, I always did a quick disappearing act when my parents had visitors. I didn't care about boring grown-up stuff. The friendly voices drifting from the living room were strangely comforting, though. I could almost imagine that we were a normal family, even if only for a few hours on a Friday or Saturday evening.

"I have no idea who you are," I tell him.

"You were very little the first time I visited your parents. You spilled Coke all over my shirt. I carried you to bed later that night."

The thought that I was in this man's arms long ago makes me shiver.

"Look, I really don't care who you are. Tell us what you want so we can all get out of here."

Alex squeezes my hand. He says nothing, but his eyes implore me to stay calm. I can hear his shallow breathing from here, then the slow exhalation, as if he's trying to steady the pain in his chest.

I clear my throat and compose myself, letting the words out slowly, carefully. "Okay. Let's talk. I'm listening. What do you want?"

"There you go. That's better," says Borsos. There is a gleeful glint in his eyes. "I knew I was right about Alex."

"What do you mean?"

"I knew that you love him. That you'd come back for him."

"How could you possibly know that?" I force myself to ask.

He shrugs his shoulders under the worn T-shirt, winks at me. "I know a thing or two about love. Something in all those in-depth news articles about you told me that you loved—that you love—Alex. There was one story in particular." He turns to Alex. "Was it one of your friends who interviewed you?"

I glance at Alex, catch the sharp frown, the aha moment as he realizes what Borsos is talking about. He looks at me guiltily. Talks to me, not Borsos. "There was one interview. Sometime after you'd left. A woman who works with me."

"You were supposed to keep quiet."

"I was pissed off. And sick of everyone nagging me for interviews. Going on about how terrible you were."

Sarah crosses her legs and looks away, into the cavernous space of the empty factory. Her jaw is set tight, her eyes unreadable.

I look at Borsos again. "So, okay, you were right. But that still doesn't explain why I'm here." I shake the cuff as though it's one of my silver bracelets. "You wanted me. I'm here now. Let Alex go. You can keep Sarah."

Borsos laughs bitterly. "This is not entirely about you. Believe it or not."

"Well, what the hell do you want, then? Why are we all here? Why this ridiculous, drawn-out game?"

Borsos's face hardens. He leans toward the bed, pointing his finger accusingly at me. "It's your father. He screwed me over years ago. Almost killed me."

"How? My father was a state prosecutor."

"That's right, yes. What you don't know is that he was also the mastermind behind a few big robberies. Big paydays. Your daddy was clever." Borsos taps his forehead. "He knew the system inside out. Knew all the right people. He made the plans. I was the hired gun. Me and another guy."

He holds up three fingers.

"Your father worked high up in the main office in Pretoria. Everyone trusted him. Told him stuff—even the bad guys, all hoping for a deal." He shuffles to the front of his chair. "He knew where the money was. Where it was hidden. Where it was going. Money is always on the move, and if you know when and how . . ." He lets the sentence hang in the air.

I shake my head. My father? A gang leader? A robber? A stupid, common criminal?

"And you have proof of all of this?"

Borsos sits back. He seems to be enjoying telling me his story. It is almost as though he has waited a long time for this audience.

He sips from the enamel mug. Takes his time to answer.

"Think, Isabel. The times your father was away from home. How often you moved to a new house and a new school, because he was feeling the heat. The rising suspicion."

"That doesn't necessarily mean . . ."

"He was a real piece of shit, your father. Come on. Admit it. That's why you did what you did." He laughs. "The rumors in some of the papers after you disappeared last year were that you shot him. That your mom wouldn't have had the guts to lift a hand against Hendrik Kroon. It wasn't suicide. Right? *Right?* You were the one who shot Hendrik Kroon? You can tell me."

Alex looks at me in astonishment, squeezes my hand again. "I thought that was just all cheap sensationalism."

I have no idea what to say to him. I never told him what happened that night. Sarah knows. Only Sarah. Because I had to tell her. She forced it out of me last year. And my mother knows, because she was there.

"Wait a minute . . ." Borsos whoops. "You never told Alex what you did? Really? You never said, 'Listen here, lover boy, I shot and killed my daddy'?"

I ignore him. I'll explain it all to Alex later. If there is a later.

"Fine," I say, trying to change the subject. "My father was an asshole. We all know that. But what does this have to do with me?"

Borsos smiles with one side of his mouth. "It has everything to do with you. Let me tell you why. I got out of prison a few years back. Armed robbery. Murder. Your father and I did a job in 1993. A cash heist. One of those armored Toyota vans. We sideswiped the van with an old Merc. It was on that road past the Pelindaba nuclear reactor, just outside Pretoria. Early morning, before anyone was around to see. We were going to split the money three ways, but Hendrik thought it would be a good idea to shoot me. Twice."

He points at his chest and stomach. "I survived. The cops called the paramedics. The other hired gun we used, a young guy named Johannes, wasn't so lucky. Two shots in the heart. Bam-bam. Just like that. Your father always loved to double-tap."

Borsos's expression turns sour. "I was going to give the cops your father's name. Tell them everything. I was busy negotiating with them in the hospital. But then I heard he'd put a bullet through his brain that same night."

He shakes his head, as if in disbelief. "And then, to top it all off, the cops thought they recovered every penny of the R1.5 million stolen from the van. They stopped searching for accomplices. They just left it there. His role in the robberies. Everything. Just like that. Gave him a free pass." He snaps his fingers. "They said they didn't believe me. And they made sure they shut me up. Repeatedly." He rubs his shoulder reflexively.

It's silent while his words sink in. I pull my hand out of Alex's grip. I have no doubt that the fact I killed my father was probably the last thing he wanted to hear about me.

Alex is the first to speak. "How does Ranna fit into all of this?" His eyes are brighter than when we walked in, his gaze more alert, even if the rest of his body is still betraying him. It's clearly taking some effort to sit upright. His body shudders when he coughs. Even after almost eight weeks of being locked up and starved, he's still the journalist.

Borsos looks at him questioningly. "Oh. Yes. I keep forgetting she's changed her name." He drinks more tea. "Ranna? Good name. Israeli?"

He doesn't wait for an answer, motions at me with his mug. "I thought it was all over. I go to jail, the money is recovered, Hendrik's dead. Justice is done. But then last year I read in the papers about Isabel Kroon. The woman who killed all those men. And I knew. The apple doesn't fall far from the tree. Just like her daddy, Ranna will do whatever she has to do to get what she wants."

"I'm nothing like my father," I say, sounding like a six-year-old.

Borsos laughs into his tea. "Just like her father."

"I am not . . ."

"Go on," says Sarah loudly. "I don't want to sit here all day."

I want to argue with her, but she's right. "Get to the point."

Borsos puts his mug down. "Right. The point. I read in the papers that Isabel inherited everything from her father. And then I read that Alex thinks she's not as bad as everyone makes her out to be, and isn't that odd, coming from someone she was supposed to have tried to kill? Maybe the two of them are friends, I thought. More than friends." He nods, happy to have been able to put two and two together about my and Alex's broken relationship.

"So, I grabbed old Alex here when he was out of town alone and called his mother with my demands. She got ahold of Sarah to find Ranna. And that's how we all come to be here now." He leans back and crosses his legs at the ankles, waves at Sarah. "It took long enough, I must say. I started wondering if this chick was ever going to find you. I was about to give up."

Sarah growls low and deep, like a trapped animal.

My eyes jump from her to Alex to Borsos. He's not as half-witted as he appears. He got me back to South Africa. Put two and two together about me and Alex. But why? It's still not clear what he wants with me. What he demanded from Alex's mother. Money? Sarah would have paid any ransom he wanted. Well, up to a point, I suppose. She is rich, but not that rich. And most of her money is illegal, which could create a number of problems.

I shift back on the bed. Consider what Borsos has said. My father. His work. That night he was so afraid, the night he gave my mother and me what I always presumed to be cheap trinkets. The night I killed him.

"Sorry," I whisper toward Alex behind Sarah's back. "My father . . . I didn't know. And his death . . . it was . . ." But I can't continue. How does one explain something like that?

"No need to be sorry," says Borsos, as if my apology were aimed at him. He waves the pistol at the three of us. Sips his tea again. "But there is something you can *do*. Something you can do for me. Something you *must* do for me if you want lover boy here to live."

I look at him expectantly. Finally. The reason we're all stuck in Sasolburg with a madman.

"There was something else in that armored van that day. Something your father really wanted. Something he was hiding from me and Johannes." Borsos wipes a hand over his bald spot. "He tagged along that day, something he never did. I should have known then that we were heading into a shitstorm. After we sideswiped the Toyota, your dad got out and told us he wanted the steel lockbox. It was smallish, like a book, hidden inside a white bank bag. He didn't even look inside. Just told us we could take the money. He didn't want any of it."

I frown. "What was in the lockbox?"

"Ah, don't lie to me. You know."

"I don't."

Borsos looks disappointed. "It wasn't in his stuff? You know, after you packed up everything when he was dead? That's going to make things difficult for you."

Wait. Maybe I shouldn't show my hand so easily. "I don't remember a metal box that size." I try to backtrack a little. "But my mother's family did the packing. She couldn't face going back to the house."

He looks skeptical. "All I know is that it must have been something big. Hendrik wouldn't have let us take the money if the lockbox didn't have something really special inside. And R1.5 mil was a big payday back then. I want to know what was so important that he was prepared to kill me and Johannes for it. He wanted us out of the picture so he could retire. Whatever he took was safe, easy money. The cops never missed that box. No one ever spoke about it. Never breathed a word."

I listen to him in growing astonishment. I can hardly believe what I'm hearing.

"You're telling me that you abducted Alex because of a small metal box, and you don't even know what was inside it? That's why we're all here?" I ball my fists. The bitter bile of powerlessness is rising in my throat.

"Unless you're lying and you can give me the box and its contents. Then it's all done. Over."

"I know nothing about any box."

"Then you're going to have to find out."

"How? How am I supposed to find a box I've never seen! It's been twenty-five years since my father died. Can you count? *Twenty-five.* My mother gave his stuff away a long time ago. Spent the little money he had left. And trust me, there wasn't much. No policies, no lovely little nest egg."

"Karla wouldn't have given away a lockbox without opening it. And her family wouldn't do something like that either. Nobody's that stupid. And you're right, I've been through all the news stories about you and your family. Every last one. I know that you and your mother didn't suddenly become stinking rich. In fact, things were quite difficult for a while, until that American she eventually married appeared on the horizon. Which means the box is still around somewhere. Maybe Hendrik hid it. In a bank? Maybe. Who knows? You need to find out. Your dad was never going to flaunt his wealth for the cops to see. He was way smarter than that."

Difficult does not even begin to describe the lean years after my father died. "And I've told you, I don't know anything about a box," I say again, wanting to scream the words. I try to remember everything about that night, but don't recall seeing a metal box of any kind.

Borsos's voice remains calm as he leans toward us, as though he is letting me in on a secret. "I don't care what you know and don't know. It's not my problem. It's payback time. Your family owes me."

"Are you deaf? Stupid? This is impossible! There's no way my mother still has that box. If she ever had it at all. And if she opened it, and there was something valuable inside, she would have spent it. I can promise you that. We ate fucking peanut butter sandwiches for weeks on end."

He shrugs. "I don't care. Get the box. Bring it to me. And if your mom sold it, you'll need to get it back."

"Sold what? Are you crazy?" I stare at him, but he doesn't react.

I realize that I may actually be right. That prison may have made him lose touch with reality.

"What happens if I can't find it?"

"Not my problem." He swings the Beretta in Alex's direction. "But it will be his." He mimics shots, bam-bam sounds exploding softly from his lips.

He gets up. "You can take Sarah with you to help you find the box. She'll be able to get all the details on the robbery so you'll know where to start looking. She's the computer geek, right?"

"You can't do this. Do you have any idea how absurd—"

"Don't care. Fuck Hendrik Kroon. Into his grave and to hell and back." He takes a final swig from the enamel mug and lets it hang from his bony index finger.

I take a deep breath, seeking some semblance of calm. "What happens to Alex while I go on this wild goose chase?"

"He'll keep me company until you bring me the box. Or whatever was inside it. And don't think you can just bring me any old box. I know exactly what it looks like. It was white and there were numbers painted on it. In black. That box was all I thought about every night in prison."

He puts his mug down on the floor and moves the revolver and the Glock farther away from us.

I yank at the handcuffs in frustration, feel them cut into my wrists. "You're asking the impossible. If you want money, ask Sarah for money. I'm sure she'll gladly pay a ransom."

"What? R50 million? R100 million?"

I stare at him, mouth agape.

Borsos nods. "That's what I want. Does your little nerd have that kind of money?" He looks at Sarah.

She shakes her head. "But I can get something worth your while. Something big, in cash. Maybe R1 million?"

He laughs. "No thanks. Get me my box."

"Take Sarah's money. I can promise you, it's the best deal you'll get. Just thin–"

"Ranna!" Alex slaps his hand on the bed several times until I look at him. "It's okay," he says urgently. "We'll work something out."

"What? How?"

"What happened to your father's stuff after he died? You inherited it all, didn't you?"

"I don't know. We left the house that night with two suitcases and never went back. Lena, my mother's sister, and Thinus, her husband, went and packed everything up afterward. My mother said they could sell everything inside, take it, do whatever they wanted with it."

"And did they do as she asked?"

"I don't know. I think they stored some stuff in case I wanted it later. My mother never told them about the beatings, so they really liked my dad. It took a while for my mom to convince them of his darker side."

"Then maybe it's still in storage."

"Twenty-five years later?" I ask.

"It's possible. Lena did a few interviews last year. One magazine discovered she's your aunt."

Borsos interrupts, his voice mock-impressed. "See? You're not stupid. If you think carefully, I'm sure you'll find what I'm looking for."

I turn to Alex. Will I ever be able to apologize enough? If it wasn't for me and my messy life, he wouldn't be here.

This is just like last year, in Dar es Salaam.

And what happens if I can't find this damn lockbox? I am worried about Alex's health. He looks bad. I don't know how much longer he'll hold up under these conditions.

"I'll go and look. I'll go now." I jerk my head at Sarah. "You can keep her."

Borsos grins. "She has no value to me."

When I see Sarah's face, I realize that we have at least one thing in common: an all-consuming fury. Well, that and Alex.

She throws her head back and stares at Borsos. "If something happens to Alex while we're gone. Or to my family . . ."

"Enough drama. Nothing's going to happen to anyone." He tucks the pistol into the back of his jeans. "And don't be tempted to do anything stupid. I'm going to move Alex as soon as you're gone. I'll contact you in a few days so I can tell you where to make the drop."

He looks at his watch. "This coming Saturday. Eleven o'clock. If you don't answer the phone, I'll kill Alex. If you show up with the police, I'll kill Alex. And if you don't find the box . . ." He turns his head, lifts his eyebrows, lets the thought linger.

"How do we know you'll keep your end of the bargain? You've lied to me once. Who's to say you won't do it again?" Sarah asks precisely what I've been wondering. "And what happens when we bring you what you want? We know who you are, what you look like."

"If I get the box, you can take Alex here and go live happily ever after."

"And if the box has documents inside? Useless documents about people long gone?"

"Then maybe we can discuss a cash payment." He waves the Beretta at us. "But I knew Hendrik. Blackmail was too much work for that lazy bastard. Bring me the lockbox. That's all you need to focus on."

"And then you'll let Alex go? Just like that?"

"Yes."

"Really?"

"I can only give you my word."

"And that means squat."

He grins, shrugs. "It's all you've got."

Sarah gives him a sour look.

He takes a bunch of keys out of his pocket and unlocks Alex's handcuffs. "Time for us to go so you ladies can get to work."

"And how are we supposed to do that?" says Sarah, tugging at her own cuffs.

Borsos ignores her, gestures with the Beretta for Alex to get up. "Come."

He stalls. "I want to say goodbye to Ranna."

"How romantic." Borsos rolls his eyes. "Hurry up. We don't have all day."

Alex steps toward me, pain creasing his face. He takes my face in his hands. He kisses me gently. Puts his face in my hair and whispers urgently, "Don't worry about your father and what I think. I get it. Maybe I have always known it deep down somewhere. Don't come back. Last time, I did what you told me to. Now I'm asking you to please do as I say. Disappear. Go back to wherever you came from."

I shake my head and put my hand on his chest. "There is no way I'm leaving you," I whisper.

"Must you always be so stubborn? When this is all done, you and I need to have a conversation. A serious one."

I don't answer him, just kiss his neck.

"I still love you," he says. "I tried, but I can't let you go."

I want to believe him, but wonder if it's possible. Maybe it's just a nice, polite parting shot. Something you say because you know you may die soon.

Fuck it, I decide. "I love you too," I whisper back. "In India—everywhere—I couldn't get you out of my head."

"That's enough. Time to go." Borsos's voice is like a whip in the echoing space.

Alex straightens up with difficulty.

I look at Borsos. "I will kill you when this is done," I say. "If I ever get my hands on you, I will kill you."

He smirks. "Just like her daddy."

He pushes Alex through the office doorway, follows him as he slowly limps across the concrete floor and into the sun that falls through the sliding door.

For a long time, it's quiet. Then Borsos comes back. He swings two keys in front of Sarah's nose. "Thanks for your help."

"Fuck you."

Borsos gapes at her in mock shock. "You've been a surprise. I didn't know you and Alex . . . ah, well, I suppose it doesn't matter. There's always something you don't see. You think you're smart, and then . . ." He turns and walks to the door.

"What about us?" I shout, rattling the handcuffs.

He doesn't answer. At the sliding door, he hangs the keys on a wooden board on the wall.

"Till Saturday!" he calls over his shoulder.

3

I don't feel like asking Sarah to fetch the keys, so I get up and try to pull the bed toward where they're hanging, but it's fastened to the floor.

"I'll do it. For crying out loud." Sarah gets up, lifting the chair she's cuffed to in her hands as though it weighs nothing.

"I'm going to kill you." I spit out the words.

The words aren't enough. I grab the bed where my arm is restrained and shake the frame in frustration. "I am going to kill you! Do you hear? There were so many better ways to get Alex out of here."

"Oh, shut up," she says. "You're going to kill Adorjan Borsos. Kill me. Violence. It's all you ever think about."

My hands are curled into fists. "Why weren't you straight with me? We could have made a plan. For Alex, and for your family."

"Like what?"

"Adriana could have helped. And that's just one example."

"Adriana knows that Alex is gone, just like everyone else who reads the papers, but he's nothing to her. She doesn't know that Borsos threatened my family. She would have gone completely overboard trying to protect them, and Alex would probably be dead by now. Anyway, if I struggled to locate Borsos, then she would never have been able to find him. Until an hour ago, I didn't even have a name or a number to trace. He knows how to stay off-grid."

"So, the thing about Alex's laptop was a lie?"

"Yes. Borsos told me he was somewhere in Sasolburg, so that I could bring you here, and then he texted me his location just before we arrived. The agreement was to be here by eight."

"Still, we could have made a plan," I insist. "But no, Sarah, clever fucking Sarah, knows best. And now Alex is . . ." I grit my teeth.

"We—me and Alex—would not have been here if it weren't for you. This is about you, first and foremost."

"It's about my father. There's a difference."

"Really?" she spits. She walks over to the keys, unlocks her cuffs, and comes back. Throws me the keys.

I unlock the cuffs, rub my left wrist. The anger is gone. I have no energy remaining to throttle Sarah. Maybe because she's right. Would any of us even be here if it weren't for me? It's not chaos that dogs poor Alex—it's me and my past.

Sarah nods toward the outside. "Come on. We need to go. We might still catch him. I can try and trace his phone."

"Now you're suddenly thinking with your head."

She stops, hands on her hips. "And what do you mean by that?"

"You know."

She turns around and heads for the door. "If anything happened between me and Alex while you were gone, it's none of your business," she shoots back over her shoulder at me. "It was you who packed up and left."

I pick up the revolver and the Glock. Wish I knew how to answer her.

I follow her out.

Borsos slashed one of the pickup's front tires. By the time we've put on the spare wheel, he'll be long gone.

Sarah takes out her computer, executes a quick trace of the phone he used to send her his location.

"Fuck! Nothing," she says. "The phone's dead."

She lights a cigarette. Turns her back on me and smokes, looking out toward the road, her whole body a brace of frustration.

I think of her mother telling me to look after her. What a joke. Neither of us knew what her daughter was planning. We completely underestimated her.

"Now what?" says Sarah, breaking the silence. She turns to me, her eyes unnaturally shiny.

I don't give a shit how she feels.

"We drive back to Pretoria. You're going to park yourself in front of your computer and find everything you can on Adorjan Borsos, and I'm going to call my mother and find out what happened to my father's stuff."

"And then?"

"Then we give the old man the box and we get Alex back. And then I hope I never, ever see you again."

"Ranna, I had no choice. Just think for a moment." She looks down at her sneakers. "He knows where my family lives, and yes, maybe it was an empty threat, but I couldn't take that chance. I can't look after all of them, and neither can Adriana. They're all over the place. Germany. At the university in Pretoria. Uncle Tiny was my only . . . I tried to make sure that at least my parents were safe."

She drags at the cigarette, throws it down, and extinguishes it with the heel of her shoe. Lights a fresh one. "I'm not stupid. I'm not that naïve to think that Adorjan Borsos would just let Alex go, but I had no other choice. You were right earlier. Borsos is a member of the 28s gang, and he's quite high up, says the prison warden I spoke to. Their reach is so wide—way beyond prison. You know that. So I weighed my options and I hoped. Prayed."

"You could have talked to me. Your parents. Asked for help."

"If I drag my parents into my 'lifestyle' again, my mom would cut me off." Her fingers make angry quotation marks in the air. "She promised me that when I went to jail, and she always keeps her promises."

No mention of why she couldn't ask me for help. "And you think they're safe now?"

"No. But hopefully they will be until we find the box and give it to Borsos."

"And then he'll just walk away and everything will be fine?"

Sarah looks at me, the sarcasm like a kick to her stomach. "No. Clearly not. But maybe you get to use that damn gun you're so fucking fond of."

I stare at her in disbelief. "Now you think of it?"

"Yes. Because Borsos said he wouldn't be alone today. That he isn't acting alone."

"And you believed him? Clearly this is his game and his game only. He's not willing to share with the 28s."

"And I knew that how?"

"Argh! Fuck it!" I run my hands through my hair. Stand still for a moment, peering at the sky. "It's too late now."

I bite back the rage I feel toward the woman in front of me. Tell myself to try and focus on Alex. Besides, I may need Sarah to find this box, despite telling Borsos otherwise.

"How did Adorjan make contact with you?" I ask. "Not today, but at the start. How did you arrange all of this? You say you couldn't trace him?"

Sarah looks relieved about the unexpected cease-fire. She drags deeply on the Marlboro, exhales a stream of white smoke. "Alex's mother. She came to see me. She said a man called her and said he had information about Alex, but he refused to speak to the police. Naturally, I said I'd help her."

"How did Borsos contact Alex's mom? Can't we trace him that way?"

"You think I didn't try? He clearly knows what I do. Alex's mom must have told him. After I told Aunt Sophia that I would help her, he called me, and that was when it clicked that he was the one who had Alex. And that what he actually wanted was you."

She points at me with her cigarette. "He's not stupid. He must have used his years in prison to educate himself about everything to do with IT. He used the phone in a grocery store in Pretoria to call me. Then I got a letter from Bloemfontein containing Alex's SIM card and a photograph of my mother standing in front of her house. Who still sends things in the mail these days? At least the letter confirmed that he did actually have Alex and wasn't making empty threats. He called one more time to find out if I was making any headway, and that call came from a coffee shop."

"How did you let him know you'd found me?"

"I had to announce your death in the *Beeld*, using a photograph of you. Your name, for that purpose, was Daisy Louw. The date and time of the funeral had to say when we'd be back in South Africa."

A photo of me? There aren't photos of me.

"While you were sleeping," says Sarah, who seems to have read my mind. "At the hotel. In Mumbai."

And this is why I don't sleep.

"What if the police had seen it?"

She shrugs.

I laugh. This whole thing seems unbelievable. A complex joke.

"And how did Borsos tell you what to do, how to get here?"

She looks away guiltily. "Two hours before the 'funeral,' he sent an email from a Gmail address. It was the first time he made contact electronically. Probably the last time too. Then he sent a text."

I turn away from her. She's right. The old man is street-smart, despite being locked up during the digital revolution. Too shrewd to underestimate. I would have preferred it if he were arrogant and stupid.

"Come on," I say impatiently, but Sarah doesn't move.

"What would you have done, Ranna?" she asks.

I don't answer her.

"Ranna," she says again.

Still I say nothing.

She mutters under her breath. Stamps the cigarette butt down with the toe of her sneaker. "We don't have much time. Let's go."

I jump into the pickup, Sarah hopping into the back seat and lying down with her shoes against the door. "I need to sleep," she mutters.

As I pull away, I hear her making a call, her voice calm and controlled, the morning's emotions neatly packed away.

"Hi, Uncle Tiny. Could you stay a little longer? It didn't quite . . . it didn't go as expected. I'll pay you and your guys double for the extra days . . . No, no, I insist. No favors."

She tries to laugh, says goodbye, and ends the call.

In the rearview mirror I see her lift her hips to jam her phone into her pocket and then close her eyes. I try to gather some empathy for her, but fail to find anything. If only she'd been honest with me.

"Phone," I say at the first traffic light, holding out my hand.

She puts it in my hand without saying a word.

I call my mother, glad that Sarah's faking sleep in the back. I check the time. Half past five in the morning over there. Fay Frost is probably on her first cup of tea for the day.

She is. Her knees kept her up all night, she tells me. She goes off to get my mother, a little surprised at the second call in such a short period of time. I tap impatiently on the steering wheel while I wait. When my mother eventually comes on, her voice is shrill with worry. "Isabel? What's going on?"

"There's something I need to find."

"What? You never call and now, suddenly—"

"It's nothing serious, Ma. Really." I force myself to speak slowly, gently. "I'm in South Africa, and I was just wondering if there is still some of Pa's stuff around somewhere. I remember you said that Aunt Lena kept some items for me in case I wanted to look at them later, when I'd calmed down about everything." The lie seems to arise from nowhere: "I think it's time. I want to look through all of it before you get here. Make peace. Move on. You know what I mean?"

"Now? All of a sudden?"

"Yes. As I said, it's time to move on."

"I . . . Of course. Yes."

"So, does Aunt Lena still have the stuff?"

"Are you sure you're okay, Isa?"

"Yes. Promise."

"And you had no issues getting back into the country?"

"No. I . . . I was able to . . ." I give up. How do you explain people like Sarah and Adriana to your mother? "Pa's stuff?"

She stays quiet.

"Ma?"

"He left everything to you," she says finally. There is a tinge of bitterness to her voice.

"I didn't want any of it."

"I had to go back to work after having been home for twelve years."

The undertone of shame makes me aware for the first time how hard it must have been for her. I was too angry for too long about the fact that she'd never left him. Have I been angry my whole life?

"I'm sorry," is all I can offer.

"It wasn't your fault."

"We need to stop with the fault thing. Please. It's been over for such a long time."

Then again, not. This whole situation with Adorjan Borsos has neatly brought me right back to that night. A perfect circle.

Somewhere, I think, Hendrik Kroon is watching me and laughing.

I overtake a truck loaded with steel pipes. I try not to sound impatient: "So do you think Aunt Lena managed to hang on to some of Pa's stuff?"

She sighs. I know the exact gestures that accompany this sigh: the crossed arms, looking away, looking down. It's the pantomime for "I'm not in the mood for this."

"Mom?"

"It's still there. Lena and I both decided to store some of his belongings for you, even though you insisted on selling it all. We hoped that one day you'd want to see it, maybe even keep some of it. One day, when you weren't so angry anymore. There were good times too, you know."

Her abrupt silence indicates that she's realized today's phone call is not going to be about forgiving and forgetting, but she knows enough not to push any further.

She clears her throat. "Your father's stuff is probably still with Lena and Thinus in Cape Town. Or maybe at their house in Paternoster."

"Do you really think they'll still have it? After all these years?"

"There wasn't much to begin with. Lena threw away a lot. And neither of us wanted to stay in the house, remember? We sold it, and the car. That's what got us through the first year or so after we settled your father's debt. So, there are only a few boxes left. Your father's desk. Things like that."

What a relief. A place to start, at least.

She scrapes together the courage to ask me, "What's going on, Isa? I mean, what's really going on?"

What can I offer her? The truth?

Why not?

"I'm looking for a flat white metal lockbox about the size of a book. Do you remember something like that? Pa would have brought it . . . he would have brought it home that evening."

I can hear her struggling with her memory, just as I had. Then she draws in a slow, calming breath. "I can't remember. I wanted to forget. I did."

Until now.

"I'm sorry. I didn't mean to tear open old wounds."

"What's wrong, Isa? Why can't you just talk to me?"

"Nothing's wrong," I say, lying smoothly and calmly. Again.

It seems truth is not for me, after all.

"Why do you want to look at your father's stuff? Now, after all these years?"

"As I say, I need to make peace."

"With a steel box? You're looking for something." The sudden smile in her voice catches me unawares. "In any case, you're not one for making peace. War, maybe. Always. Ever since you were a little girl."

"Then maybe it's time to learn." Another lie. The last thing I feel like doing is making peace. Not with Sarah. Nor with Adorjan Borsos. Nor with my father.

"I'll call Lena and tell her you're on your way."

"You can't do that. What about the police? I'm still on their wanted list."

"I'll explain."

I inadvertently hit the gas, as I suddenly imagine being caged for the rest of my life. It would kill me.

"Will she be okay . . . with me? All the news stories?" Not every family harbors a serial killer.

"I think so. She feels very guilty about not knowing what Hendrik did to us."

"I thought she and Thinus liked him."

"They did. But they were smart enough to listen to what I had to say after that night. To realize what happened. Lena saw the bruises on me. The scars."

I consider her words. "Maybe it would be good to first find out whether she actually still has Pa's stuff. Tell her you're coming to visit, and you want to go through it. And then let me know. Maybe we should keep her out of this for now. Keep me out of it."

The digital connection between us seems to drone as she considers my suggestion. "All right," she concedes. "It's probably safer. Call me again in two hours. I'll talk to her, and then I'll wait right here by the phone."

I call my mother again as I drive into Pretoria. She answers immediately. Sarah is still asleep in the back seat, no longer faking it, judging by the light snoring.

"Lena's in Cape Town. She says your father's things are at their vacation home in Paternoster. In the garage. She and Thinus stored it all there. She said she was actually thinking she might get rid of it by December. She's been wanting to clear things out since Thinus got sick. Something about starting over and living more healthily."

"Is Uncle Thinus ill?" I remember a big man with thick dirty-blond hair, a single golden front tooth, a neat beard, and light-brown eyes.

"He had throat cancer. Year before last. I'm not sure how serious it was. Lena struggles to talk about it. I think it's my fault. I haven't made an effort to visit for a long time."

"I see." I turn right, onto a street lined with jacarandas, and open the window to let in the smell of spring. "How did you explain the call to her?"

"I was careful," she says, immediately sensing what I mean. "I said Moshe and I wanted to visit her. That the vacation to South Africa was a birthday present from him." She stops talking and then asks quickly, as though worried that I may have changed my mind, "We are still coming, right? Next weekend? Moshe already bought two plane tickets. Is it still okay?"

With today's mess around Alex, I had completely forgotten about the plan to meet up with them. I made those plans before I knew the surprises Sarah was about to spring on me. Would it be better to cancel the visit?

I look at the date on my watch. No. It's Monday now. Borsos wants the box by Saturday, and my mother and Moshe are only arriving on Sunday. Whatever happens will happen.

At least there'll be someone here to attend my funeral.

"Yes, of course," I reassure her. "It's going to be fun."

The drone on the line again—louder this time, as though someone were breathing into a microphone. Then her voice, softer, more hesitant than before.

"I asked Lena whether she'd be there if we wanted to get to Paternoster earlier. We're meeting her and Thinus there. I said I didn't want her to pick us up in Cape Town. Moshe likes the drive. As you know."

I remember that about my Israeli stepfather. That and the fact that he can be somewhat pedantic, but in a good way. He fusses and cares. Never picks on anyone, never talks down to anyone, despite his wealth.

"She said it would be hard to meet us early." She speaks slowly, emphasizing every word. "That they won't be there. They're only driving up from Cape Town on Sunday morning."

Ah, now I see what she's getting at, even though she'll never openly endorse anything illegal.

"The neighbors can't let us in either," she says. "They won't be there. They're trying to sell their house. Money troubles, I think. So there won't be anyone around to help us." She clears her throat uncomfortably. "I'm just letting you know. I believe the weather . . . the weather can be bad at this time of year. That terrible wind, you know."

I roll the window up again, the promise of rain in the air. Stop at a red light. "Thank you. I appreciate it. I'll be careful. I promise."

Her voice becomes thin. "Are you sure there isn't some other, better plan?"

"I am."

"Then I trust you. See you soon." She tries to laugh. "Not long now."

I say goodbye and ring off. Look at my watch and then banish her from my head so that I can focus. All I need to remember for now—all I need to know—is that it is Monday. Monday afternoon. On Saturday morning, Adorjan Borsos wants that box, and if he doesn't have it, he'll kill Alex.

I stop in front of Sarah's gate and lean on the horn until she shoots upright in the back seat.

"What?" She looks around, confused. "Are we here? How did you manage to find the place again?"

"I have this memory thing, remember?"

She rubs her eyes with both hands, runs them through her chopped hair. Stretches, the T-shirt clinging tightly to her body, then gives an involuntary shiver. The September air is cool, and a spring rain has begun to sift down.

"We have to take the car back to Adriana," she says.

"I will. When I'm done. I need a car that's not going to attract attention, and it sure as hell isn't your Mini."

"Where are you off to?"

"I told you. I'm going to go and look through my father's stuff to see whether I can find the box. Or a clue about where it might be. My mom says my aunt stored most of his things at her house in Paternoster."

"Do you really think you're going to find it?"

"I certainly hope so."

"Do you need help?"

"We can cover more ground if we split up. Let me know about Borsos, whatever you find out. I'll take your phone. I'm sure you have more than one. Call me. Anytime, night or day."

She shrugs as though none of it is really of interest to her.

She's the old Sarah Fourie again. The unreadable woman who only cares about her people, and the rest of us can go to hell.

Just before she hops out, she looks back at me. "Those documents you got from Adriana, and the bank cards, they're the real deal. Use them. I'll pay some money into your accounts later this afternoon."

Sarah

1

I have no qualms about what I did. We're talking about my family. And Alex. Given the same set of circumstances, I'd make exactly the same decisions, without a moment's hesitation.

Well, maybe not entirely. I might try to be a bit smarter. And more careful.

And maybe I would trust Ranna more. And Adriana.

I don't know.

Point is: Alex is still that asshole's hostage. Nothing I did changed anything. All those hours in front of the computer, all those days in Lagos and Mumbai, and Alex is still exactly where he was before.

At least I have a name now. That's more than I had before. *Adorjan Borsos.*

I jerk at my apartment block's gate, but it won't open. Push my thumb against the glass reader again.

Still nothing.

Wrong thumb.

I shift the revolver to my right hand and press my left thumb to the reader. The red light turns green. I walk to the elevator and go up to the third floor. I had the front entrance bricked up when I moved here. No matter how hard I try to keep things clean, not all my clients are angels.

Megabyte dances all around my legs and then runs to sit down near the biscuit jar. They know exactly how my conscience works when I've been away from home.

I take out two dog biscuits and give them each one, rubbing their heads while they chew. Megs barks once and then goes and lies down on her bed next to the row of computers, her favorite spot whenever I'm working. Byte's still waiting hopefully for another cookie.

We can't all get what we want, Byte.

The yawn surprises me. It's almost night, and I'm supposed to be wide-awake, but fatigue is like lead in my veins. My sleep pattern is totally messed up.

I push aside the temptation to rest. It's time to work. I need to find out who Adorjan Borsos is. I get a Coke, light a cigarette, and inhale deeply. The double joy of nicotine and caffeine does nothing to ease the turmoil of the day.

Ranna was right, and that's a terribly bitter pill to swallow. I should have known better. I was so incredibly naïve. Why did I believe Borsos when he said he'd let Alex go if I brought Ranna to him? Of course it wasn't going to be that easy. Nothing ever is or will be now.

I had hope, and that is such a dumb, useless emotion. Hope never makes anything happen. It just keeps you alive artificially. Frigging ICU for the frigging heart. Like believing that Alex will one day see through that fucking woman.

His eyes gave him away today. I was no hero trying to save his life. In fact, I betrayed him by bringing Ranna to Sasolburg. That's all he's going to remember. None of the effort to try and trace her, to find Borsos. The nights in front of the computer, traveling to places I never wanted to visit, sleeping in strange, grubby cities. The constant worry about him.

Adriana is right. My mother is right. I need to let him go.

I breathe the smoke in deeply, feel my lungs burning.

And yet. If I had to do it all again, I would make the same decisions. I'm sure I would.

Maybe.

I crush the cigarette and take my sneakers off. Park myself in front of the biggest of the three computer screens. Enough. What's done is done. It's time to work. The question: Where to begin?

The license plate number for the green Sani. It had a Gauteng province tag. That might be a way to track Borsos down. I do a quick search.

No such luck. The plates belong to a canary-yellow Fiat Uno in Kokstad. Borsos plotted this down to the finest detail.

After some more work, I do manage to discover a few things about the old man. He is a Hungarian immigrant who came to the country when he was sixteen. He didn't do well at school and then fell in with the wrong people. Small things at first: leaving a shop without paying for the two cans of food in his coat pockets. Later, stealing a car in Joburg.

After a few years in jail, he tried to behave. He trained as an electrician, married a woman by the name of Jana du Toit, and became a father. Family life obviously didn't suit him. He was arrested for car theft, and, somewhere along the way, Du Toit and the kid, a daughter, left for greener pastures. It's not clear whether that happened before or after he was arrested again.

Borsos was the only one arrested in 1993 for the failed armored car heist, netting him R1.5 million for the briefest of moments. An accomplice was killed.

Seems like he was telling the truth this morning.

An ambulance took Borsos to the hospital with two 9mm bullets in his body, the same caliber weapon the security guards inside the Toyota van had had on them. The guards, ex-policemen, were shot and killed after the van they were driving was overturned. They were shot with AK-47s, the weapons Borsos and his accomplice were carrying.

The body of Borsos's sidekick, eighteen-year-old Johannes Tredoux, was found beside the road. Two shots to the heart, also 9mm.

No reports or articles mention Ranna's father, Hendrik Kroon. The really bad news is that I can't find even a footnote on a metal lockbox anywhere—which doesn't necessarily mean that the box doesn't exist, just that my sources may be inadequate. The information on the web is pretty sparse since all of this happened in 1993, before the Internet revolution.

Most of the information I'm able to find comes from scanned newspapers and magazine articles. Interviews with Borsos when he came out of jail at the age of sixty-four, after having served twenty-five years of a life sentence for double murder and armed robbery.

The main reason for his early release was cost cutting by the state, and the fact that he was deemed "old and harmless."

Bullshit.

There's surprisingly little information available about Hendrik Kroon's death from around the date it happened. A short, one-column article at the bottom of page nineteen of a Johannesburg daily. Nothing more. The most interesting articles are from last year, when journalists went all out to dissect the life of Ranna Abramson, the Black Widow serial killer, in the finest detail.

I scoff at the name. I would have thought journalists would be more imaginative with their nicknames. Black Widow is so obvious. Boring, even. If they'd known the woman, they would have come up with something far more juicy.

The article that probably made Adorjan Borsos sit up and pay attention was one about how Ranna was the only heir to deceased state prosecutor Hendrik Kroon. His widow, Karla Kroon, the article notes, says that she is happy for her daughter to inherit everything. She herself has no interest in his possessions. Neither does she respond to any questions about why she was clearly left out of Hendrik's will. The little money he'd had, in any case, had been spent a long time ago, she says.

She denies that Ranna has it in her to kill anyone. Pleads with the media to leave her and her family in peace.

Karla's sister, Lena, is a little more forthcoming in the next article I find, but she doesn't supply any new facts.

I stare at the magazine photo of the woman posing at a window. You can see she and Karla are sisters. Same tinge of regret and disappointment around the mouth. Same hazel eyes. Lena, the younger sister, is the more beautiful one, though.

A rumble of thunder draws my attention. A thunderstorm is moving over the city. It's dusk, and lightning fractures the sky. A few hesitant droplets turn into a flood of water streaming down the windows.

A second bolt of lightning motivates Byte to seek refuge under the workbench. I move my bare feet to make room for him, patting him reassuringly on his head. Turn my attention back to the screen in front of me.

I can't find any indication that anyone reported a lost or stolen metal box in the robbery, so there are no clues as to what might have been inside it.

Borsos keeps referring to forgiveness in his interviews; says that he has paid his debt to society and that he is sorry for what he did, especially about the guards he killed.

"Shit. Really?" I hit the enter button on the keyboard three times as if it will open some magic door. I stand up and light a cigarette. Become aware of the fact that I haven't eaten since this morning.

I stare at the screen, the cursor mocking my inactivity.

Where would I find more information? Why did this whole thing have to happen in the prehistoric year of 1993?

I drag at the cigarette. *Think.* I could do searches on everyone who was involved in the robbery. That might help. What might also make sense would be to talk to the policeman who handled the investigation on the case. Who was that again?

Detective Sergeant Stefan Jansen. Retired now—as a colonel—but still a resident of Pretoria.

How lucky can one woman be? I hate talking to cops, and yet it seems like all I've been doing these past twelve months.

The windows behind me shake as the fast-moving storm flashes across the city. Already I can see its moody back as it travels east toward the richer part of town.

I check the time. Past six. Speaking to Jansen won't necessarily solve my problem, I decide. I sit down again. There are a few questions I don't imagine he'll have answers for.

Why, for instance, did Adorjan Borsos tell no one about the lockbox? He could have spilled the beans to the police, even though Kroon was dead. It might have helped when it came to his sentencing. Then again, I imagine the police wouldn't want to believe anything bad about one of their own, especially if he was thought to have committed suicide that same night, leaving behind a grieving widow and young child.

I blow a puff of smoke upward and watch it disappear against the white ceiling.

There may be another way to get my hands on more information. I could go to the national archives. They keep records of just about everything that's ever happened in South Africa. Court judgments, military records, divorces, marriages.

I consider the time and date and do some calculations. There are a number of researchers who specialize in locating documents at the archives. I'll need to pay someone to find the info I want. There's no time to do it myself.

There must be something—anything—out there that might help get Alex back home.

2

I look at the Google Maps app on an old phone I retrieved from the back of my closet earlier tonight. The coordinates are right, so this must be the place.

I can't sleep, so I venture out into the night air to see where retired police colonel Stefan Jansen lives. To determine if it would be possible to speak with him.

His house is some version of Karoo-chic. Huge. Two stories high with an impressive wraparound porch. A lawn vast enough to be used as a driving range. A swimming pool that glimmers in the floodlights.

The lights aren't the only security. There are movement sensors on the walls and there's burglar proofing on the windows, in spite of the fact that the house is in a new-money golf estate in the most expensive part of Pretoria, beyond what used to be Pretoria East.

The security guards at the estate's gates are friendly and efficient. My easy access was thanks to a security system that's heavily reliant on computers. The gated community uses an electronic setup for booking visitors, and I had no hassles signing myself in before I drove here. The guards let me in without asking a single question.

I eat the last of the Steers burger and wipe my hands on a napkin. I should have bought another one. Or at the very least some fries.

When a black Range Rover drives past, I drop my head and start fiddling with Google Maps as though I'm typing in an address. I'm parked in a driveway two up from Jansen's place. The glass castle behind me is dark and deathly silent, obviously deserted. Next to a perfectly trimmed miniature lollipop tree, a real estate sign announces that the house is for sale. If anyone wonders what I'm doing here, they're likely to think me a prospective buyer or agent.

Not that many people come by here, anyway. The Range Rover was only the second drive-by in half an hour. These are, after all, the most precious commodities money buys: silence and space. All the things you certainly don't have in prison.

I lift the binoculars to my face when the door on Jansen's porch opens. A gray-haired man of medium height appears in the yellow circle cast by a light above the front door. He's wearing a thick brown bathrobe. There's a walking stick in his right hand and a cup of tea in his left. He walks, with difficulty, to a table, puts the cup down on its wooden top, and sinks gingerly into a wicker chair. He feels blindly behind him to adjust a cushion, then reaches over and picks up a book on the chair next to him.

I rest the binoculars in my lap. It's Stefan Jansen. Older, but the long, narrow face is the same as the one in the photographs I found on the net. The thin shoulders, the bony hands.

An ex-cop in a mansion. How did he come into money? No broker on earth can generate this sort of wealth from a police officer's pension. Our colonel here either inherited a pile of cash, married rich, or made money some other way.

Until I know how Jansen came by his fortune, I'm not going to risk spooking him.

I drive back to the apartment, getting nothing more than a passing tail wag from Megabyte as the two dogs settle down to sleep again. I sit down at the computer, get up again, open the windows, and put on Nina Simone. Listen as she frets and worries in a raspy voice about losing someone she loves.

Adriana would be proud. Something other than the ping emanating from my computer's speakers.

The Marlboro burns my throat. I've lost count of how many cigarettes I've smoked today.

I stub it out in the full ashtray and wander to the kitchen to make tea, glancing up at the clock as the kettle boils. Almost 10 p.m. The night seeping in through the windows is warm and brooding, the rain from earlier forgotten.

The darkness, anonymity, and familiarity it brings start to settle into my body. Soothing the brittle edges into something more confident, more at ease. More relaxed. This is the best time of the day. The air tastes sweeter, fresher. The streets have emptied, and the few echoes of other people's lives barely reach me up here. The sound of late-night movies. People having sex. Cars speeding by. The deep-throated laughter of a transgender woman and her friend, waiting on the corner for business.

I walk back to the row of computers and put my watch down next to the middle one's keyboard. I'm going to work for four hours, then sleep. If I don't get into bed at a fairly reasonable hour, I might start making mistakes.

Again.

I sit down to tackle my first problem. I still need to find someone who can do the archive work for me.

I mentally run down a list of names. Saul Nyati might be able to help. He was pretty fast the last time I needed his expertise.

I sip on the tea as I work. Decide to add four Oreos to the marvelous array of vitamins and minerals I already consumed today.

Stefan Jansen was married twice, I see, and neither of the marriages produced children. What he does have is money. Lots of it. There is R50,000 credit in his checking account, his house is paid for, and so are his three cars. One BMW, an Aston Martin, and a Volvo. Good taste in cars. Especially the Aston.

Then there's a house on Thesen Island in Knysna, in the southern Cape, and two apartments in Sydney, Australia. Plus, he owns about two percent of the shares in South Africa's biggest media company.

"Colonel Jansen," I muse. "How did you get your hands on all this money?"

I dig deeper into his finances. Until his retirement, he lived in the suburb of Montana in Pretoria North, and worked at the Brooklyn police station in the more affluent part of the city. He had a Toyota Corolla to his name. Or, more precisely, a third of a Corolla. The bank owned the other two-thirds.

Then, two years after his retirement, large sums of money suddenly started appearing in his account. Looks like it might be from two or more trusts. His ex-wives appear to be normal middle-class women, and there certainly don't seem to be any siblings who might have favored them in their wills.

That leaves me with only one possible answer to the question of his wealth: the man's a crooked cop who had to wait until after his retirement to spend his money.

But what does this mean for me and Ranna and Alex? Is it worth going to talk to him? What if he was part of the '93 cash heist? What if he, as the officer who investigated Hendrik Kroon's death, concealed the disappearance of the metal box? What if he's the one who took it?

And yet, Borsos didn't mention Stefan Jansen. And it would have been in his interest to inform us if police members had been in on the robbery, because that would help us find the box for him.

Unless Stefan Jansen wasn't involved in that particular robbery. Or Borsos doesn't know about him. Or Jansen is an honest cop and all his money comes from another source.

I stare at the screen, desperately trying to finish a puzzle with what feels like only half the pieces. Decide that the clock is the best compass through this mess. It's Tuesday morning and there's no time for subtlety.

Why not see what happens when I shake the tree? See how Jansen reacts, what he does.

I smile sourly. Sounds like something Ranna would do. Crude, with no thought for consequences.

Ranna. She needs to get ahold of me if something happens. I text her my new number, then look at the clock again. I should probably leave this for later today. Normal people have been asleep for hours, Jansen included. There is, however, something I can do before I go to bed.

I start building a spider program that can comb the net for any new communications—email, Facebook or Twitter posts, anything like that—that contain the words *Ranna Abramson*, *Hendrik Kroon*, *Isabel Kroon*, *Karla Kroon*, or *Adorjan Borsos*. It'll alert me to anyone asking too many questions about this case. Any chatter I need to be aware of.

I press enter, yawn, and lean back in my chair. The crawler may help. Or it may be a grand waste of time. The age of the people involved in this case means they are unlikely to be big fans of Instagram, Facebook, and Twitter.

A message flickers on the right of my screen. It's Saul Nyati, from the archive. He will see what he can find on Kroon and Borsos at the national archives but warns that it will take time, and he's not sure he'll be done by Friday.

More bad news, as though the day hasn't yielded its full quota yet. I switch off the light, call the dogs, and go to bed.

A cold nose wakes me in the middle of the night. It's Megs. She wants to go out. I turn away from her, but she punishes me with a wet, insistent tongue in my neck. Standing next to her, Byte gives one sharp bark.

"Tyrants," I mutter.

I suppose it's better than having no love at all.

I sit upright, searching around for something to put on. The spring night air is cool against my naked body. I pull on a pair of sweatpants and a T-shirt, grab the Marlboros, and follow the two Dobermans to the elevator.

We go down to the ground floor and exit the security gate that leads to the lawn. I wait for the dogs to finish, but they keep sniffing around, and then bark like crazy at a hovering police helicopter.

I light a cigarette, my back against the brick wall of the apartment building, safely out of the sight of the searchlight sweeping up and down the street. They're probably tracking a bunch of carjackers.

I wish I'd put shoes on. It's not warm enough at night yet to be barefoot. I look over my shoulder toward the apartment block next to mine. Daniel's room is still dark. He and his mother get up early in the mornings to travel to school, but it's too early even for them. And no one wakes up from the sound of police helicopters anymore.

I walk back to the apartment, the dogs at my heels. They snuggle down and go straight back to sleep, but I fail to do the same. Stefan Jansen, Hendrik Kroon, Ranna, Alex—they all run through my brain in some sort of weird rinse-and-spin cycle.

I get up and make myself a cup of rooibos tea. Sit down on the kitchen floor to drink it slowly. The moon is almost full as it falls through the blinds, illuminating the sparsely furnished open-plan space I don't quite yet know what to do with, even though it's been two years since I bought the building.

Alex was here a few times. Megabyte was mad about him. Says a lot.

My eyes stop at the nearest, biggest sofa. That was where he slept four nights in a row, incensed at Ranna for disappearing. He insisted I tell him where she'd gone.

The fifth night he was drunk and in my bed, snoring like a trucker.

That's how you make mistakes: you can't have what you want, so you take whatever comes along instead. Like that boy on his Ducati I challenged to a race on the N3 freeway to Durban earlier this year.

Only afterward, I realized that it was because his strong, lean body and slightly askew smile reminded me of Alex.

Pathetic.

The last of the tea disappears down my throat. I get up and start fishing around in the bread bin for something to eat. Adriana is right. Let go. For heaven's sake, just fucking let go.

I slap some peanut butter on a slice of stale bread and open a Coke. Sit down at the computer to go over the information I sourced earlier. Still very little. All I managed to do was work out that there are a lot of stubborn questions that require answers.

I write them down and paste them up on the wall above the middle computer.

Number 1: Where did Stefan Jansen get his money?

Number 2: What was inside the metal lockbox Hendrik Kroon stole?

Number 3: What if Jansen has the box? What if he's already spent/used/sold whatever was inside the box?

I'd better start raking together any cash I can get my hands on. It's better than simply hoping we'll find the box. Maybe if I get enough together, I can entice Borsos to forget about the damn box.

I light another smoke. Kill it. Curse. There are only three questions, but they feel like an exam I'm about to fail, like I failed biology at school, and all those other subjects I had zero interest in. But this time it's not about a piece of paper, as the clock in the kitchen loudly reminds me. Someone's life is at stake.

It's three o'clock, Tuesday morning.

The Suzuki sings. First a bit of throat clearing as I drive slowly through the city center waiting for the synchronized traffic lights of Pretorius Street to turn green, then, as I open the throttle, the yellow bike breaks into song.

Faster and faster.

I know what Adriana has to say about Nina Simone and Maria Callas and Leonard Cohen, but this is music. This is what clears my head. What makes me feel alive. The pure exhilaration of going so fast you could die in an instant, the brightly lit shop windows streaking past like colorful, painted panels in a superhero comic. Pow. Pow. Pow.

One streetlight after the next.

One shopwindow full of cheap trinkets and on-sale furniture after the other.

One empty bar after another.

A solitary car full of drunk people on their way home after a late night out.

Put it all behind you. All of it. Everyone. Behind you.

Sing, sing, sing.

3

After another hour at the computer, the uncomfortable truth dawns on me. Someone will have to talk to Stefan Jansen, and that someone is probably going to have to be me. As a retired police colonel, he might recognize Ranna and have her locked up. And finding out what he knows can't wait until she gets back from Paternoster.

Adriana is probably having a busy week at the restaurant. I doubt she can afford to drop everything again and rush out here to help me. But I'll ask her anyway. She knows how to talk to people, to get what she wants out of them. I don't. I don't do people, and I definitely don't do cops.

It's half past seven when I call her. I went for a short run with the dogs until I knew Adriana wouldn't complain too much about being roused from bed.

"Sarah? What's wrong?"

She knows I'm seldom awake at this time of the day. I usually only go to bed around five, after a long night at the computer.

"I need your help." I wipe the sweat off my forehead and lean my hands on my knees to catch my breath. I left Megabyte downstairs to terrorize the neighbors.

There's a short silence and then I hear sheets rustling. "What? I can't hear you very well."

"I said . . ."

I realize too late that she's mocking me. I stand up and walk to the fridge. "*Ja.* Okay. Ha-ha."

She yawns. "What do you need me to do?"

"I must . . . You need to . . . go and talk to someone, please. I need information."

I sigh when it dawns on me that I'm lying. I can't imagine Jansen will want to talk to us. Not if he has something to hide. I'm going to have to make another plan, but I still need Adriana.

I start again. "We need to get into someone's house. A retired police colonel." I open the fridge and take out a water bottle, downing half of it before I can get the name out. "Stefan Jansen."

"Why? No luck on the net?"

"Too long ago. Before everything was online. There's just too little information."

"So what do you need me to do? And be specific."

"Not much. If you can get me into his front door, I can do the rest. I need to hear what he says, who he talks to. Please."

"What happened in Sasolburg for you to suddenly say please and thank you?"

"We haven't gotten to thank you yet."

"We could."

"I'll explain later," I offer.

"Now is good."

I tuck the phone between my cheek and shoulder while I refill the bottle at the sink. "Nothing went as planned. It's still . . . Alex is . . ." I sigh.

I didn't explain to her why Ranna needed another new identity. And I haven't yet told anyone about Alex or Borsos. Looking back, that might have been a mistake.

No. It *was* a mistake. Most definitely.

"Sarah, what is it with you and this man? Why can't you let go?"

I don't know what to say. She's seen the entire Alex Derksen episode unfold from the moment he started covering my court case. She warned me early on about getting hurt.

"The restaurant is going to be busy today. Fully booked for lunch," she says as the silence lingers.

I stubbornly remain quiet, about Alex and the restaurant. We both know it's just a front. Lots of other things go on at Crow's Feet that have nothing to do with food. Adriana can afford to take the morning off. She simply has to.

"I can't believe it," she says, swearing emphatically in a language I don't know. "What exactly do you want me to do?"

"I told you: go and talk to a policeman. Colonel Stefan Jansen. Just long enough to get me in the front door."

I hear her moving around in bed, then a deep voice near her. Someone groaning and sounding half asleep.

I don't acknowledge it. Take another sip from the water bottle. "It's the only way I can get Alex back."

"Perhaps it's time to accept that you can't get back something you never had in the first place. This obsession of yours—"

"Adriana, this really isn't the time for a lecture on morals. You sound like my mother."

There is no lower blow for Adriana than to be compared to her half sister.

"If I didn't have company, you and I would be having a nice long conversation right now," she says coldly.

I might have pushed it too far. "I'm sorry," I offer. "Are you going to help me or aren't you?"

"You know I will. That's why you called." I hear her getting out of bed, closing a door, and then the kettle being filled. "What's my cover story? Why would someone show up at a policeman's door out of the blue to speak to him?"

"Retired policeman. We're journalists. I'll be your photographer. We're doing a story about a cash heist that took place years ago. It's one in a series of articles about crimes from the past and the detectives who led the investigations."

"Who's going to call him to make the appointment?"

"No appointment. He won't agree to an interview. Especially not one at his house. So we're going to crash the party, because we're not going to get an invitation."

"Who do I write for?" She opens the fridge, glass bottles clinking in the door.

"The *Cape Argus*. That's far enough away."

"He's going to check that we're not lying."

Do I really have to think that far ahead? Then again, Adriana's been smart enough never to have seen the inside of a prison before. At least, not as far as I know.

"I'll write you a biography for the *Argus* and load it onto their website."

"What if they notice?"

"I'll take it down as soon as we're done."

She sighs. The sound is exaggerated and dramatic. "Fine, then. I hope you know what you're doing. Is that all you require of me this morning?"

"There's one other thing. You need to talk to Ranna about something in her past. I'll explain later."

Silence hums over the line. Then: "Why?"

"She has this brain that remembers stuff. Remembers everything. Pictures. Details. I need you to talk to her about the night she shot her father. Tug at the knots until one loosens. Let her relax and remember. We are looking for something her father received on the day he died. She might remember something that will help us find it. I think this is the one event in her life she may have done her best to forget, but we need her to remember now."

"So, you want her to recall the night she killed her father. In detail." Adriana's voice is flat and hard.

"You would have done the same if someone's life was at stake."

"Says who?"

"Can we play moral ping-pong some other day?"

"You keep going on about morals. What have you done, Sarah? Why are you going after a retired cop? And why must Ranna go digging around in her past?"

"Nothing, dammit." I bite back other, stronger words. Adriana hates it when I swear. "It's about Alex. Getting him back."

"What have you gotten yourself involved with? Can I help?"

"You are helping. By doing this."

"I can do more."

"Not at the moment, no, but maybe later. Just help me do this. Please. Help me with the cop. Help me with Ranna."

"Will you be safe?" Her voice softens. "You know I love you."

"I'll do my best."

"Promise?"

"Yes."

"Okay, then. I'll do as you ask," she says. "When do you want me to talk to Ranna?"

I can hear she's still angry and worried. I put the water bottle down and start stretching my calves. "As soon as she gets back. She went to Paternoster. I'll let you know. Is that okay?"

"Yes. When are we going to talk to your policeman?"

"As soon as possible."

"Okay. See you in a while."

I shower and then consider what to wear. I choose my newest jeans, with the least number of rips and tears, white Nikes I hardly ever wear, and a soft green blouse. I comb my hair into a semblance of neatness and take all the silver earrings out of my ear.

Look at myself in the mirror. Nah. Still somehow look like a vampire.

4

I toss the car keys to Adriana. On our way to Stefan Jansen's house, I'll have to explain to her in more detail what's going on. I'll probably be candid, except for the fact that Adorjan Borsos threatened to kill my family. No doubt Adriana will feel obliged to do something radical, and I don't have the energy to try and restrain her right now.

Adriana catches the keys smoothly in the dusk of the parking garage and throws them back. "What journalist drives an Audi?"

She's right. Now what? I look at the cars in the garage. The Mini Cooper is the only thing that sort of fits into our cover story.

I nod toward the car she arrived in.

She sighs. "All right. But it's going to attract attention. Reassure me, at least, that the license plates are false."

"I changed them the day before I left for Lagos."

"Good. Now if you could just get rid of that unearthly roaring and we can get going."

"Ha-ha." I slip into the passenger seat. Adriana slides in behind the wheel. The soft fabric of her black-and-white dress shifts up her thighs as she takes off her heels.

I put the camera bag down at my feet. "The car's going to draw attention, but that dress isn't?"

The faint lines around her eyes deepen as she laughs. "Men know the prices of cars, not of dresses." She pulls the dress down over her knees and shoots me a prim look. "And who knows, perhaps I can get this Jansen guy to actually talk to us."

It's slow going through the morning traffic while I explain to her about Alex, Adorjan Borsos, and her new identity as a journalist. She is livid that I didn't tell her what was going on earlier.

"I could have helped you. For heaven's sake, Sarah. Why is it so hard for you to ask for help?"

"How would you have helped? I didn't know where to find Borsos. What could you have done?" She sounds just like Ranna.

"I could have been there for you."

"And how would that have helped me?"

"Sometimes you have the emotional IQ of a donkey," she hisses. Wipes a pinkie at stray lipstick at the corner of her mouth. "I could have gone with you to Sasolburg."

"And if Borsos killed Alex when he saw you?"

"I wou–"

I stop her with a firm hand. "Just stop. Ifs and buts are of little use now. Really."

She peers at me through narrow eyes. Obliges even though I can see it's almost killing her.

The uncomfortable silence lasts until we reach Jansen's security estate. Just like last time I was here, gaining entry to the estate is pretty easy. We drive in, turn a corner, and another, until Adriana parks the Mini in front of Stefan Jansen's black gate. I checked his cell signal before we left Pretoria West, and it's here, so he should be home.

Adriana switches off the engine. She makes a show of checking her makeup in the rearview mirror while she squints toward the front door.

"We have company," she says. "Window next to the front door. Someone wondering what we're doing here." She wipes under her left eye. "Come on. Let's get this show on the road."

We get out, me with the laptop backpack in my hand, my SLR camera inside, and she with her black leather handbag over her shoulder.

We open the front gate, which is unlocked, and walk down the short garden path and up the stairs to the front porch. Adriana knocks on the door.

It opens immediately.

Stefan Jansen stands before us, one hand on the doorframe, the other resting on his walking stick.

"Who are you and how did you get in here?" he barks.

Adriana smiles and offers her hand. "My name is Jolene Pinto. I'm from the *Argus*," she says as though he should know who she is.

He ignores her hand, the frown on his forehead deepening. "The newspaper? What do you want?"

He pulls his shoulders back and tries to straighten his spine, but all it does is betray the pain it takes to do so. He's still a frail old man with a walking stick and brown slip-ons, because bending over and tying laces is too difficult.

I wonder why. He's just over sixty. That's like the new fifty. Maybe his genes have caught up with him. Or his life.

With all the money he has, I'm sure Jansen must be able to employ someone to help him. I try to look past him, to listen, but there's no sound coming from inside the house to indicate that anyone's there with him. No woman, no gardener, no cleaner.

"We'd like to do an interview with you, Colonel." Adriana opens her hands, palms up, as though she comes in peace.

Hearing his rank mentioned seems to ease his frown. Perhaps it recalls a different, happier time.

"What about?" He pauses. "And how did you find me?"

Adriana ignores his question again. She takes a step toward the front door, closing the distance between them. She touches her hair, a little coyly.

"My editor wants me to do a story about the biggest crimes of the last few decades," she explains, taking another step forward. "I'd like to talk to you about that 1993 Pelindaba robbery. The one where the two guards were shot just outside Pretoria? And the two robbers. One and a half million stolen and found again. Bloody shoot-out. The whole thing resolved in one day." She inches forward again while her hands show a big headline as she announces, "'What Today's Police Force Could Learn from the Old Brigade.'"

I watch her do her thing: the smile, the innocence and harmlessness. And just like that she's already inside Jansen's front hall.

My fingers clamp around the black GSM listening device—the size of a matchbox—in my hand. I need a place, any place, to stick it. Under a coffee table, a chair—anywhere. Preferably close to where Jansen does some of his work.

I should have given the device to Adriana. She's inside already, and I'm still standing here in the bright sunshine, sweating as though I'm about to be sentenced again.

Jansen's eyes, which first flamed up in recognition at the mention of the case, have become wary.

"There are much bigger cases you could be writing about. Certainly more exciting ones." He coughs, his hand too slow to stop the trail of spit. He wipes the side of his mouth. "Not interested."

"Colonel, please. It'll take five minutes." Adriana places her hand on his forearm. He retreats as though he's been touched by the devil.

Adriana advances two more steps, deeper into the house.

"I'm not interested!"

"Please. Younger detectives could learn so much from you."

I slip past the dancing duo, and I'm inside too. There's a narrow ornate table with ivory inlay just inside the door. Opposite that, roughly ten feet into the light, airy space, are two—no, three—sofas. A coffee table with a cell phone on it. An empty plate with crumbs. A flat-screen TV.

Bingo. The sitting room appears to be one of Stefan Jansen's regular hangouts.

I lean against the side table and try to look bored with the cat-and-mouse game Adriana and Jansen are playing.

The listening device is still in my hand. I feel around under the table. Sometimes, being short is useful. I suspect I look like a bored teenager leaning against the nearest piece of furniture.

Jansen regains his composure, and his voice. “Get out or I'll call security.”

Why is this damn thing not sticking? I press harder, hoping the double-sided tape will grip the wooden surface.

Jansen's eyes shoot my way. I'm sure he can see me sweating bullets here.

“And who the hell are you?”

I swallow. “Photographer. First day.”

There you go. Stuck. I hope.

I stand up straight, look at Adriana, and nod swiftly, indicating my success, then shrug as though to say we've done what we could.

“Let's try someone else. Maybe that girl who stole all the money? That hacker?” I ask.

Her eyes register surprise, and she lifts an amused eyebrow.

I suppress a curse. I'm not great at thinking on my feet. The only option that popped into my head was my own case.

“Okay,” Adriana concedes. “I suppose we can.”

She puts her hand out to shake Jansen's, but he ignores it again. He lifts his walking stick and points it at the door. “Out. And never come back. Next time I won't be so polite.”

We walk to the Mini. Just before we get in, Jansen points a knobbly finger at Adriana. “I'm going to call your editor. Which paper did you say you're from?”

She smiles sweetly and gets into the car without answering. We drive through the main gate just as a security guard, wearing purple paramilitary togs, storms out of the control room, holding a radio to his ear, surprise and worry on his face.

Adriana drives as though we're in a getaway car. Three blocks from Jansen's estate, she releases her breath slowly.

I watch the speedometer's red needle dropping gradually: 70, 50, 40.

"That was fun," she says, turning her head to laugh in my direction. "I think I was a pretty convincing journalist, don't you?"

"I'm not sure Alex would agree. But thank you."

"Where to next?"

"Home."

She turns the Mini's nose west and switches on the radio. BB King. Dark, heavy bass rhythms fill the car.

I activate the GSM apparatus with a text message from my phone. Now the little black box under Stefan Jansen's table will alert me to listen in as soon as there are voices in his living room.

I don't have to wait long. Three more traffic lights, and the screen flashes. I press the answer button and turn the radio down, gesturing to Adriana to slow down.

The conversation is not at all what I expected. I can only just hear Jansen's voice. I'll trace the number he called as soon as I get home, but for now I'm more interested in what he has to say.

His voice is clipped, measured, angry. He sounds out of breath, either from whatever is running him down physically, or from stress. "Someone from the press was here. They wanted to know about the 1993 robbery. Hendrik's robbery."

Short silence, then: "No, of course I didn't talk to them."

He listens, then answers: "A woman in her forties. And a young woman. They both had trouble written all over them."

Silence. "I have no idea why someone would suddenly be interested in the robbery. It's over. Dead and buried."

The other person says something.

Jansen sighs heavily. "After all these years? No. I can't think of anyone who might suddenly have found out what happened. Impossible."

Adriana drops me at home. She's hurrying back to Crow's Feet to prepare for the lunch rush.

I dash through the garage and into the elevator that spits me out into the living room. The dogs are all around my heels.

I open a Coke and light a cigarette. Pringles. I want Pringles. With so much salt and vinegar flavor that it knocks the breath out of me. That'll help me think. I open a can from the cupboard and sit down at the computer to start the trace of Jansen's phone. The dogs keep milling around me, but I don't have time for them right now.

"Wait, no, Byte," I say, as he nudges his nose in under my arm. I push him away.

I read through the list of recent calls. Who did Jansen call?

There it is: 10:57 on Tuesday morning. And there's the number. He calls it often. At least two or three times a month.

I start a new search for the number Jansen calls. After a while, a name flashes up on the screen. Jaap Reyneke. The detective who investigated Hendrik Kroon's so-called suicide.

Ranna

1

I drop the binoculars into my lap and yawn long and loudly. I've been fighting it, but I'm going to have to sleep for an hour or two. It's been an exhausting sixteen-hour drive here, and I can't keep my eyes open any longer.

Thinus and Lena Prinsloo's house is about fifty yards in front of me, on the quiet bay of Paternoster. The West Coast village with its white-and-blue cottages is quiet at this time of year, with only the occasional up-country car turning off the regional road to drive down to the coast. The still, deep blue of the Atlantic is embraced by pure white sands, interspersed with the odd smooth boulder.

Paternoster started off as a fishermen's village, but I can see it's become an escape for the newly rich, who build houses that imitate the architectural vernacular but are much bigger and have air-conditioning, landscaping, splash pools, and double garages for Porsches and BMWs.

In about two weeks there will be a short school vacation, and then the place will be overrun by families, dogs, and tourists. I'm lucky the wildflower season has only begun. The rains are late this year in this part of the world, I believe.

I don't remember much about my mother's sister and her husband. They used to visit us often, but I was always ordered to bed shortly after supper. The vacations they all went on together, I spent with friends.

I pick up the binoculars to bring the house into focus again. It's Tuesday morning. The light of the new day is only just starting to slant over the horizon. My aunt and uncle's house seems unoccupied. It is surrounded by guesthouses and is almost at the most northerly tip of the bay, not far from the waves gently breaking on the sand.

I search the area surrounding the house. Most of the curtains are still drawn. Either the people of Paternoster are not early risers, or most of the houses here belong to people from Gauteng and Cape Town who only come here for holidays or long weekends.

Even better for me, the house closest to Thinus and Lena's looks empty, as though it's waiting for new occupants, just as my mother said.

Back to the Prinsloo house. It's a square two-story structure with a detached double garage, blue doors, and a blue roof. The postage stamp of a garden needs some love, as do the window frames, but otherwise it has "money" written all over it. A red-and-white sign on one wall confirms that the house has an alarm, connected to a security company.

There are no burglar bars on the windows, and a low, knee-high wall is all that separates the house from its neighbors.

I focus on the garage, somewhat hidden behind the house. That's all I'm really interested in. If my mother's information is correct, that is where my father's last earthly belongings are stored.

I have no idea why Lena didn't get rid of the stuff ages ago. I would have sold it off a long time back.

She told my mother she didn't know about my father's abuse, but I don't know about that. How could you not see? How could anyone not see? Unless they didn't want to know.

Perhaps I was equally complicit. I never mentioned my home life to anyone at school. It's as if we all bought into an intricate conspiracy of silence and pretense.

I run the binoculars over the garage slowly and carefully. It's right next to the house. The wooden entrance door is unprotected by a security gate. I could probably get in that way, but I'd have to damage the door, which would be a noisy exercise.

The garage window seems a better choice. I can't see it, but I'm assuming there's one on the other side of the building.

I run an eye over the structure again. Let's hope the garage is not connected to the house alarm. Chances are good that it isn't. The car would only be here when Lena and Thinus are here, and they're still in Cape Town.

I trace the path from the house to the beach with the binoculars. Back to the other houses.

Two fresh sets of footprints in the sand. Someone went for a walk early, and they haven't returned this way yet. Perhaps I should wait. They might return any minute. In any case, it's seven thirty, and the people who live around here are likely waking up.

I need to park the pickup somewhere and sleep. Later, when it's quieter, I'll see if there's a window that will allow me access into the garage. If not, I'll have to break open the lock on the door. If I'm quick, perhaps no one will see or hear me.

I run my hands through my hair. Wish I had somewhere to brush my teeth and wash my face. I turn the key and pull away, eager to get to the gas station I saw on the way here, in the nearby, bigger town of Vredenburg. I'll use the bathroom there, and then sleep in the car.

2

"Hello! Hey! You're not allowed to sleep here."

I'm woken by the voice and the single, sharp blow of a flat hand on the windshield.

I jump upright in the Hilux, its windows lightly tinted, and bump my head. "Ouch. Dammit."

I rub my head and check my watch. It's just past ten. I've had about two hours' sleep. I wish I could have some more. And more like this: deep and peaceful.

The bottle of Temazepam is at my feet, still unopened. I drop it back into my backpack. One day I might be able to dump it altogether.

The man hammers on the window again, his open hand leaving prints on the glass. He looks managerial in his white shirt and black trousers.

"You can't park here and sleep," he says, his voice going up an octave as a pink blush rises from his neck to his round baby face. He's hardly tall enough to reach the pickup's driver window. How old is he? Seventeen? And who is he?

I put on a cap, open the door, and get out. The air is cool. I shiver involuntarily and hug my arms. The sudden movement has stirred a headache behind my eyes. Probably dehydration. I must look irritable, because the man—boy—takes a step back. Behind him, a gas pump attendant smiles widely to reveal a gap between his two front teeth.

I don't want to be remembered for any drama, so I smile broadly. I drop my shoulders to make myself look shorter, push one hip forward, and soften my stance.

"I'm sorry. I'll go now. It's been a long drive." I point at the Gauteng province license plate. "Did the whole thing in one stretch. Family emergency." The kid's eyes are stuck on my white T-shirt.

I glance down. Ah. I took my bra off before I fell asleep.

"I'm leaving now," I reassure him.

"Fine." He turns around to the attendant and says, "Stop laughing and go and fetch her a coffee. On the house."

I park the pickup in front of a guesthouse a few hundred yards away from the Paternoster beach. I knot a light jacket around my hips, put on sunglasses and a cap, and hook the backpack over my shoulders. I hope I look sufficiently like a tourist.

The backpack holds a Leatherman, a flashlight, gloves, and the Glock. I bought the flashlight and gloves at a Pick n Pay supermarket on the way here. The Leatherman was a gift from Alex, back when we lived in Tanzania.

I take the long way around to Thinus and Lena's house, forcing myself to keep a steady, calm pace, even though what I want to do is jog. I turn right at a beach restaurant where you can sit and eat with your feet in the sand. The smell of grilled fish makes my stomach do an eager somersault. I ate a chicken pie from the convenience store at the Vredenburg gas station, but that feels like a lifetime ago.

A minute later I hit the firm sand of the beach.

"Morning," a sweaty-faced, athletic middle-aged woman in running shoes puffs as she walks by. Her Labrador stops to sniff my boots.

"Morning," I answer, stepping aside, but the dog turns to follow me.

"Come on, Rufus," she calls, plowing ahead as if she's vying for an Olympic gold medal in speed walking.

I stop. The dog doesn't budge, just pushes his nose farther into the hem of my jeans. He's probably picked up on Megabyte's scent. I clumsily rub his head. My father hated dogs, so I never got used to them.

The woman stops and turns around. "Rufus! What are you doing?"

The dog with the golden coat sniffs one more time, frowns at me, and then trots off.

I walk on, faster now. It may not be spring break or flower-viewing season yet, but there are enough people here who might remember a tall woman with long black hair.

I look back to make sure Rufus and his owner are gone. My hope was that the warm midday sun would have chased most people back inside, but it doesn't look that way. It would probably have been best if I'd arrived here at night, but I don't have much choice. Time is ticking on relentlessly. It's 11:23, Tuesday morning.

My pace slows as I approach the Prinsloo house. I look around, spotting no one as I leave the beach and turn onto the narrow tar road threading through the houses. I walk around the white-and-blue building as though I'm on my way home from a stroll.

I have to be quick. Loitering around here is looking for trouble.

On the road past the back of the house, I spot a potential problem. There is indeed a garage window, and it's open, but it's a little higher and smaller than I'd hoped it would be. What now?

I walk on, and then make a U-turn and hop over the low white wall, crouching behind it.

How small is that window? I measure it with my eyes and decide I may be able to fit. I put on the black work gloves I bought at Pick n Pay. I don't want the police discovering my fingerprints here.

My ears are attuned to the surroundings: no one's shouting or calling, no dogs barking. All safe for my next step.

I look around for something to stand on to reach the window. The garden has one or two small shrubs that provide some privacy from the houses next door; otherwise it's full of indigenous plants and succulents, spread evenly around a few biggish rocks.

The rocks.

If I stood on one, I'd be able to reach the window. There's one on my left, probably about six bricks high.

I try to roll it to the garage. It's heavier than I thought it would be, but not impossible to move. It takes a good ten minutes of keeping low and pushing to get the rock to the wall.

I pause to check for life in the white houses nearby. All quiet. Once I'm inside the garage, escaping will be difficult, so it's best to know now whether I can expect trouble. The street in front of the house remains quiet. So does the beach behind me.

I get up onto the rock, open the wood-framed window wide, and throw my backpack through. Listen. No alarm. I start worming my body in. I only just fit.

Bit by bit, I inch through the window. The garage is dark inside, but I can tell why the window was left open as the distinct smell of fresh paint greets me.

By the time my hips are through and my eyes are accustomed to the dark, I realize there's no soft place to land. Too late to do anything about that now.

The window frame cuts painfully into my legs as I bend forward, holding out my hands and then falling clumsily onto the concrete floor in an attempted tuck and roll. I groan as quietly as I can. I'm going to have crazy bruises all over my legs and hips. Not that anyone's going to see. Alex was the last person who . . .

I drop that thought and reach for the flashlight. The wall across from me has boxes stacked against it, and four or five dusty pieces of furniture, exactly as my mother anticipated. I'm so relieved she and Lena didn't listen to the eleven-year-old know-it-all telling them to sell everything.

I walk over to the boxes. Some have their contents listed on them in black permanent felt-tip marker. Probably easiest to start with those. How difficult can it be to hide a metal box?

The first box I open is full of books. My mother's books. Cookbooks and all the classics she loved. Still loves. Tolstoy. Dickens. Pasternak. Shakespeare.

The second and third boxes contain moth-eaten clothes, and the fourth has kitchen things in it. A cast-iron pot, silver salad spoons, teaspoons. Kitsch salt and pepper shakers from London in the shape of palace guards wearing tall black busbies. They were a gift my father brought back for my mother from one of his overseas trips. He often took the salt shaker with him on vacations, and even on some business trips, I remember. He always loved a midnight snack, especially heavily salted tomatoes.

I pack everything back carefully and close the boxes before moving on to others. Luckily, the tape is so ancient it no longer sticks, so it's not necessary to rip anything open.

The fifth box knocks me sideways. The yellow baby clothes in my hands are soft, and there's a blue baby jumpsuit, still packaged in the shop's plastic, with a ribbon tied around it, as though it was a gift. These must have been meant for my unborn brother.

Why are they here? Why didn't my mother take them with her? Perhaps it would have hurt too much. I put the clothes gently back into their box.

That lie I told my mother, that I want to look through my dad's things so that I can finally make peace with everything that happened? Damn impossible. Especially not now, after what Borsos told me. Hendrik Kroon's violence extended well beyond our family. His tentacles reached so much further than these pastel-colored baby clothes and a family's life packed up in boxes. He was the leader of a violent criminal gang, and he didn't hesitate to shoot people in cold blood. People who probably had wives, parents, or children.

I want to close the box and carry on with my search, but I can't. I dig around, pulling out clothes I wore as a girl. Then I find what was once my biggest treasure: a little jewelry box made of teak.

The wood feels warm, just as it did in the shop all those years ago—as though the tree it was made from were still alive. It's not especially beautiful, nor was it expensive. My father was surprised that I didn't choose something fancier and pricier for my birthday. But it was the wood, the lock, and the secret compartment at the bottom that made it so appealing to me. I could stow my treasures, hide them from him. From my mother. It was a place no one knew about. A safe place.

I take a deep breath and open it. Everything's still there. The birthday card my mother gave me on my seventh birthday. A postcard Lena sent from Paris. She was always so sophisticated. She and Thinus went to France when I was eight. I so badly wanted to see the bright lights of the Eiffel Tower and the Champs-Élysées for myself. I did, eventually, years later, when I covered a few assignments in France.

The false bottom, covered with green felt, still slides out easily. And there they are: the flat red box my father gave me that night and the handkerchief I used to wipe the blood off my face after I shot him. I'd never looked at them again.

My father's blood. Why did I keep this thing?

For a few moments I feel as if the salty sea air congeals into a heavy mass I cannot inhale. I sink to my knees. What would my life have been like if I hadn't shot Hendrik Kroon? Would I be standing here, in this garage, with no home or family, looking for something that could save the life of someone I love?

But another voice—a familiar one—reminds me of what could have happened. If I hadn't killed him, would I still be alive?

3

Nothing. Zero. No metal lockbox. No secret stashes of money. No keys. No suspicious documents.

With my back against the cool white wall of the garage, I survey the remnants of Hendrik Kroon's life with despair. I even went through all of the furniture. My father's stinkwood desk has nothing of value in it. There's also nothing hidden inside the leather chair. I cut a discreet hole in the upholstery and poked around inside.

My legs protest as I push myself up on the wall. I open the bottom left drawer of the desk again. My mother might want the photographs I found there. Thinus and Lena won't miss them.

The brittle rubber band that holds the pack together breaks into a sticky mess under my fingers. I look through the first few pictures. Family photos. The one on top is the most surprising of them all. My mother and father, sitting on the beach somewhere, young and glowing with happiness, she between his legs, back to his chest, his arms tucked around her body. Then one of my father. One of Thinus. My mother, Lena, and Thinus sitting around a barbeque pit somewhere on the coast.

The colors have long faded from these Kodak moments, but everyone looks carefree. The photos look as though they were taken in the seventies.

The next pack of photos is at a theater production of sorts. Everyone's crowded around Jana Cilliers, possibly the most famous

South African actor at the time, looking awestruck. She appears to be bearing the attention graciously. Then there's one of Thinus, fishing with my father. Hunting. He and my father in what looks like a London pub, pints in hand. My father and the man with the beard and the gold front tooth—best friends by the looks of it.

Hidden in the middle of this bundle is a smaller, square picture, which looks like it was taken in a studio by a professional photographer. It's Lena, in a swimsuit, her long blonde hair piled on top of her head, with the famous dimple in her left cheek. My mother also has one.

Lena is tall, like all of the women in our family, and she was a stunner. Probably still is. If I remember correctly, she was a finalist in the Miss South Africa competition. Lena and my mother looked the same for many years, before life took its toll and molded them into different creatures. Before my mother's life became evident on her face. The exhaustion, the wariness, eventually settled bone-deep, her self-confidence completely bled out.

The next photo is a surprise, although it shouldn't be. My father and a younger version of Adorjan Borsos, arms slung across each other's shoulders and grinning, with fat cigars plugged into their mouths. Next to them is a young man I don't know.

Adorjan wasn't lying. He'd been to our house. The photograph was taken in our old sitting room. I remember the ugly brown carpet and the beige curtains.

I shuffle the pictures into a neat pile again, wondering whether my mother will be happy to have them. Probably not. But then again, do you throw away your entire past if one person poisoned it?

I almost laugh at the irony of the question.

I put the photos in my backpack. Outside the garage window, the day has faded to inky blackness. I've been here for hours, and I'm none the wiser. Time to call Sarah and give her the bad news. Maybe she has, in the meantime, found something that could help us.

I pull the desk chair to the window. It might reveal that someone's been here, but I can't think how else to get through the window.

My backpack plops into the sand outside. I hoist myself into the opening and check around for movement and sound in the cool evening air. Nothing. I start to wiggle my body through the tight, rectangular space.

Shit. Problem. How do I get out of here and not hit the rock I used to climb in here?

I hold my breath, inch forward until physics fails to hold me any longer. I extend my hands in front of me, push away from the rock, to the side, and land with a thud on the hard ground next to it.

Thank heavens for long arms.

I lie on the sandy soil, waiting to make sure no one's seen or heard me. Two or three houses down the road, I hear people laughing. The smell of meat on a fire must be coming from the same direction. I look up at the sky. The first stars are out. The sky is that dark pewter it always is just before the night turns black. My eyes close. Sleep is so tempting . . .

No. Closing my eyes is a luxury I can't afford right now.

I get up, jump back over the wall, and jog past the houses toward where the pickup is parked. As I run past a house where loud voices spill out of the open front door, the smell of barbeque makes my mouth water. I look at my watch. Tuesday evening, just before seven. Time is running out, but I am desperately hungry and tired. Perhaps I should just stop and eat something. There are lots of lovely restaurants in Paternoster.

A low-throated growl close by stops me dead in my tracks. In the front garden of the party house, yellow eyes sparkle in the moonlight.

The yellow eyes approach me. The growl turns into a bark.

Shit. The wall between us is as useless and ornamental as the one at Lena's house. Easy for a big dog to clear.

The barking intensifies as the dog bounds over the wall. Stands in front of me.

I can't remember what you're supposed to do when a dog threatens to attack. Run or stay put?

"Rufus," someone shouts from the house. "What are you barking at?"

Rufus? It's the woman from the beach, and the Labrador. Aren't Labradors supposed to be friendly dogs? All those toilet paper ads make them out to be floppy lugs of happiness.

"There now, Rufus," I whisper. "Shh. You remember me, don't you?"

I don't want the woman to spot me and point me out in a police lineup later.

Run or stay?

Rufus barks, happier now, as though he's recognized me.

"Rufus!" the woman shouts.

A door opens and hasty footsteps sound across concrete.

I turn around and run, Rufus in jubilant pursuit. Isn't he exhausted from his walk this morning?

I increase my stride, my soles slapping the tar loudly. Where's the car? There, parked under a streetlight between two German sedans. I unlock it as I approach and jump in.

Rufus stops next to the Hilux and gives me a disappointed look.

"Sorry, boy," I say. "Go home. Home!"

He stays put, giving a single, sharp bark. In the bright moonlight, I can see he is panting. His mouth is open. It almost looks like he's laughing at me.

4

I drive to the Vredenburg gas station again. The same attendant from this morning recognizes the pickup. He waves a greeting and points to an open parking spot under a long carport. I roll down my window to acknowledge him.

"He won't be in again until around eight tomorrow morning," he says, anticipating my concern about the crotchety manager. "That's if we're really unlucky. Boss's son."

I nod my thanks and get out. I withdraw money from the ATM using the bank card Sarah gave me and buy two sandwiches and two cups of coffee, one each for me and the attendant. Tip him handsomely for cleaning the windshield.

The sandwich is fresh, but what I really want is a hot meal and a shower. Something like the barbeque I smelled earlier, or the home-cooked lunch Sarah's mother served on Sunday.

I hope they're safe. Not Sarah. Her family.

I try my best not to think about Alex. That just won't do right now.

When I'm done eating, I wash as best I can in the sink in the ladies' restroom. The brightly lit space is spotless, and I have it all to myself. Not a lot of women on the road at this time of night.

I put on the clean clothes I brought along. As I brush my wet hair back, I spot three gray wires by my temple. I lean toward the mirror and look at the woman staring back at me. Exhausted, worried eyes. Deep lines around the mouth.

Bitter lines?

I gather my things and walk back to the car, weighing my options for the night. I could book a room at a guesthouse, but that would waste time. I only want a few hours' rest, and then I need to hit the road again. Besides, I might just draw attention at a bed-and-breakfast, especially showing up at this hour without a reservation.

I'd prefer to limit the risks and accept the attendant's friendly invitation to sleep here.

Back in the pickup, I call the number Sarah texted me earlier. She answers immediately.

"Did you find the box?" she asks.

"No. I found my dad's stuff, right where my mom said it would be, but there was nothing."

"Fuck. Where's the fucking thing?"

"No idea."

"What are we going to do now?"

"Have you found anything interesting?" I ask, squinting at the lights of a Ford Fiesta as it pulls in to fill up.

"Not much. The robbery happened before everything went digital. I did find out, though, that Stefan Jansen, the policeman who investigated the robbery at the time, knows Jaap Reyneke, the detective who investigated your father's death. By the sounds of it, they're old mates."

Reyneke. I vaguely remember the name. He had a gentle smile, if I recall. "Which means . . . ?"

"I don't know. Not yet. But I'll find out."

"We might not have time to find out." A young man gets out of the Fiesta. He looks slightly inebriated.

"Maybe. Maybe not."

"Maybe it's best to focus on establishing what was inside the box, and to then offer something similar to Borsos," I suggest.

"But Borsos said he knows exactly what the box looked like. That he wanted that specific lockbox and what was inside it."

I hear Sarah lighting a cigarette.

"The box might have been lost," I offer. "Damaged. We can make something up. It's better than nothing. Or we can lie. Say we found it. Maybe have the cavalry there when we do the exchange." I rub my tired eyes, look on as a young woman gets out of the Fiesta and heads for the bright lights of the KFC across the road.

"That's our last option," Sarah concedes. "And I can offer Borsos whatever money I can lay my hands on." She blows the smoke out loudly enough for me to hear the slow hiss of air.

"There's something else that may be worth chasing," she says gingerly, the raspy bravado from before replaced by a hesitant question mark.

Sarah never uptalks. I sit up straight. "What?"

"I think we might need to dig around inside your head." A moment's silence. "I asked Adriana to talk to you. About that night, about what happened. You might know something you didn't realize you knew that could help us. You might have seen the box, but you just don't remember it."

Protestations rush up my throat and jam in my mouth. "I don't want . . . I don't have to . . ."

"You have to do this. It's important. We have to get Alex back."

The young man from the Fiesta returns to his car. I manage to lip-read the string of curses he lets loose when he sees the woman has disappeared.

"Would you want to remember every detail from prison?" I ask.

"If it would help my family, then yes, I would."

"There's nothing to remember. I know what happened."

"Can you swear to that? I mean, one hundred percent swear that you remember every detail?"

I close my eyes. "Why Adriana?"

"I trust her, and I don't trust a lot of people." She takes another drag on the cigarette. "Besides, Adriana knows how to get information out of people."

"Sounds painful."

"Could be," she says dryly.

"Okay," I say. What else can I do? It's not as though I have a better plan. If the box isn't in Paternoster, I don't know where else to look.

"I'll arrange it," Sarah says.

I'm not about to say thank you. "I'm going to try and catch up on some sleep before I drive back. What are you going to do?"

"Keep digging around. See if somethings pops. Damn well hope so."

"And if you find nothing? And I remember nothing?"

The young woman from the Fiesta darts across the road to the gas station, fast-food bags in hand. I feel kind of sad when she gets in the car again, apologizing to the driver.

"Then we'll do what you suggested and think up a story about the box's contents," says Sarah. "Maybe we could even have one made. Borsos might be lying about his excellent memory."

When she speaks again, she sounds dead tired, as though she hasn't slept for weeks. "We might have to use those weapons of yours after all."

I remember Sarah with the revolver in her hands. She's likely to accidentally shoot me or Alex.

"Let's try and avoid that."

Exhaustion washes over me. I put the front seat back and stretch my legs. "Cheers. See you tomorrow," I say, but the connection is already broken.

I throw the phone on the passenger seat, miffed at her and about this day that delivered nothing useful. "Someone should teach you manners," I tell the phone before I shrug into a jacket and close my eyes.

Alex

1

Why.

And yes, where, who, when, and how are all important when you write a news story, but the "why" is often the most important question. And the most interesting one. Nothing fascinates people as much as human nature, after all.

When you're little, your parents first ask you what you did, so that they can try and limit the damage, but the second question is almost always why, to establish what could possibly have motivated you. As if they need to know that it wasn't their fault—no failure on their part to try and raise a decent member of society.

We want to know the "why" of news stories because we need to confirm that whatever happened wasn't something we would have done. That we're not like that. Oh no, not us.

I can understand why Ranna shot her dad. I've been tempted to do the same many times to my own bastard of a father. Itching to just pull that trigger . . . but I never did. I've taken my revenge in other ways. I've always wanted to show my father what I could become in spite of him, knowing that the satisfaction of that would last so much longer than the fiery one-second revenge a bullet could offer.

Doing something like that must seriously mess you up. Destroy some part of you. That bullet hits you too, and sits there, like shrapnel, festering for the rest of your life.

I suspect I've always known what Ranna did. It was impossible not to, not after all the newspaper articles, after what Sarah had told me. But I didn't want to believe it until I heard it from her own mouth.

Does it change how I feel about her, knowing that she killed Hendrik Kroon?

Don't think so. I've seen the hospital reports on Ranna's mom the newspapers dug up last year. Her long-running list of injuries was horrendous. She would have died in that house. Ranna too, quite likely.

I am still mad at her, though, for running away last year after Tom Masterson died.

I think.

Somehow I've lost some of the clarity I had on that one. Maybe that's what happens if you're locked up with your own thoughts for eight weeks, constantly reliving the events that ended with you being chained to a rusty hospital bed.

Next why: Why didn't Sarah trust Ranna and ask for her help? Why did she sell her out, just to have it backfire spectacularly? I know Sarah doesn't like Ranna, but what she did is unlike her. It seems stupid and shortsighted.

Was she jealous?

I suppose I must admit what I've suspected all along, that I know exactly how Sarah feels about me. Should I have been firmer with her? Stated my lack of interest in her more loudly and more clearly than I've done in the past?

Well, maybe I've done that now, when we were all at the factory.

Third why: Why does Adorjan want that box containing who-knows-what?

That one's easy. I grin, pleased with my own little game of twenty questions. Greed.

And number four: Why did Ranna come back to South Africa?

Because Sarah misled her.

Because she wanted to help me.

It was a pretty stupid move, though. She could so easily be spotted and turned over to the police. She'd be thrown in jail for a very long time. And if she ends up in prison, what would the point have been of running away last year? Then we've both just wasted our time. And a lot of drinking money.

I swing my feet over the edge of my new bed. Another steel hospital bed, just like the one in Sasolburg. Adorjan is a planner. He had more than one hiding place picked out.

I hold my bruised left side with my right hand and look around my newest prison cell. It's an eight-by-eight zinc shack with one tiny, high window, through which I can see that it's dark outside.

How did I get here? How did I get to Sasolburg? How did an old man manage to keep me locked up in one cage after another?

That first blow in Welkom, the one he delivered to the same place the bullet hit, gave him a head start, that's for sure. My ribs are broken. Or at least cracked. I'm also increasingly struggling to breathe. My chest feels as though someone with enormous hands is squeezing it. It hurts whether I sit or lie or stand. And my lungs itch.

It's hard to imagine running in this state. If I'm lucky, I might get one more opportunity to escape. Just one.

If I mess it up, though, Adorjan will probably sink my feet in concrete and leave me to starve to death.

He unlocks the cuffs every evening for ten minutes so I can walk around. We're no longer in Sasolburg, but the routine's the same. He always takes me outside just after we've played chess.

How far I'd be able to run is a different question altogether. The diet he's put me on isn't doing my body any favors: bread, rusks, and sweet tea. I long for a piece of red meat. My mother's baked potatoes. Ranna's coffee. And water. Lots and lots of sweet, cool water.

Five days left. No. I look at my watch. It's Tuesday evening. Four days.

What happens if Ranna and Sarah fail to find that lockbox? Will he shoot me? Feed us all to the sharks?

I keep imagining that the far-off droning I hear is the sound of the ocean.

Adorjan gave me a bottle of Coke in the Sani, and I fell asleep immediately. I know I shouldn't have drunk it, but I couldn't help myself. He keeps me dehydrated. Weak. I only woke up again this morning, here—wherever here is—with a lazy tongue and a thick head.

I don't feel much better yet. I can't shake the cobwebs in my mind, the persistent headache that slows my thinking to a ridiculous pedestrian pace. I've stopped trying. All I know is I need to get out of here. Before Ranna and Sarah get here and do something stupid.

Ranna's arrival solved at least one very important why—finally, after two months. It was never me Adorjan wanted, after all. I'm just leverage to force Ranna to do something for him. A dancing monkey in a cage. That's me. Nothing more. Nothing less.

2

"You're quiet this evening." Adorjan takes a sip of tea, assessing me over the rim of his cup. His slurping drives me insane. It's not that hard to drink properly. Open your mouth. Close it. Swallow.

We're sitting in a second zinc construction, much larger than mine, where Adorjan seems to stay. His shack has power—no idea where he's getting it from—so there's a bright overheard light, a small fridge and microwave in the one corner, and a bed with a small TV in the other.

"My chest hurts." I shift to try and get more comfortable on the green camping chair he's chained me to, my handcuffs clanking against the aluminum of the frame.

He says nothing as he moves a pawn into a defensive position.

"I want a painkiller," I say.

He rubs his cheek. He's shaved since Ranna and Sarah showed up. And he's bathed. I wish I knew why. It's like he's waiting for something or someone. Something other than money.

He moves his queen closer to my king. "The pain will remind you to behave. Pain is good. It keeps the memory sharp."

I move a pawn right up to his knight, ready to pounce. Usually I hold back to let him win, but I'm not feeling charitable tonight. The sooner I kick his ass, the sooner we'll go outside for that walk.

I got up onto my bed earlier to try and look out the window. I couldn't see much. Just miles of white sand in two directions. The sea is close, I have no doubt now. There's a saltiness to the air, a trace of it on my dry lips. And if the ocean is close by, there might be a road. And a road means cars. Cars mean people.

Well, I suspect it's the sea. It could also be tinnitus. Or dehydration catching up with me. The pills Adorjan gave me are strong. For all I know, we could be on another planet in a different galaxy.

I turn my head. Drop it into my hand when a sudden spell of dizziness descends. I'm struggling to focus properly. The chessboard is swimming a little before my eyes. What the hell was in that Coke?

"Ha!" Adorjan moves his queen forward with a flourish, as though he realizes I'm playing a different, more aggressive game this evening.

He smiles. Slurps more tea. Caresses the Beretta in his lap.

"Why?" I blurt out, the drugs apparently muting all my efforts at diplomacy.

This time I don't want to know why he's holding me hostage. I want to know about Ranna. About her father.

He doesn't answer, just sits there as though I didn't even speak, his eyes nailed to the chessboard.

I refuse to give up. "Why are you going after Ranna? She's not the one who shot you."

He looks up, straightens his legs. "Well, you know what it says in the Bible: you will pay for the sins of your father. Ranna is the only one left who can make this particular payment. Not my fault her mother is on the other side of the deep blue ocean."

"You can't punish Ranna for something her father did."

"Of course I can. My father made me pay. All the time. He was always pissed about something. This bill. That bill. My mother who left us. The buses that were late, all the cars on the road, the radio that didn't work, the news. How much a pack of cigarettes cost. The price of beer."

"Ranna is not your father."

"But Ranna killed that guy . . . What's his name again? Tom Masterson. She also has sins to atone for. Many of them, by the sounds of it."

"Nobody's perfect." I brush my hand through my dirty hair and gnash my teeth when the movement sends a shock of pain through my chest. "And most of us never have to pay for our sins."

"What are you, His Royal Highness, the King of Karma? How sweet. Punish where you see fit, and sweep everything away where you think it doesn't belong?"

"I'm not the one playing God here. You are. Why Ranna? It's been decades since Hendrik Kroon died."

He finishes his tea and puts the enamel cup down on the ground next to him. "Money," he says curtly. "Family. People I love. Sanity."

He pushes the pistol into the back of his faded black jeans. I can see the buckle on his belt has moved along to a new hole. Probably all those Aeros he's been eating. Man loves his sugar.

"Family?" I ask, hoping this pushes his most sensitive button.

"Yes, Alex, I also had one of those. My daughter must be close to fifty now. That's old. A long time to be without a dad. A long time for me to have been locked away with nothing more to my name than an orange jumpsuit and a toothbrush. I can't even remember the last time I had enough money to buy her a birthday gift."

"You have no guarantee that there's going to be money in that box you're after. You're wagering everything on something that was locked away in a metal box twenty-five years ago. It's gone by now. Surely you know that."

"Does it seem to you like I have anything to lose?"

"You haven't done your math properly. You're still breathing. Eating. Walking around freely."

He laughs. "I've done my math very well, thank you. I want what's inside that box. I want to know why it was worth my life. And Johannes's life. I want to know why someone I thought was my best friend betrayed me like that. And since I can't screw him, I'll screw his family."

Anger flashes across his face.

"Get up," he says, gesturing to the door. "This is a pointless conversation. You were probably a fancy white-bread-and-cheese kid." He holds up both hands when I open my mouth to speak again. "You wouldn't understand, Alex. You can't. Hendrik was . . ."

His words dry up. He moves the bony shoulders inside his thin, faded sweater, as though he's trying to shake off his anger. "Not much longer. Then I'll have what I want. I'll have my money, and you get that racehorse of yours back. Ranna." He grins. "Good name. Ranna's much better than Isabel."

He takes the handcuff keys out of his pocket and throws them to me. The Beretta appears in his right hand again.

"Let's go. Move it. Outside. We can carry on with the game tomorrow."

I unlock the metal bracelet and slowly straighten up out of the chair, freezing halfway to let the pain subside. Then I cough and have to pause again for the pain.

My breath is shallow when I talk. "What if there's no money in the box? Or if it's old money and the banknotes have expired? You know, like the notes we used before we became a democracy? Or what if it's information? Documents? Useless pieces of paper about the men who no longer rule this country?"

Adorjan shakes his head, waves the gun to show me to walk. "You know nothing. When Hendrik shot me, I asked him why. Just like you keep doing now. He said it was money. More than me or Johannes could ever dream of."

Outside the shack, the night is cool, and the sound of waves more distinct. The smell of the sea is unmistakable. Sweaty and salty. The breeze pushing up against me carries the promise of fish. And something else. Stronger. The smell of seals? Birds? How far off, I can't tell.

I glance over my shoulder. Our two shacks have a neighbor, about twenty feet to the left. Looks like an outhouse of sorts. I can't see any other lights or signs of civilization. The whole setup makes me think of a road construction camp, or something equally nomadic.

I wish I knew where we were. I know we drove far. Adorjan gave me the Coke yesterday just outside Sasolburg, but we only got here today. I was completely out of it, stumbling to bed and falling asleep immediately again. I woke up shackled.

How far is Sasolburg from the sea? About six hours if we're near Durban, especially if there are no trucks on the road, but we're definitely not in the tropical KwaZulu-Natal province. How long did we drive for? Sixteen hours? That means we could be anywhere in the Eastern, Western, or Northern Cape provinces.

Why so far?

Possibly because this is the last place Sarah and Ranna would think to look. Not in the city. Not in Johannesburg. No. Here. In the middle of what looks like a desert. I go down on my haunches and touch the sand. The texture feels familiar. Are we in Namaqualand? Near Namaqualand? Farther south? How close might we be to the farm? My mother?

She probably thinks I'm dead by now.

I start walking around and around in the sand, Adorjan patiently waiting in the bright light by the door of his shack. Every time I look at him, I lose what little night vision I've gained. Probably why he chose to stand there.

I turn, blink my eyes to adjust to the dark. Wonder whether I could make a run for it. A wave of nausea washes over me. I try to spit the sudden bitterness out of my mouth. The sleeping pill, or whatever it was, hasn't worked itself out of my system yet.

I turn around and look at the wide-open space around me. Tune my ears to pick up anything like traffic—the sound of tires on tar perhaps—sifting through the noises until I find it: the drone of an 18-wheeler or something gearing down in the distance.

There's a road nearby. I'm sure of it. Not a busy one, but a road all the same.

Tomorrow. Tomorrow I'm going to make a run for it. But I have to eat first. Sleep to clear my head.

Tomorrow.

Sarah

1

I stick the last sheet of paper up on the wall, making sure it lines up precisely with the others. I stand back and measure it in relation to the tiles on the floor. Neat.

This is the only way my head can function properly. I can't bear it when information is disorderly, when I can't see or understand the pattern.

If anyone found out I used paper, I'd never hear the end of it.

I sit down again, feet on the table, and stare up at the list of names and the photos of everyone involved in this mess in some way or another.

Nothing jumps out at me.

I can't believe these useless pieces of paper are the only things I have to work with. Stefan Jansen didn't call Jaap Reyneke again after the first time and the spiderbot also delivered nothing, much as I expected.

I look again, starting with the papers on the left. Top of the list is Hendrik Kroon. Ranna's dad. State prosecutor. Successful. Criminal. Wife beater. Ranna shoots him when she's eleven. His sins are all wiped away when he dies.

Karla Kroon. Hendrik's widow. Ranna's mother. Former teacher. Married, for a long time now, to Moshe Abramson. Lives in New York.

Moshe Abramson. A longtime friend of one of the old apartheid cabinet ministers. Meets Karla in a shopping center and buys her coffee, according to Ranna. Surgeon at a big hospital in New York.

Thinus and Lena Prinsloo. Lena is Karla's sister. Thinus and Hendrik were big buddies. Got along really well. Lena was a receptionist at a doctor's office, but stopped working years ago. Thinus ran his own business. Long-distance transport. Has terminal cancer.

Adorjan Borsos. Hendrik's stooge. Hendrik Kroon shoots him during a robbery and takes a metal box that no one misses but leaves a lot of money, possibly to reassure the police that it was a botched job and that nothing was stolen.

Johannes Tredoux. Borsos's fresh-faced sidekick and only eighteen years old when Hendrik Kroon shoots and kills him. Never finished school.

I get up and make a little cross next to his picture. I need more info about him.

Next to Tredoux's school photo are two personnel pictures of Gerhard Jooste and Braam Willemse. They were the two ex-policemen who were in charge of transporting the money and the metal box.

Jooste and Willemse, employees of a private security company, were on their way to a Pretoria city bank. A newspaper article reports that a jeweler from Johannesburg, Eitan Blomstein, was "extremely relieved" to get his money back. His expression in the photograph doesn't look happy, though.

Then there's Jaap Reyneke. The retired detective who investigated Hendrik's death and declared it a suicide. There's also his colleague and friend Stefan Jansen, the detective in charge of the robbery investigation.

Next profile.

Ranna Abramson, aka Isabel Kroon. Shoots her father after he attacks her mother yet again. By coincidence, it happens on the evening of the day Hendrik Kroon returned from the robbery, apparently with a small metal lockbox in his possession.

What is inside the box? No one knows. Where is the box? Same answer.

I get up and walk over to the window. Walk back again. "Fuck Adorjan Borsos."

I am still no wiser. Equally bad is that Saul Nyati had to leave the national archives empty-handed earlier today. Apparently, their systems crashed.

I sit down. I'm missing something. Something big and obvious. What is it?

Borsos. Johannes Tredoux.

Hendrik Kroon. Borsos.

Stefan Jansen. Borsos.

Hendrik Kroon and Jansen could have been colluding. A state prosecutor and a detective might have plotted robberies together. Jansen has too much money for a policeman—there's no doubt about that. And perhaps Jaap Reyneke was in on the game.

Reyneke and Jansen could have given Kroon information about where and how money was being transported, and then Kroon, in turn, could have arranged for Borsos and Tredoux to do the dirty work.

If that's how it was, then it would have been convenient for the two policemen to have Kroon dead and Borsos behind bars. It might have suited them perfectly that everything tied up so neatly in the end. Clean and simple.

Does that mean that Reyneke and Jansen also knew about the metal box?

And what's with this Eitan Blomstein guy? Would he also have known about the existence of the box? Did it belong to him? But then why not admit that it was missing?

What the hell was inside that box?

I nudge the computer out of its slumber, yawn, and look over my shoulder at the fridge. Then bend down and count the cans in the wastebasket under my desk. Eleven. I'm way over my limit already.

And the Pringles are all gone too. It looks like real food is my only option now.

It's nine o'clock, Tuesday evening. Time for Uber Eats.

"I don't believe it."

Yet, there it is, in black and white, on the screen in front of me.

Byte is still watching me hopefully, trying to bum a piece of pepperoni-and-chili pizza, but Megs is asleep already. I push his cold nose away.

"No, stop it now." I point at his bed. "Go and lie down. You can't eat this crap."

I look back at the screen. Jansen and Reyneke worked together for a number of years at the famous Brixton Murder and Robbery Unit, with Jansen a rank higher than Reyneke at the time. Then something happened, and both were transferred to other units. Problem is, there is no record of what that something was.

And if Reyneke has the kind of money Jansen has, he is a lot more conservative with it. I can't find any signs of extravagance, nothing that doesn't square with the life of a retired policeman. He buys alcohol, mostly beer and rum, on his credit card, and two months ago he spent quite a lot of money on a big-screen television and two tickets to the Bulls rugby match at Loftus.

He still pays for the same private medical insurance plan he's had for the past twenty years and fills up his old Honda once a month.

It looks as though Reyneke's and Jansen's paths crossed Hendrik Kroon's a number of times, although the Kroon family moved around quite often. Kroon was the prosecutor in a handful of cases the two cops worked on.

Two of these cases are quite interesting. In the first, a Joburg businessman was robbed of R350,000 cash, and in the second a group of armed men stole three dockets from the Boksburg police station, each one handpicked from the hundreds on offer. The two cases made it into the papers, and into the courts, and, miracle of miracles, both articles are digitally available.

I scan through them quickly. Seems the cases were thrown out of court due to a lack of evidence. Smells fishy. Does this mean Kroon, Jansen, and Reyneke were in cahoots all along, helping out their criminal friends whenever possible?

Perhaps Kroon was meant to share whatever he stole on the day of the robbery with Jansen and Reyneke.

Half an hour later, I have a tiny bit more information about Johannes Tredoux.

The tall, thin, blond boy went to high school in Alberton, but left when he was sixteen, having failed grade nine twice. He was good with his hands: woodwork, welding, fixing cars. When he died, no one could trace either of his parents for the funeral.

Eitan Blomstein doesn't deliver much either. The jeweler who almost lost R1.5 million in a robbery that ended in a shoot-out died not long after when a truck flattened his BMW. He was sixty-seven. His sons sold the business and went back to Tel Aviv.

Just as I'm about to give up on this evening producing anything of value, my phone rings. It's the listening device. Seems Stefan Jansen has guests.

There are two voices. Jansen invites someone inside. There's a shuffle of feet, the door closing, and then Jansen greeting someone by name.

Jaap.

Could it be Jaap Reyneke, visiting his former boss?

"I tried to trace the Mini," Reyneke says. He speaks quietly and calmly, his voice younger and stronger than Stefan's.

"And?"

"False plates."

"I knew it. They weren't journalists." Silence for a second or two. "The car was special. Customized. Did that help at all?"

"No one I spoke to worked on a car like that."

"Shit," Jansen says.

"What now?" Reyneke sounds worried. "What if they really were journalists? What if they find out about Hendrik? Us? What if they put it in the papers? I've only just started making peace with all of it."

"How would they find out?"

"I suppose you know that Borsos is out. He got out a year or so ago."

"Borsos?" Jansen gives a short laugh. "He knows nothing. He's never known anything. They always made sure he was kept in the dark."

"Are you sure about that?"

"Yes. But I'll go and look for him. And see if you can find the women. The older one seemed familiar. The one with the body and the scar. She did all the talking."

Their voices fade until I can no longer hear them. I call Adriana.

"You need to be careful. Those former cops are looking for you." I explain to her what's going on.

In the background, the restaurant sounds busy. Voices. Cutlery. Heavy jazz. Adriana can't stand elevator music.

"Jansen said you looked familiar." I wonder whether I dare to ask. "He isn't perhaps one of your . . ."

"No," she says quickly. "I would have remembered. And I definitely wouldn't have turned up on his doorstep if he had been."

"And what happens if he turns up on *your* doorstep? I'm sorry I dragged you into this."

"Don't be." She laughs mirthlessly. "He can come. I'll be ready."

"Adriana . . ."

"You just find Alex. I'll be okay."

I take a deep breath. "Be careful."

"I will be."

The restaurant din is replaced by the sound of a sizzling grill. She must have stepped into the kitchen. "When is Ranna coming to see me?" she asks.

"Tomorrow evening. It might be late. She's only just leaving Paternoster. Is that okay?"

"Can't wait."

There's something in her tone I don't like.

"Adriana, don't . . ."

She laughs before I can finish my sentence, much warmer this time, sends a kiss over the line, and tells me to sleep tight.

As if that would even be remotely possible.

Ranna

1

I've woken the redhead. I can hear it. She coughs, barks something indecipherable, and then puts down the phone.

The pickup idles while I wait for her to open the gate. It's Wednesday afternoon. Overhead, thunderclouds promising rain sag low in the sky. Now and again the jacaranda trees rear as the wind staggers through Pretoria's streets.

All-in-one weather. That's how Alex described it once.

Suddenly my body misses him. Not my heart. Not my head. My body. My mouth. My neck. My back. My hips.

A groan escapes me. Desire. Frustration.

Same thing.

The gate to Sarah's castle opens just in time to check my self-pity.

I drive into the basement, the elevator ready for me as I park the Hilux. I grab my backpack, lock the car, and step inside. It moves, without instruction from me, to the top floor. I wonder, as I did the last time, what happens on the second floor.

It's quiet inside the flat. The dogs must be elsewhere. Perhaps Daniel took them for a walk. Sarah's alone in the kitchen, wearing a cropped T-shirt and ripped jeans. Her hair is standing up in every direction. Seems like she never takes those earrings out.

For a moment we stop to stare at each other. The last time we were together was the day she betrayed me. Now it's two days later, and neither of us has achieved anything that might help Alex.

The temptation to lash out at her is so strong I turn and walk to the nearest sofa. I remind myself of Alex, chained to that bed in Sasolburg. Focusing on him is the only way Sarah and I are going to survive this mess. The only way we are going to survive each other. We are just going to have to keep thinking of Alex. Then I can kill her.

Except, I promised her mother I'd look after her.

I put the backpack down and start unpacking its contents onto the black leather. The photographs I took from my father's desk, the baby clothes, a few of my mother's books, and the jewelry box. I leave it all there and turn back toward Sarah.

Her face is a mask. Her hands—ridiculously small—are balled into fists. If I had to hit her, she'd be flat on her back. On the other hand, I doubt I'd be able to keep up with her if she took off. She probably runs like a greyhound.

"I need to do some laundry, and I want to shower," I say.

She jerks her head toward the kitchen.

"Washing machine's there."

"And I'm hungry."

"There are eggs in the fridge. And chicken salad. I went shopping."

I nod and turn to pick the last pair of clean underwear out of the mess in my backpack. There should be one fresh T-shirt and a pair of clean jeans left in the suitcase I brought from Mumbai.

The dress I flew in is still in the suitcase, I remember. And the come-hither shoes. I'm going to put those on as soon as Alex and I are together again, I promise myself. And I won't need any underwear then.

I carry my things to the bathroom. On the way there, I wave at the couch: "Lunch first. Then you can look through those."

I don't wait for a response.

When I get out of the shower, Sarah is on the couch, paging through the photos. There's a plate on the kitchen counter piled high with chicken salad and, next to it, black coffee steaming in a mug.

I take a sip of coffee and make a face. Instant. Better than nothing. The salad looks delicious. Everything is so fresh. Looking for a fork, I almost laugh out loud when I open a drawer to find the revolver lying on top of the cutlery.

"The gun is of no use to you here. You have to keep it where you can get to it."

She carries on looking at the photos. "You need to get to Adriana's. The sooner, the better."

I dig into the salad. "But you and I are having such fun together."

When she looks up, her eyes are icy. "Stop it, Ranna." She points at her watch. "Stop being a bitch. And stop pretending you don't care. We have three days left, and we are not an inch closer to that fucking box."

"It's way too early to start panicking now."

She snorts, the photographs still clamped in her hand. There's a suppressed rage in her today, almost too much for her tiny frame to carry. It oozes out with every blunt gesture.

I turn my gaze to the motorbike helmet on the coffee table, as if not looking at her might assist me in being civil. I try to soften my voice, strip the sarcasm from it. "Maybe you should go for a ride. It'll help you relax."

She folds her legs in under her. "I already have. And I've been for a run with the dogs. It didn't help. Nothing helps."

"Sleep?"

"I'm sleeping as badly as you."

"Your mom and dad okay? Your brothers?"

"Why do you care all of a sudden?"

I ignore her. I poke the fork into the salad and mix it all up, then point the fork at her. "Tell me what you found out."

"Stefan Jansen and Jaap Reyneke are bad news."

"How so?"

I carry on eating at the kitchen counter while she tells me everything she discovered.

"You're right. They could be trouble. We're going to have to be extra careful."

"They just need to stay out of our way until we have Alex back. That's all."

She puts the photos down on the coffee table. Then picks them up and starts going through them again, as though she's determined to get an answer out of them.

"Go and sleep," I say. "You're exhausted."

She doesn't answer.

I pick up the coffee and go and sit down on the sofa next to her. "I've got Temazepam," I offer.

"No way." She tosses the photos down on the table again. The faded images fan out like a pack of cards. Two fall on the floor. My mother. Thinus and Lena on the beach.

When I look at Sarah again, she seems older than her twenty-three years.

"I promised his mother I would find him." She rubs her hair, her eyes. "And I'm going to keep that promise."

"Is Sophia okay?"

She gives a half-hearted smile. "She is. Except, of course, for the fact that her son is gone."

I finish the coffee and put the cup down. "And Alex's dad? Is he sober enough to care?"

"Don't know. Aunt Sophia moved in with someone in town when she heard about Alex."

"And Francois is okay with that?" Alex's father beats his mother. Always has, probably always will.

"He showed up there once, but she called the police."

This makes me smile. "Good."

Sarah looks at me with tired green eyes. "I have never broken a promise before, Ranna. Never."

"Then you haven't made enough of them."

She looks away testily.

"Must you always do that?"

"What?"

She gets up. "I'm going back to bed. You should rest too. Go and see Adriana as soon as you wake up. Take the pickup and bring the Mini back." She waves a hand to the left. "You know where the spare room is. It has its own bathroom."

She walks toward her bedroom.

"I don't need to speak to Adriana. I know what happened that night."

She stops in her tracks. She turns around slowly, placing her hands on either side of the doorframe.

"You don't know what you can and cannot remember. I've been through your school reports. You . . ." She hesitates, as though it will take too much out of her to say something good about me. "There is something . . . You're smart. You remember things in detail. I told Adriana what to do. She'll find something. I promise you that."

"And if I don't want to remember?"

"We can't afford that luxury."

"It's not 'we' who have to remember—it's me."

She looks out the window at the dark clouds moving by without dropping any of their rain on Pretoria West. "That's true."

"Why can't you talk to me?" I ask. "One person who knows too much about me is more than enough."

She scoffs. "You're not going to tell me anything. You want me dead. If it weren't for Alex, you'd have killed me by now and left me in the nearest ditch."

She's right. But it's also a handy excuse. "Why are you so bad with people?" I venture.

She frowns sharply, as though that was not what she was expecting to hear. Then she smiles slightly. "Don't tell me you think you're good with people."

2

I'm about to turn around and go back to Sarah's when Adriana opens the front door of her Sandton penthouse, the classical music I heard a moment ago suddenly silent.

Her straight brown hair is tied in a sloppy ponytail. She's wearing a spaghetti-strap dress of deepest red. Her fingernails are unpainted, her feet bare. There's a yellow pencil between her teeth. She takes it out and pushes her black-framed spectacles up her nose.

"Sorry for making you wait. I was busy."

She gestures for me to come inside. It's one in the morning, but she looks wide-awake.

I walk to the kitchen, dump my backpack and the Glock from the back of my jeans on the counter. As was the case the last time I was here, something is simmering on the stove. Some kind of stew, by the looks of it. And I smell coffee. Good coffee. Like she's just ground the beans. The full, fresh aroma fills the apartment.

"Let me get you a cup," she says, without asking if I want any.

While hovering at the breakfast counter, I try to decipher the writing on a blackboard on the wall behind her. A number of symbols are chalked up around a list for onions, tomatoes, and Madagascar vanilla. It takes me a while to place them.

"The second law of thermodynamics."

She looks up from behind the Italian espresso machine. "Indeed. I want to see whether it's possible to translate it into music."

I consider the symbols again. Would that even be possible?

She holds out one of the two red mugs in her hand and invites me to follow her. We walk to the living room. She sits down next to a cello leaning against one of the purple sofas. The gray cat from before pads out of the bedroom and rubs its body against Adriana's legs.

She shoos him away. "No, Hosni, now is not the time."

I remain standing, pointing my chin at the cello, silently asking the question.

"Beautiful, huh? I'm crazy about Jacqueline du Pré," is her response. "The sounds she could string together from a piece of wood. I wish I could do the same."

"I can come back later, if you want," I suggest, wondering how much venom Sarah is likely to spew if I skip this little exercise she invented for me. I really can't imagine what more I might remember from that night. Certainly nothing that's going to be of any value to us. The only thing I can see this doing is hurting like hell.

"Why would you want to do that?" Adriana asks, smiling. The throaty sound is low and warm. "Now is perfect. Come on. Sit down. Please."

"Perfect for what?" I say, playing dumb.

"Whatever your heart desires," she says, playing along.

"Nothing," I say, serious now, before this conversation goes places I may not be willing to explore. "That's what my heart desires: for nothing to happen. I want peace and quiet. For once in my life."

She laughs. "You'd die of boredom within two days."

I hate that she's right.

I walk over to the window and look at the city lights sprinkled out there, wary of the woman behind me. She's different tonight. More direct. More curious. Less careful. Maybe it's because Sarah isn't here.

I shouldn't have come. I'm not in the mood for games. In any case, the more I see of Adriana, the clearer it becomes that there's a lot more to her than she will have you believe. Alex would call her Chaos-with-a-capital-*C*.

"What are you, really?" The question pops out before I can stop it. I blame the journalist in me.

She considers her answer. Says, "Happy. Mostly."

"Crow's is a front."

"For what?"

"For your business."

"Crow's is a business. Your statement makes no sense."

I turn around, finish drinking my coffee. "In other words, we're not going to talk about it tonight."

She shrugs lightly. "You're right. Another night, maybe. I'll cook for you."

"Sounds good. Especially if . . ."

"Wait, let me guess," she says, holding her hand up. Hosni hops onto her lap, demanding affection again, and she rubs his back while she thinks. "Venison. Kudu? Lots of green vegetables. No salad."

"Not bad."

"And no red wine. Beer. And very bitter dark chocolate for afterward, with a double espresso."

I sigh in mock surrender. "I'm so transparent."

She shakes her head, smiling. Puts her glasses back on her nose. "So? Are you going to relax now? Come and sit. It won't be that bad."

"Promise?"

She waves her hand toward the sofa opposite her. "I suppose it depends on your frame of reference," she says.

"My frame of reference?"

"Yes. What's the worst thing that's happened to you?"

I think for a moment. Was it the night I shot Hendrik Kroon? Was it when I killed Tom? When I left Alex? That first morning I woke up in Lagos?

I sit down across from her, kick off my shoes, and curl up on the couch. I push my hair back behind my shoulders. Refuse to look her in the eye.

The silence becomes a quiet hum between us.

"Okay. I'll give you my worst, if you give me your worst," she offers.

I nod. "Okay. The day my father kicked my unborn brother to death." The day Hendrik Kroon flipped the fight switch in my mind, waking some primordial being I sometimes struggle to control.

Adriana doesn't skip a beat. "Mine is the fact that my family wants nothing to do with me. That Sarah's mother believes I'm a bad influence on her." She looks away for a second. Then asks, "The happiest?"

"Happiest?"

"Every scale has two extreme points."

This time I don't hesitate. "My very first camera. And Alex. The night he fell asleep on my couch in Dar es Salaam." The memory makes me smile.

"And you?" I ask quickly, worried that she thinks I'm not interested in the happiest thing that's happened to her.

Sometimes pleasure is harder to explain than pain, especially when you imagine you know the one more intimately than the other.

Adriana's face softens, the scar on her cheek seeming to fade. "My father. Definitely. He told me never to care what other people thought of me. He said it was the only way to become my true self."

I smile. Then I close my eyes for a moment, taking a deep breath. "Okay. I'm ready."

Adriana nods. "We're just going to sit and chat and see what you remember. That's it. You can stop me at any point. The power is yours."

And Sarah's. And Borsos's. But hey, let's pretend it's all hunky-dory.

"Sure." I know I don't sound convinced. I can hear myself breathing anxiously, feel my hands starting to sweat.

"Would it help to lie down and close your eyes?" Adriana offers.

"You sound like a psychologist."

"Not in a million years."

"I don't like this one bit."

"It's not my favorite pastime either."

"Let's leave it, then."

"Ranna." The single word is soft but firm, like a parent admonishing a willful child.

I have the power. Yeah, right.

"Okay. Fine."

I surrender, sinking deeper into the couch and closing my eyes.

"Let's start at a specific point that evening. When your father came home." Adriana's voice is calm and quiet. "Where are you?"

I hesitate one last, long moment—my final, pointless rebellion against this thing I've been forced into—then I dive into the deep, dark waters of my memory.

"I'm in the kitchen. I'm helping my mother. I'm peeling potatoes, and she's cutting them to make chips. It's her birthday, but she's making my father's favorite food."

"What time is it?"

"It's just after five." The kitchen clock is brown and white. "Eleven minutes past five."

"Where is your father?"

"He's just walked in the front door."

"Is he early? Earlier than usual? Late?"

"I'm not sure. He always comes home at different times."

"That's fine. Just say if you don't know or don't remember."

Adriana is quiet. After a while she speaks again. "What does your father look like? What's he wearing?"

"Black pants. Black shoes. Golf shirt."

"Golf shirt?"

I'm just as surprised as she is. Why am I only remembering this for the first time now?

"It's the one he always kept in the back of his car. His just-in-case shirt, he called it."

"What's he doing? What's his mood like?"

"He comes into the kitchen. He's restless. And he looks stressed. More than usual. The last two weeks have been different. He tells my mother he spilled something on his shirt and threw it away."

"Do you think that's what really happened?"

I open my eyes and look at her. "Did Sarah tell you about the robbery?"

I know immediately it's a stupid question. Adriana de Klerk knows more about me than Sarah does. She knows everything about me that Sarah's told her, plus everything she's taken in with those all-seeing eyes of hers.

She makes a soothing gesture with her hands. "Yes, I know about the robbery. And your dad. Sarah finally decided to be honest with me. And now we're all just trying to help Alex. Nothing more. Promise."

I lift myself up on an elbow, searching for pity or judgment in her eyes about what happened that night my father died, but there's nothing.

She waits for me to settle down again.

"Think about the shirt again."

"Okay."

"Is there a chance your father might have changed into the golf shirt because the other one had blood on it?"

I nod. "It's possible, but it's just a guess."

I hoist myself to my elbow again. "Sarah's right, you know. You are good at this."

"Ranna . . ." Adriana sounds exasperated. She swings her glasses back and forth in her left hand. "I know this is hard, but you need to cooperate. Please. You can't keep jumping up with every question."

"Okay, okay. Sorry." I sink back down again.

She gets up and walks over to the kitchen to pour herself a glass of wine and comes back. "Close your eyes."

I do as she says.

"Your father comes home. What does he have with him?"

"I leave the kitchen when he comes in, but I remember there are keys in his hand. Car keys. And a wallet. His briefcase is in the hallway. It's one of those big black ones lawyers always wheel to court."

I stop. There's a new memory. I frown, trying to pull it into focus. Could it be?

"What can you see?" Adriana asks.

"A white bag," I whisper. "It's resting between the briefcase and the wall. Something like a flour bag, or a money bag. Thick, strong, off-white cotton. There's something in the bag. I don't know what."

"How big is the bag?"

I show her the length of my forearm. Borsos mentioned a white bag, and I realize now that it would have been big enough to hold the metal lockbox he described to us.

"Okay, good," says Adriana. "What happens next?"

"I go to my room."

"How are you feeling?"

"No." I open my eyes, wagging a warning finger in her direction. "You don't need to know that."

She takes a sip of wine and tucks an errant strand of hair behind her ear, her brown eyes suddenly darker. "Okay. When do you see your father again?"

"At the dinner table."

"Retrace your path back to the dinner table. Where is the briefcase now? The white bag?"

"The case is there, but the bag . . . it's gone."

"You sound surprised. Have you noticed something else?"

"Yes. There is an extra case at the door. A suitcase. I think I might have heard my father tell my mother he had to go away for business."

"Is the suitcase big or small?"

"Big."

"Bigger than an overnight bag?"

"Yes. It's not the one he usually packs when he goes away for a night or two. It's the big red suitcase. And usually . . . usually he only leaves in the mornings when he's going to be away. Not in the evening."

"What do you think it means?"

I rub my eyes. This is more tiring than I thought it would be. And more painful than I ever imagined. It feels as though there's a slab of concrete on my chest, making it difficult to breathe.

"Maybe he wanted to go on vacation." It's a guess.

"Without you or your mom?"

I clear my throat, not wanting to say what I really think.

"Ranna . . ." Adriana's voice is soft. She puts her wineglass down, gets up, and settles on the coffee table in front of me. She rubs my arm. Her hand is warm; the touch is light and caring. "Do you think he was planning to leave you and your mom? Is that how it felt? How it feels now?"

I sit upright to get away from her. Tuck my knees up under my chin. "If I say that—if I admit it—do you know what that means?"

"No."

I laugh. "You know exactly what it means. It means I shot my father for nothing. If I'd just waited a few hours, he would have been gone. Out of our lives." I take a deep breath. Rattle through the thought: "And maybe I knew it. Maybe I didn't want him to escape."

Adriana gets up to make me a fresh cup of coffee. The red mug arrives on a tray, a square of something chocolaty next to it. She squeezes my shoulder.

"Eat. I made it at the restaurant and brought some home. It's a dark-chocolate brownie with almonds. A bit of coarse salt on top. I think you'll like it."

"Thank you."

I break the brownie in two and dip one half in the coffee.

Stop thinking. Stop thinking. The refrain hammers inside my skull.

It doesn't work.

What would have happened if I had just waited that night for Hendrik Kroon to take his suitcase and leave?

I shake my head, annoyed. What is the point of brooding over what's done? No one has the answer, and no one ever will. Not even Adriana, no matter how many questions she asks, or what kind of advice she offers.

I get up, mug in hand, and walk to the row of windows looking down on Sandton. Watch the lights burning in towering office blocks and apartment buildings. The twenty-four-hour McDonald's on the corner. The only car on the road, a silver BMW, skipping red traffic lights one by one. I run my hand through my hair, rub a stiff muscle in my neck.

"You probably want to get to bed." I don't look at Adriana. She sees too much. Knows too much. And I know nothing about her. That kind of imbalance always makes me wary. And, suddenly, irritable too.

"Not really," she says. "I'm not much of a sleeper."

She comes and stands beside me, her wineglass full again. We watch the traffic light on the corner go from red to green to yellow. Then I turn and stare openly at the scar on her face.

"How did you get that?"

She touches it, the fine muscles in her forearm rippling briefly.

"Call it a souvenir. A daily reminder to watch my back."

"That doesn't tell me how you got it."

"Now is not the time."

"But you want me to spill my guts?" I return my gaze to the traffic light. Green. Yellow.

She turns toward me and steps into my personal space, so close I can smell her expensive perfume, something woody and earthy.

I step back and am immediately irritated with myself.

She smiles, but it's tepid. Disappointed, even. She steps back to face the carpet of lights outside the window again.

"You want Alex back. You want the metal box. You don't really want to know about me."

"Maybe. Maybe not."

The smile warms a bit. "I'll tell you sometime. When everything's over. I'll invite you and Alex to dinner."

"That would be nice." Red. Green.

She turns and motions toward the sofa with her glass. "So, what do you think? Shall we try again?"

I sigh, resigned now. "Why not?"

She touches my arm. This time, I don't flinch.

"We react to things that happen." She takes a sip of wine and then pulls a face, as though it's lost its appeal. "Especially when you're a child. When things are going badly, you don't react to what you think might happen. You do what your instinct dictates." She gives my arm a gentle squeeze. "No one is judging you for what happened. Not even Sarah."

"She's . . . difficult. Sometimes I could strangle her."

"Her mother is first in line for that job. Trust me." She offers a mischievous smile. "Come, let's get on with it."

I nod, turn, and settle back down on the sofa.

This time Adriana sits down on the coffee table, as though to prevent me from running away.

Her dark voice is soothing, like when you speak to a child. "Get comfortable. Relax."

I close my eyes.

"All right. You're in your house. You see the suitcase in the hall. When you see your father again, it's for supper. Do you eat in the kitchen?"

"Yes."

"Do you all eat together?"

"Yes. We're at the table. My father seems okay, but then there's a sound in the backyard, like something falling over. He jumps up and walks to the window. He looks out. I don't think he sees anything because he comes back to the table. Then he jumps up again and walks to the front door and makes sure it's locked."

"Why do you think he does that? Does it happen often?"

"No. It's the first time I've seen him do this. Except, maybe, earlier that week. Once."

"And what is your mother's reaction?"

"She seems surprised."

"And then? Does anything else strange happen?"

"No."

"Okay. You're done eating. You get up . . . ?"

"My mother and father go to the living room to watch TV. I go to my bedroom."

"And then?" Adriana's voice is almost a whisper, urging me toward the moment I most dread. The moment that buried every other memory from that night.

"After a while, my father calls me to the living room."

"Yes?"

"I close my book and go to them. He's had a lot to drink. He tells me to go to the study. There's a surprise there for me."

My throat tightens. I clear it loudly and cough, though it's not really necessary.

"Okay. You go to the study. Your mother stays in the living room?"

"Yes."

"What can you see in the study?"

I can feel my breathing getting faster, my hands are feeling clammy. "There's a . . . hmm . . . The safe is open."

"The white bag?"

"Not inside the safe."

"What's inside?"

"A revolver. And . . . the passport that's usually there is gone." I say this with astonishment.

"Okay. You're doing fine. What happens then?"

"My father wants me to open a red box, bigger than my hand, on his desk. I wonder why, because it's my mother's birthday, not mine."

"What's inside the box?"

I shake my head. I can feel my father's hot booze-breath on my neck as he tells me to open it. It's a gift. I should be grateful.

"I don't want it. He yanks me by the arm, tells me to be grateful."

"What do you think it is?"

Adriana's voice stays even, though I can hear mine becoming increasingly shrill.

"I never opened it. Can you believe it? I guess it's jewelry. Maybe like the earrings my mother got that day. Maybe it's a bracelet or something. But it'll be cheap. His gifts were always cheap garbage. Saying sorry or saying well done never had much meaning, coming from him."

"What might he be apologizing for? Or was it a reward for something?"

"He never had any interest in my report card. So, the gift would have been a sorry."

"For what?"

"Maybe because he was leaving? Because he'd hit my mother the week before? He'd aimed a blow or two my way as well for the first time, but I'd run away."

"Are you afraid?"

"I was afraid. Then. I was afraid things would start changing, that I'd be next."

"And the night in the study?"

"I am angry. A bit scared," I concede, "but mostly angry."

Adriana's hand rests on my arm again. I let it be.

"Look around the study," she says. "Is there any sign of the metal box? Something that looks like it? Is the white bag there?"

"No." I concentrate to bring the room into focus again. Wooden desk. Wooden bookshelves. Cream-colored carpet. Worn brown leather chair. "No. Nothing."

I sigh. This is frustrating.

"Just hang on," Adriana urges. "Take it easy. And relax. We don't have to talk about the actual shooting. It's not necessary."

I sigh again, this time with relief.

"Let's jump ahead a bit. The shot goes off. Then what? What happens next?"

"He is on the ground. I put the revolver in his hand. I lift his arm and fire a shot in the direction of where my mother had been standing. I drop his arm. I leave everything as it is. I want to go to the bathroom. I want to stand under the shower, although I know I mustn't. My mother says we have to go to the kitchen. She tells me not to say anything more than that I had been standing next to him when he shot himself. That he had me by the arm, keeping me there. She's calm. More calm than I've ever seen her."

"And then?"

"The police come. There's a lot of noise. Cars and lights and sirens."

The same cold, dead feeling wells up in me again. The unnatural indifference that carried me through the night.

"No one asks me anything. A policeman wants to give me a drink. Tea, I think. But I don't react. I'm standing next to my mother, my hand in hers. Dead still. Just as she told me. She says we were all in the study, me included. My father had me by the arm. He shot at her. Then he shot himself. She tried to stop him, but she couldn't. They believed her."

The words of an overzealous constable come back to me now. “Someone said something about knowing that he’d been under a lot of pressure. Some sort of investigation. My mother knew nothing about it.”

I struggle to breathe. I force myself to inhale, exhale, through the sounds and smells from that night. The gunpowder. My own sweat. Blood. My mother’s eerily calm voice. A policewoman asking whether I was all right, was I hurt. I had blood on my face, on my lips.

And there were lights. Lots of lights. Blue-and-red lights. Round and round and round they spun, all through the house, reflecting off the open front door, the ceiling, the windows.

Adriana’s hand squeezes my arm. “Two more questions,” she says gently, “then I promise we can stop. Just two more.”

“I don’t want to . . .”

“Just two questions. Please.”

I close my eyes. Force myself to calm down with the same thought I had back then. It’s over. Over, over, over.

“Was there a logo or anything else on the white bag? The one the box was in?”

Good question. The answer is even better.

“Yes. Little logos, a whole lot of them, all over the bag.”

“Remember what they looked like. When we’re done here, I want you to draw them and give the drawing to Sarah.”

I can’t imagine what the next question’s going to be.

“When and how did Detective Jaap Reyneke arrive at the scene? The policeman who investigated your father’s death—do you remember him? What did he look like? Could you read his mood?”

I remember what Sarah said about him and Colonel Stefan Jansen, that perhaps they’d worked with my father.

I remember Reyneke well. Average height. The beginnings of a belly bulging over his belt. Broad shoulders, sloping down like a tired swimmer’s. Ash-blond hair. Strong fingers. Bright blue eyes that looked curious and interested. Warm smile.

He wanted to talk to me that night, but I just stared at him. I was standing next to my father when it happened, I told him. A nugget of truth. Please may I go and bathe?

He said I could. He told me I was very brave.

We were standing in the kitchen when he spoke to me. Exactly where my mother had stood while we were waiting for the police to arrive. Detective Reyneke was there before everyone else. He arrived just before all the bright lights did.

I remember the clock in the kitchen after we called the police. The loud tick of the minute hand. The neighbors gathering by the front door, whispering, hiding their curiosity behind fake concern.

None of them had ever rushed over when my mother had screamed in pain.

"He got there at twenty-six minutes before eight. Seven minutes after we'd called the cops. He was angry. Livid."

"Seven minutes? That's fast. Are you sure?"

My eyes fly open. "Yes. Seven. Almost like he was close by. Waiting." Suddenly something else surfaces from that muddle of a day. "And when everyone was finally gone, so was the suitcase. And the black briefcase."

Adriana's eyebrows shoot up. "Gone?"

"Gone. Like my father."

And then, before I can stop myself, I start crying. Without a sound, chin on my chest, Adriana's arms around me, soothing sounds coming from her mouth.

Alex

1

I feel slightly better after Adorjan shared some of his chocolate with me, but it's not going to last. It's just a sugar rush storming through my veins after weeks of bread, rusks, and tea.

Now. It has to be now.

I win the first round of chess. Adorjan is peeved, but it's his own fault. His head's not been in the game. He keeps looking at his watch, as though willing time to move faster. No matter how often he does it, it remains Wednesday evening. Three days before Ranna and Sarah have to bring us the metal box and its mysterious contents.

"Go to sleep," he snaps after I win the second round too.

He slams his cup down on the hard ground. The milky tea sloshes over his hand. He licks it off and then rubs his neck, where a naked woman reclines with a pair of aces in her hands.

I get up as far as the cuffs on the camping chair will allow. Cough long and hard. "What about my ten minutes outside?" I ask, when I can finally talk again. I shouldn't have beaten him at chess.

Adorjan shakes his head. "Take your chair and go to bed."

"Come on," I say sharply, realizing it sounds like a curse. I try again, more gently. "Please."

He considers for a moment.

"Three minutes. That's all," I say.

"Fine, but hurry."

He throws me the keys to the handcuffs, his pistol, as always, at the ready. I unlock the cuffs and almost jog past him, trying to get out before he changes his mind.

The moon is bright. Too bright.

I stop indecisively in the sand just outside the door. Look up, as though I'm breathing in the night air. Why couldn't there be some cloud cover tonight? For fuck's sake.

Adorjan is waiting at the door of his shack, pistol in hand. I start ambling while I keep an eye on him. He looks tired and worried. The last few weeks must be starting to take their toll.

All those dreams while he was behind bars, trapped inside a metal box two women have to find for him, because its contents are the only thing that can ease his last few years on earth.

Hope. That's all he has.

There's no guarantee the box even exists anymore, let alone whatever was inside it.

But it could also be revenge driving him. Though maybe *justice* is a better word. You get the feeling Borsos really believes he can make Hendrik Kroon squirm in his grave.

But dead is dead. I wonder whether that enters into his mind at all.

My back protests when I stretch it gingerly. The pain is duller today. Can a single chocolate bar make that much of a difference? Or is this a side effect of my own crazy, stupid hope? A tiny shot of adrenaline?

I glance at the old man again, casually. He's chewing his left thumbnail, the weapon in his right hand. There's a little ridge in front of me. It's about 130, maybe 160, feet high. To the left and right is the dusty plain with its low brush and dirty white sand. I need to get over that ridge, which is where that low hum is coming from. My hope is that it's a road that runs parallel to the sea.

Adorjan spits a piece of fingernail to his left, swears.

Now.

I run like I'm sprinting in gym class. Every square inch of my body protests at the sudden action.

"Hey!" Adorjan notices sooner than I expected he would.

Thirty strides to the ridge. The first shot explodes into the sand on my left. A warning.

I start climbing. Up, up, up.

The pain in my ribs screams.

Another shot. Closer.

Bastard shoots well in the dark.

Thirty feet more and I'll be over. My lungs are on fire. I can't. I can't.

I have to.

Up. To the top.

Another shot. Blood. Sudden and warm. On my arm. My chest?

Six more feet.

One.

I dive over the ridge and roll down the other side. Get up. Fall down. Get up. Run.

Don't look around.

I can hear the old man's breathing just behind me. Or is that my breath?

Where's the road? I can't see it. I must be confused. It should be to the right somewhere. To the left maybe? The only thing I can see is the silver of breaking waves.

I stop. The pain is too much. My hand digs at the fresh stab in my shoulder. Things are starting to get fuzzy.

No. I can't. Not now. Not yet. Please.

A moment of clarity descends, as if someone answered my silent prayer.

I can hear Adorjan toiling up the ridge. I look his way and back again. Stare at the sea. Look to where the road may or may not be. Glance back again to see Adorjan's gray head bobbing over the ridge.

"Come back!" he yells. "I'll kill you. I swear I'll fucking kill you!"

I take six, ten steps. Into the icy black water.

A shot. A shout. The ice-cold West Coast water closes over my head.

Ranna

1

I sip my fourth cup of coffee, though I crave something much stronger. Lots of it. But if I do that now, I'll return to a place I never really liked much. A place I tried to leave behind in Dar es Salaam when I met Alex. A toxic, self-destructive place.

I put the mug down on the coffee table. Blink tiredly. Drop my head into my hands and listen to the music. Adriana's playing the cello. I asked her to. Maybe I needed her to reveal something of herself. An attempt at equalizing the little game of show-and-tell I was forced to play.

It's four in the morning and the ghosts won't rest. They have feet and hands and they're scaling the scaffolding of my brain, reaching even the safe and happy places. They're like willful children. Your own children—not someone else's. Created by you and you alone, the guilt and the noise all of your own making.

A knock at the door surprises both of us. It's soft, hesitant even. It's followed by another one, slightly more insistent, as though the person outside decided the first attempt was too polite for this time of the day.

Adriana's face reveals so little, you'd think she was used to early morning guests. She points toward a bedroom, and I go there without argument. Sarah told me that Stefan Jansen thought he recognized Adriana, though it's not clear how that would be possible.

I stand behind the door in the bedroom, which is smaller than I imagined. Or perhaps it's the colors she's chosen: red and brown, intimate and earthy. It seems like a guest bedroom, I gather from the moonlight seeping through the windows.

The light spilling through the space between the open door and the frame allows me to watch Adriana. She's in the kitchen, taking a knife out of the top drawer. She walks to the front door, the sharp blade openly on display as though she's in the middle of chopping something. She opens the front door, but keeps the safety chain on.

The man there is much older than I remember. The neatly clipped ash-blond hair is now completely gray, and age is dragging at his jawline and his stomach. But the hands and the voice are still familiar. The light-blue eyes, the sharp but sagging shoulders.

It's Jaap Reyneke.

"Can I help you?" Adriana's voice is friendly, light. "Is the music bothering you?"

"No. Good evening." He looks at his watch. "Morning, I should say." He takes in the knife in her hand and raises his eyebrows.

Adriana lifts the blade into the air, laughs. "I was cutting carrots."

"Carrots?"

"I'm making soup. For a funeral." She pulls her shoulders back, as though daring him to challenge her. She shifts her weight so that a well-shaped leg slips through the slit in her soft, flowing dress.

He doesn't question why she's cooking in such a fancy outfit. I suddenly wonder whether she ever wears casual clothes.

I see her rising up on her toes as the silence grows between them, the knife in her hand a light, familiar instrument.

She knows this is no visit from a neighbor complaining about the noise. Good thing she has a weapon.

Weapon. Shit. I left the Glock and backpack lying on the kitchen counter. If Jaap Reyneke comes in, he's going to wonder about the gun. He might even be able to see it from the door.

Reyneke finally breaks the pregnant silence. He gestures down the corridor. "I live one floor down. I wanted to check if everything was all right. I heard strange noises." He shrugs sheepishly, flashing her a charming grin. "You sleep lightly as you get older."

She looks him up and down, surveying his day clothes of chinos, black golf shirt, and a sports jacket that could be hiding who-knows-what. "It must have been the music, then. I'm sorry. Did I wake you?"

"No. Don't worry. I don't sleep deeply anyway."

It's quiet again as they look at each other, both of them knowing the other is lying. Reyneke's hands hang motionless by his side. He could whip out a gun before Adriana manages to do any damage with her knife.

If only I could get to the Glock without Reyneke seeing me. He'll recognize me immediately. I have no doubt.

"It's been a long day, and I need to get to bed," says Adriana, her voice a notch cooler.

"That's understandable. It is almost sunrise."

The knife's blade taps a steady, impatient rhythm against her thigh. The light from the kitchen catches the blade and reflects it into Jaap's eyes. He blinks and tips his head to the left.

"I haven't seen you around here before," Adriana says. "Are you new in the building?"

"Yes." He gives her a tight little smile. "This is the first time I've seen you too. Do you live alone? Big place for a single woman."

Enough.

I step back and look around the room. Slam the en-suite bathroom door and call, "Adriana? Where're you? Everything okay?"

I walk to the door and look through the slit again. Jaap has stepped back, his hands in his pockets.

Adriana deserves an Oscar. She smiles over her shoulder in my direction and then at Jaap. "I'm sorry. I really must go. I have a guest."

He nods slowly. "Of course. My apologies. Nice to meet you. See you around."

She closes the door and locks it. I come out of the bedroom.

"It's Sarah's Mini," she says. "Jansen must have traced it. I would have noticed if anyone followed me."

"I thought Jansen recognized you."

"That's what Sarah says, but I don't know. I'm a hundred percent sure we've never met."

"How did Reyneke get in here? This is supposed to be a high-security building."

"Maybe he used his old police credentials. Maybe he bribed someone."

She picks up her phone. "I'm going to make sure it doesn't happen again."

She dials a number. Speaks Russian, or something that sounds like Russian. I catch four words: *Stefan Jansen. Jaap Reyneke.*

"Who were you talking to?" I ask when she ends the call.

She sweeps the hair from her face, puts the knife down on the kitchen counter. "No one."

"I'm not three years old."

"I didn't say you were."

Perhaps it's better not to know. I pick up the Glock and throw the backpack over my shoulder. Then I put it down again. I'll have to wait awhile to make sure Reyneke is no longer hanging around the building before I head back to Sarah's.

I need to do something with the information Adriana mined out of my head. The logo. The fact that Jaap Reyneke had arrived at our house that night so quickly, as though he'd been hanging around nearby, expecting something to happen. The fact that my father was planning to run.

I look at Adriana. It's not safe for her to stay here. "You should come with me. They know where you live."

She opens the fridge and peers at the contents. "Jansen and Reyneke will drop their little investigation. I'll make sure of that. Don't worry about me. I'll be fine."

Down on the street a car alarm goes off. Someone shouts.

I shake my head. "Enough people have been hurt already."

Adriana closes the fridge without taking anything out of it. She laughs, but it sounds bitter. "That's the problem when you topple one domino, Ranna. You should know that. When the first one goes, there's little you can do to stop what follows. It's a law of nature. Cause and effect."

I know what she means. I wish I didn't. My whole life feels like one long chain of dominoes that started toppling the night I shot my father.

Is it really necessary for more people to get hurt? Alex. Tom. My father. Isn't it enough? "You can't," I say.

"Can't what?"

For goodness' sake, is nothing sacrosanct with her? I say nothing.

She slips the knife back into the drawer.

"Exactly. The less you know, the better."

2

At first, Adriana digs in her heels, but finally I convince her to come with me. I'm worried about her. What if Reyneke's plan is to return with the cavalry in tow? Besides, if we're both at Sarah's, I can keep an eye on her. Make sure she doesn't do anything irresponsible.

We leave the Mini at her building in case the retired cop is waiting for us outside. We search the streets as we drive off in the pickup, but see nothing suspicious.

I head north, against the early morning peak-hour traffic. Adriana and I discuss the night's events for a while, then she reclines her seat as we reach the freeway to Pretoria. I watch enviously as she drops off quickly and easily.

She looks different in jeans, but still curated to a T. Flawless, earthy makeup hides the scar on her cheek. The tight-fitting, light-yellow sweater over a white blouse. Ankle boots made from soft, expensive-looking leather. Italian, I suspect. I can't help wondering who this woman is and how she made her money. She'd make for the subject of a damn interesting profile.

I suppress a yawn and remind myself to stick to the speed limit. No need to attract attention. No one's recognized me yet, but that could change in an instant.

When we pull up outside Sarah's gate, I touch Adriana's shoulder lightly. Immediately she's awake and alert.

She stretches, yawns, and smiles. “Good morning.”

The elevator opens as we park. We get in and, as before, it moves automatically to the third floor.

Sarah is waiting for us at the top. The stress of the past few days is visible in the dark circles around her eyes. She registers our arrival a second too late, her body, usually fighting to look bigger, leaning hunched against the wall.

As we step out, she pulls back her shoulders, the pink T-shirt straining against her breasts. She walks over and greets her aunt with a kiss on her cheek. Like all physical contact with Sarah, it is quick and awkward.

The dogs ignore me for a change, milling around Adriana instead. She greets them both with wide smiles and a quick rub behind their ears.

“Why are you both here?” Sarah asks after putting Adriana’s suitcase down in the spare room.

I guess that means I’ve just been downgraded to the sofa.

Adriana ignores the questions. She walks to the kitchen counter and puts on the kettle. She opens the windows to let the fog of cigarette smoke clear.

“Jaap Reyneke paid us a visit,” I inform her.

“What?” She makes an almost military right turn in her combat boots.

“He must have traced the Mini back to the penthouse. Or to me,” Adriana concedes. “There are a few policemen who sometimes eat at Crow’s.”

“Fuck,” Sarah says, her voice a whisper. “I’m sorry I dragged you into this.”

“Don’t worry about it.” Adriana taps her gold watch and points at the spare room. “It’s Thursday morning. We don’t have much time. I’m going to unpack while you and Ranna work through what she’s remembered. I have to make some phone calls too. I have a business that needs to make money, even if neither of you seems to think so.”

There's a flicker of hope in Sarah's tired green eyes as she looks at me.

I don't want her to get her hopes up: "It's not much. One small thing, maybe two."

She rubs her head and then her neck with both hands. "Well, that's more than we had a minute ago."

"It was something like this," I say, passing Sarah the pencil and paper she'd given me. She looks at it with a frown. Turns it this way, then that.

"Sure?"

"Yep."

We both stare at the two fleurs-de-lis lying back-to-back. There's an extra curl here and there, but it's definitely recognizable as the outlines of two lilies.

"I'll scan it and see if I can get a hit. We might get lucky." She puts the sketch in the scanner beside her computer. While it does its job, she says, "So our thinking is that this is the bag the metal lockbox was in when your dad took it from the Toyota van?"

"Yes. Borsos spoke about a bank bag, didn't he?"

"Okay." She retrieves the sketch from the scanner. "What else did the two of you come up with?"

I tell her what Adriana and I discussed on the way here. "It's a possibility the police may have been onto my dad. We think someone suspected he was up to no good. It may also explain why he wanted to get away." I tell her about the packed suitcase I saw the night he was killed. About Jaap Reyneke showing up so quickly, as if he'd been keeping an eye on Hendrik Kroon.

I consider some of the other options we'd put on the table. "It's also a possibility, though, that Reyneke wasn't investigating my dad, but that he actually wanted the lockbox. My father's suitcase disappeared with the police—with Reyneke, I think—that night. It wouldn't have been considered evidence. He was shot in the study, not in the entrance hall."

She looks at me and shakes her head. "Another dirty cop? Can we not get a lucky break? Just one. That's all I ask. One frigging lucky break."

I push on with the bad news. "It gets worse. This morning's episode at Adriana's apartment means that Reyneke and Jansen realize something's up."

"We knew that already." Sarah bites her lip. "They've been in contact since Adriana and I showed up at Jansen's front door."

"Yes, but now your aunt is in the firing line too. They know where she lives."

Sarah stays quiet.

"Do you think she's going to be okay?" I prod gently. "Is she going to forgive you for this mess you've gotten her into?"

Sarah looks up at the note of worry in my voice. A shadow of a smile plays across her face. "Who are you really worried about? Me or Adriana?"

I lean back in my chair. "Let's just get Alex back." I do my best to sound nonchalant. "I'll go back to being mad at you when we're done."

The smile deepens, the lines of her body softening. "Adriana will be fine. But we'll owe her." She points at me. "Not me. You *and* me. Us. For better or for worse."

"Really? I don't have any money."

Sarah raises one eyebrow. "Oh no. Not money. One day she's going to call you and ask for your help, just like we called her. And you're not going to be able to say no."

Fantastic.

I look at my sneakers. Decide to focus on today. On what's happening now. Tomorrow will have to look after itself.

I suppress a yawn. "So, back to Reyneke. If he and Jansen took the lockbox, they must have sold what was in it a long time ago. Or spent it. You say Jansen has too much money for a retired policeman? Maybe Reyneke just hides his money really well."

Sarah nods. "That's what I thought too."

"That investigation Reyneke led into my father's death. Did you find anything about it?"

She shakes her head, and her body seems to slump again. "It's hard to find anything about your dad. Or anything about what happened, in fact." She throws her hands in the air. "Not everyone digitized their stuff. There must be a pile of documents somewhere with information about Hendrik Kroon, but I can't get to it quickly enough to help us."

Her voice grows louder with every word. Byte jumps off his bed and trots over to us. He growls at me as though I've just done something to Sarah.

She reaches out and rubs his back to calm him. "Isn't there anything else you remember that can help us?" she asks, her eyes grazing over the gallery of photos and notes on the wall in front of her.

I get up and look at each of the faces in turn. "I don't think it matters what we know anymore. There's too little time."

She crumples the dog's ears in her hands. "Then I suppose it's time for plan B."

I turn around. "A second box with some of your money in it?"

She nods. "I've already called Uncle Tiny and asked him if he'd be able to make something similar. We paint numbers on it and add a lock. Put some cash in it. Hopefully Borsos won't realize the serial numbers are way too advanced for it to be from 1993. Maybe if he sees the money, he'll think it's better than nothing."

"So we're going to hope that Borsos's memory lets him down about the numbers on the box? What the whole thing looked like?"

Sarah moves to the computer. Opens the image of the fleurs-de-lis. "We better hope so, because this here is just a wild goose chase. Borsos is setting us up to fail. This stupid, fucking box . . ." Frustration kills off her words.

I don't like having to agree with her, but she's right. We're chasing shadows. Faraway, long-forgotten ghosts. And they may just get us all killed.

3

Adriana, in a silk bathrobe of deepest blue, is towel-drying her hair. Seems like she decided to take a shower while Sarah and I worked through the memories Adriana had dislodged from my mind.

The past few hours have caught up with her. Tired lines down the sides of her mouth accentuate the scar on her cheek, a perverse smiling arc across a face that has seen too much. Perhaps went looking for too much. Not all trouble is uninvited, after all.

I wonder again who she called in her apartment earlier. The person she spoke Russian to, or some language of equal flavor. What's going to happen to Jaap Reyneke and Stefan Jansen? Should I tell Sarah?

Probably not. The redhead has only one thing on her mind right now, and I don't want to distract her.

She's sitting at the long white workbench in front of her computers, staring at the screen, Coke in hand, as though willing something to pop out as the machine sifts through the Internet for the fleur-de-lis logo.

The game she'd been playing earlier is frozen on a screen on her left. A mercenary with arms like tree trunks is holding an automatic rifle. Nina Simone's "If I Should Lose You" bleeds through the speakers.

Someone who called earlier, Saul Nyati, pushed her into an even darker mood than usual. He told her the files on Borsos and my dad had been removed from the national archives. The last time they were requested was a few years ago, but no one in the archive is willing to say more than that. Apparently, they're unable to do so until they've completed their investigation into how such a thing may have happened.

I look at my watch for what feels like the hundredth time. It's almost nine in the morning. Thursday morning. The day after tomorrow, we're supposed to give Borsos what he demands. And if it can't be the box my father stole twenty-five years ago, it has to be one that looks like it.

"I'm going to make us breakfast, and then we're all going to sleep," Adriana announces. "Staring at one another with murderous intent isn't going to make anything happen."

"We're not . . ." I stop. Look down. Her comment is aimed at me. And she's right. In spite of what I said earlier, I'm still struggling to forgive Sarah. Worse than that is the guilt eating away at me. She was right that day in Sasolburg: if Alex had never met me, he wouldn't be in this mess right now.

Sarah looks at Adriana as though she's speaking a foreign language. Then she shrugs, as though nothing matters. And for her, nothing does, I suspect. Nothing but Alex.

"Breakfast would be nice. Thank you." I kick off my shoes and lie back on the couch.

After a while, I get up to fetch the Temazepam from the backpack. I put the pills down on the sofa's arm. I'm going to do as Adriana says and try and get some sleep as soon as we have eaten.

I sit down. Become aware of Adriana holding the kettle in her hand and looking expectantly at the sleeping pills, as though she's waiting for me to take one. Sarah swings her chair around and looks from me to Adriana. Laughs.

"Don't ask," she says, circling two fingers at her temple. "She's trying to mess with her own mind."

"At least I have a mind."

Sarah looks at me as though I were six years old. Even I know I'm being childish.

She gets up and walks to her bedroom. Comes back with a thick blue book, which she puts down beside me.

"Leave the pills. They're poison. I need you alert and present."

I pick the book up. It weighs a ton. *Linux Programming Manual.* She's right. If this doesn't put me to sleep, nothing will.

Just as I put the last forkful of egg in my mouth, Sarah's computer beeps. She drops her toast and jumps up. "There's a match for the logo."

Adriana and I follow her to the workbench. We all stare at the words on the screen.

"Can that be?" Adriana looks from me to Sarah and back again. "Is that the logo you remember?"

I nod.

I flop down into Sarah's chair. Touch the image on the screen as though that would help me. "I don't know it." I shake my head, the hope I had that the logo would deliver some kind of answer dashed. "I don't know the company at all."

ALEX

1

The water is frigid. I'm as cold as I was on those winter mornings on the farm when I got up early to go for a run and it had been raining.

No. Colder than that. It's Copenhagen cold, when I was there two years ago and it was fourteen degrees Fahrenheit. The snow was something out of this world for a Namaqualand farm boy. Waist deep. Never seen anything like it.

The cold shocks me to clarity. I shakily draw a breath. The air burns as though I've swallowed lava, shooting fire through my lungs. I cough. Squint in the light, brighter than I expected. To the left of me are rocks. To the right, sand. A beach. I'm lying on my back at the edge of the waves. The tide is coming in. Another coughing fit makes me turn over. Spit and blood pour out of my mouth, coloring the water around me pink.

How did I end up here? What's the time? Where am I?

Above me, the sun is flickering uncertainly through clouds on the horizon. It's early morning. Then I remember. Ranna. Sarah. Adorjan.

I move carefully to feel if everything's still in working order. I need to get out of here. My fingers dig into the sand for traction. Trying to sit upright hurts. Why?

I drag my body through the sand until I am half sitting, half lying by the rocks.

Adorjan. Gunshots. I gingerly search my chest. My shoulder, which hurts like hell. I gasp when my fingers touch a wound. I look at my fingertips. Red.

I gently probe. Relief surges through me. It's just a graze. Thank goodness.

I rest my head on the rock behind me. Count to ten. Twenty. Thirty.

I need to get away from the beach, find somewhere warm and dry. I'm going to die of cold if I stay here.

I grit my teeth and start crawling. My body feels like lead, my head thick and stupid. I look ahead. I need to keep going. Toward the . . . single row of footprints on the sand? Footprints going only one way, far into the distance. If someone's been past here, they might pass by again on the way back.

Darkness laps at the edges of my consciousness. I swat at it as if it's a lazy fly.

Not now. Not yet.

I put out a finger and write in the sand, next to the footprints. Slowly. Clearly. Then I turn on my side, my back, and fall asleep.

Sarah

1

When this whole thing is done, I'm going to hit Adorjan Borsos where it hurts. Where it really, really hurts. If money means that much to him, I'm going to take it all. Every last cent. Car, house, clothes. Everything. And if he doesn't have debt, I'm going to push him so deep into the red a lifetime won't be enough to pay it off. I'm going to blacklist him. Break him, little by little, until he has to stand on the street and beg for a piece of bread.

I turn the music down. Dial the familiar number of the man who taught me to ride a motorbike. My dad has always believed in four wheels. He hates the Suzuki. Thinks it's dangerous. That I'm a reckless driver.

"Uncle Tiny? It's Sarah."

I told him yesterday to take a break from watching my family and asked him instead to begin making me a metal box according to specifications I could only guess. He didn't ask any questions. He knows not to. We understand each other. And I pay well. Everyone knows that.

He says the box will be ready tomorrow. Friday. A day before Ranna and I have to bargain for Alex's life.

I wonder what we should do once we have the box. Deciding what to put in it seems harder than trying to work out what it should look like. Should the contents be heavy or light? If you shake it, should it sound like it contains paper or Krugerrands?

Krugerrands. Hadn't thought of that. Good option.

I look again at the fleur-de-lis logo still flickering on the screen. Trippers Transport. I rub my eyes, gritty from staring at computer screens for hours on end. I glance at the clock, gnawing away at the time. Thursday afternoon. Twelve thirty.

Time to sleep.

What the hell?

Something's making a noise. It's shrill and loud and insistent.

Phone. My phone, the one Ranna gave back to me when she returned from Paternoster.

I open one eye slowly. It's a number I don't know. I grab the bright screen in the dusk of the bedroom. I'm unusually devoted to it these days, desperate for it to be Alex. Or Borsos, saying it's all over, Alex is free.

"Sarah."

It's him, the old man. But his voice is too hard and impatient for it to be good news.

"You're early. It's Thursday."

I come up on my elbow and look at the clock on the bedside table again. Yes, two o'clock, Thursday afternoon.

"You should have the box by now," he says.

"It's harder than you think. It's too long ago. How . . ." I furiously ward off Megabyte, who has just come tumbling in the door.

"I want to see you sooner. I'll call you later tonight with a time and date."

"Wait . . ."

He ends the call.

Ranna's in the doorway. "What is it? Is it Alex?"

"No. It was Borsos. He wants to move up the swap."

Ranna rubs Megs's head as the dog pushes against her legs. She looks worried. "Move it up? Why? What changed?"

I sit upright, pulling the bedding up around my naked body. "He's impatient? I don't know."

She rubs her arms as though she's cold. "We can't. We have nothing to give him. Not even the fake box. Why the hell would he want to move up the exchange?"

I don't answer.

Ranna takes a sharp, worried breath. "Unless . . . what if . . . what if Alex is dead? What if he is scared we'll find out?"

"For fuck's sake. Must you always think the worst?" How did Alex ever fall for this woman? "We're getting the box," I say. "Uncle Tiny's bringing it tomorrow afternoon. He has to make it by hand to be as sturdy as the ones they used in the early 1990s. Then we'll have something we can bargain with. I'm going to put in a mix of Krugerrands and paper money. Adriana has Krugerrands."

"When does he want to make the swap?"

"He didn't say. He said he'd call later. We can push him to make it as late as possible."

"And if that doesn't work? If he insists that it must be done tomorrow?"

"Then we'll have to resort to your Glock. Which should make you very happy."

I open a Coke. The first sip leaves a burning trail down into my stomach. It was bound to happen eventually. I pour the contents of the can down the drain.

"Tea?" comes the laconic question.

Adriana's making food again. Salad this time. Ranna grabbed her camera to go and take photographs at the Union Buildings. Said she couldn't sit here anymore waiting for something to happen.

I told her it was really stupid to be out in public right now, whether she has a new identity or not, but she went anyway. I really can't afford for her to get locked up at this point.

"Sarah? I asked if you wanted some rooibos tea."

I nod, sad at the prospect of a day without caffeine. "That'll be nice, thank you."

I walk to the workstation in my bare feet and start a quick search. No luck. The phone Borsos used to call me is still dead. For an old man who was stuck in prison for a long time, he's pretty sharp when it comes to technology. He must have switched the phone off immediately and taken the SIM card out. He clearly knows that every cell phone is basically a GPS device. The phone isn't his either. It belongs to a woman in Johannesburg. Probably some hapless biddy who hasn't yet figured out that her phone is gone.

What I do know is that he was somewhere in the Northern Cape when he called, but what help is that to me? The Northern Cape is huge, the biggest of all nine provinces by land area. And he would have left the spot he called from ages ago. If he knows to switch the phone off, he'll know to keep moving around.

Adriana puts a cup of tea down next to me, and a salad with nuts and blue cheese.

"Where did you get all this stuff? I didn't have any of this in my pantry."

"The plate or the food?" She wipes her hands on her Guess jeans, looks at me with one raised eyebrow.

Honestly, sometimes she sounds just like my mother. "The food."

"I went to the store earlier. The two of you were still asleep. It's a miracle you haven't died from scurvy yet."

The building's security allows Adriana access everywhere, something I made possible a long time ago.

I demolish the salad and ask for more tea.

Adriana eats while she pages through the newspaper. When I'm done, she comes and stands next to me, holding out a hand for the teacup. I give it to her, but she doesn't move.

She rests a hip against the table and looks at me. She leans down, pushes an errant strand of hair from my face. It's a gentle gesture. Tentative. She looks older today. I think we all do.

"Do you remember when you were in prison? When I came to visit you? That first time?" I wonder where this is going. She smiles. "I told you that you couldn't show any fear. Not in there. And I said that you would be better at surviving than you imagined."

I nod.

"I didn't mean for you to take it to heart for the rest of your life." She rests a hand on the table, searching for something in my eyes. "It's okay to show how you feel now and then. Something other than rage. And it's okay to touch someone again. To touch a man. Not now, I mean. But soon." She smiles. "And give your old mother a hug now and then. I'm sure she could do with one. I could."

I look down at my feet, biting my bottom lip. Reach out my hand to squeeze her arm, but it feels clumsy and wrong. I drop it back down on the keyboard. Fiddle with the escape button. Push the control button.

"It's okay, Sarah. It doesn't have to be now. One day. After this mess. After Alex. That's all." She bends her head toward the elevator, as though Ranna's waiting on the other side, about to come striding in. "Her head and your body play the same game: they pretend you guys don't care. I don't want you to be that way. You have your whole life ahead of you. Don't become her. How long will it be before your body convinces your mind too that nothing matters? That no one really matters?"

I clear my throat. "Okay." Why doesn't my voice sound stronger?

"And try and have a bit of compassion for Ranna. I know it's there. You're allowed to show it. She didn't have your family. Your mother and your father."

"She'd laugh if she heard you."

"I'm sure she would."

Adriana puts her hand on my shoulder. Stares at me until I lock eyes with her. "The other thing, the second thing I said that day in the visitors' center, in prison?"

"That I'm better at surviving than I think I am?"

"Yes. Whatever happens, you'll survive this. We'll make sure of that."

Adriana makes Ranna a salad when she gets back. They sit down on the sofa and go through the photographs Ranna took from the desk in Paternoster, looking for something they may have missed earlier.

Adriana's phone rings and she goes to her room.

I sit at the computer, wishing away the hopelessness of our predicament. What can we do other than wait? Wait, wait, and wait once again. Nothing to do until Borsos calls.

I touch the mouse to wake the screen. The Trippers Transport's website is still open. With nothing better to do, I start working through the tabs on the site: *Contact us. Who are we? What do we own? Company history. Business opportunities.*

Wait.

Back to company history.

I read through all the information again.

Something drifts to the surface of my mind. I grab on to it, before it disappears again, drawn down by stress and a lack of sleep.

Can this be possible?

I shoot forward in my chair. Read. Read again. Slowly. Every syllable.

It is. It really is possible.

Alex

1

The sun's so hot. I feel like my blood is about to boil. My face and my arms are burning on the outside, my lungs are on fire on the inside. There's a deep pain somewhere I can't reach. I spit blood. Salt water. I'm conscious enough to know that I've already done this once before. How long have I been lying here? I blink until my eyes focus.

Now I remember a little better. Adorjan. Ranna.

I've been lying here for quite some time. The waves have almost erased the footprints in the sand. They're still only going in one direction. The words I wrote have almost been washed away entirely. *Phone Ranna.*

Did I write that? I rub it away. That's one way to get her into trouble. And who the hell would understand it anyway? It's too cryptic. I need to get higher. Write again. Write better. My name. Sarah's number. And then I need to move. Walk until I find people. A phone.

I roll onto my side and then onto my back again. Reach for the new shard of pain among all the others I've become accustomed to recently. My fingers locate the wound. My first diagnosis was right. There's a furrow tearing through the skin, and it's not bleeding anymore.

I sit up slowly. Suddenly I'm overwhelmed by the thought of a warm shower. Coffee. Meat. Ranna's body slowly moving beneath mine, her nails digging into my back, her fast breathing in my neck.

Fuck, I'm delirious.

I shake my head gingerly, trying to get rid of the cobwebs without igniting the pain. There's nothing around me. Just long stretches of beach on either side of me. No houses. No signs of life. On the water, not far away, an old fishing boat is anchored in the shallows, but there's no one on board. Behind me there's a low dune. What's beyond that, I have no idea.

It's time to move. Write a message, I tell myself. Bigger this time, away from the waterline. And then go and look for a phone. Water. Food. In that order, if possible.

As I get up, a figure appears on the horizon, about two hundred yards away. Someone walking and looking down, like when people comb the beach for shells.

Great. Maybe they can help me. Maybe they have a cell phone on them.

I get up, gritting my teeth through the pain. Cough. Start waving my arms.

The figure looks up. It's a man. He takes something out of his pocket.

No. He's taking something out of the back of his pants. What can it—

Impossible.

I start running. Stumble. Crawl. Claw my way up the dune. Get to my feet and run inland, away.

It's Adorjan Borsos.

Ranna

1

"Hang on. Wait. Start again. Slowly this time."

I get up off the couch where I've been sitting, flipping through my father's photos, desperate to find something that could help us.

Sarah's standing by the computer. She looks exasperated with me, but honestly, no normal human being would have made sense of the tsunami of words that just gushed out of her.

"Trippers Transport," she says slowly, as though speaking to a child. "The company whose logo was on the bag? The one with the box in it? I couldn't find any connection between the business and the people on the list." She jabs a thumb at the pictures on the wall above her workstation. "So, I went back into the history of the company. And guess what? Your uncle Thinus owned the business at some point in the past. He sold his majority share just after your father's death."

"Thinus? As in Uncle Thinus and Aunt Lena?"

"Yes. Him," she says, nodding her head excitedly.

I think of the photos. Thinus and my father by the fire, arms around each other. Best buddies.

"But what does it mean?" I say, something else occurring to me. "And what about the retired cops we've been chasing? Reyneke and Jansen?"

Her excitement wavers for a second, and a shadow crosses her face. Then she brightens up again. "Forget about them. I think your father robbed your uncle."

"That doesn't make sense. And you can't just forget about them."

I pick the photographs up off the coffee table and walk over to show Sarah the pictures of my father with my uncle.

"They were close friends. Good friends. Look. Isn't it more likely that they worked together?"

Sarah takes a sheet of A4 paper lying by the printer and hands it to me. "Could be. But look here." She points to the second name on a list. "Look who had a thirty percent share in Trippers Transport way back then."

I follow her finger. Grab the paper. Eitan Blomstein. I recognize the name from Sarah's notes. The jeweler whose money almost disappeared in the robbery.

Thinus. My father. Eitan Blomstein. What does it all mean? And how do the policemen fit into all of this?

A theory slowly takes shape in my mind. "What if . . ."

"Yeah?"

"What if my father and Thinus tried to rob Blomstein? They were friends. Maybe Thinus knew about my father's extracurricular activities. Thinus might have given him information on Blomstein's money, revealed how and when he was going to transport the cash. Maybe Thinus even arranged the transport for Blomstein. Was it a Trippers van that was robbed?"

"Nope," says Sarah. "The company never moved cash, but it's a good theory. And Thinus could have recommended the use of a certain company to Blomstein. The security guys traveling with the money were ex-cops. Maybe your dad knew them. Told your uncle to recommend them. Maybe they were all in on it, and your dad betrayed everyone."

Something about the theory is tripping me up, though. "But why leave Blomstein's money and take the box? And who's to say the box belonged to Blomstein?"

"Let's assume it did. It was in a bag with the Trippers Transport logo on it."

"Okay. But that still doesn't explain why my father left the money. R1.5 million was a lot of money back then."

"From what Borsos told us, nobody knew about the lockbox. All the police cared about was the money. That seems to indicate that the money was on the books and on the transport manifest, but the box wasn't. There must have been something illegal in it. Something valuable. Blomstein was a jeweler. It could have been precious stones. Diamonds. Lots of them. Illegal ones. Or it could have been jewelry. Illegal gold that had been turned into jewelry, maybe. I imagine there was lots of smuggling happening from the gold mines in 1993. Probably still is."

I nod eagerly. "You could be right. My father came home with jewelry that night. One box for my mother and one for me. I thought it would be cheap rubbish, because that's what it always was. But what if it wasn't? What if his plan was to give us something of value before he left? What if that lockbox was full of jewelry? Eitan's jewelry."

"So your father gives you and your mom something, keeps the rest for himself, and then disappears?"

"Exactly."

"And Thinus?"

"Maybe my father was meant to meet him somewhere later that night. Or maybe you're right and he was planning a major double cross to screw everyone over."

I consider our theory, warming to it by the minute. "Do you think Thinus is in on Alex's kidnapping?"

Sarah shakes her head. "In the beginning, I considered that Borsos might have a partner, remember? Or that some of the members of the 28s gang were working with him, but after Sasolburg I suspect he works alone. And anyway, didn't Thinus store your father's stuff in his garage for all those years? It might have been in the hope of locating the box. And it didn't seem as if Borsos knew your dad's stuff was at Thinus's house."

The frustration. It's like we're on the edge of finally breaking open the case, but we just can't see where to head next. "Then why . . ."

Sarah dismisses my question with an impatient hand. "The box is the only thing that matters. And what's inside it. We don't have time to work out who's implicated and who isn't. Where's the jewelry your father gave you? Do you still have it?"

I dig in my backpack and take out the teak box, open the secret compartment, and hold out the flat red box to Sarah.

"What's in it?"

"I don't know."

Her hands freeze. "I thought you'd opened it . . ."

She stops talking when she sees my face, notices the black spot—blood—visible on the red fabric. She puts it down as though it's going to bite her.

"It was on the desk when I shot him."

"Ah."

We stare at the red box on the pristine white work surface.

"Open it," she says.

"You do it."

She snorts irritably. "Isn't this some sort of psychological thing? You know . . . looking your demons in the eye. That sort of thing."

I almost laugh nervously, but then, looking at the box, I consider that she may be right. A bit of *boere* voodoo. Why not?

The box is light. As light as I remember.

I open it.

We both gasp, though I suspect neither of us really knows what we're looking at. We do know it is beautiful and that it must be valuable.

"Oh my."

It's Adriana, finished with her phone call.

She pushes between us and takes the box out of my hand. She removes the pendant with the big yellow stone in it and rests it in the palm of her hand, her eyes glittering as she inspects the intricately cut diamond. She holds it up to her throat, above the soft black fabric of her blouse.

"This is at least seventy carats. And I'm guessing it's a yellow diamond. Rare. Very rare. More valuable than most yellow diamonds, I'd say, because the color is so unusual. It's almost daffodil yellow."

"How do you know so much about diamonds?"

"Every woman knows diamonds."

"Not like that."

She folds her hand around the stone. "It is beautiful. And I'd say worth a fortune, and not a small one either."

She holds the pendant out to Sarah but appears unwilling to let it go. "I suggest that you take a picture and see if you can find something similar on the net. Maybe something like this has been stolen in the past. It's an exceptional stone. It's likely to answer many of your questions."

"My mother got earrings that night," I say.

"Same size?" Adriana asks.

"No, quite a lot smaller. But I think they went with this."

"Good heavens," Adriana says.

"Where are they?" Sarah asks, practical as always.

"New York? I don't really know what she did with them."

Sarah looks at me. "If we can give Adorjan the earrings and the pendant, perhaps he'll let Alex go. Maybe he'll forget about the box then. Like Adriana says, they must be worth a fortune."

"If the box was full of jewels like this and Adorjan wants all of it, you won't have a hope in hell," Adriana comments. She points at the pendant. "Especially not if there were more fancy vivid yellow diamonds with no cracks or impurities. I'm not completely on top of the price of diamonds anymore, but my rough guess is that this thing is worth around R40 million. If not more."

2

"I have an appointment."

Adriana's in the doorway of the guest room, wearing sandals, jeans, and a black blouse buttoned down so that just the smallest scrap of delicate lace shows. A silver dragonfly in flight nestles in the hollow of her throat.

"Okay, see you later," says Sarah, her eyes nailed to the computer screen, where she's launched her search for the diamond.

"Okay?" I say, in disbelief, looking from her to Adriana. "Forget about the pendant for a second. It's blinded the both of you. Jaap Reyneke knows where Adriana lives. And he and Jansen probably already know about the restaurant too."

"Adriana knows how to look after herself," Sarah says. "She'll be fine." Yet her eyes dart to her aunt. "You can't go to Crow's. And you know you can stay here until everything's over."

Adriana laughs. "My arsenal is much bigger than both of yours put together. As is my circle of friends, let's call them." She looks teasingly at Sarah. "Much, much bigger."

Her niece waves the remark away and turns back to the screen. "Go out. But sleep here."

"I will." Adriana says this as though she is being generous, guileless, as though she is simply agreeing to do what Sarah says in order to keep her happy. "See you later."

At the elevator she turns back to us. "I'll be back later today. Don't do anything stupid."

Sarah bangs repeatedly at the enter button. "Stupid just about sums up every single thing we've done so far."

"Everything you've done," I say with emphasis.

Adriana checks her mascara in the steel reflection of the elevator doors. Sighs. "Let me rephrase: Don't kill each other while I'm gone. Because that would be really stupid."

She turns, waves, and disappears through the elevator doors.

Sarah grumbles, walks to the fridge, and takes out a Coke without offering me one.

I sit down at the kitchen counter and take a closer look at the pendant. I hold the diamond between my thumb and forefinger, watching as it bends and breaks the light streaming in through the windows.

"What if this is not from the box? What if my father bought these gifts legally?"

The Coke pops open. "Is that really what you think?"

"No." I probably just wanted to hear what she thought.

She drinks from the can, pulls a face as if she's hurting somewhere. "Did you really never suspect what your father was up to?"

"No. I didn't want to know anything about him. I just wanted to get out alive."

"And your mom?"

"She might have suspected something, but she's never mentioned anything."

Maybe my mother's goals were the same as mine. Survival.

Sarah rolls the can between her palms. When she speaks finally, it's in a slow, cautious tone—her I'm-about-to-ask-you-a-shitty-favor voice.

"Do you think you could get your mother to bring the earrings here? Maybe, if she knows what happened, about Alex, your father . . . maybe she'd be willing to give them to us."

I look at my watch. I've thought about it too. It's quarter to five on Thursday afternoon. My mother is supposed to be flying to South Africa this weekend. I could call and ask her to bring the earrings, but the thing is, Borsos wants us to meet soon and she won't be here yet.

"I suppose I could, but not even a courier would arrive here in time."

"We could always promise them to Borsos."

"I'll call and ask," I say.

What I don't say is that I have to call her anyway. She and Moshe can't come to South Africa. I can't see this mess ending well.

3

“Are you all packed?” I ask.

“Yes, but it’s hard. Moshe says I’m only allowed three pairs of shoes.” Karla Abramson’s voice is a little breathless, excited. Then her tone changes, as though she suspects something’s up. “Is everything all right?”

I use the gap she’s given me. “Not really. I think we may have to postpone our visit.”

“Why?”

“I’m struggling . . . Things are . . .”

“What’s wrong?”

“I’m sorry. Things have really gone sideways here.”

“I’m coming anyway,” she says stubbornly. “So is Moshe. Even if I only end up seeing Lena and Thinus.”

“Why not wait awhile, just a few weeks, until I’m free to see you too?” I don’t want her near her sister and her brother-in-law right now, not until I understand how Thinus fitted into my father’s life.

“The plane tickets were expensive. And you asked us to come,” she says accusingly.

“Please, Ma. I’m serious.”

“No. We’re coming. And it would be really wonderful if I could see you too.” Her voice softens. “Please, Isabel. Don’t do this to me.”

“Is it going to help to argue with you?”

She keeps quiet.

"Okay, then," I agree, sighing. "I'll make a plan."

I can almost see her relieved smile through the phone.

If she insists on coming to South Africa, she may as well help. And be here for my funeral. "Those earrings Pa gave you, that night when he . . . you know. Do you still have them?"

The silence that meets the question is shocked. This must be the last thing she expected me to ask.

"What on earth do you want to know about the earrings?"

"Will you trust me if I ask you to bring them with you?"

"That rubbish? I don't even know why I kept them. What on earth do you want them for? I've never worn them again since that night."

"Please?"

"I'm not even going to ask you what's going on." Her voice has hardened into something flat and cold.

"How did he give them to you that night?" I'm suddenly thinking aloud, wondering what she remembers about her birthday so many years ago.

"What do you mean how did he give them to me?"

"Were they in a metal box? Was the metal box in a white bag, by any chance?"

"You've mentioned a metal box before. I don't remember one. But he did take them out of a bag. A white bag, like the bank bags we used years ago. And it's possible there may have been a box inside the bag."

My heart beats faster. Something concrete, finally.

"Was there anything else in the box? Or in the bag?"

"I really can't remember. More jewelry? Something he wanted to give you, I think." She sighs. "I'll give it some thought. I tried . . . Your father didn't like it when I asked him anything. Said I was being nosy. It made him furious."

"Did you ever wonder about them? About the earrings? Where he got them?"

"He was always bringing stuff home. Strange things. Mostly cheap. I just lost interest eventually."

It's quiet for a while before she asks again: "What's going on, Isabel?"

"I can't tell you, not yet."

"You can tell me on Sunday, when I see you."

When I say nothing, she asks, "Am I seeing you this weekend?" There's a gentle stubbornness in her tone.

"I'll do my best," I offer. "I'll . . . You'll be careful, won't you? Your arrival might draw attention. I'll text you a number from a phone—a friend's phone—that you can use to contact me when you're here."

"Promise? I haven't had a way of contacting you in years."

"Promise. In fact, I'll do it straightaway."

Alex

1

Nothing. No people, no cars, no houses. No one to help me.

My feet get heavier with every step, pushing through, rather than stepping on, the thick sand. Like that injured lion I once, long ago, wrote a story about. My fourth article, when I was still a rookie reporter. We followed the wounded animal into the bushveld for three days as he left a trail of destruction going for easy kills on farmsteads and in small rural villages. It was out near Polokwane. I watched him die. Some jackass hunter had injured him instead of killing him with a clean shot.

I lost Adorjan a while back. I move faster than he does, but I wonder how long that will last. The bullet might only have glanced off me, but the wound has begun to bleed again. And the stabbing pain in my chest is getting worse. It's like I've swallowed a piece of glass.

If I don't get help soon, if Adorjan's gone to fetch the car and decides to track me with the off-roader, I'm going to be a sitting duck. If . . .

I lick my rough lips with a dry tongue and add another thing to the list of potential threats: if I don't get water soon.

I keep walking with the sea on my right. The sun is warmer than it should be. It's September, but it feels like December.

If this was Namaqualand, as I first thought, then there'd still be flowers around. I look right. I see none of the veld flowers the district is so well known for. Just sand and patches of stony ground. Bushes. Small shrubs.

Where's the road? Any road?

I focus on my feet, willing them to keep moving. One step.

Another one.

Another.

I start humming. A silly little song from my childhood about sleep and the tiny man who delivers it. One my mother used to sing to me as we sat in my bedroom, with its blue blanket and green curtains.

I cough. Look at the blood on my hand. Wipe it on my filthy jeans. I want to sit and rest awhile. I need to rest. To sleep.

No.

Focus, I tell myself.

If you sleep now, you die, Alex Derksen. And you fucking well know it.

Sarah

1

My phone rings just after seven. The call is from an unknown number. Must be Borsos.

I answer and put it on speaker. Ranna comes to stand beside me at the workbench.

"Tomorrow afternoon," the old man says. "Friday. Three o'clock. Lambert's Bay, up north on the West Coast. There's a yellow house at the end of the beach. South. Out of town, on its own. Easy to find. I'll see you and Isabel there. No cops."

"Is Alex okay?" Ranna asks before I can.

"Three o'clock. Tomorrow."

"That's too little time," I say, trying to keep him on the line so that I can track the call. "What happened to doing this on Saturday?"

"It's Thursday evening. It's enough time. And if you're not there, Alex dies."

He ends the call.

I look at the computer. Work in silence for a few minutes. The phone he used belongs to someone with an address in Cape Town. A sixty-seven-year-old man. Probably stolen or borrowed. And dead as a doornail now.

Ranna looks at me hopefully.

I shake my head. "Nothing."

"Fuck it. Fuck, fuck, fuck!"

"What now?" I ask.

"We go. We take what we have, and we go to Lambert's Bay."

"And the box Uncle Tiny is making?"

"There's no time. We can't leave here tomorrow, it's too far," Ranna says.

"We could fly," I suggest. "We'll get tickets. Then we can rent a car down there."

"Too risky that things could go sideways. And we'll only be able to fly tomorrow morning. That's two hours in the air. Plus three hours of driving. And what if the plane gets delayed? I'd like to get there early and check things out a little. See if there's a chance we can find Alex before three o'clock. At least we now have a place to go looking for him."

I don't think it's going to be that easy. "Borsos is not going to sit around in Lambert's Bay waiting for us. He's smarter than that. He uses a different phone every time he calls, and he calls from a different place each time. He's in the Western or Northern Cape, and that's about all we know for sure right now. I don't think he's going to be at that yellow house before exactly three. My guess is it's an empty vacation home."

"Okay," she concedes. "You're probably right. But everyone makes mistakes, and he must be tired by now. It's hard work guarding someone."

"Is that why you think he's moved up the schedule?"

"I don't know what happened to rush him like this."

"Well, something happened," I insist.

Ranna looks at me, something akin to hope on her face. "Maybe Alex escaped. Maybe the old man is scared Alex will get to us or the cops before we do the swap."

I don't want to ask the question, but someone has to. "If that's the case, why hasn't Alex popped up somewhere, then? What if you were right earlier? What if he's dead? What if he died, Ranna?"

Ranna puts her hands on her hips, shakes her head vigorously. "Nope. You said we're not going there, so we're not. My money is on Alex. He's tough as nails. He can outlast almost anyone."

I take a cigarette out of the pack and fiddle with it while I think. "Will the pendant alone satisfy Borsos?"

Ranna sits down on the chair next to mine. Gestures at the computer. "Have you been able to trace the diamond?"

"Not this specific one. But in 2011, a yellow diamond that was 110 carats was sold for $12.3 million. It came from South Africa. It was described exactly the way Adriana described it: fancy vivid yellow. So her ballpark price for the diamond is probably on the low side. I can't find anything on your specific pendant or the diamond. It was never recorded as stolen or missing. Clean, in other words. Same with the earrings, as far as I can see."

"The pendant will just have to be enough for Borsos. It's a lot of money. And we can promise him the earrings as soon as my mom delivers them." Ranna gets up and walks to her backpack. She starts throwing clothes into it as if she's in a hurry to leave. She looks up suddenly. "Why would my father give me something like that? Something that big?"

Why is she asking me? "Maybe he was sorry about everything he'd done."

She scoffs bitterly. "Maybe. Or maybe the other stuff in the box was just worth so much more."

She closes the backpack and throws it over her shoulder.

"Hang on," I say, when I realize she's ready to hit the road. "I have to phone Uncle Tiny to look after the dogs and then see if Daniel can take care of the garden. And maybe we can get Adriana to help us? Maybe she can come with."

"I'm game."

I call her number, but she doesn't pick up.

Ranna looks at me expectantly.

I shake my head. "No answer."

"We can't wait."

"I know."

I leave a message, telling Adriana where we're going.

It's probably best this way. I don't really want to put anyone else in the firing line.

Ranna looks at me with a wry smile. "Just the two of us, then."

"Yes. She's probably busy on the restaurant floor." I stand up. Stretch my back. "Let me quickly shower and grab something to eat before we go. And make those other calls."

Ranna puts the bag down reluctantly. "Why get this uncle of yours to look after the dogs? Why don't you ask your mother to pop in every day and feed them?"

"When I got out of prison, my mother forbade me from ever using a computer again."

"So, she doesn't know about this place?"

"No. I have a house in Faerie Glen. Suburban bliss."

"Faerie Glen? Fancy Pretoria East?" She laughs.

"Don't judge."

While I call Daniel, Ranna puts on the kettle and starts making sandwiches.

Three minutes later, the intercom buzzes. Daniel is at the gate. I open it and send the elevator down.

Ranna quickly walks to the coffee table and hides the Glock in her backpack. Back in the kitchen she starts eating her sandwich as she pours milk into her coffee. She chews slowly and deliberately, as though she doesn't want to eat, but knows she must.

I look at her photographer hands with their prominent veins. The grim anticipation of loss around her mouth. All of it disappeared, briefly, on Monday morning when she saw Alex.

I should have trusted her more.

I *should* trust her more. She'd do anything for Alex. And there is no way this meeting with Borsos will be a straightforward swap. I can't imagine he would want to leave any witnesses alive.

I push the thought aside. It's too late now. If I'd wanted to trust her, I should have started doing so in Mumbai. And I can't help wondering whether she isn't going to shoot me as soon as Alex is safe. Anything is possible with this woman.

Daniel pushes his thick black-framed glasses up his nose and glances at Ranna surreptitiously. She's standing at the elevator, impatient to get going.

I hand him the keys he needs and give the dogs each a good head rub.

"How did you get that tall?" Daniel asks with a frown.

Ranna doesn't budge, just carries on staring out in front of her, rocking back and forth on her heels.

"Ranna," I say, calling her back into the room. "Your question. Definitely not aimed at me."

"Excuse me?"

"Daniel wants to know . . ."

"How did you get that tall?" he asks again, always ready to do his own talking.

Ranna smiles, a bit sourly. "Unfortunately, I think it's in your genes."

That's not the answer Daniel hoped for. He sighs dramatically, pushing his glasses up again. Looks at me. "So, you don't think Jungle Oats will do it?"

"Is that what your mother says?" I ask him, adjusting his collar, which is sticking up on one side.

"Yes. And I hate oats. I'd eat them if I knew it was going to help. Everyone in my class is taller than I am."

"Maybe your mom's right." I have to try and stay on her good side. "What you eat does make a difference. Healthy food makes you grow properly."

"Hmph." He puts the keys I handed him in his pocket and holds out his hand. "You owe me a hundred bucks. I got ninety-six percent on a math test."

I fetch the money from my backpack. "Well done."

"Have you stopped smoking yet?"

Ranna laughs.

I shoot her a venomous look. "No."

He smiles. "So, I don't owe you anything yet."

"No. But one day you will. Soon."

While we get into the elevator, I explain to Daniel that Adriana's going to sleep here, and that she will keep strange hours. I didn't want to tie her down to being here at Megabyte's mealtimes.

In the parking garage I walk straight to the Audi. Speed and safety. That's what counts right now.

I put the radio on as we pull away. Then turn it off again. People making meaningless remarks about meaningless events. The weather. Politics. I switch to music, downloaded from Adriana's collection. Muddy Waters.

At a red light on the way out of town, I surprise both of us.

"I know . . . ," I blurt out suddenly.

"Know what?"

"I know you and Alex . . . I know. I've known from the beginning. The way he spoke about you. Everything."

She looks at me, but I can't read anything on her face. "Then you know more than I do."

"What do you mean?"

I move along with the stream of cars and turn right at the next street, just to have to jam on the brakes. The traffic's moving like cold syrup, though it's dark already. My right foot is itching. Lambert's Bay is a fourteen-, fifteen-hour drive.

"To love someone is one thing," Ranna says. "Living with them is something else altogether. It's not always the same mechanism. Sturm und Drang and brilliant sex and then what? Routine, work, movies, and watching sports on TV?"

"What do you mean? You can't . . ." For goodness' sake. She's not going to run away again, is she?

"I'm a serial killer, Sarah. How do you think this story's going to end? It's not exactly fairy-tale material."

The traffic thins out slowly, and finally we're on the highway, the open road ahead of us. I put the car into sixth gear. I've never been fond of automatics. The speedometer climbs steadily.

"So what are you going to do after we get Alex?"

"If we get him," she corrects me. "I don't know." She sounds tired. "I don't know anything anymore."

2

The road through the Free State is quiet and boring. On the long straightaways, where I can see miles into the distance, I swing the Audi to the left, then to the right. I open the window. The air is fresh and cool, like someone just cut the grass along the shoulder. The spring rains were on time this year in this part of the world.

I blink to fight off the tiredness that threatens to overwhelm me. These past few days have been trying. They've felt like weeks. Ranna has no idea what it was like, the uncertainty that gnawed at me until I found her. The constant fear.

What a ghastly word. *Fear.*

There are few people I'm close to because there are few people I trust. Alex is one of the few. If I had to lose him . . .

Before Alex, it felt like no one saw me. Really saw me. They saw my face and my body. They might have been able to imagine me in bed. I learned that early enough: I was fifteen.

Other people saw my work, what I could do with a computer. Saw how they could exploit me. Seventeen.

Then I finally made a friend. A real friend, who never wanted more than friendship, although I did. Eighteen.

Perhaps I should be grateful that I learned all these lessons early. Other people never learn, according to Adriana.

I close the window and turn Natasha Meister louder. The red numbers on the clock read 10:28 p.m.

How long to Lambert's Bay?

Hours later, somewhere in the Karoo, I stop. I'm so tired, I can hardly keep my eyes open anymore. Ranna needs to take over the driving duties for a while.

Outside the car is a different world. The air is cold, the sky a bright blanket of jewels. The plains on either side of us are so spacious and empty, you can almost hear the earth breathing, content with the lack of people.

I walk around the car and listen to the near silence. I could live here. I could live with the breeze that stirs the sparse, dry vegetation now and again, the far-off bleating of sheep. With the sound of a windmill's rusty wheeze as it pumps water into a farm dam.

No voices. No people. Bliss.

Ranna is still in the Audi. I expected her to ask for the keys and walk to the driver's side. She seems to be fishing for something under the passenger seat. She leans over and flicks on the headlights, diffusing the dark around us, and gets out.

"Here."

I stare at the matte-black metal she's holding out toward me. It's the .38 revolver. She's got the Glock in her left hand. It looks so comfortable there, just as it did back in Mumbai.

"I'll take it later. When we get there."

Ranna shakes her head. "No. Now."

I take the weapon from her.

She points at the road unfurling like a gray ribbon ahead of us in the high beams of the Audi. Her eyes move from the windmill to a weather-beaten sign about thirty yards ahead of us that reads *Calvinia 140*. She points at the sign. "Aim for the word."

"I told you I can shoot. It's just not my favorite thing to do. Someone always gets hurt."

"I need to know how well you can shoot. Otherwise I'm going to be worried about you the whole time. And about myself. I don't want to be shot. Not by you, in any case. And Alex would never forgive me if something happened to you."

The wind rears up again, blowing dust into the air. Then, bored, it drops it and moves down the road. When I bite my bottom lip, there's fine Karoo sand on it. Ranna could be right. This is no longer a fight for computers and fancy algorithms. It's about these things now—weapons. Things that kill.

I look at the gun in my hand. "Right. Okay, then."

Ranna tucks her hair behind her ears. She stands beside me and lifts the Glock to shoulder height, ready to shoot. She turns her head around quickly, surveying the quiet landscape around us.

"Ready?" she asks.

It's dark, but I can hear the adrenaline in her voice. The life. The lack of fear. That wretched thing that I suspect Alex is so fatally attracted to. Even worse: I've begun to understand it, though I don't want to, or can't, explain it.

I cock the gun. The sound is not nearly as dramatic and loud as in the movies. I look around me. I know the night, know how far sound travels.

"Someone's going to hear the shots," I warn her.

Ranna laughs, nods. "Yes. Probably. But we'll be long gone before they get here. Five shots each. That's how many bullets the Taurus holds. Remember that. You can reload in the car."

I look from her to the road sign. Ranna drops the Glock to her side, points with her right hand. "Aim for the *C*."

I hesitate.

"Imagine it's my face," she says.

The first shot hits to the right of the *C*, nearer the *l* on the other side of the *a*.

The sound is deafening. Ranna rolls her eyes when I look at her. I blow my breath out and take the second shot. Looks like I hit the *a*.

"Yes!"

This feels so good after the tension of the last few days. Finally. A straight answer. No matter how brutal.

I shift, redistributing my weight. The third shot is just outside the *C*, but the fourth and fifth land neatly in the heart of the capital letter.

Ranna nods. She looks around one more time to make sure there are no cars, people, or animals nearby. She pulls the trigger five times. As the sound rolls away over the veld, she doesn't even look at the board. She holds out her hand for the car keys.

I give them to her. But I'm curious, even if she's not. I jog over to the sign.

Every one of her shots is through the last, small *a* of *Calvinia*. It looks like it's been attacked by a swarm of angry bees.

We stop at a Total gas station in Calvinia and buy coffee, Coke, and ham-and-cheese sandwiches. I'm not at all hungry, but I know I need to eat. The Coke is a joy, though. I lean my back against the hood and breathe in the smoke from my cigarette, feeling the nicotine drop into my system like a silver coin.

I try not to smoke in the car. Because of Ranna. Her disapproval is almost tangible, just like my mother's.

She's on the other side of the car now, at the driver's door, coffee in hand, watching the small rural town waking up. I wonder what she did in India, why she's such a brilliant shot. Or is this an old skill of hers? She did, after all, start at the age of eleven.

A new cigarette. A second Coke.

A truck groans by, then a pickup with a double bed strapped on to the back. Across the road, a butcher shop opens its doors.

Ranna clears her throat. I look over my shoulder. Her hands, around the to-go cup, are resting on the roof of the car.

"Why Alex?" she asks.

Fuck. I turn back, pull on the cigarette. "What do you mean?"

She laughs, as though she knows I'm playing dumb. "Why Alex?"

"I don't know."

"Really?"

It's not a question, it's sarcasm. What I really, really like about computers is that they are never sarcastic.

I look at her again. She's gazing at me with unreadable eyes. I still can't figure out what goes on inside her head.

"I wouldn't have said Alex was your type," she says. "The only thing he uses a computer for is to type up his articles. Google searches. Send mail."

"So, I am nothing more than a computer junkie?"

"That's not what I said. Tell me what you like. What makes you like a certain type of man. What makes you like Alex?"

I turn my back on her again. Flick the ash off the cigarette. "Sex or love?"

"Start with sex."

"Sweat."

"Sweat?"

"Yep. Run-jump-ride-fix-things-dust-mud sweat."

"Ah. All those macho boere things."

"Maybe. But I don't expect the guy to speak Afrikaans."

"Love?"

I blow the smoke out slowly and drop the cigarette, killing it with my boot. "I don't know. I know that what wakes up my body doesn't necessarily entertain my brain. According to Adriana, that's my problem. I like a sharp mind. Someone who makes an effort. Who looks to see beyond the obvious."

"Was Alex the first . . . brain one?"

Would she have wanted to know if he was the body one?

"Yes. He saw. He looks in order to see. You know that." Another Marlboro. To keep my hands busy.

"You?" I ask, before she asks another uncomfortable question. "Sex and love?"

"Sex and love are the same thing for me, but that's only now that I'm older. Straight-talking, honest, decent men. And they can't be afraid, of me or of the world's chaos. And if he knows how to make his own rules and stick to them, I'm pretty much sold. It means he thinks for himself. Rare."

"Alex?"

"Alex."

An old Golf with Gauteng plates drones by. A young man in a yellow T-shirt leans out and whistles at me and Ranna, makes a crude gesture with his hand. His friends in the back seat cackle.

Ranna finishes her coffee. "I thought you and Alex would . . . you know, while I was gone." She stumbles on: "I . . . I thought it would be a good thing. If it happened."

Really? I keep my eyes on the colorful clothing shop next to the butcher's. Must be Chinese. No one else seems to be into manufacturing these days.

"But then you came back," I say.

"You brought me back."

"It wouldn't have made a difference," I say. "Nothing would have. Yes, Alex might have gotten married eventually. Maybe even have had children. Messed around. Who knows? But he would never have loved like that again."

"How do you know that? You can replace anything. Anyone."

I flick the half-smoked cigarette away. It's time to get going.

"Because that's what he told me."

3

Just outside Calvinia, my phone rings. I look at the number. It's the bug in Stefan Jansen's house.

There are two voices, so it can't be a phone call. It's someone who came knocking on his front door at the rather impolite hour of nine o'clock in the morning.

I've missed the first part of the conversation.

"He asked us to let you know," says the unknown voice. "Apparently, he has no other family."

"He has a son in Australia. And a sister on a farm in the Cape somewhere," Jansen says. He sounds tired and upset. "How did it happen?"

"He was robbed."

"In the early morning, outside his home?" His voice is brimming with anger.

"Yes."

"How serious is it?"

"He was conscious when they put him in the ambulance. He asked the paramedics to contact you. That's why I'm here. He's in the ICU now."

Adriana. Whatever this is, it's Adriana. I'm sure they're talking about Jaap Reyneke. As far as I recall, he has a son in Sydney.

I look over at Ranna to see how much of the conversation she can hear. None of it, it seems. Her hands are clamped on the steering wheel, her eyes pinned to the road.

The guilt gnaws at my insides. I led Adriana onto this path. Brought Reyneke and Jansen straight to her door with information that now seems to have been irrelevant.

Or not. Why did the retired cops keep tabs on Borsos all these years? Where does Jansen get his money? There's something we're not seeing, some connection we're not spotting.

The men walk out of earshot of the listening device. A few minutes later they return to the front door.

"Thank you for driving here to deliver the message, Constable," says Jansen. "I appreciate it. I'll let his son know." A door opens with a creak. "How's he looking? Did you see him?"

"No. But the doctors say the next day or two are critical. They're trying to establish whether there's any brain damage. Whoever attacked him is very strong. And angry."

"It seems to me everyone's angry these days."

Jansen says goodbye to his guest. "Thank you again, Constable. I appreciate your effort." Footsteps, a closing door, and then the lonely, fading sound of a walking stick on tiles, followed by silence.

I put the phone down. Try to gather my thoughts. Realize I'm tapping my fingers like crazy on my legs, like I tend to do when I crave a cigarette.

"Bad news?" Ranna glances my way. "You okay?"

I avoid her eyes. "Mm-hmm."

"Who was it on the phone? You didn't say anything. Was it the bug in Jansen's house?"

She's pretty alert for someone who's been awake most of the night. "Yeah. Reyneke's in the hospital."

"Shit." Her hands grip the steering wheel. "Adriana?"

"Probably."

"So what do we do now?"

"What do you mean?"

"Are we just going to leave it there?"

"What do you want us to do?" I ask.

"Tell Adriana to back off until we know what's going on. Before she goes after Jansen too."

"Okay," I agree. "We can do that."

Ranna grumbles something unintelligible.

I take out my phone, start typing a message. Push send. "Done. Happy?"

"No."

"Look, we really don't know what's going on," I say, trying to protect Adriana. "We suspect Borsos is working on his own, but what if he isn't? What if they are all knee-deep in this mess? Reyneke, Jansen, Thinus, and Borsos—all of them?"

She doesn't look at me.

"If it will make you happy, I can ask someone to trace Jansen's money. I looked, but it would have taken a shitload of time and it wouldn't have helped us find the box, so I didn't spend too many hours on it. All I saw was a number of companies and trusts with strange addresses that own many of his assets. I could probably also try and find out where Reyneke's hiding his money, if he has any. Will that make you feel better?" I do my best to sound reasonable.

"Do that," she says. "Please. Just so we know."

I wonder if she's ever said *please* to me.

"As long as you know that it's not going to make any difference in terms of Alex's situation. None at all. It's way too late for that," I remind her, then relent. "But I'll do it."

I pick my phone up, call Saul Nyati again. It's going to cost me a small fortune, but if it will buy Ranna some peace of mind, it'll be worth it. And to be honest, I wouldn't mind knowing myself.

The sun is quite high in the sky when my phone beeps me awake. It startles me out of a sleep that's left me stiff and sore from my crumpled position in the passenger seat.

I dreamed about Alex. Alex, who used to call me after our interviews to hear whether I was okay with the articles. Whether there was anything he could do for my parents.

Decent Alex.

Ranna's Alex.

I look at the phone. There are two messages from Adriana. One promises to leave Jansen alone if he leaves her alone. She doesn't admit to attacking Reyneke. The other sounds pissed because we left Pretoria without her.

I try to placate her with an apology. As I put the phone away, it starts to ring. The number on the screen is too long to be a local one. And it looks slightly familiar. This can only mean one thing. "I think it's for you."

Ranna frowns at me.

"Phone?" I say, holding it out to her.

She takes it from me, answers.

"Hello?" Then: "Ma?" She's quiet for a while, listening. First, she looks worried, then her entire body stiffens.

"Really?" She looks at me, excitement sparking in her eyes. "Are you sure? . . . Thank you!"

She ends the call and passes the phone to me. "We have to go to Paternoster. I know what was in the lockbox and where to find it. My mother . . . She saw something that night."

"Paternoster?" I look at my watch. "It's ten o'clock. And we're almost in Lambert's Bay."

"Aren't you listening? I know what was in the box. We can find it and give it to Borsos."

After so many days of searching, the words almost sound impossible. "Really? Are you sure?"

"I'm telling you. I know."

I calculate how much time we'll need to make it to Lambert's Bay to do the swap with Borsos. "We're going to have to hurry. And we still need to work out how we're all going to walk away from this thing alive."

"Don't you worry. We'll make sure we're on time."

ALEX

1

I look at the white house with the green roof slowly coming into focus. The clouds gathering behind it hold a real promise of rain. Then I look at the train crawling past me on the right, a long red-brown caterpillar edging toward the simmering horizon.

It's the iron-ore train traveling to the Saldanha harbor. The same train that mangled Tom Masterson's body last year.

At least I know where I am now. Northern Cape, by the looks of it.

I glance at the solitary house again. The train's last cars slowly pulling past me. The house.

My lips are cracked and bloody. I lick them, try to spread a little of the spit that's still left inside my mouth. I look longingly toward the sea, which I can hear but not see, hushing on the other side of a dune. Any water would be nice now. Even seawater.

But that would probably be a mistake, I think. It's a bit hard to get anything useful out of my brain at the moment.

As the house solidifies into more than just a vague outline on the horizon, I start to move faster. There has to be a phone. There must be. Even if there are no people around, a phone means I can call. I can call Ranna and Sarah and ask them to come and fetch me. Not that I know where I am. Somewhere on the West Coast, and it can be a big, empty place when you don't know it.

If there's a cell phone in the house, Sarah can find me via GPS. She's done it before. Done it for me before.

From somewhere I draw the strength to jog. To ignore the pain.

I can't see anything suspicious as I draw nearer. No green Nissan Sani. No Adorjan. No one moving around or inside the house.

The place looks old and in desperate need of TLC. The rusted zinc roof needs a new coat of paint. So do the flaking green window frames. Someone—maybe a husband for a wife—tried to make a garden a long time ago, something to look at from the kitchen window while you do the dishes. All that remains are three or four dried-up shrubs in a dusty flower bed surrounded by Cape marigolds that have probably sprung up on their own.

There's no fence around the square house. I approach slowly and, with my back to a wall, shuffle to a window to check inside. There's no car around, but someone clearly still lives here. There's a teacup next to a sagging, grimy cream-colored sofa. The *Sunday Times* is open on the coffee table to a page with a large photograph of former president Nelson Mandela.

I hold my rasping breath. Listen. Still no movement from inside the house. No dogs barking from the back.

I weigh my options. I'm dressed like a hobo, and I certainly smell like one. I have no doubt I'll be mistaken for a burglar if anyone sets eyes on me, and I don't want to be shot for trespassing.

No. There will be no calling out for help. Besides, Adorjan Borsos has surprised me once too often for me to just walk into the house.

I move to the next window. It's the kitchen. The back door is open. A sweat-stained baseball cap hangs over a dish towel on a hook. And—fuck, yeah!—there's a cell phone next to the sink.

I take a deep breath and try to muster my thoughts. I can't carry on walking. I need water. And I need that phone.

I sneak to the open kitchen door. Step inside. The house smells dank and moldy, as though it's been closed up for a long time. I walk in and grab the phone off the Formica countertop. Turn to a yellowing fridge in the corner and open it. There's an almost-empty gallon of milk in the door, and an apple on one of the shelves next to a pack of hot dogs and a Lunch Bar chocolate.

I finish the milk, push the apple into my pants pocket, and fill the milk bottle up with water at the tap. While I'm doing that, I call Sarah's number. She made me memorize it once. Said she didn't want to be a contact on my phone.

The call goes through, but she's on another call.

No, wait. The number on the screen isn't right . . . I've dialed the wrong number. I sift through the fog in my brain. Drink water from the bottle. The lukewarm, brackish liquid tastes like the best beer I've ever had. I open the packet of hot dogs and start eating.

Sit down at the rickety kitchen table. More water. I dial again, this time swapping the last two numbers.

It rings again, but a man answers. Fuck.

I look around me. I need to go. I'll take the phone with me and keep trying as I move. I'm not far off, I know that. Just got to remember those last two digits.

Go.

I will my legs to move, to stand up, but they refuse.

That sofa in the living room looks so welcoming. And if there's a bed . . .

Forget it, Alex. Move.

I stand up, turn on my heels, and grab the baseball cap off the hook. It might help against the sun. I call the number again. The first three numbers are 083, not 082. That's the mistake I was making.

The phone rings. Thank goodness.

Sarah answers just as Adorjan Borsos appears in the doorway, binoculars in one hand, Beretta in the other. He smiles, proud to have been able to shepherd me home.

"I see you found my house. Well done."

Ranna

1

I could scream. I look at the white double-cab pickup in the driveway at Thinus and Lena's house. I can't believe it. They're home for the weekend, probably preparing for my mom's visit.

Should have thought of that. Should have known my luck always runs out.

Sarah and I park the Audi around the corner from the beach house while we come up with a plan.

"What are we going to do?" Sarah asks impatiently. "We don't have time to sit around like this."

She's tapping her thighs with quick, irritable fingers. Possibly something she does when she needs to smoke. It's driving me insane.

Her phone rings. She looks at the screen, frowns sharply, and answers. She says hello again and listens, but then disconnects. "Must be a wrong number."

We look at the house.

"We go and knock on the door," I offer.

She looks at her watch and mumbles something. We both know exactly what the time is: 11:16 a.m. And once we have what we need, it's another two hours to Lambert's Bay. Time is being stretched so thin it's almost transparent.

"What if they call the police?" she asks. "What if Thinus knocks you over the head?"

"Then you shoot him."

She grimaces. "I'll go and knock if you want me to. They don't know me. I can spin some story, get inside."

"No. It's not safe for you to go in alone. Thinus might be sick, but he could still be dangerous." I lean down and retrieve the Glock from under Sarah's seat and hand her the revolver. "Let's hope he doesn't call the police the minute he sees me. Let's cross our fingers for a bit of family loyalty. Possibly some fear too. I am the Black Widow, after all."

"Isn't he going to be suspicious if we suddenly appear out of nowhere and knock on his front door?" Sarah holds the revolver like a piece of rock she discovered in her garden. "And why on earth would we want to dig through your father's things? He's going to know something's up. Something big."

I unclip the seat belt.

"We could sit here going through the ifs and buts all day, but time's running out. My suggestion is that we go and knock. Ask if we can look for photographs among my dad's stuff. She knows by now that my mother is coming to visit. I'll say I want to surprise her with a photo album she can take back to New York."

I open my door before Sarah can argue again. "You can sit with them and make small talk while I look. Make sure they don't call the police. And keep the Audi's keys ready. If something happens to me, go. Try and get Alex back with what we've got."

She hesitates.

"What now?" I ask.

"I tried to leave you behind once before. In Sasolburg."

"I would have been fine," I lie.

"Sorry."

The word doesn't bring nearly as much pleasure as I thought it would.

"Don't say sorry now. It makes me think something's going to happen."

I tuck the Glock into the back of my Levi's, making sure my shirt covers the weapon. I take off my sunglasses and hook them into the front of my shirt. The wind sweeps through my hair. Storm clouds have gathered out over the ocean and they're heading straight toward us.

I look at Sarah, giving her a gentle nod. It's go time.

The woman who opens the door looks like my mother. Or rather, the way I remember my mother from when I was a child. Long blonde hair, stubborn chin. Hazel eyes.

Lena is the younger of the sisters. How old does that make her—late fifties? Sixty? She's still tall, though her shoulders are struggling to retain their earlier grace.

She's had work done on her face. The lines on her forehead and around her eyes have been smoothed to a sterile landscape. Same with her mouth, which seems to struggle to produce a tight smile. But her hand, thick and ropy with arthritis, betrays her age as it flies to her mouth and then flutters down to her chest to fidget uncomfortably with the sea-green scarf around her neck, showing off perfectly manicured red fingernails.

"Isabel! Goodness. Hello."

"Hi, Aunt Lena."

She looks me up and down. Takes in the jeans, the loose white shirt, the silver bangles. I turn my face into the breeze and try to smile, careful not to make any sudden moves.

"Please don't be afraid," I say, my hands in the air.

Sarah inches forward a little to stand beside me.

Lena takes a step back.

"This is Sarah," I say, trying to sound as reassuring as I can.

Lena nods, still dazed. She knits her fingers together, starts fiddling with her wedding band.

Then something like relief appears on her face. Happiness, even. "So, this is why Karla's coming to visit!"

I let my breath out quietly. "And to see you. She misses you." I look past Lena into the house to see whether I can spot Thinus.

"Please don't be afraid," I try again. "The newspapers . . . It's not true . . . really . . ."

She shakes her head. "Don't worry. I've never believed the newspapers. I've known you since you were born. I'm your godmother, for goodness' sake."

Of course. I'd forgotten.

She invites us to step inside. "Let's go and sit down. What a surprise!"

Can it really be this easy? Did my mother really work this hard to keep things on an even keel with the only family we have left here in South Africa? Can there really still be people who believe in me? Who trust me?

I glance at Sarah. There's a wary look in her eye, but then she points discreetly at her watch and signals me to go inside.

We follow Lena into her spacious seaside home. I blink in the darkness of the large, cool space, the entrance hall that leads us to the living room, where white sofas provide a vista on to the brooding ocean. Three of the walls are painted a light brown and the fourth an azure blue. Seashells are displayed on a single bookcase, magazines on the coffee table.

"Come. Make yourselves comfortable," says Lena.

She chooses the sofa nearest the kitchen. Crosses her legs under her long white skirt and looks at us attentively. "I'm sorry, I wasn't listening properly before. You're . . ." She looks at Sarah.

"Sarah," she mumbles.

I sit down, wondering how to move the process along without upsetting Lena's sense of hospitality.

Sarah sinks down next me, her combat boots primly parked next to each other on the floor. She crosses her arms and clears her throat uncomfortably, but says nothing.

"Can I offer you some tea? Coffee? Or are you in a hurry?" Lena frowns. "I take it you're here for a reason. Karla won't get in until tomorrow." Her face softens. "Or are you in need of a place to stay? I suppose it must be hard with the police . . . You know."

"No, we're fine, thank you. I'm talking to the police. It really has all just been a big misunderstanding," I lie.

"Really? That's nice to hear. Your mom will be so happy."

I edge forward on my seat. Glance at the black clouds hurtling toward us, the breeze picking up speed by the minute. "Aunt Lena, I'm sorry to arrive unannounced like this, but I've been wondering about my father's things. I'm sure there must be photographs in one of the boxes you have kept in storage for me. My mom and I left without taking anything. I want to make an album for her that she can take back to the States with her."

"That is such a nice gesture." She nods. "Of course. You are welcome to go and see what you can find."

I nod my gratitude.

"Where's your husband?" Sarah suddenly asks, pointing at the black-and-white family picture in the bookcase of a seventies wedding with big hair and bushy mustaches. She even remembers to smile.

Sarah's right. Where is Thinus? He might not be as friendly as Lena.

A gust of wind shakes the house, and a door slams somewhere.

Lena's shoulders move stiffly. "He's here. In the bedroom. Resting. You can go and say hello in a while."

Relief washes over me. "I heard about the cancer," I offer. "I'm so sorry."

"Life happens to all of us." Lena smiles wanly, flicks a few strands of her blonde hair out of her eyes, and folds her hands over each other.

Turns her wedding band around and around. The ring, like the clothes and the furniture, is expensive but old and somewhat worn.

"Was my father's death a shock to him?" I venture, not sure how to urge her to move along.

"It was. A bad shock. Really terrible." She hesitates for a second. "The police were here last year. They wanted to know about you. About that night Hendrik—your dad—died. The last we heard . . . the last we read . . . was that you were in India. Are the stories . . . That man . . . Those men . . ."

"I'm not a serial killer," I say gently.

Theoretically speaking, that's true. Only my father and Tom count. Two people. Not three. Three makes you a serial killer, right?

Lena's mouth forms a perfect circle. "Oh." There's a flicker of uncertainty in her eyes. A slight discomfort in her stooped shoulders.

Time to get out of here. Good old Afrikaner courtesy has brought me this far, but it's starting to evaporate.

I look at Sarah. She nods. She gets it: she has to stay here and make sure Lena doesn't call the cops. We have no guarantees about what she'll do once we're gone, but we'll deal with that problem later.

"Tea? I'll go and put the kettle on," says Lena, breaking the silence.

"I'll come and help you," announces Sarah, jumping to her feet. "Ranna's told me so much about you. About how good you were to her and her mother after her father's suicide."

The change in Sarah is astonishing. She sounds warm and friendly—human almost.

Lena gets up. "Karla should have left him long before all of that."

She heads for the kitchen, Sarah and me in tow. She reaches inside the pantry cupboard and takes out a bunch of keys. Gives them to me.

"There are a few pieces of furniture in the garage and about ten, eleven boxes. I brought everything here from a storage facility in Cape Town a year or so ago, but I haven't looked at any of it since the day we packed up your house. Maybe you'll find photos. Take whatever you want. I'll talk to you later about what we should do with everything. When your mom's here. You're coming back on Sunday, right?"

She smiles, and suddenly she looks exactly like the woman in the faded photographs. The beautiful Miss South Africa finalist. The wife of a successful businessman. My mother's sister.

2

Walking in the side door of the double garage is much easier than wriggling in through a tiny window. I switch on the light. It's looking dark outside now, the rain falling unevenly, driven on by gusts of wind.

Everything looks exactly as I left it. Dusty and almost empty except for my father's things up against the wall.

I won't be here long. I already have the photos I lied about coming to get in my backpack, and I can just show them to Lena when I go back inside.

I don't want to think about Sunday. Tomorrow morning my mother and Moshe land in Cape Town. I must call and warn her about Thinus seemingly being in cahoots with my father. About what happened today. What's going to happen. The police are likely to be on my ass by tomorrow, and they are definitely going to want to talk to her. I can't imagine Lena's planning to keep this surprise visit to herself, no matter what she says.

At least Alex will be—could be—safe by Sunday. We'll just have to play hardball and refuse to give Borsos anything before he hands over Alex.

The box I'm looking for is next to the desk, under two of the same size. I put them aside and open it. I have to force myself to work patiently. Being in storage for so many years has weakened the box.

I sift through the loose kitchen stuff. Pans. Plates wrapped in ancient newspaper. Where is it?

Ah.

I take out the salt shaker, the one that looks like a British palace guard. Open it and throw the contents into my palm. Grin with satisfaction. The last time my mom said she saw the white bag was on the kitchen table when my father filled the salt shaker, just before supper.

He chased her away to go and iron two shirts he wanted to pack for his so-called business trip.

She also remembers a metal lockbox in the kitchen dustbin, later, when they were watching the news and he'd finished the brandy and she had to open a new bottle.

He never thought much of her, saying she was stupid. *But look who's kicking your ass today, Hendrik Kroon,* I whisper.

I throw the salt and its treasure back into the shaker. I struggle to stuff the red-and-black soldier into the pocket of my jeans, though it would be much better to carry it in the backpack.

After the past few days, I want it right on my person, so I can feel it against my body.

I pack everything back as I found it and close the box. As I'm about to stack the other two boxes on top of it, something catches my eye. A handprint in the dust on the desk. My hand? I put my palm down. No. Then my fingers. Also no. The impression is smaller than mine.

Come to think of it, the boxes aren't stacked as neatly as I left them either. Lena said that neither she nor Thinus had been in here. But someone has. Someone who leaned on the desk while they searched through the desk drawers?

I imitate the action as I imagine it.

Yes. Someone searched the drawers.

I stare at the imprint. Think of the photos in my bag, the salt shaker in my pocket. The boxes neatly stored for so many years. The window, which was so conveniently left open when I was here earlier in the week.

I look up, to my left. The window, which is closed now.

Lena and Thinus.

Adorjan Borsos.

My father.

My mother.

Can it be?

Sarah

1

Lena's hands are light and quick as she takes out the cups. She pours boiling water into the old-fashioned white porcelain and dips the teabags in and out, in and out with a dull silver teaspoon.

Milk? Sugar? With every question, she raises her neatly plucked eyebrows.

"Please," and "three spoons," I say. "Nothing for Ranna."

"You know her well."

"I'm not sure anyone knows her well."

Lena passes me a cup and saucer with pink flowers on them. I hold them as though they're going to break. I stir the contents and then put the saucer down on the counter and the delicate spoon in the sink. I've got my computer backpack over my shoulder. The revolver's in the front compartment for easy access.

I know I look preposterous, standing here in this woman's kitchen with the bag over my shoulder, as though I don't trust her. As though I can't wait to get out of here. The fragile cup isn't helping any. I put it down. "Let's go and say hi to your husband. He's probably wondering what's going on."

"We can in a while. I just need to make a quick phone call."

My heart picks up speed. Call? Not a good idea.

I step closer to the woman, who is almost as tall as Ranna but less imposing.

Lena must have read my face. “Don’t worry. I’m not calling the police, I promise.” She smiles gently, her hands trying to placate me. “It’s an old friend coming around for a visit. I want to tell her to come later. She might recognize Isabel. Then there’ll be trouble for the two of you.”

I step back, but keep a wary eye on her.

Lena picks up the cell phone lying next to the bread bin and looks for a number. Dials it. Shows the screen to me.

It’s not 10111, the police emergency response number.

I nod.

She talks quickly, cryptically, smiling. It sounds like a normal conversation between friends.

“Yes, yes. You know how it is—sometimes people just arrive,” she says. “Come around later, though. Please. I’m sorry about the inconvenience.”

She says goodbye and rings off.

“Okay?” She puts the phone on the counter and pushes it toward me. I pick it up and look at the number again.

“Sorry,” I mumble. It’s raining so hard now that I have to raise my voice. “It’s just . . . we have to be careful. And Isabel . . . she really is innocent, even though the cops don’t believe it.”

“Don’t worry. I believe you.” Lena points at a room down the hall. Then fidgets with the scarf around her neck again. “Shall we go and say hello to Thinus? He might be awake now.”

We leave the tea and walk to the main bedroom. The wind plucks a window open somewhere in the house with a bang. A gust of cold air howls through the kitchen and sweeps down the hall. A sudden chill fills my lungs. I wonder whether stopping here was such a good idea. But did we have a choice, really?

Too many things are out of our control. Since Sasolburg. Before that. Adriana. My parents. Welkom. And there are just too many discrepancies. Things that don’t fit. Like now. Who says Thinus hasn’t climbed through the window and taken off? And this woman with her restless hands, she's making me nervous, whether she's Ranna's godmother or not.

In the master bedroom, it becomes clear that Thinus isn't worth worrying about. The long, narrow room with its cream-colored carpet, worn thin in places, smells strongly of sweat, unwashed bed linens, and disinfectant.

Lena adjusts the sheets around her husband's atrophied body. She walks around the hospital bed to do the same on the other side. "He doesn't really know what's going on around him anymore. The cancer's spread to his lungs and liver. The doctors say any day now."

"I'm sorry."

The words sound banal and useless.

"Don't be."

"You've been married a long time."

I wish Ranna would hurry. It's starting to feel like I can't breathe in here. And something else is bugging me. Something I saw in the kitchen. What was it?

"Being married for long does not equal being happily married." Lena smiles, but the emotion doesn't reach her eyes. She walks to one of the built-in cupboards in the corner of the bedroom and starts looking for something in a pile of blue towels.

I remember what it was that bothered me. That number on Lena's screen. The friend she called. It was the same number that called me just before we walked in here. How is that possible?

Lena turns around. The black pistol gleams dully in her hand.

ALEX

1

The phone rings. Adorjan answers. He doesn't drive any slower while he talks, just speeds ahead on the gravel road to fuck knows where. I flinch at the pain threatening to rip my insides apart. I cough and the metallic taste of blood fills my mouth.

At least the milk and food helped to restore some of my strength. And Adorjan gave me a fresh T-shirt. He made me take my shoes and socks off, though. To teach me a lesson.

The hot, stony semi-desert surface had burned my feet as we walked to the Nissan Sani. I've asked where we are, where we're going, but he hasn't answered me.

"Give me about two hours," he says on the phone now. He sounds angry. "I'm still outside Lambert's Bay. I was on my way to the exchange location. I wanted to be early to see what those chicks were planning. Don't worry. I'm on my way."

He kills the call, mutters something unintelligible. The Sani slows down, as though he's fallen into deep thought.

Lambert's Bay. At least now I know exactly where we are. My friends and I used to come fishing here sometimes when I was in high school.

The gravel turns to tar. The white clouds become a steely gray. I consider the Sani's speed, the landscape. I wouldn't survive jumping out. Especially not with my hands cuffed behind my back. I doubt I'd even be able to reach the door handle.

At least this time I'm not drugged. Adorjan probably needs me awake.

"Are we on our way to see Ranna and Sarah?"

"Yes."

"Did they find the box?"

Adorjan grins. "Looks like it."

"What's in it?"

"You'll see. We'll all see."

I look at the veld around me. The familiar emptiness. The heavy clouds we're driving toward. My mother's not far, just in Vanrhynsdorp. Practically around the corner.

"And then? Are you going to let us go? All of us?"

The grin melts away. "It seems there are some unforeseen complications."

"What complications?"

"Not what, who. Maria Magdalena Prinsloo. Never been an easy lady, that one."

Ranna

1

I open my backpack and leaf through the photos. My mother and Lena. Thinus, Borsos, and my father. My father. Another one of him. And then the photo of the woman with the long blonde hair and my father. The one on the beach in which they look so happy, she resting between his legs on pristine white sand. The one where my father's smiling like I hardly ever saw him smile.

The shard of happiness I thought belonged to my mother was Lena's. It's not my mother in the faded photo. The eyes aren't right, the curve of the neck. Seeing her here, now, after all these years, has made me realize that.

My father and Lena had an affair. The way they are entwined in the photo . . . it's intimate. And Lena is looking at the camera with something like respect in her eyes. Admiration. My mother would never have been able to muster that emotion with Hendrik Kroon around.

I sit on the desk, trying to gather my thoughts.

Someone was here, in the garage. Someone knows I was here. Someone came looking for something. Came to see what I'd found. *If* I'd found anything. Someone who knows about Borsos and Alex?

Or am I imagining things? This is a garage. Lots of people store stuff in garages and then come looking for things.

Except none of the stuff in here belongs to Thinus or Lena.

I get up again and look at the side door, the closed window, the black sky beyond. The rain drawing a dark curtain across the ocean, the house.

How could Lena betray my mother like that?

I pack the photos back into my bag. It doesn't matter now. What matters is the salt shaker and its contents. And that we drive to Lambert's Bay and get Alex back.

It's still raining when I sneak in through the back door. The kitchen is empty. Where are Lena and Sarah?

I walk to the living room. Voices drift from the far end of the house. One stands out—Sarah, speaking louder than she usually does.

Is she trying to warn me, or amplify her voice above the rain on the roof?

I throw the backpack over my shoulders and pull the straps tighter in case I need to run. The voices draw me deeper into the house. I follow the sound down a hall leading to the bedrooms.

The dust makes me want to sneeze. I stop, take a deep breath, and pinch my nose. Inch forward again.

They're talking in what looks like the main bedroom at the end of the hall.

"Who was that you called? Borsos?" Sarah's throaty voice rasps.

"He's on his way." Lena.

I stop.

Adorjan Borsos and Lena. What about Thinus, then?

I peep through the opening between the door and the frame. Something—a smell—sticks in the back of my throat. I blot it with my tongue. Recognize it immediately. It's the smell of death, tired of waiting. It's the smell everyone knows, even when they've never smelled it before. The odor of decay and disinfectant and a body that hasn't seen the sun in a long time. A body fighting itself, devouring itself.

Thinus.

"Do you even know how to use that gun?" Sarah says to Lena.

She *is* trying to warn me.

"Of course I do. And I'm pretty damn sure you do too. Isabel's always had wild friends. So why don't you put whatever you have down on the ground?"

Lena's voice is cold, miles away from the courteous woman who met us at the door.

I hear Sarah fiddle with her backpack, drop the revolver.

"Kick it here."

I hear Sarah's boot connect with the metal. What now?

If Borsos is on his way here, we don't have much time. I need to turn the situation around. Right now, it's just me against Lena, but in a few minutes it might be my Glock against Borsos's Beretta and whatever Lena's got in her hands.

I walk into the bedroom with three long strides, Glock in hand.

Sarah swings around, but Lena moves just as quickly. She's fast for a woman no longer in her prime. And strong. She steps behind Sarah and jerks her back by her shoulders. They step back, once, twice.

Sarah tries to pull free, but Lena, tall Lena, digs her nails into Sarah's shoulder. The other hand lifts the gun to Sarah's temple.

"We were just waiting for you." Lena laughs. It sounds hard and unnatural. "I can't believe you just walked up to the house and knocked on the front door. I'd hoped you'd found what you were looking for that first time. Weren't you glad I left the garage window open for you?"

I aim the Glock at Lena. She is much taller than Sarah, leaving her head and shoulders exposed. The bad news is that the pistol in her hand looks comfortable there, as though she would easily pull the trigger. Plus, she and Sarah are half hidden behind the foot of the hospital bed.

The skeletal body between the sheets must be Thinus, spun into a web of tubes and wires. He is barely recognizable as the jovial man from the photos. He is pale, emaciated. His breathing is uneven, broken.

"You and my father had an affair," I say, quietly measuring the distance to her forehead.

"Yes. He was leaving that night. To be with me. One last job and then we were going to disappear."

I think of the lockbox, the robbery near Pelindaba. Trippers Transport. "My dad stole from Eitan Blomstein, and you betrayed your husband. Did Thinus give my dad the information about where and how Blomstein was moving his goods that day?"

Lena doesn't answer.

"Come on. You can tell me."

Lena pulls her shoulders back, her hand clamping Sarah's shoulder harder. "They worked together for many years. Thinus cleared the stuff Hendrik's team stole across the border in his trucks. Except this time. This time your father and I were going to take everything and leave for Switzerland. Just the two of us."

Sarah looks at me pointedly, then taps her watch surreptitiously, as though trying to signal me to hurry up.

"And Adorjan Borsos?" I ask. "How did the two of you partner up?"

"I'm not in the mood for chitchat, Isabel. Where's the stuff that was in the box? The box isn't among your dad's stuff. Thinus and I looked so many times. And Adorjan and I have been through it a hundred times since he was released. Did Hendrik leave you a clue? Tell me!"

"I want to know why we're all here today. Then we can talk about the box."

"I want the box," she says, clipping off every word. "Where is it?"

"Forget about it. Tell me about you and Borsos." The Glock emphasizes the question. "Or the box disappears forever."

Lena's mouth becomes an almost impossibly thin line. "Adorjan fell in love with me the moment he laid eyes on me. We met at your parents' house. Nobody suspected Hendrik and I were in a relationship. Not Thinus, Adorjan, or Karla. I knew about the robberies, about Hendrik's and Thinus's business. Your father never trusted Karla, but he was different with me. I knew. I wanted to know."

She laughs sourly. "Your father and Thinus told me to be gentle with Adorjan. They told me to"—she hesitates—"to keep him happy because he would be difficult to replace. So when Adorjan came out of prison, he called me, angry that Hendrik betrayed him and Thinus. Thinus was sick. Hendrik was dead. I played along and said I was equally upset. I gave Adorjan a few thousand rand because he kept quiet about Thinus for my sake when he went to prison. And then . . . well. Then the news revealed the real you."

Her eyes shine with something like wonder. "You kill all those men and you're on the front page of every newspaper and website, and Adorjan says he knows about this metal box that will ensure that the two of us can retire in peace."

Her nails look like claws digging into Sarah's shoulder. "I've always known about the box. I just didn't know what happened to it after Hendrik's death. It was ours. Mine and your father's. Our retirement fund. I told Adorjan I didn't know about it. That I never came across it when we packed up your house. That your mother said she knew nothing about any box. She never lived as though she'd suddenly stumbled across a load of money. I said it had to be here somewhere. I told Adorjan to see if he could find it. He went through your father's stuff, but no luck. He even dug around a few places I didn't know about. Then he decided to abduct Alex and lure you back to South Africa. He was convinced that you or your mother would figure out where it was if you put your heads together. You were the last people to see Hendrik alive."

I nod toward Thinus without taking my eyes off her, seeking confirmation about the house's neglected state. "Your money's all gone."

"Thinus got cold feet after your father died and decided to go straight. He said we were lucky no one came for us after Hendrik's death. He always was spineless."

Sarah moves her head slightly and pulls a worried face as she again points at her watch.

I nod slightly, deciding to push Lena into a corner.

"If my father trusted you so much, loved you as much as you imagine, you wouldn't have needed me. He would have told you what he'd done with the box. Where it was hidden. What was inside."

Lena's eyes ice over. She jerks Sarah back roughly. Sarah has to step wildly not to trip. In the process, they end up hidden behind the bed entirely.

"You know what I mean, Lena. You were just another woman in my father's bed. There were many others. Trust me. All cheap and ugly. Every one of them."

"Your father trusted me." She spits out the words. "More than he trusted anyone else."

"Not enough to tell you where he hid the box."

"He never had the chance to, that's all." Her mouth is twisted bitterly. "Hendrik always said he didn't trust you, that you were far too smart for your own good." She frowns, something like revulsion in her eyes. "He almost sounded proud of you. He thought of you as a younger version of him. I could never understand it."

I try to ignore her last words. Borsos had said it too: *your father's daughter.*

"He was right not to trust me," I say.

"In the beginning, I was convinced it was Karla who'd shot him," Lena says. "That she'd found out about us."

I shake my head. Sarah's right. We're running out of time. "Nope. It was all me. I killed him. He was a bastard. He never really loved anyone but himself. All he did was use people."

Rage reddens Lena's neck, shakes the hand that holds the gun. "He loved me! Your mother was a whore who—"

"Leave my mother out of this. She's a far better person than you could ever hope to be."

Lena's fingers turn white around the gun she is holding to Sarah's head. She pushes it against the messy red hair, just above her ear. "How did you shoot him? Like this? Up close?"

I try not to think about that night. I have to focus. I have to find a clean shot. One that won't hurt Sarah.

One that won't kill Lena.

The thought startles me.

Is this really the best time to get soft?

Outside, the storm rages with a new intensity, rain battering the windows.

"Where's the box?" says Lena, raising her voice over the howling wind. "Adorjan tells me you found it. That you're ready to make the swap. Is it here?"

"No, of course it isn't. There's no box."

Sarah's head jerks under the violence of Lena's rage.

"Ranna . . . ," Sarah says, her hands in the air. "Think of Alex. Forget about me."

"I will shoot her. I swear!"

"Okay, okay, just hang on. There's no box, but there is this." I hold up my right hand. Move it slowly to extract the salt shaker from my jeans. Hold it up for Lena to see.

Her eyes widen with interest.

"My father filled it that night, just before we ate."

"Thinus and I have been through everything a thousand times . . . Adorjan . . ."

"You were after a box. A clue. You didn't know my father at all."

I put my teeth around the rubber plug on the underside of the shaker and pull it out, pouring the contents onto the carpet. The fine white is followed by diamonds. One after the other.

Sarah gasps.

"How did they operate?" I ask. "Did Thinus steal the diamonds and Blomstein cut them and turn them into jewelry? Sell them legitimately?"

Lena nods, her eyes shiny with greed. "I knew it was diamonds. Thinus bought the diamonds from illegal miners on the West Coast. He drove to Namibia now and again for business, up along the coast. The miners knew him as someone they could sell their stones to at a fair price. He gave them to Eitan for a share of the sales of the jewelry. Hendrik wasn't involved in this venture, but he knew about it. Adorjan was completely oblivious about it all."

All three of us stare at the diamonds on the carpet, especially two big bluish stones that must be worth a fortune.

"And the rest?" Lena's voice is almost shaky with excitement. "Where's the rest?"

I look at her in mock surprise. "What do you mean 'the rest'? What are you talking about?"

"The other stones. Thinus said he had hit it big with a miner who sold him fancy stones from Lesotho. Big stolen diamonds from a mine in the Maluti Mountains that would draw attention if they weren't handled properly. Apparently, Eitan was very excited about the jewelry he'd made with those diamonds. That's why Thinus decided to end his partnership with Blomstein and get his hands on the jewelry."

"Ah. The rest." I pick through the salt and diamonds with the toe of my sneaker. "I've been thinking, you know. You never told Adorjan what was in the box. You acted ignorant. Why?"

Her eyes narrow. The pistol's barrel moves an inch away from Sarah's head as she focuses on me.

"Were you worried that Adorjan would get greedy if you told him?" I ask. "That he'd make his own calculations and decide you weren't that pretty anymore? Not that important?"

"Shut up."

"What about the exchange in Lambert's Bay? Alex for the box? You would have gone along, and then what? You'd shoot Adorjan? Us?"

A twitch around her mouth gives her away.

"I think Adorjan is on his way here," says Sarah quickly. "She made a phone call just now."

Lena again thrusts the barrel into the side of her head. Sarah closes her eyes under the pressure.

"Ah." I nod, the tension inside ratcheting up a notch. "And I'm sure you don't want him to see the diamonds. You want them all for yourself."

"Shut up. Just shut up."

In the bed, Thinus suddenly stirs, mumbles. Opens his eyes.

"I don't care about those stones." Lena points her chin at the salt and diamonds on the carpet. "Where are the earrings? The pendant? Hendrik said Eitan had made something special with three rare yellow diamonds."

I think of my father and, for the first time, a twinge of regret stirs inside. A morsel of respect for his last deed before he meant to leave us.

Alex

1

Thunder rumbles overhead. It starts raining. Slowly at first, then harder and harder, as though the storm is in a hurry to move on to another part of this semi-desert.

Adorjan puts the windshield wipers on and drops the Sani's speed down to forty, then thirty-five, miles per hour.

Maybe this is what I need. One last opportunity. Because fuck knows, we're almost there. The end. The last page. The last word. And I can't let Ranna or Sarah get hurt.

My wrists strain against the cuffs. I shift my hands, behind my back, to where I can just reach the red release mechanism on the seat belt. I keep my hands ready.

Adorjan's eyes are nailed to the two-lane road, water eddying over its surface now in the downpour. The Sani's too old for this weather. The headlights reach thinly into the storm's dimness, the windshield wipers fighting a losing battle.

Over the next hill, a field full of flowers reveals itself. Closed up daisies and marigolds. Sheets of them, bowing their heads under the relentless shower.

Adorjan slows down even further, the determination in his expression tempered now by the concentration required to keep the SUV on the road.

I loosen the seat belt and hold it so it doesn't reel in. I slowly shuffle to the right in the seat, in Adorjan's direction. I dig my feet into the footwell and launch myself toward him.

"What the . . ." His head swivels in my direction, startled.

My forehead hits his temple with a loud smack.

Still holding on to the seat belt, I swing my right foot to his side of the car, wildly searching for the brake pedal. Step on it as hard as I can.

Adorjan doesn't move, doesn't make a sound.

The Sani spins across the road, out of control. I try to find something to hold on to. The seat. The door. But there's nothing.

Adorjan groans.

I struggle against the speed of the car, which is trying to pin me against the door, and lean right. Knock him with my body again. His head hits the window on his right.

Blood on the window, dark red against the gray thunderclouds and battered flowers. Round and round we go.

Spinning, spinning, spinning.

SARAH

1

Karma's a lie. Never believed in it. Reap what you sow? Complete bullshit. You're either lucky or you're not. End of story. I didn't end up in prison because of some cosmic joke. All those women in prison—me included—were there because we got caught. Because we made stupid mistakes.

Live and learn. Now that's a motto I can live with.

No one's keeping score.

But now I'm not so sure anymore. Now there's an angry, jittery woman behind me with a gun to my head, and Ranna's in front of me with her Glock trained on me.

Feels like karma. Like paying for what I did to Ranna.

Ranna with a gun.

Aimed at my head.

Ranna is not me. She isn't about to hand her weapon to Lena and start haggling for my life. Not like me with Borsos in Sasolburg. When you've lost enough, losing doesn't scare you anymore.

I'm pretty damn sure that's Ranna's motto.

I look into her dark-blue eyes. No. Violet. The color they turn when she's really angry. Like in that abandoned factory in Sasolburg.

Outside, it seems to be raining even harder.

"Shoot," I mouth at her.

Ranna blinks in surprise.

I'm surprised too. But what else can we do?

"Shoot," I urge her again silently. I'm sure she'll understand. *Calvinia 140*. A swarm of bees. She can make the shot without putting a bullet through my head.

She frowns, shakes her head almost imperceptibly.

For the first time ever, I wish I were shorter. I shrink against Lena's body, trying to make myself smaller, but the woman's fingers, digging into my shoulder, keep me upright. It almost feels as though she's trying to draw blood. And that gun against my head. I'm one hundred percent sure she'll pull the trigger if Ranna continues to piss her off with her game of twenty questions.

"I want the jewelry, Isabel," Lena says, "or I will shoot your little friend here."

"My name is Ranna."

"The jewels. Now."

"I don't play those sorts of games."

Lena gives a harsh, ugly laugh. A speck of spit lands on my cheek, and the barrel of the gun digs into my skull. "Such a beautiful woman. How would she look with a hole in her head? A hole like your father's. Just here, below the ear."

Ranna doesn't even lift an eyebrow. In fact, there is no emotion on her face.

"Shoot her," she says, with a little shrug. "Now that I know what's going on, I don't give a shit anymore. I'm going to sell the jewels. I need the money." She drops the Glock a bit. "Sarah betrayed me. You're wrong if you think I care about her. In fact, do me a favor and kill her."

I can feel Lena's nails drawing blood, the heat of her anger in a succession of short, rapid breaths.

"Wait a minute. Just wait," I plead.

"Shut up." Lena shoves me forward. I feel like a puppet. The barrel's pressure is suddenly lighter.

"It's fine she means nothing to you, Isabel. I'll shoot her and then move on to that boyfriend of yours. He'll be here soon. And then Moshe. And your mother."

"I told you to leave my mother out of this."

Ranna pulls the trigger.

"You shot me."

"Mm-hmm."

I watch the blood blooming on my jeans, like a red lily.

"I can't believe you shot me."

"Lie still."

I put my head down on the carpet. The pain's not that bad, but the shock is making me shiver. Ranna shot Lena in the leg, and the bullet grazed me.

"You shot me," I say again. "On purpose."

"Shh," says Ranna, kneeling next to me. She's taken a towel out of the cupboard and is pressing it to my wound.

"Ouch!"

"It's just a scratch."

"It's not . . ."

"Stop complaining and hold this," she says, flicking her eyes to the towel. "We have to stop the bleeding."

I drag myself into a sitting position against the cupboard so that I can do as I'm told.

I wonder how long it will be before the cops arrive. The rain, though it's coming down hard, could surely not have dampened the sound of a gunshot.

"Ranna, someone will have heard."

"I know."

She's moved over to Lena. Lena dropped her pistol when she fell, and Ranna kicked it over to my revolver near the door. Lena is lying at the foot of Thinus's bed. Her breathing is shallow, blood pooling under her left thigh and sinking into the carpet. Her eyes blink open and shut, fear and shock on her face.

Thinus doesn't move. He just stares at us.

No. Past us.

Ranna puts a towel on Lena's wound and says over her shoulder, "Call an ambulance. The bleeding won't stop."

"What about Alex? He and Borsos are on their way here."

"We'll go out and wait for them. There's only one road into Paternoster."

"And if he doesn't show?"

"We can't just leave her like this," Ranna argues. "Call an ambulance!"

I'm tempted to say something about her father, but I don't. "If Borsos finds out that you shot Lena . . . if she means that much to him . . ."

Ranna wipes at her nose. Her chin. "I'm going to tell him Lena is fine. And she is, for now. We can use her to get Alex. Alex for Lena. Borsos doesn't need to know she's gone to the hospital. We'll take her phone. All the phones. Make sure he can't reach her."

Lena groans. Her eyes flutter open.

"Okay," I concede. "I'll call, but then we have to hurry."

I dial the number, watching the two women.

Lena reaches out and grabs Ranna's hand. "Your father . . . Why? Why did you have to kill him? I loved him so much."

Ranna's eyes go dark again, like just before she pulled the trigger. "You could have had him."

"Your mother . . ."

"I'm going to tell her everything. Warn her to stay away from you. If you do anything to put her in danger, if you say anything about me or Sarah, I will come back, and I will kill you. Alex and Sarah will tell the police that Adorjan acted alone in kidnapping him. What Borsos says will be up to him."

She pushes down on the wound, as though she wants to make sure that Lena understands her.

Lena groans.

"My mother can't lose anyone else," says Ranna. "And there will not be any new stories about Hendrik Kroon, and her, by extension. This one is not for you. Your miserable life belongs to my mother."

"I have nothing left," Lena murmurs, her face ashen. "Nothing."

Ranna pulls her hand out of the woman's grip. She places Lena's right hand on the wound and pushes a towel in under her head. "The ambulance will be here soon. If you behave, I'll send you a few diamonds, once I know for sure that you're going to keep your mouth shut about everything. Me, Sarah, my dad. *Everything.*"

"What do I tell the police?"

"You were cleaning the gun. Fired an accidental shot. Think of something, and you get to walk away from this mess."

Ranna gets up, glares at the woman by her feet. Then she looks at Thinus, his eyes brighter than they were a minute ago.

She nods.

He does the same, slowly and painfully.

She walks to the bedroom door, picks up my revolver and the Glock's shell, and then fishes the diamonds from the salt pile and hands them to me. Pushes the salt around on the carpet with her shoe. With a towel wrapped around her hand, she picks up Lena's pistol and puts it down near her.

She helps me up. "You're wrong, you know," she says to Lena over her shoulder. "The only thing you've ever loved is money."

2

We use the back door to leave the house. The gunshot has left me with a limp, the bullet probably tearing through a muscle somewhere along the way.

The rain is coming down almost horizontally, and we're drenched within seconds. Ranna peers around the house to where the Audi is waiting. No sign of Borsos or his green Sani. Everything is quiet except for the beating rain. She looks at me as though she's weighing me.

"Oh no," I say quickly. "If you're thinking of carrying me to the car, we're no longer even."

"Who says we're even?"

"You shot me!"

"It's a scratch."

Ranna puts her right arm around my shoulder and hooks her hand into my armpit. "Come on. Let's get to the car as quickly as we can. The ambulance could get here any minute."

She helps me out of the garden and down the road to the Audi. She holds out her right hand for the keys, unlocks the car, and helps me in. Puts her backpack on my lap. Then she gives me a concerned look, the rain pelting her in the face.

"Are you sure you're okay? Do we need to get you to a hospital?"

"No. I'm cool. Don't worry." I inspect the tear in my bloody jeans. "It's not really even bleeding anymore."

That's not entirely true, but there's no way I'm going to the emergency room now.

Ranna jogs around the car, gets into the driver's seat, and pulls away. She motions toward my backpack and the laptop inside.

"Can you send my mother a text and an email? It's fine if she only gets it when she lands. Tell her to stay away from Lena until she's spoken to me. Tell her to go to the place where my father proposed to her."

I unzip the bag and take out my phone. Ask: "Are you going to meet her there on Sunday?"

"Yes. If we find Alex by then."

She slows down to navigate a flooded intersection. Paternoster's streets are empty, except for a bedraggled dog of questionable breeding hiding under a restaurant awning. Ranna gives me the cell number and her mother's email address. I type the messages and send them. Let's hope Karla Abramson turns her phone on when she gets to Cape Town International Airport.

At the next street an ambulance goes by, driving as fast as the weather will allow.

Just outside Paternoster, Ranna parks the Audi on the side of the two-lane road and switches on the hazard lights. She turns to me.

"Borsos has to be able to see me, and the rain's going to make that hard. I'm going to get out and wait next to the car and look out for the Sani. I need to wave it down. Stay inside. Keep the revolver handy. And the diamonds and the pendant."

I can't believe this is the best plan we have. "We should have waited at Lena's house. What if we miss him?"

Ranna's eyes grow dark. "And let Lena die?" she explodes. "Haven't you had enough of all the killing? Because I certainly have. And as I said, there's only one road into town. Borsos will be here."

She gets out of the car and slams the door. Walks to the front of the car and parks her backside on the hood.

Hopefully she has nothing sharp in her pockets.

I slick my wet hair back and inspect the wound again. The bleeding has finally stopped. I shudder, lean over the driver's seat, and switch on the heater. Swallow the rising panic that all of this might have been for nothing. That Alex might die anyway.

The minutes tick by slowly. The windows mist up. I try to wipe them with the bloody towel.

The phone vibrates in my hand. Borsos?

Not that lucky. It's Adriana.

"Are you okay? Neither of you has let me know what's going on," she says. "It's almost three o'clock."

"Sorry. Things are insane here. We've . . . Everything's fine," I lie.

I'm surprised by a wave of emotion, pushing my voice into a higher register. I take a deep breath to ease the tightness in my throat.

"Sarah? Sarah, are you okay?"

"I am. We're waiting for Alex now."

"I wish I was there," she says softly. "I should have been there. Why didn't you wait for me?"

"Things just happened too quickly, and Borsos wouldn't have you around anyway."

"I'll be waiting for you," Adriana says. "I'll be at your apartment. Call me as soon as it's all over."

"I will."

"Please be careful."

"Will do."

Just before she rings off, I say, "Adriana?"

"Yes?"

I don't wonder why. Just say it without thinking about it too much. "Please tell my mother I love her."

ALEX

1

The world comes into focus ever so slowly. The dark sky. The driving rain. Flowers?

Something sticky is running down my mouth, my eyes. I want to touch it, but my hands won't move. Something's holding them. Something cold. I try and jerk them free, but they're clamped.

Then I remember. The cuffs. Adorjan put handcuffs on me.

I shake my head, rub my bearded chin against my shoulder to wipe down what I suspect is blood. Stop when it hurts too much. There's a noise in my ears, a dull, almost electronic, beep.

I blink against the blood dripping over my left eye. Feel it running down my cheek.

Where am I? I try to sit up. Bad idea. It's like a knife sliding into my lungs, arresting air going in.

I realize I'm no longer in the Sani. Somehow I was flung from the vehicle. I look to my left. Flowers bending under the rain. Right. A man lying among the flowers. Not moving.

Adorjan.

I struggle to my bare feet and stagger over the muddy ground toward him. Flinch when I step on something sharp.

With my hands locked behind my back, I angle myself so that I can put my fingers on his neck.

I can't find a heartbeat.

Where's the Beretta? I pat down his pockets, search around his belt. Nothing. I need to find it. Fucker's not going to lock me up again. I get up, even though the pain feels unbearable. I lick the rain off my lips. The thirst is overwhelming. Cold is seeping into my bones.

I take in the landscape. The Sani's about twenty yards away, the doors open, its headlights cutting a weak beam through a curtain of water.

I walk to the pickup. Turn back when Adorjan starts groaning. It's loud and persistent.

Where's the gun? I jog to the passenger seat and look around. Papers. Empty soda cans. Chocolate wrappers. Ah. The phone. I turn around and grope for it blindly. Grip it eventually and slide it into my back pocket.

Still no pistol, and no sign of the keys for my handcuffs.

I shuffle over to the driver's seat and bend down carefully so that I don't bump my head on the steering wheel. As expected, the cuff's keys are on the set of keys in the ignition.

I turn around and lean back through the door, frozen fingers feeling for the keys.

There's a dull click as the keys come out of the ignition. I grip them tightly. Can't afford to drop them. I glance over at where Adorjan's lying, as I try to open the cuffs. He's turned onto his stomach. His left leg is out at an unnatural angle, but that's not stopping him. He is slowly, painfully crawling through pools of muddy water. Where the hell's he going? There's nothing . . .

The Beretta.

It's lying in the flowers, eight or ten yards in front of him.

He starts laughing as he gets closer. A high, hysterical cackle.

The cuffs. I need my hands. I struggle to pick out the right key.

Shit. Shit. Fuck.

I free my left hand and drop the keys. Run.

Adorjan is four yards away from the gun now. Three. Two. I kick the Beretta out from under his fingers. Land on my knees, lunging forward to grab the weapon.

I turn around and fall on my back, gun pointed at the old man.

"Don't move, you fucking bastard."

When the pain in my chest has subsided to something below the maximum level, I struggle upright and slowly walk back to the Sani, leaving Adorjan lying in the rain.

My body is smashed. His leg is broken, and the right side of his face is badly swollen. His eyes, when he looked at me, were hazy.

I sit down on the ground next to the car, watch as water dams up around my frozen feet. I stare at the raindrops like I'm hypnotized.

Eight weeks with that man. Almost nine. Eight weeks in a cage. Eight weeks in handcuffs. I choke down the words I want to scream at Adorjan, the urge to murder him. I rest my head against the metal behind me, opening my mouth greedily to the rain.

Finally, I take the phone out of my pocket and call Sarah.

Ranna

1

The rain is letting up slightly. Not that it matters. It drowns out the rising panic. The sheer terror at the thought of getting this wrong. Of missing Borsos. Of Alex getting killed because I couldn't open that red box sooner. My selfishness in wanting that passport first. My father, coming back to haunt me so many years after his death.

Maybe I should have left Lena to die.

But when is it enough? How many people have died because of me? When does it ever end?

I stand up straight when a car approaches through the downpour. Sit back down on the Audi when the Golf drives by, a woman behind the wheel.

Behind me the car door opens and slams shut. Sarah appears, limping, her weight on her right leg. I must have been less accurate with that shot than I thought I would be.

Or maybe I did intend to hurt her.

Then I see her face.

I'm almost too afraid to move, to ask. I get up, hands covering my mouth, dread surging through my body, paralyzing every coherent thought.

"God no, please, Sarah. Not Alex."

"He called." Her lips twitch into a smile. "We have to go and fetch him."

"He called? How did he . . ."

"I don't care." Her eyes shine with tears, and suddenly it's as though something has lifted. Something she's been carrying since I first saw her in Mumbai.

I close my eyes for a second, swallowing back the bile that has pushed up into my mouth. Alex found a way. He found a way. "Where is he?"

She wipes at her eyes. "Not sure exactly. Not far from here. I think."

I help her back into the car and get behind the wheel.

I drive the way Sarah usually drives. I don't care about the weather and the traffic rules; I just follow the directions she's giving me.

We take a wrong turn once, but then we're there.

The clouds have begun to lift, the rain has slowed to a steady shower. Under a steel-colored sky, I spot the green Nissan Sani from Sasolburg on its back in the veld, deep skid marks following it off the road. A short way off, someone's lying in the mud. I jump out of the car, halfway to the body lying motionless in the flowers, but then stop.

A figure is struggling up off the ground next to the vehicle. I reach for the Glock, but then I see who it is.

Alex.

I stare at him. Realize Sarah's not beside me. I'm torn between running there and jogging back. I decide to check if Sarah is okay. Maybe that wound is more serious than she's let on.

I open the Audi's door, leaning into the leather interior, slick from our wet bodies.

She's sitting, hugging herself, her eyes glued to the man stumbling toward us.

"Are you okay? Are you coming?"

She shakes her head, refuses stubbornly to look at me. "You go. I'm coming."

"Sarah . . ."

"For fuck's sake, Ranna. Please."

She looks up at me, her green eyes unguarded, the loss clear. The letting go.

I nod, slam the car door, and run through the veld toward Alex.

Halfway there, he lurches forward, resting his hands on his thighs, spitting what looks like blood. Then he wobbles and collapses onto his knees.

No.

I run.

"Alex!"

I kneel next to him in the mud. He looks up. Past me. Points to somewhere behind him. "Adorjan is there. Ambulance."

I turn his face toward mine. Kiss him on his lips, blue from the cold. His bearded cheeks. His eyes. I put my arms around him.

He drops his head against my shoulder and mumbles something.

"What? Alex? Are you okay?"

He talks softly, tiredly. I struggle to decipher the jumble of words.

"I'm pissed off at you," he says. "Very. Last year. You left. Very."

"Now's not the time."

"Just saying."

"I hear you."

He starts to shake as though he is freezing. Looks up again, searching my face, as if he can't believe his eyes. The lopsided, familiar smile appears. The ever-so-slightly cocky one I fell in love with in Dar es Salaam.

The scar on his cheek stands out vividly.

He folds his hands around my waist, drops them to my hips possessively, as if he's never letting go.

"Are we just going to sit here in the rain, or are you going to call the cavalry?"

2

We follow the ambulance to the hospital in Vredenburg, urging it along as it navigates the debris of the unexpected torrential downpour.

I don't know why I'm tagging along, exactly. My time with Alex is going to be short. Perhaps it's already over. It won't be long before one of his colleagues arrives. His mother too, probably. And the police won't be far behind.

But first, he needs help. That's all I desire. To know that he is safe and cared for. He looked close to death when the two hefty paramedics put him into the ambulance. He groaned every time they moved him. And he coughed way too much, like someone who couldn't breathe.

Adorjan is dead. Nothing anyone could do about him. No one to shed a tear.

I don't know how Lena's doing.

I yawn while I'm driving. I could sleep for a week. Even if it means swallowing a handful of Temazepam. Sarah has her head against the side window, like someone who's drifted off, but I can see her watching the lines in the road ahead of us like she's counting them.

Just as we're about to walk into the ER, the younger of the two paramedics comes out, the one who looked so uncertain about what to do with Adorjan's body at the accident scene.

"Going already?" I ask.

He shakes his head. “Sounds like a woman in Paternoster shot and killed herself. And her sick husband. Bullets everywhere. She went berserk when they tried to treat her. Tried to claw one of our guys’ eyes out. They need another ambulance. I don’t know what’s going on around here today.”

“Lena,” Sarah whispers as he rushes to his vehicle.

“Could be. Probably didn’t believe me about the diamonds.”

“She should go to prison for the rest of her life. I don’t know why you’re suddenly so nice.”

I shrug.

Before we walk in the door, Sarah places a hand on my arm. “I think you need to get out of here. I’ll stay and make sure everything’s okay.”

“I just want to see if Alex is okay.”

“I’m sure he’s fine. I’ll let you know as soon as I know anything. It’s too dangerous for you to be here.”

I cross my arms and tuck my hands into my armpits. The rapidly subsiding adrenaline is allowing the cold in bone-deep.

“Go and book into a hotel somewhere. Get out of those wet clothes. Shower. Sleep. Eat something. I’ll call you as soon as I can. Take my phone.”

I know she’s right, but I don’t want to go. I look at the hospital doors. So close, and yet so far.

“What about you?” I ask.

“I’ll be okay. I’m sure they sell Coke here somewhere.” She hands me the Audi’s keys. “Go and meet your mother. I’ll phone you as soon as I can. Trust me, Ranna.”

I can’t help smiling. “I assume you mean that.”

She doesn’t answer, just rubs her upper arms to warm herself.

“Sarah . . . tell Alex . . . explain to him . . .”

“I know. I will.”

She walks toward the glass doors. Just before they swallow her, she turns and says, “But if you disappear again, I’ll kill you.”

3

My father proposed to my mother in the kitchen of a restaurant on Long Street. I don't know why. I never asked. Their story wasn't a fairy tale I wanted to hear about or attempt to copy in any way.

The restaurant's still there, though it's no longer an Italian place. These days the busy spot is run by a Malawian making traditional African dishes with ingredients that bring adventurous backpackers streaming in but keep the fussy locals away.

Music is blaring through speakers in front of the restaurant, loud enough for the manager of the coffee shop next door to have come in twice to complain.

I'm sitting at a booth in the corner, my back to the wall and my eyes glued to the front door. The place is fairly empty, probably because it's still morning.

The police are going to follow my mother once she's landed. I'm sure of that. They'll be eager to see whether she's meeting me. They will have worked out by now that I'm not in India or Vietnam. Any cop worth his salt would wonder why I'd go to that much trouble if I wasn't up to something.

I'm the only family my mother has left, except for Moshe. Lena is dead. She had no children. By some miracle, Thinus is still alive. A news report on the radio said this morning that it looks like a family murder, brought on by a lack of money and the stress of serious illness.

I was relieved at Lena's death at first, but then came the remorse and the worry. The police haven't released specifics, but I'm sure her gunshot wound is going to make someone suspicious. No one trying to kill themselves is going to shoot themselves in the leg. And small coastal towns like Paternoster, full of rich, retired people, love drama. People are going to speculate. Someone's going to remember seeing me in town. And, if there's a thorough investigation, DNA and ballistics may reveal that I was inside Lena's house.

And then someone's going to wonder why Alex Derksen, my ex, the abducted journalist, was found so close to the scene where my aunt committed suicide.

And then, bam, suddenly it's three murders, and I truly am the Black Widow. My father. Tom. Lena.

What does that say about me?

The police will pin Lena's death on me, I think bitterly. And the media, my erstwhile colleagues, will follow their lead.

Which is why I'll be gone long before the story breaks.

It looks as though Alex is going to be okay. Sarah called on a new encrypted phone she gave me. She says Alex is dehydrated, three ribs are cracked and two are broken, and he has pneumonia. But he's responding well to treatment. The doctor says a less stubborn man would have died long ago.

When my mother eventually walks into the restaurant, I feel a jolt of emotion. A mix of regret and love. When last did I see her? Ten years ago? More?

Her eyes are softer than I remember. And her body has grown more fragile. Her sixty-four years are etched in the lines around her eyes and in her neck. Long gray curls cascade down around her face.

My hair. My body.

She's alone. Adriana's plan must have worked. Again the woman from Joburg helped when I needed it most.

My mother and Moshe left the airport in a car Adriana arranged for them. A black Mercedes-Benz with heavily tinted windows. The radio was "broken," so they were unable to listen to the news. I want to be the one to tell my mother about Lena.

The car took them to the V&A Waterfront to do some quick shopping. My mother went to the restrooms near the Woolworths where a different woman, tall, dressed like her, and with a wig similar to her hair, was waiting to walk out and get back into the car with Moshe.

Now Moshe is driving around Chapman's Peak on this clear, sunny Cape Town day with a strange woman. They are taking it slow and easy, like two old people taking in the beautiful landscape, talking about how the old country has changed.

I get up. My hands are sweaty. I wonder whether I look okay. I cut my hair yesterday. Bought some new clothes. Slept for hours and hours.

As she approaches, I see that there are tears in my mother's eyes.

My hands feel too big, my body as awkward as a teenager's. Too tall again. Too clumsy.

Then she makes it easy. "Isa," she says, holding out her arms and walking toward me.

She's shorter than I remember. She fits just under my neck, the crown of her head level with my chin. The last time we said goodbye it was different. Our eyes were almost level as I explained why I had to go away.

"I have missed you so much," she says as she steps back, taking my hands in hers. "This is the best birthday gift ever. You look beautiful."

We sit down. She holds my hands across the table. The Malawian is on his way over with menus, but then seems to reconsider.

"I see Adriana got the message to you in time. I was so worried you wouldn't be prepared to play along. Especially Moshe. I'm so sorry, Ma."

"Moshe is a good man. Neither he nor I would do anything to put you in danger. Not after . . . not after your father."

"That debt has long been paid."

She shakes her head as though she doesn't want to hear, her hair falling over her face. She sweeps it back in a gesture that suddenly seems intimately familiar—like I'm staring at myself in the mirror years from now.

"Ma. Truly. I mean it."

Deep lines pleat around her hazel eyes when she smiles. Her shoulders seem to shed some unseen weight. The right one, the one my father broke, looks like it's still stiff. I hope that's her only reminder of her early life. That, and me.

"Really?" she asks.

"Really."

She smiles again, and I wonder whether this isn't the happiest smile I have ever seen on her face. I can't remember something this bright in all the years we were together.

What a pity I have to take it away again.

But do I really have to do that? What am I going to tell her about Lena? The truth? Or just a part of the truth, as it was announced on the radio this morning? Lena Prinsloo committed suicide and tried to kill her terminally ill husband. An unusual Romeo and Juliet story. Something that won't destroy her love for her only sister, or the brittle peace she's made with Hendrik Kroon and the past.

Maybe that's exactly what I'll do. Perhaps it will also pay off the debt for my years of silence, my steadfast absence from her life.

I push my own hair back behind my shoulders. Wave the owner, hovering behind the counter, over with the menus.

"Ma, before we order, there's something I have to tell you."

4

"You bought a ticket to Caracas." Sarah is standing outside my Pretoria hotel-room door, hands stuffed into the pockets of her black leather jacket.

"How do you know that?"

"That's your question? Really?" She pushes past me into the room.

Something is different. Perfume? Something with a heavy, spicy presence. And something else, though I can't put my finger on it.

Behind her, Adriana's coming lightly and quickly up the stairs.

I look from her to her redheaded niece. That's what it is. Sarah's ubiquitous combat boots have been replaced by neat, sharp-toed boots.

Sarah lifts a foot when she sees me noticing them. "Adriana and I have been shopping. These give me an extra inch. Almost."

She slaps my shoulder when I grin. "That's a lot!"

"Why didn't you get yourself some Jimmy Choos with real heels?"

Adriana takes off her Audrey Hepburn sunglasses and shakes her head as though she wishes I hadn't asked. "Seven sales assistants, Ranna. Seven," she whispers. "And I practically had to bribe the last one. This was enough."

She walks to the window of my cozy four-star hotel room. The weather in Pretoria is as inclement as it was when I left Cape Town the day before yesterday. Spring feels like winter. It's been two weeks since

I saw my mother for the first time in years and three days before I plan to start packing again.

Adriana turns around and parks her backside on the windowsill. The dragonfly pendant dips toward her cleavage, framed by a deep-red blouse. Her black skirt looks comfortable. Expensive. As always.

"Why are you going to Caracas?" she asks. "We were just getting to know each other."

"I know. And I am aware of how deeply indebted I am to you. I can pay with some of the diamonds, if that's okay with you?"

"I don't want your money. I know you owe me, and I'll call in the debt when the time comes, don't worry." She fleetingly, softly, touches the scar on her face. Smiles to soften the words.

I wish she'd take the money, but it's no use forcing it on her. As if I could, anyway.

Sarah sits down on the bed and raises her eyebrows at me. She wants an answer.

I give in. "What kind of a life would Alex and I have here in South Africa? I can't stay. And I can't ask him to come with me. What about his career? His mother?"

"And you?" Adriana asks. "What about what you deserve? Or are you not allowed to be happy? Alex is a big boy. He can look after himself."

I shoo Sarah off the bed and straighten out the bedding again. Fluff the pillows. Move the bedside lamp.

"I'm happy. Travel is good for the soul," I say curtly.

"You sound like a self-help book." Sarah sits down at the chair by the writing table.

"For fuck's sake," I snap. "Don't be so damn difficult."

"We can work something out so you can stay," offers Adriana. "Your documents are the real thing, the best that money can buy from the Department of Home Affairs. And there are one or two other things we could do. Things that would make it very difficult to prove that you're actually Isabel Kroon."

There's only one thing to say to this. "DNA. The cops may have my DNA from the knife we . . . I used to kill Tom Masterson. What if they match it to something from Lena's house?"

"There's no noise yet on Lena's death. It seems the cops bought the suicide story. And besides, we could manage that too if it happens, I think."

"Don't be a coward," Sarah chips in.

I refuse to be provoked.

Sarah sighs. "Let's talk about it tomorrow. I can't deal with your crap right now." She jumps up. "I'm off to watch *Top Gear* with my father. He recorded yesterday's episode for me. And I have some accounts to pay. We're still doing dinner tomorrow night, right?" She looks at me.

Maybe not. "When's Alex getting out of the hospital?" I ask.

"He'll be back in Pretoria the day after tomorrow."

That gives me a day before I have to get out of here. I sigh, resigned. "Okay. See you tomorrow evening." I suddenly think of something. Look to Adriana. "Are we going to Crow's Feet? Am I finally getting to see this famous restaurant of yours?"

Adriana slips on the sunglasses and smiles. "If that is what you'd like, then that's what we'll do."

5

The Wilgers hospital smells like all hospitals. No one seems to have been able to think of a way for the sterile linoleum halls to smell less like death's dirty hands.

The man in the bed before me is breathing evenly. Tubes in his nose are feeding him oxygen, while an IV drip in his arm is feeding him something else. The young nurse at the nurses' station told me—his "daughter-in-law"—that his prognosis was good. As far as they know, no one's been arrested for the violent mugging. And, she adds inquisitively, they were told his son couldn't come to visit from Australia. Did he send me?

I nodded, said nothing. This was the only way I could get into the intensive care unit—I had to be related to Jaap Reyneke.

The older man's hand is cold under my fingers, the skin transparent and elastic. His body is thinner than I remember, his face gaunt.

I lean closer and hope that he can hear me. "I'm sorry," I whisper.

Adriana was out of line, even though I still can't figure out what the retired cop was doing at her apartment in the middle of the night. Maybe I came here hoping for answers. I squeeze his hand and turn to leave. I'm not going to get any answers today.

I'm halfway to the door when I hear "Stay."

The single word is soft, mumbled.

I turn back to his bed, though I'm not sure why. Maybe I know how it feels to be scared and alone. Reyneke must be starved for human contact. The nurses do what they can, but they don't have time to act like family.

I put my hand on his again.

He opens his eyes slowly. "Isabel."

It takes me by surprise that the detective who investigated my father's murder recognizes me. I want to retreat, get away, but his hand stops me with a surprisingly strong grip. The heart monitor beside his bed flickers, peaks, and then settles again.

"You know," he says in a low, rasping voice, "I understand."

"Understand what?"

"What you did. Your father. Why. I can't forgive . . . forgive myself. Tried for years to get to the big fish and let everyone else around him . . . drown."

"You knew about him? Who he was?"

"Suspected."

He closes his eyes and licks his dry lips. He moves his head toward the bedside table. There's a little bowl of ice there. I put a piece in his mouth.

"Thank you," he says breathlessly.

It's quiet for a while. His hand relaxes. I wonder about what he said, whether he's delirious from pain meds.

"We were investigating your father," he begins again. "Me and Stefan. Hendrik Kroon was bad news. I know. I knew it then. I should have done something. You and your mother . . . if we'd been one day earlier. If we hadn't . . . if we hadn't waited, all those people would be alive. The guards. Johannes."

Tears well up in my eyes unexpectedly. Someone saw. Another person saw. Knew. Realized. Chose to do nothing.

But is it their job to do something? I wonder as I so often do. Aren't you supposed to save your own life?

I squeeze his hand, grateful for the unexpected empathy. "Why did you come to Adriana's apartment that night? I don't understand."

He coughs painfully. "You're friends with her? I thought so. Watch out for her." He fiddles clumsily with the tube in his nose.

I retrieve his hand, before he does something to alert the nursing staff.

"The case still bothers us. Me and Stefan. Suddenly Hendrik's dead. And everyone else. The money found. Too neat. Something wasn't right. Then this woman—these two women—arrive on Stefan's doorstep"—he gasps for breath—"wanting to talk about the case after all those years. Didn't make sense. We always thought there was someone in the picture we didn't see. Something happening we didn't know about."

"There was. My mother's sister. Read the news when you get out of here. We were . . . Adriana was trying to help me. Alex Derksen?" I blow out a slow breath. The guilt over what Adriana did—what we did—weighs heavily. "I can't really tell you more."

He frowns, coughs again, then nods slowly.

"We were curious about Stefan's money," I venture, eager to get Adriana to back off for good. "Where did it come from? We thought the two of you might have been involved in my father's business."

He shakes his head, his eyes fluttering closed. "His girlfriend. They never married. He didn't want to marry again. She was a speculator. Property. Died. Heart attack a few years ago." He tries to laugh, his breath straining in his throat.

I rub his hand. "That's enough. You need to sleep now. Maybe I'll come by again later," I lie. "Then we can talk some more."

I wait until his breathing deepens before I get up and call Adriana.

6

There's a knock on my hotel room door as I'm getting out of the shower. Probably Adriana and Sarah. I look at my watch. They're early. Can only be Adriana's influence. Can't imagine Sarah would be on time for anything.

"Hi," says Adriana as she walks in. Sarah gives a silent wave.

"Hi." I tighten the towel around my body.

"I still don't understand why you don't just stay with Sarah," Adriana says as she sits down at the desk.

I glance at Sarah, who is staring at her boots. Adriana rolls her eyes at us.

I start towel-drying my hair.

Adriana looks at the jeans I've put out on the bed. Her eyebrows shoot up crossly. "I hope that's not what you're wearing."

"What's wrong with them?"

"Everything."

Adriana points at herself. She's wearing a charcoal pencil skirt and a white shirt with a stiff collar. Five-inch black heels. Then she points at Sarah, who's wearing her new boots, tight jeans, and a light-blue blouse. And Sarah's definitely wearing perfume again.

"All right then," I give in. "I get it. I can probably make a plan."

I take out the blue dress and shoes I bought in India. Makeup would be a good idea. And I could probably blow-dry my hair into something less unruly.

"Give me twenty minutes," I say, and head back to the bathroom.

A half hour later we're on our way, after Adriana gave my outfit an approving nod.

We take the Grayston turnoff on the M1 freeway and head deeper into Sandton. Sarah speeds through Johannesburg's northern suburbs, past dense stands of trees, perfectly manicured lawns, and six-bedroom mansions glimpsed through towering eight-foot gates. Money lives here. Lots of it.

We turn left onto a narrow street and stop at an enormous farmhouse with a red roof, two black chimneys, and an inviting porch. It looks as if it was built in the sixties and recently revamped.

I open the car window when we stop at the gate. The week's bad weather has moved north, to Mozambique, to make room for the rich promise of summer.

The evening smells of jasmine and roses, the rich fragrance of tilled soil and freshly cut grass.

Crow's Feet, a sign announces in elegant letters on a high white wall surrounding the house. Painted next to it, two silhouetted crows sit on a wire.

"Where does the name come from?" I ask, craning my neck to see her in the back seat.

Adriana smiles but doesn't answer me.

I sigh dramatically. "One day you and I are going to sit down and have a nice long chat."

"Maybe," she says. "But not today."

"Liar. I don't think I'm ever going to see that day."

She smiles again, a deep and satisfied smile, filled with pleasure.

A switch flips in my head. It's the same feeling I used to get when I was in a crowd of protestors looking for the perfect shot. That moment, almost frozen in time, just before the crowd turned on me and my camera.

Something's wrong. Something's . . .

"What's going on?" I ask.

Sarah tenses in the driver's seat. She stops looking for a better parking spot and maneuvers the Audi under a tree between two other, more expensive-looking cars. Kills the engine.

"I'm not getting out until I know what's going on."

"Relax," says Adriana, reaching out to touch my shoulder. "There," she says, pointing to the left.

A tall man steps out of the shadows into the glow of the fairy lights winding up the trunk of a white stinkwood. His face is thinner than it should be. He's shaved. His brown hair is curling, as always, on his neck. The only things that are not familiar are the tailored blue pants and the thin blue tie. I've never seen him in a tie before.

"I'm going to kill you." I look at Sarah. Turn to Adriana. "And you too."

Sarah shakes her head. "You're not going to Caracas. Stop this bullshit of always running away. Adriana and I will work something out." She opens her door. "Consider this the last installment on my Sasolburg debt."

"What was the first installment?"

"Oh, you enjoyed shooting me. It was written all over your face."

"That's not true."

She gives me a meaningful look.

"Okay. All right. I did."

Adriana gets out and opens my door. "Come on. We don't have all night. Sarah and I have work to do. The two of you have kept me so busy this past while, I can't make any promises about the service around here anymore."

Alex places the cutlery neatly on his empty plate, wipes his mouth with the crisp linen napkin, and puts it back on his lap. Fiddles with his beer glass.

"So, where to from here?" he asks.

I take a sip of the Stellenbosch cabernet Adriana opened for us earlier and pretend I don't know what he's talking about. "What do you mean, 'where to from here'?"

"With you."

"You're taking me home, aren't you?" Under the table, tucked away in a private corner of Crow's Feet, I run a high-heeled shoe up his leg. "I've had too much to drink."

"We don't have a home."

"Not yet. But I do have a hotel room."

"Not yet? Does that mean you're staying?" He looks at me, a mixture of distrust and curiosity in his green eyes.

I've been trying to avoid the topic of me and him—of us—all evening, but it's clear his patience has run out.

"How can I?" I ask. "It's not safe here, Alex. Not for you and not for me."

"Are we talking about the police?"

"Yes. Remember? I'm a serial killer. It's still who I am. The Black Widow who kills and devours men."

"According to the police." He loosens the tie and undoes the top button of the white dress shirt. He leans over the table and takes my hands in his. "But I know who you really are."

I pull my hands from his grip, sit back. "And who am I really? I'm the woman who fucked up your life. Tom Masterson's death? The last few weeks? Lena, Borsos? All the media interviews you've been avoiding and the lies you've been telling the police, saying that the abduction was linked to your investigation of a gold syndicate? How can you just move on from that? You will wake up at night, look at me, and think, It's her fault I don't have a nice cushy job in Brussels covering the European Union."

"It wasn't your fault. None of it. Tom did what he did out of some obsession with you, and what happened to me was your father's fault. And who says I want a nice cushy job in Belgium?"

He reaches for my hands again. I relent, place them in his. They feel strong, sure.

"So, you're not angry?" I ask.

"No." He hesitates for a second, and it feels like my heart stops while he does. "But the secrets have to stop. You could have told me about your father."

"Most days I couldn't even admit what had happened to myself."

He gives a gentle nod, a hint of the familiar crooked smile flashing across his face. "Is there anything else I should know?"

"No. Not that I can think of."

He raises a lazy eyebrow, his gaze drifting from my eyes to my neck. Lower.

I withdraw my hands from under his, aware of the sudden electricity from his touch reaching every part of my body. My cheeks feel warm.

I touch my face self-consciously, hoping he doesn't notice.

"I'm not going to beg," Alex says. "Yes, you're staying, or no, you're leaving. But know that leaving isn't some act of heroism to save me. You have to stop making decisions on my behalf, like you did last year."

"That's not what happened."

"Really? Not from where I'm standing." He takes a sip of his beer and puts the glass down hard. "Sarah will make a plan to keep you safe, and so will Adriana. They say it's possible, even after what happened to Lena. Thinus is too sick to say anything. No one knows you're here. They can speculate, but they don't know."

"That's what you all say, but I'm going to be the one looking over my shoulder all the time. You too."

"Stop the bullshit, Ranna." A note of anger has slipped into his voice. "What's worse? Being alone and looking over your shoulder, or being with me and looking over your shoulder? Because those are your choices, and you know it. Leaving me doesn't miraculously solve your problems."

"But you'll be safe."

"I don't want to be safe. I'd rather have this thing with you, even if you drive me insane sometimes. Something like this only shows up once in a lifetime, if you're lucky, and you know it."

He cuts to the bone with his relentless honesty, as he always does. And he knows me better than anyone.

I push my wineglass away and wave at a passing waitress. I feel like a beer.

After I've ordered, I look at the man across the table. The strong, decent man, for whom there is no facsimile. And he is right—I would know. There have been too many airports and too many empty beds for me not to know.

"You don't even know whether I can cook," I say.

He shakes his head. "I know you can't, and that's okay. The only thing I'm not going to negotiate is that the right side of the bed is mine." He sweeps the same possessive glance over me as he did earlier.

I cross my arms. I need to think. With my head.

"There are many ways to put bread on the table." He gets up and walks around the table. Holds out his hand for mine and then pulls me up and into his arms.

"I still have the diamonds," I offer.

"That's blood money. You can give them away for all I care."

That'll be the day. "What will we do to make a living?" I kick off my heels so I can look him in the eye.

"I suspect I'll freelance and learn to take fantastic news photographs to go with my articles," he says softly. "A hobby to remember my long-lost love. To fix my broken heart."

He spins us around, as though there's music playing that only he can hear. "I'm going to write stories, and I'm going to take photographs of . . . ," he says into my neck, waiting for me to finish the sentence.

I take a breath. Think for a second.

"Wildlife. Rhino poaching. Elephant poisoning. Canned hunting. Small towns and the people who live there."

"Exactly. I'm going to take photos of wild animals, small towns, and the people who live there."

I rest my head against his. Drop it onto his shoulder, inhaling his familiar aftershave. Feel the stubble against my face.

I run my hands over his back, mindful of his injuries. Too thin. He's still way too thin.

"You're going to be so busy. All that work. Too much for one person," I say.

"I know. Poor me."

"Poor you."

And then I kiss him.

Acknowledgments

I have many people to thank for making this book possible, including the fantastic team at Amazon Crossing—Gabriella Page-Fort, Michael Jantze, Megan Meier, Lauren Grange, Kristin Lunghamer, Jacqueline Smith, Erin Calligan-Mooney, and Shasti O'Leary Soudant.

Also, Karin Schimke deserves more than my heartfelt gratitude for her patience and generosity as she worked to translate this text. *Baie, baie dankie!*

About the Author

Photo © 2017 Rudi de Beer

Irma Venter is a journalist and thriller writer. She loves traveling, Labradors, good coffee, excellent whiskey, and expensive chocolate—not necessarily in that order. She writes books about strong women, interesting men, and that fascinating space between right and wrong. She lives in South Africa.